She grabbed a proper ~~~~~~~ joke compared to Eovath's axe—for her right hand and somebody else's eating knife for her left. Then she edged forward.

Her foster brother snorted. "Truly?" he asked.

She didn't bother to answer with words. She simply rushed in, and the axe whirled to meet her. She ducked the horizontal stroke and kept coming.

The low ceiling was already awkward for Eovath, and getting in close seemed the best way to further turn his size into a handicap. At that distance, big warriors had difficulty hitting smaller ones.

Or at least that was how it was supposed to work. But Eovath was an expert combatant, and after the hundreds of times they'd practiced together, he understood exactly what she was doing and why. He strove to keep his distance and, when she got close anyway, met her with elbow strikes and jabs with the butt of the axe. Meanwhile, his vest of boiled leather stopped her stabs and slashes from reaching his vitals. As often as not, the attacks failed to penetrate at all.

Eovath chopped at her head. She stepped back out of range, caught her ankle on something, and staggered, struggling not to fall.

The giant charged . . .

had finished a long carving knife – it verged on being
a weapon, even though it seemed like a bad

The Pathfinder Tales Library

Called to Darkness

Richard Lee Byers

Called to Darkness © 2012 Paizo Publishing, LLC. All rights reserved. No part of this publication may be reproduced, stored in a retrieval system, or transmitted in any form or by any means digital, electronic, mechanical, photocopying, recording, or otherwise, or conveyed via the Internet or a website without prior written permission of the publisher, except in the case of brief quotations embedded in critical articles and reviews.

Paizo, Paizo Publishing, LLC, the Paizo golem logo, and Pathfinder are registered trademarks of Paizo Publishing, LLC; Pathfinder Roleplaying Game, Pathfinder Campaign Setting, and Pathfinder Tales are trademarks of Paizo Publishing, LLC.

Cover art by Michal Ivan.
Cover design by Andrew Vallas.
Map by Robert Lazzaretti.

Paizo Publishing, LLC
7120 185th Ave NE, Ste 120
Redmond, WA 98052
paizo.com

ISBN 978-1-60125-465-8 (mass market paperback)
ISBN 978-1-60125-466-5 (ebook)

Publisher's Cataloging-In-Publication Data
(Prepared by The Donohue Group, Inc.)

Byers, Richard Lee.
  Called to darkness / Richard Lee Byers.

  p. : ill., map ; cm. -- (Pathfinder tales)

  Set in the world of the role-playing game, Pathfinder.
  Issued also as an ebook.
  ISBN: 978-1-60125-465-8 (mass market pbk.)

  1. Hunters--Fiction. 2. Betrayal--Fiction. 3. Imaginary places--Fiction. 4. Good and evil--Fiction. 5. Fantasy fiction. 6. Adventure stories. I. Title. II. Title: Pathfinder adventure path. III. Series: Pathfinder tales library.

PS3552.Y428 C35 2012
813/.54

First printing December 2012.

Printed in the United States of America.

For Amber

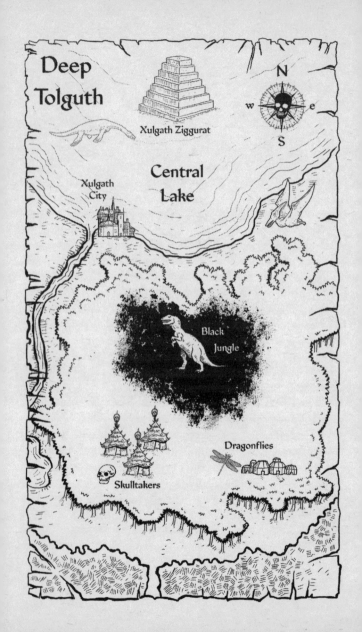

Chapter One
The Last Feast

For a moment, everyone fell quiet at once, and Kagur heard the wind howling outside the Blacklions' meeting tent, a long, peak-roofed shelter pieced together from the tanned hides of mammoths, giant sloths, and other enormous beasts. Then the wood burning in one of the fire pits *cracked*. Yellow flame leaped, sparks flew upward, and as if that had broken a spell, the whole tribe resumed its clamor.

Annik struck up a fresh tune on a harp shaped from caribou antler and strung with reindeer gut.

Grinning like one of the snow foxes that had given its fur to make his tunic, Roga told a joke. Kagur couldn't catch it all, but like most of Roga's pun-laden humor, it must have been awful. It elicited groans and prompted Taresk to peg a well-gnawed elk bone across the trestle table at him.

Zonug held up his silver-chased drinking horn, and eight-year-old Dron came scurrying. When the boy failed to fill the vessel all the way to the brim, Zonug made a show of peering inside it, mock scowled, and bellowed, "By Gorum's blood-red eyes! Who's pouring here, Ganef of the Fivespears?"

That sally *did* make people laugh. The chieftain of the Fivespears tribe was much disliked for his stingy, conniving ways.

In fact, Kagur reflected, Ganef was the antithesis of all that a proper Kellid chieftain should be—which was to say, the antithesis of her father. Sitting straight and tall, the gray eyes of a Blacklion keen and his mane of hair raven-dark despite his advancing years, Jorn turned and told Eovath to tap another cask of Tian brandy.

Even more than their generous, valorous leader, or the preserved skull of the gigantic man-eating cave lion their first chieftain had slain generations before, Eovath was the emblem of Blacklion pride, for only the bravest tribes captured and adopted frost giants. Twice as tall as a man but with a build so thick and muscular he nonetheless looked squat, Eovath had long, straw-colored hair, eyes to match, and skin the blue of the sky at dusk. To Kagur, his features looked less brutish and more intelligent than those of other frost giants, and she sometimes wondered if the love and care of humans had so improved him that the benefit even showed in his face.

For much of his life, Eovath had sat by Jorn at the head of the table. He needed to be where the ceiling was highest to keep his head from bumping against it. Still, when he rose in response to his foster father's command, it did anyway, even though he didn't straighten up all the way. Moving with care so as not to jostle anyone or anything, he picked up the brandy cask. His prodigious strength and enormous hands managed it easily.

Kagur considered staying and sharing the brandy. After all, the liquor and wine that came over the Crown of the World were rare treats. If the tribe hadn't fared exceptionally well hunting this past season, amassing fine wolf and bear pelts and caribou hides in abundance, her father couldn't have afforded to trade for it. It would certainly warm the blood on a frigid winter night.

But she didn't actually need drink to warm her, or the flames in the fire pits, either. Stroking her thigh beneath the table, Dolok's hand was more than sufficient.

She liked Dolok. He had a quick, crooked smile, and was nimble and clever enough to make her work at sword practice. He obviously saw something to like in her as well, and they'd grown amorous in recent weeks, kissing and fondling until she made him stop.

She'd already decided that tonight would be the night they wouldn't stop. Once the feast was in full swing and everyone was tipsy, they'd slip away unnoticed.

She'd just as soon avoid the bawdy jokes of the rest of the tribe, good-natured though they would be. And as for her father, well, it was one of the great mysteries of life how he knew perfectly well that she was a grown woman—indeed, one of his ablest warriors and hunters—yet could only see her as a fragile little girl whenever lovemaking was in the offing.

She nodded toward the nearest exit. Dolok grinned in response. They rose and made their way toward the end of the tent.

As Dolok untied the rawhide knots that secured the flap, Kagur glanced around to see if their departure really was going unremarked. Pouring brandy into the leather wineskins in the hands of Dron and the other child servers, Eovath looked back at her.

She might have expected a smirk, a wink, or even a reflection of their father's characteristic frown of disapproval. Instead, he looked . . . relieved? About what?

Dolok pulled back the flap, and a blast of cold wind and swirling snowflakes blew the question out of her mind. She hastily followed him out into the night.

The snowdrifts were halfway to her knees and crunched as she waded through them. Clouds covered the moon and stars, and the other tents were merely shadows in the dark. So were the mammoths standing shaggy and stolid, impervious to the worst the blizzard could do.

Kagur took Dolok's hand and drew him into a supply tent. "Whew!" he said, smiling. "It's not much warmer in here!"

"I know what to do about that," she said.

They clung together and kissed for a while. His mouth tasted of the bison he'd eaten and the ale he'd drunk.

She started unlacing and unbuckling his clothing of fur, hide, and leather, and he did the same for her. When their garments were open, and they could touch in ways they hadn't before, they lay down together.

At that point, he took the lead, kissing and caressing. Content for the moment to be passive, she closed her eyes and enjoyed it.

Someone screamed.

"What was that?" Kagur gasped.

Dolok lifted his head. "What?"

"Someone cried out."

He grinned. "That was you, honeycomb."

"Someone *else* cried out."

"Then it was the wind. It's howling like a pack of wolves."

He was right. Perhaps her imagination was playing tricks on her. Surely no enemy would come raiding on a night like this, and if one did, the mammoths would trumpet a warning.

She smiled. "The wind. Yes. Sorry." She settled back, inviting him to resume his attentions. But as soon as he obliged, she heard another shriek.

When she tensed, Dolok frowned. "What now?" he asked.

"You must have heard it that time."

"No."

"Then my ears are sharper than yours. Get up!"

"Curse it, Kagur!" But he did as instructed.

When they mostly had their garments refastened against the cold, she hurried back out into the night, and he followed. On first inspection, the meeting tent looked no different than before.

"See?" Dolok said. "Everything's fine."

"Maybe." But she led him onward anyway.

Another scream shrilled, louder and unmistakable now that they were closer.

"Lord in Iron!" Dolok said.

Floundering in the snow, they ran to the tent flap. Kagur tugged the edge back, and they peered through the crack.

Every human in the tent was down, either slumped across one of the tables or sprawled on the ground. Some moaned or stirred, barely, like swatted flies still clinging to a trace of life. Some were utterly still, and a number of the latter group lay hacked and dismembered in pools of blood.

Grinning, his yellow eyes shining like molten gold in his blue face, Eovath was doing the chopping with a huge axe the Blacklions had taken as a trophy on the same day they'd seized the giant himself. Gore dripped from the weapon's edge and stained his arms all the way to the elbows.

This is a dream, Kagur thought. He *couldn't* do this. He's my brother.

Then Eovath turned toward Annik, who lay on her side with her fingers still tangled in her harp strings, and raised the axe. Kagur's incredulity shattered. This horrible thing *was* happening, and if she didn't intervene immediately, Eovath would murder Annik and then move on to another victim, and another after that, until no human in the tent was left alive.

But what could Kagur do? Kellids were a warrior race, and none more than the Blacklion tribe, but even so, neither she nor Dolok had carried weapons to the feast.

The only option was to *talk* to Eovath. Talk, stall him, and hope that, as she'd always believed, he loved his foster sister.

"Arm yourself," she whispered to Dolok. "Take him from behind." She gave him a shove to start him moving.

Then she yanked the gap between the flap and the rest of the tent wider and squirmed through. "Wait!" she shouted.

Eovath pivoted and looked her over. Then he sighed and lowered the axe slightly. "When you left without drinking the poison, I thought you were out of it," he rumbled in a voice deeper than any human's. "I thought the Rough Beast had granted me a favor."

"'The Rough Beast?'" That made no sense, either. The Blacklions had raised Eovath to revere Gorum and, to a lesser extent, Desna, the same as they did. Only the worst and maddest people worshiped Rovagug, god of annihilation and wrath—a being so mighty and infinitely malevolent that, at the dawn of time, both good and evil deities had combined forces to imprison him, lest he destroy the world. Even that hadn't rendered him entirely powerless, and from time to time he still created earthquakes and terrible beasts to ravage the lands of men.

The frost giant nodded. "He talks to me. In my dreams, mostly, but sometimes I hear him even when I'm awake."

"How could that be?" Kagur asked. Blood dripped from the edge of a table. Across the tent, someone retched. "You're not a shaman."

"No," Eovath said, "but I will be. It's part of his plan for me."

"Listen," Kagur said. "You're confused, and it's making you do bad things. You're killing your own tribe. Your family."

Eovath spat. "My family died a long time ago."

It took her a moment to guess what he meant. "The other giants? Your blood kin?"

"Who else? You've heard the story often enough. How your father and the rest of the Blacklions slaughtered my tribe and carried me off into slavery."

"You're not a sla—"

"Don't lie to me!"

She took a breath. "All right. It's true, that's what they call it. But Father raised you like his own son."

"To make me forget my real father and turn me into a traitor to my own kind."

Kagur felt like she was saying all the wrong things. What did she know about reasoning with lunatics? Where in the name of keen iron was Dolok?

"Eovath," she said, "brother . . . humans raid giants, but giants raid humans, too. It's just the way things are."

"But not the way they have to be."

She hesitated. "I don't understand."

"Down in the depths, a sun shines in the darkness, and a pyramid rises under the sun. That's where I'll find what I need to do my work."

"What does that mean?"

He grinned. "I don't know. But the Rough Beast will guide me, through the Earthnavel and beyond."

"Can't you hear how crazy you sound? But if you want to go on a journey, just do it. You don't need to kill all the people who love you."

"Yes, I do. Rovagug wouldn't help me if I didn't sacrifice to him, and even if he would, the spirits of my *real* tribe are calling out for vengeance. They won't be satisfied until every human is driven from the tundra."

She stared into his yellow eyes. "Even me?"

He winced. "I told you I wanted to spare you. I still do. Just go to one of the other tents and don't come out till morning."

"You know I can't do that."

"I suppose I knew you wouldn't." He lifted the axe and advanced on her, stepping over the dead and the helpless, leaving footprints in the pools of blood.

Kagur reached past a corpse with a smashed skull for a wooden platter. The grilled ribs of an aurochs tumbled off as she grabbed it up and skimmed it at Eovath's head. Not even breaking stride, he knocked it aside with a flick of the axe.

She grabbed a stool and flung that. He chopped and again prevented the blow, but he ended up with the stool stuck on the blade of the axe. With a scowl, he started to shake it loose.

At that instant, when he was at least partly distracted, Kagur grabbed a knife smeared with grease and flecks of bear meat. It wasn't a proper weapon, just the kind of tool every Kellid carried for eating, mending harness, and whittling tent pegs. But it was a length of steel with a point, and she hurled it at Eovath's heart.

It only had a short distance to travel, but even so, he jerked to the side, and the spinning knife only pierced his left biceps. He bellowed, shook the remains of the stool off the axe, and charged.

With the walls of the tent hemming her in, Kagur only had one place to go. She sprang and rolled over the tabletop, upsetting trays and dishes in the process. For an instant, she found herself gazing into the glazed gray eyes of Roga's severed head, and then momentum carried her onward. She tumbled off the other edge of the table into someone's lap—she didn't see whose, or if he was alive or dead. He toppled backward, and they crashed to the ground together.

It knocked the wind out of her, but she didn't dare let it slow her down. She scrambled to her feet just as Eovath grabbed the long, heavy tabletop between them. With a grunt, he flipped it up off the trestles and sent it spinning at her.

She flung herself backward, and the makeshift weapon just missed her. Unfortunately, it couldn't miss all the incapacitated Blacklions sprawled on the ground. A woman cried out as the weight smashed down on her.

Kagur resisted the urge to look down and find out who it was. She kept her eyes on her foe.

Who, intentionally or not, had just cleared a larger space for the two of them to fight in. With bodies, severed limbs, benches, trays, drinking horns, and chunks of roast meat strewn about, the footing would be treacherous. But that was true of the rest of the tent as well, and maybe with a little more room to maneuver, Kagur could use her speed and agility to at least hold out until Dolok returned.

She glanced at a table next to the open space. She grabbed a long carving knife—it verged on being a proper weapon, even though it seemed like a bad joke compared to Eovath's axe—for her right hand and somebody else's eating knife for her left. Then she edged forward.

Her foster brother snorted. "Truly?" he asked.

She didn't bother to answer with words. She simply rushed in, and the axe whirled to meet her. She ducked the horizontal stroke and kept coming.

The low ceiling was already awkward for Eovath, and getting in close seemed the best way to further turn his size into a handicap. At that distance, big warriors had difficulty hitting smaller ones.

Or at least that was how it was supposed to work. But Eovath was an expert combatant, and after the hundreds of times they'd practiced together, he understood exactly what she was doing and why. He strove to keep his distance and, when she got close anyway, met her with elbow strikes and jabs with the butt of the axe. Meanwhile, his vest of boiled leather stopped her stabs and slashes from reaching his vitals. As often as not, the attacks failed to penetrate at all.

Eovath chopped at her head. She stepped back out of range, caught her ankle on something, and staggered, struggling not to fall.

The giant charged. The axe flashed at her, she twisted, and the weapon passed so near that it snagged in her mantle and ripped free.

Eovath hesitated, as if he imagined he'd actually struck her. Kagur recovered her balance and darted in. She stabbed his hip where the vest didn't cover and lunged on by.

He roared and whirled with blood already welling from the puncture. They glared at one another, circled, and then he let go of the axe with his left hand and gripped it with the right alone.

Evidently, Kagur decided, the knife still jutting from his left forearm was bothering him. At first, he'd scarcely seemed to notice the wound, but now it must be painful enough that he needed to let the damaged limb dangle.

Which meant Kagur should attack his left side. It would be harder for him to swing the axe across his body to hit or block her there. Only a little bit harder, but little advantages were all she had.

Pivoting, fixing her gaze on the crook of his right arm, she raised the carving knife as if for a throw. He sneered but also poised himself to bat the blade out of the air.

Instantly, she charged at his left flank. She'd cut even lower this time, hamstring him and dump him on the ground, then slash his throat as it came within reach.

She could see the sequence of events so vividly it was like it was already happening. Perhaps that was why it caught her so completely by surprise when Eovath's left arm, the one she'd thought useless, snapped into motion.

She tried to stop short, but it was too late. Looking like a sliver in his enormous hand, Eovath's dagger drove into her midsection. It didn't exactly hurt, but she felt a kind of shock all through her body, like she was made of shattering ceramic. She stumbled back and fell with the blade still buried inside her.

She struggled to understand what was happening, but it didn't make any sense. She was supposed to outwit and outfight Eovath, and he was supposed to fall down. Everything was the wrong way around.

She looked at the hilt of the dagger and realized she knew it well. Her father had fashioned it himself, carving it to look like a crouching cave lion and staining the pale bone dark. Then he'd presented it to Kagur to give to Eovath as a token indicating that the tribe now trusted him with weapons.

The giant gazed down at her with tears running down his cheeks, washing away the specks of gore that had splashed that high. "I'm sorry," he said.

She could see he meant it, that he truly did love her. Insane though it might be, she felt a surge of love in return. Somehow the emotion managed to well up inside her without in any way diminishing her horror, grief, and rage. She'd never known it was possible to feel so many different things at the same time.

She was still marveling at it when she glimpsed Dolok creeping up behind Eovath. Her lover had armed himself with a longsword and a round shield of wood covered in leather.

The sight of him cut through the daze her injury had engendered. She struggled to control her expression lest it change and so warn Eovath of the peril at his back.

Apparently, she managed it. Her foster brother just kept looking down at her and weeping. She felt a kind of vicious eagerness—another emotion to add to the stew—to see Dolok cut him down.

But the toe of Dolok's boot bumped a wooden cup lying amid the gory litter on the floor. The cup rolled and clicked against a platter.

It was a tiny sound, and Kagur insisted to herself that Eovath wouldn't hear it over the wail of the wind outside the tent. But he plainly did, for he started to pivot.

Dolok charged, and his sword flashed yellow in the firelight. Eovath finished turning just in time to parry the cut with his axe.

The giant struck back, and Dolok blocked with his shield. He had it angled to make the axe glance off, yet even so, Eovath's strength knocked him backward.

Eovath advanced and struck again immediately. Step by step, he pushed his opponent back. The relentless pressure kept Dolok from making many attacks of his own, and when he did, the axe deflected the sword with a clang of steel on steel.

I have to help, Kagur thought. I have to! But when she tried to stand, agony ripped through her middle and paralyzed her.

With his back nearly against the wall of the tent, Dolok finally landed a cut to Eovath's wrist. Then, at last, the frost giant faltered. At once, Dolok bellowed, feinted to the knee, then spun his sword up for a slash to the torso.

Undeceived, Eovath stepped in and brushed aside the true attack. Then, not even bothering to chop with the edge, he simply rammed the top of the axe into Dolok's face. Bone crunched, and the human flew backward into the wall of the tent, bounced back, and collapsed. Blood flowed out around his head.

When Eovath turned back around, his face was once again a mask of malice, without a trace of the love, regret, and perhaps even guilt Kagur had seen there previously. He was ready to finish off the rest of the tribe, and she was helpless to prevent it.

Or nearly helpless. She couldn't save anyone else, but if she played dead, perhaps he wouldn't feel the need to hack her to pieces.

She tried it, and rather to her surprise, it worked. Eovath didn't hurt her any further. But she still had to endure the thuds of the axe striking home, to listen to the occasional truncated cry or whimper without crying out and giving herself away.

She felt like the slaughter would never end. And in fact, she passed out before it did.

Chapter Two
Stand Up and Walk

In good weather, following game, the Blacklions often didn't bother to pitch their tents. Maybe that was why, lying on the soft summer grass, Kagur could hear the prisoner weeping.

Father said the blue-skinned giant boy needed to cry, and that they should leave him alone to do his grieving. He'd said, too, that for the time being Kagur shouldn't go near him by herself. But the choked sobbing pulled at her. It bothered her that someone was so sad.

Quietly, to avoid waking her parents, she rose and crept past other sleepers snoring on the ground. But when she neared the captive, she hesitated.

He *was* a boy. A person could tell it from his face. But he was also as tall as a grown man and had broader shoulders and bigger muscles than any warrior in the tribe. Father was right; he could hurt a little girl if he got his hands on her.

But Father also said Blacklions didn't balk in the face of danger, and anyway, the giant seemed too wretched to muster the resolve to hurt anybody. Kagur continued her approach.

The grownups had the boy tethered with a braided rawhide rope to a bone stake driven into the ground. That seemed cruel, but it gave her something to say: "Father told me you'll only have to be tied for a little while."

He didn't answer, just peered back at her. In the dark, she couldn't really make out the color of his eyes, but they still looked pale and strange.

"Did you try to get loose?" she asked. It was what she would have done in his place.

He looked at her for a while longer. Then, haltingly, he said, "I got . . . no place go no more."

She hadn't anticipated he'd have difficulty talking to her. Human speech must be his second language.

That seemed strange, too, but in an interesting way, not a scary one. Now that she was up close, there was nothing menacing about him, just abundant evidence of the aching misery that made her want to comfort him.

"It's nice here," she said. "My father—*our* father, now—is nice."

He stared at her like she'd said something crazy.

"I'm your sister Kagur," she continued, determined to break through, "and *I'm* nice. I'll show you."

She slipped her hand inside her deerskin shirt with its dangling fringe, brought out a cloth bag, and shook out a round piece of candy. In the dark, she couldn't tell if it was a red one or a purple one. She offered it to the prisoner.

He looked at it like he suspected it was something intended to hurt him. Or maybe like a part of him wanted to slap it away.

"They're good," she said. "Father got them from a trader. They're like berries, only hard. Suck on them, and they last a long time."

Or so the merchant had claimed. Kagur didn't know firsthand. After a little while, she always succumbed to the urge to crunch them up.

The giant boy took the candy and put it in his mouth. His cheeks hollowed as he sucked, and then, for just an instant, his lips twitched into the slightest of smiles. "Good," he said.

With a twinge of reluctance, but only a tiny one, she said, "You can have the ones I've got left."

"I have something for you, too," he said, and suddenly he was neither tethered nor a grief-stricken child anymore. He was so huge she felt like a mouse in comparison, and he lunged at her with a knife and stabbed it into her stomach.

She looked down at the stained bone hilt and said, "This isn't right. I don't give you the dagger until winter."

Then a stab of pain tore the dream apart. Kagur gasped, and her eyes flew open to a reality more horrific than the nightmare.

Her wound throbbed, and the air was cold. The fires in the pits had burned to embers. With Eovath gone and everyone else chopped to pieces, there hadn't been anyone to feed them.

The dead stared at Kagur. *Your fault*, they whispered. *Your fault*.

No, curse it, it wasn't. She'd done her best to save them, and they weren't really accusing her anyway. It was just her wound, her pain, her impending death playing tricks on her mind.

For a moment, the thought of death enticed her. It would end all the pain, the searing pulse in her guts and the anguish of loss and betrayal.

Then a spasm of anger revealed the temptation for the contemptible thing it was. Weakling! she thought. Coward!

She *had* to live. There was no one else to avenge the tribe.

She hadn't been able to leap up when Eovath and Dolok were fighting, but maybe she could haul herself to her feet now, before she bled out or froze to death. She strained to flop over onto her side.

That small motion spiked even fiercer pain through her midsection, making her gasp and blurring her eyes with tears. But she was halfway to shifting herself onto her hands and knees. Teeth gritted, she heaved herself over the rest of the way.

The dagger hanging straight down from her abdomen, she crawled to the nearest table. She gripped the edge and dragged herself to her feet.

The stress of that exertion was so great that the tent spun around her and the dimness grew even darker. She held onto the table with what little strength remained to her to keep from falling back down or passing out.

After a few moments, the dizziness and faintness abated, although she could sense them hovering close, like beasts waiting to pounce. Still holding onto the table, she inched toward the nearest tent flap, past one corpse after another.

A part of her didn't want to look at them, but she forced herself. She needed to know *exactly* what Eovath had done. The knowledge would feed her outrage, and her rage would give her strength.

As she should have expected, Eovath had desecrated their father's body more thoroughly than any of the others. All four of Jorn Blacklion's limbs were severed, and even his torso lay in multiple pieces. The fragments of his cloven head sat in a splash of blood and brains.

Seeing him that way was unbearable. Kagur yearned to go to him, tend to him, and somehow restore some measure of his dignity. But she couldn't spare the strength or the time.

Eventually, she neared the tent flap. She drew a ragged breath and took her hands off the table. She swayed but didn't fall back down. Careful not to trip over anything, she shuffled to the wall of the tent.

Her trembling hands were as weak and clumsy as the rest of her. She fumbled with the knots securing the flap for what seemed like forever. Why hadn't she picked up another knife from the table? She was nearly convinced she'd have to turn around and get one, even though the prospect of taking even a couple extra steps was ghastly, when the lashings finally came undone.

Now for the hard part.

She shuffled out into the night. Shrieking, the frigid wind slammed into her and tried to knock her down. She staggered and kept her feet, but again the effort made the pain in her guts even more excruciating.

She wondered if the dagger shifted in the wound and cut her a little more every time she moved, then scowled the demoralizing thought away. Even if it was true, she couldn't do anything about it. She knew better than to pull the blade out. That was apt to kill her on the spot.

Hunched against the wind and the drumbeat of agony in her middle, she stumbled onward to find that forcing her way through the snowdrifts was like wading through a freezing quagmire. The snow wasn't really trying to clamp tight around her numb feet and calves and lock her in place, but her feebleness and addled senses made it seem that way.

In fact, her progress was so torturous that it soon became impossible to think of anything but the next step, and then the one after that. When she lifted her eyes and found the mammoths looming in front of her, it took a moment to remember they were what she'd been laboring to reach.

"Lift," she croaked, not caring which of the huge shaggy beasts responded. Unfortunately, none of them did. They hadn't heard the puny rasp of her voice over the wail of the wind.

She staggered closer. "Lift! Lift!" She was still wheezing, not shouting like she wanted.

His curving tusks ringed with the dyed leather bands she'd placed there, Grumbler padded forth from within the herd. He and Kagur were fond of one another, and he evidently hadn't needed to hear her call to come to her. It had been enough to catch her scent.

Curling, his trunk sniffed and nuzzled at her. For a mammoth, he was gentle about it, but the nudging still nearly dumped her in the snow. He made a low, querulous sound when he sensed that she was hurt.

"It's all right," she said. "Lift!"

Grumbler raised his right foreleg.

Kagur took hold of the mammoth's ear. She tried to step up onto the animal's fetlock, but couldn't heave her left foot high enough.

No! She could. She would. She hadn't made it this far only to fail at the final task.

Snarling against the hammering pain in her middle, Kagur strained and finally got her foot planted. Grumbler immediately lifted his leg higher. It was what he was supposed to do, but she still nearly lost her grip on his ear and spilled back onto the ground.

Nearly, but not quite. She hauled herself onto his back, turned him to the north, and bumped him three times with her heels to start him running.

I'm coming for you, brother, she thought, and then fell unconscious again.

Chapter Three
A Guest of the Fivespears

Near the pond, the summer grass was tall, and the saber-toothed cat had found a low place in the ground to hide. Despite his skill at hunting and tracking, Kagur's father failed to notice the spotted beast. Nor did he hear it when it broke cover at his back.

Thirty paces away, Kagur had paused to admire little pink bog rosemary flowers growing intermixed with stringy white reindeer moss. Still, she saw Jorn's peril, and she had an arrow fletched with goose feathers already nocked. As the saber-tooth started its charge, she drew and loosed.

Her arrow plunged into the cat's shoulder. It stumbled but then kept running.

Kagur drew another arrow even though it was too late. Quick as she was, she didn't have time for another shot.

Fortunately, she didn't need one. The cat staggered again, although she couldn't tell why, and then fell down thrashing.

Father heard that. He pivoted, pulled back his own longbow, and drove an arrow into the saber-tooth, whose convulsions then subsided.

Kagur ran toward the fallen beast while Eovath did the same from the opposite direction, his long legs eating up the distance. He must be the one who'd stopped the cat.

Along with their father, they scrutinized the animal, making sure it was really dead. Then Kagur asked, "How?"

Eovath showed her and Jorn the rock in his callused, enormous hand. "All I had that would carry across the distance."

Father grinned up at him. "Good throw."

It was an understatement, but Kagur couldn't take pride in Eovath's feat the way her father did. Frost giants were notorious for the deadly force and accuracy with which they hurled stones, and despite the circumstances, it suddenly seemed like a hideous portent that Eovath had inherited the knack.

"Why?" Kagur demanded of him. "Why save Father on this day if you meant to kill us all in the end?"

"Who are you talking to?" Eovath replied.

Except that it wasn't his deeper-than-deep rumble coming out of his mouth. It was a reedy voice she'd never heard before.

Her eyes snapped open.

She was lying on one bearskin and under another in a tent with a gaunt old man kneeling beside her. Sticking out every which way, long wisps of white hair ringed his otherwise bald, spotted head, and an assortment of carved bones, feathers, and polished stones dangled around his scrawny wrinkled neck. The fetishes suggested he was a shaman—the healer she'd fought so hard to reach.

Looking up at him, however, she wondered how ably he could tend her or anyone. Milky cataracts all but masked the pupils of his eyes, and it seemed unlikely he could see out any more clearly than she could see in.

"How badly am I hurt?" she asked. Her throat was dry, and the question came out as a whisper.

He held a clay cup of water to her lips. The cold liquid brought a surge of pleasure; her body was eager for it. A bit of it escaped her mouth and dribbled down her chin.

"Not too much at once," the shaman said, lifting the cup away. "You asked how badly hurt you are. That's something we need to figure out together. Do you know me?"

She shrugged, and her stiff back popped. "You must belong to the Fivespears tribe." She'd pointed Grumbler toward their camp. It was the only one within reach.

"Yes, but do you know *me*?"

"Should I?"

"I'm Holg. I took the dagger out of you and tended you thereafter. You've been awake—well, give or take— and spoken with me several times. But you never remembered it afterward."

She grunted. "I will this time. My head is clear. Give me more water."

He tried to bring the cup back to her mouth. She hitched up onto one elbow so she could hold it for herself and was pleased that it didn't require any great effort and only produced a slight twinge in her abdomen. Blind or not, maybe the healer knew what he was doing.

"You *are* making more sense," Holg told her as she drank. "And the fever's broken, so there's no reason you should still be delirious."

"The fever?"

"I know prayers to close a wound, but you had yours for a while before you reached me. It festered."

"But it's all right now?" She realized she was naked between the bearskins. She gingerly felt her stomach and found a short, ridged scar.

"It was touch and go for a few weeks, but I believe so."

She glared at him. "A few weeks! Couldn't you work faster?"

He frowned. "Believe me, I *wanted* to hurry it. I have a keen interest in whatever it is you have to tell me. But I could easily have hurt you."

"I need to get up."

"I recommend you go on resting. We can still talk with you lying down."

"You're not the one I need to talk to. Where are my clothes?"

"Gone for rags. They were so bloodstained, it's all they were fit for. I found you some new ones." He indicated the pile with a wave of his hand.

She threw off the top bearskin and stood up. It made her lightheaded for a moment, but after that, she was all right.

She started to pull on the clothes and found several ways they differed from the ones she was used to. The lacing that threaded through four eyelets on a side instead of five. The belt that was too narrow and had an unfamiliar pattern hammered into the leather. Gauntlets lined with the fleece of a mountain sheep rather than the wool of a mammoth.

Little differences, but they signified that she was wearing garments made by Fivespears, not Blacklions, and they brought the reality of her situation crashing down on her. Father, Dolok, everyone gone! She averted her face to keep Holg from discerning her anguish.

"I have this, too," the shaman said. "Although I don't know if you'll want it."

She looked around. He was proffering Eovath's dagger. He'd found a black leather sheath for it that nearly matched the inky stain on the hilt.

"I want it," she said. It would gall her every time she noticed she had it, and the sting would spur her onward. She started to buckle the sheath to her new belt.

"I'd put it somewhere less conspicuous," said Holg. "For now, anyway."

She scowled. "Am I a captive?"

"You're an honored guest of the Fivespears tribe. The traditions of hospitality say so. Still, you have my advice."

Given what he'd just said, Kagur had no idea *why* it was his advice, but she had more important things to do than stand here trying to elicit an explanation. She slipped the dagger inside her shirt. "Satisfied?" she asked.

He shrugged.

"Then take me to Ganef."

"All right." In an unhurried fashion that made her jaw clench, he put on his cloak, pulled up the hood, took up a short staff covered in intricate carvings, and finally preceded her out of the tent. The sunlight made her squint.

The camp was much like that of the Blacklions, only with standards made of five spears fanning out from a single base planted in the snow and most of the tents round and stained a muddy red. Holg led Kagur toward the central meeting tent. He swished the butt of his staff back and forth in the snow in front of him, and she realized he was partly feeling his way. Apparently, it was a useful trick, as she watched him step neatly over guy ropes without tripping.

A mammoth trumpeted. Kagur turned. His trunk still upraised, Grumbler stood with a couple of the Fivespears' animals. Unlike him, the other beasts had no leather rings on their tusks and bore five vertical crimson stripes dyed into the wool on their flanks.

Kagur owed the faithful creature her life, but even so, she was too set on her purpose to stop to scratch the leathery hide beneath the thick brown hair or find him a treat. Soon, she promised, soon.

The air was cold, but not bitterly so, and the meeting tent had the flaps thrown back to admit the daylight. A lanky man with dark, close-set eyes and a pointed gray beard, Ganef sat at the far end drinking from a leather jack.

Trophies Kagur recognized—an orc banner with a three-eyed demonic face on it and the great cave-lion skull itself—hung or reposed around Ganef, just as if his own tribe had taken them in battle or the hunt. Spears, bows, shields, pots, and a smith's tools sat here and there, perhaps awaiting distribution or an opportunity to trade. A longsword with a round black stone in the pommel—Jorn's blade and the blade of his fathers before him—hung from one corner of the Fivespears chieftain's high-backed chair.

Evidently Kagur's arrival had prompted some of the Fivespears to visit the Blacklion camp, and when they'd discovered the carnage there, they'd looted whatever took their fancy. It felt like an affront, an attempt to erase even the memory of the slain, but she took a breath and told herself it was nothing compared to Eovath's treachery.

Ganef beamed at the sight of her. "Kagur!" He must have recognized her from trading visits and those rare occasions when Varnug, the Mammoth Lord of their particular following, called together those tribes that had accepted his leadership.

"Chieftain," she said, advancing.

"Are you well?" Ganef looked past her to Holg. "Should she be up?"

"No," the old man answered. "But since she refuses to stay down, it doesn't matter."

"I'm fine," said Kagur to Ganef. "Thank you for taking me in, and thanks to the healer here for tending me. Now—"

Ganef raised his hand. "Please, before anything else, you must let me welcome you properly. Sit."

She wanted to snap that she didn't have time to waste on courtesies. But it would be foolish to offend him, and so, biting back her annoyance, she settled herself on a bench and waited while he poured a second jack of ale, pricked his fingertip with a dirk, and squeezed a drop of his blood into the beverage.

"Drink," he said, "and you will be one of us for as long as you remain."

She drank. "Thank you."

"Now, please, tell me what happened at your camp."

Finally! She began a terse recitation of the tale.

Relating and so reliving the horror scourged her with fresh waves of grief, and once again, she tried to keep the emotion from showing. Her pain wasn't a spectacle for strangers.

But there was no humiliation in letting them see her anger, and so she focused on that until it shivered inside her and made it impossible to stay sitting. She jumped back up and finished the story on her feet.

"I am so sorry," Ganef said. "I wish there were something I could do."

"There is!" Was he so thick that he didn't understand what she required of him? "You, your warriors, and I need to track down Eovath and kill him."

He fingered a tuft of his beard. "Hm."

"The Blacklions have to be avenged!"

"Of course," Ganef said, "ideally. But how are you going to find him when the trail is so cold?"

"We'll find a way."

"I'm sure you'd try. But he must be high in the Tusks by now, and has likely found a new home with his own kind. It would be foolhardy to attack a tribe of frost giants on their home ground in the midst of winter."

"My tribe has done it and won. Are the Fivespears afraid to try?"

Ganef frowned. "No, but we aren't stupid, either."

"Think of it as you like. If you won't help, I'll hunt down Eovath by myself."

"I can't let you attempt that. You've been deathly ill for weeks."

"I'm better now."

"Not enough to survive alone on foot on the plains with only the clothes on your back."

She stared at him. "What are you talking about? My mammoth is here. Everything the Blacklions owned is here. You can't begrudge me what little I need."

"No one 'begrudges' you anything, but we have to think about what's fair. We fed you. The old man there spent his prayers on you, magic that might otherwise have benefited the tribe."

"So I have to pay for *hospitality*?" Much as she'd always disliked Ganef, she'd never dreamed he could stoop this low.

"Yes," he said, scowling, "if that's what it takes to keep you from throwing your life away. Instead, you'll recover the full measure of your strength and, when you're ready, repay our generosity by hunting along with the rest of the tribe."

"Then you're enslaving me."

"We're *adopting* you, idiot. Giving you new kin and a new life. And I don't care how sick you were and how the fever cooked your brain. Your ingratitude is starting to rankle."

Kagur drew breath to snarl that she'd rather die than join a tribe of thieves and cowards. But before she could get the words out, Holg cleared his throat.

Ganef turned his glower on the shaman. "What?" he snapped.

"It's kindly of you to seek to look after this warrior." Holg's tone was dry but stopped short of overt sarcasm. "But you still don't understand the situation." He turned to Kagur. "Tell him about the sun in the deep and all the rest of it."

A chill oozed up Kagur's spine. How did the old man know about Eovath's ravings? She'd left them out of her story because they didn't seem worth repeating.

She supposed Holg's mystical talents were responsible. Anyway, it didn't matter. If *he* thought repeating Eovath's gibberish might throw a scare into Ganef, she was willing to give it a try.

Attempting to act like she took it seriously, she laid out the giant's threat to do further harm, his claim that Rovagug spoke to him, and all the rest of the craziness. But when Ganef smirked, it was plain he wasn't impressed.

"It does sound mad," said Holg, demonstrating that he too somehow perceived the chieftain's skepticism. "But occasionally mad things happen."

Ganef sighed. "And your spirits are whispering that this one will?"

"In a sense."

"Well, if you hear from our Lord in Iron, let me know."

Holg shook his head. "Your god has no quarrel with the powers I serve. I've never understood why one of his worshipers feels the need."

"Perhaps if the spirits' servant didn't question and second-guess me at every turn—" Ganef took a deep breath. "But our guest doesn't need to hear us bicker." He smiled at Kagur. "It's obvious you're too sensible to believe the ravings of a lunatic—and a lunatic giant, at that—so you'll understand why I don't, either. In other words, my decision stands. You'll bide with us. Now, have the old man find you something to eat."

It was clear she couldn't change Ganef's mind. Kagur turned, strode out of the tent, and, fists clenched, looked around for something or someone to hit.

Unfortunately, there was nothing and no one within arm's reach—or rather, no one but Holg emerging behind her. And she wasn't quite disgusted enough to punch a blind old dodderer who'd saved her life.

"You should understand," Holg said, "Ganef knows of your skills with sword and bow. He's heard stories and seen your prowess for himself when the following united."

"So what?"

"So your talents would make you a valuable addition to the Fivespears. And since he doesn't believe Eovath poses a threat to his own tribe . . ." He shrugged.

"But you do believe?"

"Yes. I think that when the giant spoke of performing the task that Rovagug set him, he meant he'll continue as he began and wipe out other human tribes. Maybe even all of us. That's certainly the kind of thing the Rough Beast might want a follower to do."

"Still, why do you take Eovath's ravings seriously? How do you even know about them? Did your familiar spirits tell you?"

He smiled. "No. You did. I told you we've talked before today, even though you don't remember."

So he had. She felt stupid for not figuring out the actual—and thoroughly mundane—explanation.

"But I don't need prompting from the spirits to take the danger seriously," Holg continued. "I have other reasons. So the question is, what are we going to do about it?"

The answer to that was obvious. "We" weren't going to do anything.

Kagur unclenched her fists and sighed. "What can I do? Your chieftain is a worm, but he's right. I'll never find Eovath, and if I did, I couldn't kill him without a band of warriors at my back. There's nothing for me to do but try to make a new life with a new tribe. It's what my father would have wanted."

Holg snorted. "You're not—"

"I need to go to Grumbler. My mammoth. No doubt your people have taken good care of him, but I need to see for myself. After that, I would like some food."

And that was nothing less than the truth. She needed to eat, rest, and gather her strength if she were going to escape come nightfall.

Chapter Four
The Sword of the Blacklions

Kagur lay in her bearskins listening to the noise of the camp subside. When everything was quiet, she rose and pulled on her new boots and cloak. Lying in a tangle of his own sleeping furs, Holg didn't stir. Good. That was one problem avoided.

The next was presumably lurking somewhere outside. Shortly after her conversation with Ganef, she'd noticed a warrior trailing Holg and her at a distance. No doubt the chieftain had ordered the spy to keep an eye on her.

But she hadn't let on that she'd noticed him, which meant he had no reason to expect her to exit Holg's tent except in the usual way. And if he'd positioned himself to watch the flap, he couldn't see the opposite side of the shelter.

Using Eovath's dagger, she slit the bottom of the tent wall. Then she crawled out the hole and on through the frigid snow for several paces thereafter.

With luck, no one would now associate her with the captive in the shaman's tent. In the dark, the Fivespears would mistake her for one of their own. She stood up, brushed the snow off, and headed for the meeting tent.

It was even darker inside. She had to grope among the clumps and piles of stolen Blacklion goods. One by one, though, she found the items she needed. A pack and a waterskin. Venison jerky. Flint and steel. A longbow and a quiver of arrows. And then, to her delight, her own shield and leather armor.

The round shield had come off the body of an orc raider out of the Hold of Belkzen who'd likely obtained it by similar means himself. It was made of steel, not wood and hide like the ones the northern tribes fashioned.

The armor, on the other hand, was Kellid work, but Kellid work of the highest quality. Kagur had paid a considerable price in ermine pelts to commission it from a craftsman of the Hawkwing tribe, whose skill with leather was unrivaled. The armor fit looser than before, and she realized she'd lost weight during her recuperation.

Still, she felt more herself once she had it on, ready to meet any challenge. Unfortunately, that was a satisfaction that lasted only until she crept through the gloom to the end of the tent and discovered her father's longsword no longer hung on Ganef's chair.

Evidently, it was no longer the property of the Fivespears tribe as a whole. Ganef had claimed it for his own, and when he'd returned to his personal tent, he'd naturally carried the blade with him.

Kagur told herself it didn't matter. There were other swords here for the taking.

But like her shield, Jorn's weapon had come from some land of master metalworkers beyond the tundra. The steel was more resilient and held an edge better than any blade a Kellid smith could forge.

Even more importantly, it had been her *father's*, and his ancestors' before him, back as far as anyone remembered. Kagur couldn't leave it in the grasping hands of a conniver like Ganef. She just couldn't.

She slipped back outside and looked around for the second largest tent. That would be where Ganef slept.

When she peeked in the flap, what she saw surprised her. The Blacklions had possessed furnishings for their meeting tent, tables and benches that came apart to make it easy for a mammoth to carry them, but otherwise they'd sat and slept on the ground like Kellids always had. Apparently, that wasn't good enough for the chieftain of the Fivespears.

Ganef and a woman who was presumably his wife lay in a bed, a box-like object Kagur had heard tell of but never seen before. A swaddled infant shifted restlessly on the other side of the wife, and, stained red by the glow of the coals, a small, curly-headed boy made do with a pallet of wolf pelts near the fire pit. Maybe not everyone in the family was effete.

And maybe Kagur had more urgent things to do than reflect on their sleeping arrangements. She cast about for the sword.

Apparently Ganef believed in keeping a weapon close. He'd draped the baldric over the bedpost nearest his head, where it was too far away for Kagur to simply reach in and grab it, or even hook it with the end of her bow.

Careful not to bump anything, she tiptoed inside. Deciding it would be easier to step over the boy on the ground than maneuver around him, she hiked up her cloak to make sure it wouldn't brush across him.

Slowly, scarcely daring to breathe, she lifted the sword and its harness off the conical finial at the top of the bedpost. Grinning at the thought of Ganef's reaction when he woke and realized the valuable weapon was gone, she slung it over her shoulder, turned, and headed back the way she'd come.

She made it two steps. Then the baby started crying.

She had no idea why. She hadn't made a sound. Possibly, hunger had woken the infant. Or a bad dream. Of late, she knew all about those.

Whatever had done it, she prayed the baby's wailing wouldn't rouse the rest of the family immediately. If it did, perhaps she could still make it to the exit. She quickened her stride.

The little boy sat up from his wolf skins. "Mama," his high voice whined, "the baby's cry—" His head snapped around toward Kagur, and even in the dark, she could see his eyes widen. *"Thief!"*

Kagur sprang over him, lunged onward, and burst out into the night. Precarious as her situation was, she had collected her gear. Now she just had to make it to Grumbler on the other side of the camp.

But as she ran in that direction, a figure came pounding through the snow to intercept her. She assumed it was the man Ganef had assigned to watch her.

Whoever he was, he had a long, narrow face, with a drooping mustache that accentuated the mournful look of it. He halted when they were still a few steps apart. "You're a guest," he said.

"Then get out of my way."

"Can't," he answered, and while he was still articulating the word, she rushed him.

Alas, the sudden action didn't startle him into immobility. He caught her cut on his shield and riposted by slashing low. She pulled her front leg back, removing it from the path of his blade, and sliced his forearm.

He managed to come back on guard, but blood streamed from the gash, and the sword in his hand started shaking. She gave him a moment to surrender or run away. Then, when he didn't do either, she advanced with her shield out to the side where it didn't protect her, daring him to attack.

Bellowing a war cry, he obliged with a head cut. She parried with her sword, not the shield, a defense that many Kellids wouldn't anticipate, and started to step forward for a slash to the throat.

"Halt!" someone shouted.

She had no reason to heed the call. Yet it seemed to hang and echo inside her skull. Her lurching, aborted step made her attack awkward, and her opponent avoided it by reeling back out of striking distance.

She glanced around and saw it was Holg who'd cried out. She bared her teeth at the realization he'd balked her with a spell.

"If you kill anyone," the shaman shouted, "you're starting a blood feud! The Fivespears will hunt you like you mean to hunt Eovath!"

Curse him, he was right, and she couldn't have that. It would make her task even more difficult.

She rushed her opponent, caught his feeble sword stroke on her shield, stepped in close, and hammered the black stone pommel of her blade against his temple. He gave a little grunt and collapsed.

As soon as she was sure he was finished, she looked around and winced.

A half-dozen other warriors, some only partly dressed, were converging on her. There'd been too much noise, and they'd scurried out of their tents to investigate.

Their emergence made Holg's counsel, sensible though it was, impossible to heed. Kagur couldn't fight against such odds if she weren't willing to kill. She'd be lucky to prevail regardless.

Holg chanted and stabbed the end of his staff at the warrior closest to intercepting Kagur. The man went rigid like he'd frozen solid in an instant. Momentum nearly pitched him forward into the snow.

"Run to me!" the shaman called to Kagur. "I can help you!"

Maybe he could at that. She sprinted toward him. The other warriors, all but the paralyzed one, closed in on them—but, wary of the old man's magic, they did so more deliberately than before. It gave Ganef himself time to scramble forth from his tent and join them.

"There's no need for this," the chieftain growled, advancing with a longsword of Kellid manufacture in his fist.

"I agree," Kagur said. "Just let me go."

"I explained why you need to stay, for your own sake!"

"And she," Holg said, "explained why he has to find the giant for everyone's sake, including ours."

Ganef glared at him. "If I didn't know you're at least half senile, and if I didn't believe poor Droga back there would be all right when your spell wears off, I'd declare you a traitor and kill you here and now. If you don't hold your tongue, I'll do it anyway."

"Chieftain," Holg replied, "you have my word that no one cares more for the well-being of the Fivespears than I do. Think how diligently I've tended the sick. How I saved your own wife and unborn daughter when you feared you'd lose them both . . ."

As he spoke on, his voice fell and became such a singsong drone that Kagur lost the sense of the words. She jerked, blinked, and realized some power concealed in the recitation had nearly dulled her into somnolence.

It had done precisely that to most of the Fivespears warriors, who stood listening with slack-jawed fascination. But, with a snarl, Ganef roused an instant after Kagur did. Another warrior slapped his own scarred, square face to clear his head.

"That was it, old man!" Ganef said. "That was the last time you'll disrespect me!" He started forward, and the other man followed his lead.

"Stop them," crooned Holg, making the words a part of his recitation. "I can't. I have to hold onto the others."

"Back away," Kagur replied. The shaman did so, commencing a slow retreat. But it was still going to be tricky to keep both Ganef and the other Fivespears warrior away from him, especially if she couldn't kill or maim anybody.

She interposed herself between her two opponents and Holg and backed up along with the shaman. Ganef and his ally spread out to flank her or simply swing wide around her to get at the old man. The warriors caught in the snare of Holg's magic shuffled along too, like sleepwalkers.

Kagur maintained her defensive posture until, she hoped, both her opponents were certain she'd decided to hover close to Holg. Then she rushed Ganef. One of the sleepwalkers stepped obliviously into her path, and, slipping in the snow, she struggled to veer around him. She jostled and bumped him off balance anyway, but without waking him from his daze.

She attacked Ganef furiously, but with small preparatory movements intended to give a competent warrior just enough warning to defend successfully. Warding himself with his shield, Ganef did so, but the onslaught still provoked a wordless cry of alarm. *He* didn't know she didn't intend to kill him.

His comrade, a spearman, scrambled to help him. In the Fivespears warrior's place, Kagur might have opted to catch up with Holg, silence the old man's recitation, and rouse those he'd entranced. But maybe the spearman was afraid Kagur would kill Ganef in the moment that would take.

Whatever he was thinking, now Kagur could fight the two of them without needing to shield Holg at the same time. Though it was still going to be difficult, she could manage it.

But not if she let Ganef's ally come up behind her. As his running footsteps thudded in the snow, she dipped her shield to invite a cut to the head. Ganef obliged.

She lifted the shield again. Steel rang on steel, and before Ganef could ready his sword for another stroke, she spun past him. She whipped the flat of her blade against his knee.

He cried out, staggered, but didn't fall. His thick leather breeches had blunted the force of the blow.

Still, at least both Kagur's adversaries were in front of her again. And when Ganef shifted sideways to flank her anew, he limped.

She laughed. "I guess I am still a little weak. I meant to cut the tendons. I'll get them next time."

"Bitch!" He took another hobbling sidestep.

She launched herself at him, blocked the cut he whirled at her face, and rammed her shield into his.

The impact knocked him reeling and dumped him on his backside.

She spun back around just in time to parry the other Fivespears warrior's spear thrust with a downward sweep of her sword. She shifted in close and bashed him in the face with her shield.

The spearman gasped. His eyes rolled up, and his legs gave way beneath him. Kagur pivoted and found that, as she'd hoped, Ganef's injured leg had delayed his reentry into the fight. In fact, he was still floundering to regain his feet in the snow.

Why give him the opportunity? Kagur charged him, knocked his sword out of line, and kicked the bad knee. Ganef fell back down and clutched at it.

Kagur backed away and watched him. When she was satisfied he was going to stay down, she turned to catch up with Holg.

Only to find herself pivoting right into an axe cut that threatened to shear into her guts. As Ganef had predicted, Droga had recovered from the paralysis with which Holg had afflicted him. Then he'd crept up behind her.

She flung out her shield and blocked—poorly. The full force of the blow jolted her. But the axe hadn't cut her, and that was what mattered.

Startled, angry, she riposted to the face and only remembered she meant to avoid doing irreparable harm when she saw blood splash. Thank Gorum, Droga was nimble and had tried to leap out of harm's way. As a result, the stroke had merely gashed his cheek from ear to jaw. With luck, he ought to survive.

For now, though, the shock of the wound robbed him of the will to fight. He lowered the axe and stood with his mouth opening and closing. Blood dribbled through his teeth and down his chin.

Kagur ran after Holg.

The blind man was still drawing the warriors he'd entranced along, and they still looked harmless. But new Five Spears were emerging from their tents to see what all the yelling and banging around were about.

Kagur sheathed the sword of the Blacklions and pulled her longbow off her back. She strung it, nocked an arrow, and drew the string back. Then she pivoted back and forth in the slim hope that the threat of a shot would deter further hostilities.

Until she had a better idea. She aimed at the nearest of the spellbound shufflers. The fellow didn't even seem to notice, but the Fivespears in their right minds did. They faltered at the threat to a kinsman too close for her to miss and helpless to take any action at all to defend himself.

"Go back in your tents!" Kagur called. "Otherwise, I'll kill the sleepwalkers one after another!"

The rest of the Fivespears didn't all scuttle obediently back into the shelters. That would have been too much to hope for. But no one risked a bowshot of his own, and though some warriors tried to steal closer when Kagur was looking the other way, they froze whenever she swung back in their direction.

That was good enough for her to reach Grumbler. "Lift!" she said, and the mammoth made a ladder of his foreleg. She scrambled onto his back as hastily as possible, so she could quickly re-aim her bow at the addled warriors.

"Now me," said Holg, still weaving the words into his soporific crooning. The recitation had acquired an underlying wheeze, like the effort was wearing him out.

"What?" Kagur asked. Meanwhile, she kept her eyes moving, watching for any hotheaded Fivespears who succumbed to the urge to make a move, and never mind the helpless kin in danger.

"How can I stay here after this?" the old man asked. "You need to take me with you."

She didn't want to, but she supposed he was right. "Lift!" she repeated.

Like any Kellid, Holg must have ridden mammoths ever since he was old enough to walk, but he was still clumsy clambering onto Grumbler's back. Kagur had to leave off drawing the bow again to haul him up.

To her relief, her luck held. Perhaps unable to discern the opportunity quickly enough in the dark, none of Holg's fellow Five Spears sent an arrow streaking in her direction.

She pointed Grumbler away from the camp and set him running. Snow flew up around his pounding feet.

Chapter Five
A Bargain

As dawn painted the eastern sky gold and red, Kagur headed Grumbler up to the top of an ice mound. Unless a traveler was nearing the Tusk Mountains, such a gentle rise was about as much of a hill as the windswept Ginji Mesa had to offer.

She halted Grumbler at the top and gazed back the way she'd come, out across the tundra. Here and there, some of the taller shrubs protruded from the snow, and in the distance, the frozen surface of a pond gleamed. Nothing was moving.

"We'll stop and rest here," she said. "Lift!" Grumbler obeyed the command, and she hopped to his fetlock and then to the ground.

Dismounting slow and stiffly but without need of assistance, Holg said, "I take it you don't see anyone chasing us. If the tribe's not on our trail by now, it likely means they aren't going to bother."

"Good," Kagur replied, "Now I just have to find a safe place to leave you."

Holg snorted. "No, Blacklion, you don't. Haven't you wondered how I showed up just when all those warriors were closing in on you, fully dressed and with a bag slung over my back?"

Feeling foolish, Kagur scowled. "I had other things to think about."

"From the moment you woke, I tried to explain that I'm coming with you. You were just too preoccupied to hear. But I'd guessed you'd try to slip away in the night, so I decided to meet you when you went to retrieve your mammoth. I hoped finding me there would persuade you I'm clever enough to be useful. If not, I'd threaten to raise an alarm unless you took me along."

"Only Ganef's son raised it first."

"Is that who it was? At any rate, when the yelling started, I surmised you might need help and came as quickly as I could."

"Thank you. But I can't take you with me."

"Why not?"

"A blind old man will slow me down."

"Like I slowed you down when Ganef and the others came after you?"

Kagur frowned. "What you did was useful. But I suspect things went as well as they did because you knew the layout of the camp. How would you fare on a battlefield where nothing is familiar?"

"Throughout my life, I've acquitted myself well on a number of them. There's more than one kind of sight."

"Maybe. That still leaves the question of your age."

"Does it? I rode Grumbler here mile after mile through the cold without complaint." Holg reached out and scratched in the wool on the mammoth's flank.

The shaman had an answer for everything. Kagur found it annoying, like they were practicing swordplay and she couldn't penetrate his guard. "Curse it, old man, I don't understand why you *want* to accompany me."

"Then you really didn't listen to a thing I told you. I take Eovath's threats seriously."

"But *why?* You admitted the spirits didn't tell you."

"Not in a clear, unmistakable way, certainly. Nor recently, nor in words. But the ancient powers don't always communicate by speaking."

"What do they do, then—send visions?"

"In this case, more of a feeling."

Kagur snorted. Grumbler nuzzled her, and she stroked his trunk. "A feeling."

Holg surprised her by chuckling. "I know how dubious that sounds. But at least it's a feeling of long standing.

"When I was younger than you are now," the shaman continued, "I left the tundra to see the southlands. In Varisia, I fell in with a band of self-proclaimed 'adventurers,' fools who made it their business to go places sensible people shun and meddle with things better left alone. Somehow, I knew I belonged among them, and I shared their fortunes for many years."

Despite her impatience, Kagur felt slightly intrigued. "But not forever, plainly."

"No. In time, my hair fell out, and my joints started to ache and creak. The company endured, but that was thanks to new, young warriors replenishing the ranks. One by one, my old comrades retired or died."

"And you came home."

"Yes. I missed my tribe and all that I'd known as a boy, but that wasn't the whole of it, even though I thought so at first. Years before, I'd sensed I belonged with my southern friends, and on my journey back north, I finally realized why. My time among them prepared me for a task I would one day have to undertake to help my own people."

"And you thought that when I showed up, that was the task beginning?"

"Yes, and I still do."

Kagur hesitated. "If I were an old warrior and had done mighty deeds in my youth, age might weigh on me. I might yearn for one more great battle, and even persuade myself the gods meant for me to have it."

Holg nodded. "That's a reasonable thing to think, especially in a time when the weave of things has come undone, and omens and portents of any sort are scarce and unreliable. Even I wondered whether I'd simply deluded myself, as the years passed and nothing extraordinary happened."

"It still hasn't," Kagur said. "I'm not extraordinary." A chilly breeze gusted, fluttering her mantle and Holg's.

"You are now," the old man said. "By rights, you should never have reached me alive with Eovath's knife in your stomach. You should never even have made it to Grumbler or managed to haul yourself onto his back."

Kagur frowned at the implication that she herself had become somehow uncanny. "I couldn't die. I have a score to settle."

"At times, mortal stubbornness and the will of the spirits act in concert."

"I don't know what that means."

"Then maybe this will make more sense: When Eovath spoke of the Earthnavel, you may have assumed he was babbling about something imaginary. Most people would. But, bleeding out, freezing, you nonetheless found your way to one of the few people on the mesa who knows differently. In this land and everywhere I wandered, I've spent my days collecting lore the way other men seek—"

"*The Earthnavel's a real place? And you know where it is?*"

"Yes."

"Then we know where Eovath went!" She was still convinced it was for a crazy reason, but what was the difference? "Tell me how to find it!"

"No. But I'll take you to it."

Anger flared up inside Kagur, and she took a long breath to cool it. "You just said the spirits want you to help me. Point me to the Earthnavel, and that will satisfy them."

"No, it won't. They—and you—need more from me. Think about it: How does *Eovath* know about the Earthnavel and the depths underneath it? How, unless Rovagug—or something that presumes to speak for Rovagug—truly is guiding him?"

"To the sun shining underground."

"I don't understand how such a thing could be, either. But supposedly, the Darklands are full of wonders and horrors that make a mockery of what we think we understand about the world."

"The Darklands."

"The place where Eovath has evidently gone. The true underworld beneath the little caves we humans occasionally explore. Layer upon layer of tunnels and vaults twisting through the roots of the earth. I've never been there, but I once spoke to the son of a man who had. The lad shared his father's stories."

"And secondhand tall tales make you an expert?"

Holg scowled. "They make me as close as you're likely to find hereabouts. They make me canny enough to know the Darklands are a maze as big as our whole world. Alone, you could never pick up Eovath's trail, not if you searched for a thousand years. But with my prayers to aid you, you have a chance."

Frowning, fingering the hilt of her father's sword, Kagur considered until Grumbler resumed nudging her with his trunk. Probably, the mammoth simply wanted attention, but it felt like he was urging her to accept Holg's offer.

If so, he was a wise beast, for what other choice did she have?

"This is how it's going to be," she said. "We'll hunt Eovath together. But if I decide you're slowing me down, you'll tell me what you know, and I'll go on alone."

Chapter Six
Into the Tusks

Grumbler stopped of his own accord just before the place where the trail became narrower and steeper, snaking its way up an escarpment with icicles hanging from the ledges.

Though mammoths were creatures of the plains, Grumbler had carried his riders safely through the foothills of the Tusks. But he was unlikely to do as well on the actual granite mountainsides looming before them, and he had the good sense to know it.

Kagur knew it, too. "Lift!" she said, and she and Holg climbed off Grumbler's back.

It was likely they'd never see the animal again. He'd linger here for a while, hoping for Kagur's return. He might even wander back from time to time. But like the nomadic hunters who tamed them, mammoths had to keep on the move or starve. That was especially true in winter, when they had to find their forage beneath the snow.

Kagur stroked Grumbler's head, and he nuzzled her with his trunk. Her vision blurred, and she blinked the tears away.

She told herself it was ridiculous, *weak,* to cry over a mammoth, even one she was fond of. But Grumbler was one of the last remnants of her life as a Blacklion, and the only one that was a living creature. She gave him a final pat, then turned away.

"I'm sorry we have to leave him behind," said Holg, hobbling to restore flexibility to legs stiff from the ride. "He has a faithful heart."

It shamed her that even a blind man could perceive her distress. "He'll be fine," she snapped. "Worry about yourself. Are you sure *you* can handle the mountain trails?"

"I'll count on you to keep me from stepping off a cliff."

Though he was presumably joking, Kagur could easily imagine him plunging to his death in just such a mishap. But in the hours that followed, he surprised her.

He *didn't* have trouble keeping clear of the drops, nor did he need to stop and rest at annoyingly frequent intervals. When they came to an especially daunting slope or narrow icy ledge, he chanted a prayer and twirled his staff through mystic passes. The carved swirls in the wood gleamed like gold—sometimes his flesh did, too—and then he negotiated the treacherous stretches slowly but capably.

Afterward, he sometimes appeared winded, as though drawing down power was taxing in and of itself. Still, Kagur had just about conceded he was acquitting himself adequately when they came to a fork in the trail.

The branch to the left climbed steadily. The one on the right dipped down, then rose again. But both twisted around the mountain and out of sight, and Kagur could see no reason to choose one over the other.

Apparently, neither could Holg. Panting a little, his wrinkled face ruddy, he squinted uncertainly back and forth.

"Well?" Kagur asked.

Holg shook his head. "I'm not sure. The spirits will have to advise us."

"You claimed you knew the way!"

"I do, give or take. I paid close attention to the wayfarer who told me how he stumbled on the place. But that's not as good as if I'd gone there myself."

Kagur felt like he'd deceived her, although perhaps that wasn't strictly true. She took what she intended to be a calming breath, and the cold, thin air stung her lungs and made her cough.

When the fit subsided, she asked, "*Will* the spirits tell you?"

"Watch, and you'll see. This is the same sort of magic that will guide us underground."

He stood and pondered for a moment, then removed two of the fetishes strung around his neck, an amber bead and the fang of a wolverine. He laid the former in the snow at the start of the trail on the left and the latter at the beginning of the one to the right.

Then he clutched his staff with both hands, planted the butt on the ground, closed his cloudy eyes, and whispered. Kagur couldn't make out much of what he was saying, but she caught enough to notice that the lengthy incantation looped back on itself. The last line was the same as the first. If he wished, a shaman could thus recite it over and over without arriving at an endpoint.

As it turned out, that was what Holg had in mind. As he muttered his way through for the seventh time, the eighth, and then the ninth, the westering sun dropped behind a peak, and twilight turned the white snow misty gray. Her jaw tight with impatience, Kagur wondered if the old man's magic had failed and he was just too stubborn to admit it.

Then she heard a faint rustling sound at her feet. She recoiled a step, reached for her sword hilt, and then released it without drawing. The phenomenon that had produced the noise appeared harmless even if it was uncanny.

Slithering like a snake, the wolverine fang fetish crawled down the trail on the right. Meanwhile, the amber bead and its knotted thong lay lifeless as before.

"We see the sign," said Holg in a normal voice, startling her, and the tooth pendant stopped moving. He went to pick it up. "I told you the spirits would point the way."

So he had. She only hoped she could trust them.

She had no real reason to believe otherwise. Except that Holg was the only shaman she'd ever met who didn't worship the Lord in Iron or the Song of the Spheres and who didn't seem interested in nattering on endlessly about the glories of whatever it was he did venerate.

That made her curious, and a trifle wary. She decided to see what she could pry out of him once they stopped for the night.

With an outcropping shielding them from the wind, their meager campfire crackling between them, and wolves howling somewhere to the northeast, she asked,

"Why do you serve these spirits of yours? What's wrong with Gorum?"

Holg swallowed his mouthful of salty, leathery jerky. "Nothing. But these"—he gestured toward his cataracts—"generally grow in the eyes of the elderly. They came on me when I was very young. Perhaps you can imagine what that was like. All I wanted in the world was to be a hunter and warrior like my father. Suddenly, it was never going to happen. I was never really going to have a life at all."

"Your parents must have sought a healer to cure you."

"Of course, and he was a powerful one. He traveled with Lord Varnug himself. But for some reason, his prayers didn't work, and afterward, I decided to slash my throat. At least that way, I wouldn't be a burden and an object of pity for all the long years stretching out in front of me.

"Fortunately," the old man continued, "I was still getting up the nerve when the spirits started whispering to me. Well, not literally, but 'whispering' suggests the way it feels. They promised that if I became their servant, they'd give me talents to make up for my murky sight. I'd grow up as capable as any man, and more able than many. Naturally, I took them up on it." He smiled a crooked smile. "It never even occurred to me until years later that perhaps they'd ruined my eyes themselves to bend me to their purpose."

Kagur scowled. "*Is* that what happened?"

"I still don't know. Nor do I really care. They kept their word. They gave me all I needed to live as a Kellid should."

Picking a scrap of jerky from between her teeth with her thumbnail, Kagur mulled that over. She decided that in Holg's place, *she* would have cared about the answer. And had it been the wrong answer, she would have found a way to retaliate.

"You never speak their names," she said. "Is it forbidden?"

The old man chuckled. "No, I just don't know them."

"How can *that* be?"

"These particular spirits are ancient. Maybe so ancient they came into being before anything *had* a name, although some of my learned southern friends would say such a notion is blasphemous. Be that as it may, if they do they have names, they don't confide them to mortals. I suppose it ensures no witch or wizard will call them forth and try to order them around."

The more Kagur heard, the stranger it all sounded. Holg had walked with the spirits for most of his long life without ever really coming to know them at all.

"Anyway, they're friendly," she ventured at length.

"Somewhat. They often don't care what happens to men and women. But when they do take an interest, they come down on the side of good-hearted folk like the Blacklion tribe, not evil giants and minions of Rovagug. Which is what you want to be reassured about, isn't it?"

Feeling vaguely discomfited, she shrugged.

"I understand," he said. "Every shaman learns there are two kinds of people: the many eager to imagine spirits and gods take a keen interest in every trivial thing they do, and the few who chafe at the thought of it. You're one of the chafers, so the secrets I have to tell you make you ill at ease."

"I'm not 'ill at ease.' I'm just out to do my duty to my tribe, which is to cut Eovath to pieces. It doesn't help me to listen to crazy prattle."

"Well, there's one way to shut me up. You know most everything worth knowing about me. I know scarcely anything about you. Tell me something before we lie down to sleep."

"What do you want to hear?"

"Anything. Perhaps something about Grumbler, or that sword you prize enough to risk stealing it back from Ganef."

Kagur was reluctant to oblige him. Since waking in the Fivespears camp, she no longer cared for talk except to accomplish some practical purpose.

But for good or ill, Holg was her comrade now. He'd answered all her questions, and a blunt refusal to respond in kind would be rude. She tried to select an anecdote for the telling and so discovered something awful.

Prior to the slaughter of the Blacklions, her life had yielded an abundance of pleasant memories. Her mother singing and playing cat's cradle with her. Riding a mammoth all by herself for the first time. Her first kiss, from a skinny boy of the Blueice tribe at a muster of the following. Winning the prize for swordplay at a similar gathering four years later.

It had always made her happy, or at least happier, to recall such moments, but now the memories hurt like sharp stones grinding inside her. Eovath figured in so many of them. His betrayal had even murdered the past.

He truly left me with nothing, she thought. Nothing but the need to end his life.

To Holg, she said, "I'm too tired for stories. Maybe in the morning."

To her relief, the blind man didn't press her to make good on that. As the sun rose, they simply gnawed more jerky, rolled up their sleeping furs, kicked snow over the embers and gray ash of their little fire, and then trekked on up the trail.

Kagur kept an eye on the peaks and ridges, on the gnarled pines, boulders, and even snowdrifts that an ambusher could use for cover. She still only had Holg's word for it that Eovath had passed this way before them, and if the shaman was correct, her foster brother had had no reason to linger. But these silent, frozen heights were frost giant country beyond a doubt.

Yet even so, no hulking marauders appeared to block the way. Unfortunately, when Kagur labored to the top of a grade and got a clear look at what lay beyond, she discovered the way had blocked itself.

She knew how to spot a trail, even one buried in snow, and there was none to take her to the top of the scarp looming above her. Perhaps there had been once, but if so, an avalanche had swept it away. Suggesting such a collapse, dark scree dotted the white slopes below.

Wheezing, Holg climbed up to stand beside her. He squinted at the cliff for a time and then asked, "What do your eyes see that mine can't?"

"That your crawling fetish led us astray."

He sighed. "I don't want to believe that, but it's possible. Sometimes, the spirits speak, and men misunderstand. If there's no way to make the climb, I suppose we'll have to double back and try the other path."

How long would that take, and what if the other trail didn't go where they needed it to? Scowling, Kagur took another look at the cliff.

Truly, it was mad to imagine anyone could scale that sheer expanse of rotten stone glazed with ice. Still, a climber could at least make a start here, and that bulge farther up would do for a step . . .

"Give me the rope," she said. Holg had brought a line because *he'd* known from the start they were headed into the mountains, and they'd already used it to belay themselves together on some of the more dangerous stretches of trail.

Alas, the same precaution was unlikely to preserve anyone's life on the scarp. In fact, the opposite was true. If one climber fell, he or she would probably jerk the other loose from the cliff face.

Kagur took off her shield, bow, quiver, pack, and baldric and hung the rope in their place. "When I make it to the top, I'll drop the line. Send the gear up and then climb up yourself."

"Let me strengthen you before you start." Gloved hand manipulating the air like he was determining the shape of some invisible object, Holg murmured the beginning of a prayer. It was the same charm he used to facilitate his own climbing.

Kagur felt an impulse to step back. Like many Kellids, she appreciated it when shamans closed cuts and cured sickness but was leery of other forms of magic, even those supposedly sent by Gorum.

At the moment, though, she was likely to need all the help anyone, even a strange old man and his nameless familiars, could give her. She stayed put while he finished the prayer and gripped her forearm.

Warmth shivered through her limbs. The sensation was exhilarating, and she smiled. Then she remembered who she was and everything she'd lost, and that instant of pleasure felt like disloyalty. Hoping Holg hadn't noticed, she twisted away from him and toward the bottom of the scarp.

With the shaman's power quivering inside her muscles, it wasn't too difficult to clamber up a little way. After that, though, she had to inch and hoist herself along on a diagonal. A zigzag course was the only way to the top.

Despite the cold, she sweated until it soaked the garments next to her skin. Her fingertips ached, and as often as not, the ridges and outcroppings beneath her groping feet felt narrow as the edges of blades.

Worse, she moved with an unaccustomed lack of certainty that brought home to her that she was as much a creature of the tundra as any mammoth. She wondered if she was making mistakes any accomplished climber would know to avoid. If so, she might well pay for it with her a bone-shattering tumble to the ground.

But maybe she wasn't entirely inept, for in time she came to the flat, featureless spot that had looked like it would be the most dangerous of all to negotiate. The fingers of her left hand wedged in a shallow crack, the toes of her left foot barely planted on a convex bit of rock, she stretched out her right arm. Her right foot dangled.

As she'd hoped, she was just able to touch the lump of stone on the other side of the flat space. She brushed the snow off it and found ice underneath.

She told herself it didn't matter. She still had to try. She gripped as tightly as she could, and, with an awkward sideways hop, abandoned her other points of support.

Despite her augmented strength, her right arm throbbed all the way down to the shoulder. Her body banged into the rock face, and her fingers started to slip.

But there was a trace of a ridge under the handhold. She'd spotted it from base of the cliff.

Or at least she'd imagined she had. As she scrabbled with her feet and couldn't find it, she wondered if she'd actually seen a shadow or a streak of discoloration.

Then her left foot landed on something solid. That enabled her to find it with her right one, too.

Her fingers were still slipping. But with her toes on a perch, albeit a narrow one, she dared to release her grip and heave herself to the right once more. She flailed out with both hands and caught a larger outcropping that—thank Gorum!—was both bumpy enough for easy clutching and free of ice.

Once she had hold of it, her body didn't want to let go. Still, after a panting, shivering moment, she forced herself to look up, find the next set of holds, and clamber onward.

The warm inner vibration of Holg's spell died away when she was just shy of the top. Fortunately, at that point, the hand- and footholds were substantial. Grunting, she dragged herself up into the notch between two peaks, then slumped on her belly in the snow.

"Are you all right?" Holg called.

Sighing, wishing he'd held his peace for another moment, she rose up on her hands and knees, hitched herself around, and looked back over the edge. Holg was small with distance, but even so, it was odd how the climb didn't look as long now that she'd already made it.

"I'm fine," she yelled. "I'll drop the rope as soon as I catch my breath." But first, she wanted to see if she could spot any sign of what she'd just risked her life to attain.

She didn't expect to. As she waded through snow to the other side of the notch, doubt welled up in her again, whispering that there was no such place as the Earthnavel. As addled as Ganef had suggested, Holg had simply latched onto her description of Eovath's raving and incorporated it into his own delusions.

But the view beyond the notch stunned her. As she'd told the shaman she must, she caught her breath.

Chapter Seven
The Earthnavel

Beyond the notch, the trail resumed, switchbacking its way down into a valley. Kagur kept reminding herself that the steep, snowy descent was dangerous. Otherwise, she might have succumbed to the temptation to rush.

As it was, she and Holg reached the foot of the trail around midafternoon. From there, it was only a short hike to what she assumed to be the Earthnavel itself.

As they peered over the rim, Holg said, "Please, tell me what you see."

Not sure she could do the sight justice, Kagur took a moment to consider her words. Then: "The pit is round and several javelin tosses across here at the top. It narrows as it goes down, like the mark of a giant fang except that the sides aren't smooth. There are tiers going down like stair steps."

"Thirteen of them, if the account I heard is correct. Can you see anything else?"

"Yes. Skulls and other bones set in niches along the walkways. The ones on the top couple levels belong to cave bears, saber-toothed cats, mastodons, and such, but the ones farther down . . ."

"Yes?"

"I don't recognize them. I can only tell you they get bigger the deeper you go. I see a skull with five curved horns that's bigger than a mammoth all by itself."

Holg sighed. "I know I said I was content with the gifts the spirits gave me. But this is one of the times when I wish I could see as others do."

"Who made this?" she asked. For plainly, even if it had started out as a natural feature, someone had shaped the descending rings and emplaced the bony relics.

"No one remembers. It wasn't Kellids, certainly, nor frost giants, either, unless they were once very different than they are today."

She grunted. "I don't suppose it matters anymore. We just need to find a way down."

That turned out to be easy enough. The builders had dug out stairs leading from the surface to the first tier and from one level to the next. In some places, time had worn the steps smooth, but the sloping surfaces that remained still allowed a person to clamber safely.

The one real inconvenience was that the various sets of stairs didn't line up, and so Holg and Kagur couldn't go straight from the top to the bottom. They had to walk past dozens of the skeletal displays.

Kagur did so with sword and shield at the ready. She doubted Eovath was lying in wait in one of the recesses. But he could be, nor was it beyond the realm of possibility that a wild beast—a living one—had made its lair in one of the artificial caves.

But her caution still didn't make her as slow as Holg, who paused repeatedly to squint at an enormous bone or a grotesque skull with the wrong number of eye sockets or jagged, crooked tusks jutting up from a jaw that stuck out farther than the rest of it. Eventually, sensing Kagur's growing impatience, he said, "I understand our task is urgent. But your father won't hold it against you if you take a few moments to drink in one of the marvels of the world."

"Don't talk about my father," she replied.

On first inspection, the circular patch of ground at the bottom of the pit had nothing to show them but the layer of snow that had fallen on top of it. But, stepping warily, Holg tapped with his staff, and Kagur did the same with the end of her bow, until the probing dislodged the snow at the center of the space. With a hiss, it spilled down into the hole it had covered over.

"Behold the actual Earthnavel," said Holg.

Kagur stared at it in dismay, which then clenched into anger. She rounded on Holg. "You blind, doddering . . . look how tight the hole is! A human being could slip through, but a frost giant, never!"

"Then Eovath must have found a different entrance into the cave under the hole. This *is* our path. It has to be."

Well, perhaps that was true. After all, Eovath had told her he meant to descend via the Earthnavel. "Give me the rope," she said.

She moved to belay the line to a yellowed skull like two heads fused together, with double sets of fanged jaws protruding side by side from the central mass. The mass of bone was far too huge for the dangling weight of a human to shift it.

The question was how to secure the rope. If she rigged it to pull free afterward, she and Holg would have it to use in the caves. But then it wouldn't still be hanging here to allow them to climb back out the same way they'd come in.

She realized it was an easy choice. Finding and killing Eovath was all that mattered. She didn't care what happened afterward.

She sent Holg down the rope first, then followed. Shining in at an angle, the afternoon sun cast a hazy diagonal across the darkness, but without revealing anything of the walls. Intuition told her she'd climbed down into a space at least as long and wide as the ceiling was high, but unless she groped her way around, there was no way to truly know.

"We need torches," she said. Her voice sounded hollow, like it had almost echoed.

"No," Holg replied. Though standing just a pace or two away, he was merely a shadow in the gloom. "We could never carry enough. But I have something better." He chanted, and the curling, crisscrossing lines incised in his staff glowed red. He touched it to Kagur's shield, and the steel burst into flame.

She gasped and started to fling the shield away, then realized the rippling yellow fire wasn't burning her. It wasn't putting forth any heat at all, just light.

"Next time," she growled, "warn me before you do something like that." She hesitated. "But this should be all right."

He smiled wryly. "For you. For just a moment, I saw everything around me clearly, without straining, and now it's all foggy once again."

"You see better in the dark?"

"Much. The darker, the better. But since you absolutely have to have light to find your way, your needs take precedence."

She pondered that as they prowled through the caves that opened endlessly before them, one after another, a number with crude carvings—representations of men or a race resembling men—hacked into the walls. In some chambers, the floors were slippery and foul with guano, and masses of bats hung overhead. At other points, the walls pinched together, and she had to divest herself of much of her gear and turn sideways to squeeze through.

It was all unfamiliar and unsettling, but she told herself she could cope with it. What should concern her was whether she and Holg were going the right way.

Eventually, she said, "We keep coming to places where we have a choice of paths. But you aren't casting any more spells."

He snorted. "You didn't seem all that pleased at the way the last divination worked out."

She grunted. "It got us here."

"That it did. But I can't ask the spirits for guidance every time the path forks. It would slow us to a crawl, and I'd run out of magic quickly."

"So we still have to proceed like any hunters on the trail of their quarry. We have to watch for sign."

In other words, the search might be even more difficult than she'd imagined, but the realization had the paradoxical effect of making her feel a little more at ease. It was somehow reassuring that her own skills were still necessary even in this alien, dark, and claustrophobic place.

Sometime later, she caught a whiff of decay from somewhere off to the left. She crept in that direction, and the flickering light of her fiery shield flowed out ahead of her to reveal three motionless forms, each the size of a wolf.

She stalked closer. The bodies were unlike any she'd ever seen: brown, cricket-like things mottled with mushrooms and fungus. Curiously, the growths appeared to be withering, not flourishing in rotting flesh like she might have expected. But the important thing was that, smashed and split with pieces of needle-toothed mandible, feeler, and leg lopped off, the insects had been hacked apart by a giant's axe.

Kagur smiled. *I truly am on your trail, foster brother, and you'll never shake me, no matter what.*

Not far beyond the crickets, she and Holg came to the largest chamber they'd seen so far. Along its walls capered an abundance of the graven stick figures they'd noticed before, and black spots, the stains of ancient fires, dirtied bits of the floor.

At the far end, the floor and lofty ceiling both angled downward. The walls drew in, but only a little.

In fact, all in all, it looked like the beginning of a particularly promising tunnel for descending deeper into the earth. Here at the mouth, at least, even a frost giant could traverse it without having to worry about bumping his head or getting stuck. Kagur started toward it.

In the darkness, something whispered.

Chapter Eight
The Dead

Kagur whipped out her sword and turned. The light cast by her shield flowed over the stick figures on the nearest wall. The carvings almost seemed to twitch and shift in the wavering yellow glow. But they were all she saw.

"What's wrong?" asked Holg, hefting his staff with both hands.

"I heard a whisper," Kagur replied, keeping her own voice low. "But I don't see anything."

"Noises can carry a long way underground," the shaman said. "If you truly heard anything—"

"I did."

"—it may be in a different chamber altogether. Still, stay alert."

She scowled. "I don't need you to tell me that."

They prowled onward. For several steps, everything was quiet. Then another whisper made her halt.

"I heard that one, too," said Holg. "But I'm not sure how much we're hearing with our ears. The whispers may be all inside our heads."

"What does *that* mean?"

"That we should be quiet and move. Don't run, though. Running might provoke it."

They didn't run, but they did quicken their pace. Kagur caught more whispers. Although she still couldn't make out the words, she somehow discerned the tone—malice as cold as the bitterest winter night.

She could also tell she wasn't just overhearing one mad, spiteful voice muttering to itself. She could distinguish several different voices. How could there be so many foes stalking her without her catching so much as a glimpse of any of them?

An answer of a sort came when she and Holg reached the middle of the chamber. Murky figures with foxfire eyes appeared around them, not emerging from cover, just clotting from the ambient darkness. The light of the shield dimmed like it was shrinking from them, and the air grew colder.

Her hackles rising, Kagur reminded herself that she was a Blacklion warrior, and a Blacklion showed no fear to any foe. She still had to swallow away a sudden dryness in her throat before she could ask, "Are these ghosts?"

"Ghosts or something like them," Holg answered. "Something dead. This is where they lived, and apparently they resent intruders."

"So we have to fight?"

"I hope not. Let's try talking to them." He squinted out at the circle of shadows. "I'm Holg, shaman of the Fivespears tribe. My friend is Kagur of the Blacklion tribe. Who speaks for your tribe?"

A smoky figure either stepped forth into the firelight or simply thickened out of the gloom. It was taller than any living man or any of its fellows, and for an instant,

Kagur wondered if it was Eovath, slain and reborn into undeath. It wasn't, though. Its build was nowhere near bulky enough, and the head was too narrow as well.

Holg inclined his head to the tall wraith. "We don't mean any harm," he said, "nor do we wish to linger. Please, let us pass, and you'll be rid of us in a matter of moments."

Kagur waited to see if the ring of shadows would part before them. It didn't.

"I told you I'm a shaman," Holg persisted. "If any of you crave rest, I may be able to help."

The spirits just glared.

"Do they even understand you?" Kagur whispered from the side of their mouth.

"The big one revealed itself when I asked for their leader," Holg replied. "Still, who knows? I have a prayer that should ensure they understand, but I hesitate to spend the power. I may need it if we have to fight."

"Then don't cast it. You aren't going to talk our way out of this. These things hate us. But they haven't attacked, so maybe they're leery of us, too. Let's go forward. Maybe they'll clear a path. If not . . ." She shrugged.

The old man turned his milky eyes in her direction. "It isn't easy to make yourself walk right up to things like that, especially if you've never done it before."

"They're in my way." She strode forward, and Holg followed.

She *did* find it hard to approach the phantoms, less because of the danger they presented than the sheer, palpable wrongness of them. They felt like festering sores in the substance of the world itself.

Better not to dwell on that. Better to make sure she kept her eyes shifting so she'd catch it if one of the spirits made a move.

Four paces. Five. Six. Then, with the ghost of a war cry, faint as the whispers that came before it but somehow jolting as well, several of the phantoms sprang into motion at once. They rushed Holg and Kagur with shadowy spears leveled and the murky hints of hatchets and knives upraised.

The two travelers pivoted to fight back to back, and something throbbed through the air like the note of a horn. The sensation made Kagur feel strong and fresh, but the onrushing phantoms staggered, and one simply frayed away to nothing. Holg had blasted them with magic.

Kagur advanced a step and slashed at a wraith while it was still doubled over in pain. Striking it was like cutting fog, and yet her blade whizzed through its target without resistance. She must have hurt it, though, for the dark form broke apart.

Evidently recovered from Holg's attack, a different wraith jabbed at her with its spear. She blocked with her shield, and the triangular blur of the spearhead plunged through the burning steel as easily as her sword had sheared through the substance of a ghost. The incorporeal weapon slid into her biceps, and a wave of dizziness and weakness swept through her. As she stumbled backward, the wraith gave a whispered cry of satisfaction.

It would surely press the attack as well. Shaking off the sickness that had assailed her, or at least refusing to succumb to it, Kagur covered up with her shield just as though she had yet to understand it was no protection.

The phantom took the bait and tried a second thrust through the shield. Spinning out of the way of the attack, she whirled her sword through the wraith's neck. The spirit crumbled into nothingness.

Another dark figure rushed her, and a second burst of Holg's power tore streamers of darkness from its head and torso. The wounds looked like tongues of black fire. Kagur sidestepped the spirit's spring and hatchet strike and drove her blade into its middle. That didn't finish it, but a follow-up cut to the head did.

Taking a chance, she lunged right through it before it had quite finished dissolving. She felt a pang of cold but nothing worse, and the reckless action seemed to catch one of its fellows by surprise. It faltered, she cut into its torso, and it burst apart into scraps and vapor.

So far, so good, especially considering that Kagur's shield and armor provided no defense. But where was the big phantom? If she could slay it, maybe its followers would flee. She looked around for it, then cursed.

The tall wraith was still standing back from the two mortal intruders, and now it was swirling its murky hands through mystic passes like the shaman it had likely been in life. Apparently, it retained at least a portion of its magic.

Kagur charged in to destroy or at least distract it before it could finish casting its spell. Unfortunately, two of the lesser phantoms pounced between them and cut her off.

She and her shadowy opponents traded attacks that everyone ducked or dodged. Behind its defenders, the tall wraith swept its arms wide, then clasped its murky hands together in a final dramatic gesture.

The cool flame rippling across Kagur's shield blinked out abruptly. Darkness as profound as it was unexpected nearly shocked her into immobility.

Nearly, but not quite. Her father had once told her how to fight while blind—a useful trick in one of the tundra's white-out blizzards, or perhaps with a gashed scalp bleeding into one's eyes. Strike hard and fast from side to side, so no adversary can safely slip in close enough to attack.

The defense kept her alive for the moment, long enough to notice pale spots floating in the blackness. Was she truly seeing the spirits' phosphorescent eyes, or were the bits of luminous blur just tricks her desperate mind was playing on itself? She decided it scarcely mattered when there was nothing else to aim at.

She cut at one pair of spots, and they disappeared. An instant later, a surge of cold and sickness made her stagger. Her foot caught on something, and she fell.

She imagined the wraith that had just struck her standing over her and poising its insubstantial weapon for the deathblow. She flung herself sideways, her shield clanking on the stone floor as she rolled.

Then—thanks surely to more of Holg's magic—light burned away the darkness. Dazzled, Kagur nonetheless spotted the wraith scuttling after her. She heaved herself up on one knee and thrust her sword at its midsection. The phantom couldn't stop in time to avoid impaling itself, and its form smoked away to nothing around the blade.

The violent action cost her, though. She felt faint, and the floor seemed to tilt beneath her.

She'd shaken off the effects of one blow from a spirit weapon, but weathering the second was more difficult. The ghostly spears, knives, and hatchets didn't cleave flesh or spill blood, but they plainly poisoned a person somehow.

But she mustn't succumb to it. She tried to brace herself with battle cries: "Blacklion! Blacklion! Blacklion!" The first was only a gasp, but the second came out as a snarl, and the third, a roar.

She leaped to her feet and charged the tall wraith. One of its fellows moved to intercept her, and she slashed it into nothingness. Magic vibrated through the air, and another phantom crumbled.

As she neared the hulking spirit, a shadowy war club appeared in its hands. Eyes gleaming in its blur of a face, it brandished the weapon like it expected that to daunt her.

She sneered up at it. "You're nothing to me. Just practice." She advanced.

As she'd intended, that provoked the wraith into striking down at her. She sidestepped, and the insubstantial club hurtled down beside her and right into the floor. Before her foe could lift the weapon up again, she slashed through its wrist. Then she rushed in, sliced it across the belly, scrambled behind it, and kept on cutting at its spine and knees.

Her heart hammered, and her breath rasped. The stamina on which she'd always unthinkingly depended was gone, stolen by the weapons of the phantoms. Yet for that very reason, she judged that she mustn't stop attacking for a moment. She had to dispatch her opponent before her strength gave out.

Such relentless aggression made her vulnerable to counterattacks, and she suspected a single blow from the war club would obliterate all that remained of her vitality. But she kept on the move, circling, shifting, dodging, ducking, and the oversized weapon kept missing her, albeit sometimes by no more than the length of her little finger.

Faking right, then darting left, she managed to get behind the tall wraith again. She cut into the small of its back. She'd landed strokes to the same spot before, but evidently this was the one that counted.

The war club slipped from the spirit's grasp, started to drop, but melted away to nothing before it reached the floor. The phantom itself staggered a step, half lifted its hands, and then it too dissolved.

Kagur looked around for lesser wraiths. She didn't see any, only Holg, panting and dripping sweat like she was, leaning heavily on his staff, but alive.

"We should rest," she said, "but not here."

"I agree," Holg wheezed. "We need to get farther down the trail. Let's hope we can find a good resting place before something else finds us."

like to think my soul and mind are as strong as they ever were. But when I channel the might of the spirits, particularly when I do it many times in succession, the vigor of the body comes into it, too, and that . . . well, as you've noticed, I'm not a sturdy young cub of sixty anymore."

She frowned. "You didn't have to cure me while I slept. You could have waited and rested."

"I didn't want you to wake up weak and sick if anything unfriendly came wandering through the passage."

She looked back the way they'd come, for the little distance she could before the firelight failed. "Has there been any sign of trouble?"

"No. Killing the dead is often an uncertain business, but we may actually have done it. If not, perhaps the wraiths can't pursue anyone beyond the boundaries of their territory. Or maybe once somebody cuts her way through them, it takes them a while to reconstitute themselves."

Kagur took a pull from her waterskin. "That would explain how Eovath made it through the cave, and yet the dead were there again to bother us."

"You may be right," Holg replied. "Although not even a giant could have hacked his way through the wraiths unless his axe was enchanted like your sword."

Midway through a second drink, Kagur choked and sputtered. "What?"

"Didn't you know?" the old man asked. "It's why you were able to hurt them."

"But . . . the blade has been in my family forever!"

Holg chuckled. "With each passing generation apparently oblivious to the fact that it owes its exceptionally keen edge and resistance to rust to a wizard's arts. Or else the clever ones who suspected didn't let on."

Kagur eyed the sword lying ready to hand beside her. Naturally, it looked the same as ever.

Holg cleared his throat in the manner of one who realizes too late that perhaps he should have kept something to himself. "I, uh, hope I haven't made you mistrust the blade. As best I can tell, there's no curse or geas bound up in the steel."

She scowled. "I know that! It's my father's sword, and I'm proud to bear it! It's just . . . one more surprise. First, my brother runs mad. Then, it turns out there's enough truth in his madness to lead us both underground. Now, it seems that Jorn Blacklion, who spat and made the sign against the evil eye whenever anyone mentioned wizardry, wore it on his hip every day of his life. What's next?"

His clouded eyes catching and splintering the firelight, Holg smiled. "Everyone asks that from time to time. In these days of failed prophecy, at least, no one can ever know the answer."

"Maybe that's better if it means we're free to choose our own fates."

"Learned men say we always were. It's a paradox, I know."

Kagur unbuckled her pack and rummaged through it for the jerky. "You're fond of strange words, storyteller."

Holg laughed. Not particularly loudly, but the sound still echoed away in the dark.

"Then let me try to say something you might find more meaningful. We can never truly know the future, but we can recognize the patterns and cycles in life."

Kagur twisted a piece of jerky until it snapped, then handed him half. "Like the changing of the seasons? Geese flying south in the fall and coming back with the spring?"

"Well, yes." He bit off a chunk of jerky, chewed, and swallowed. Unlike some of the old people Kagur had known, he still had strong teeth. "Partly. But there are other rhythms and repetitions than the ones we see in nature, subtler ones that play out in human life."

"Like what?"

"Well . . . the Blacklions killed Eovath's tribe. He in turn killed all the Blacklions but you. And here you are, tracking him so you can kill him."

Kagur glared at the shaman. He was lucky he was old and blind and that she needed him. Otherwise, she would have driven her fist into his wizened face.

"My father and his men slew enemies honorably in battle," she gritted. "They weren't betraying folk who loved and trusted them, and they didn't use poison."

"I know," Holg said, "and I didn't mean—"

"My father was nothing like Eovath! *I'm* nothing like him!"

"I didn't say you are. I was simply . . ." He took a breath. "If I've given offense, I apologize. It's been a long time since I had to fight the dead. Perhaps the excitement loosened my tongue."

"Perhaps." She was still angry, and it was as close as she could make herself come to accepting his apology.

They finished their meal in silence save for the tiny chewing, smacking sounds they were making themselves. Noise might carry long distances underground, but it wasn't doing so at the moment, and the cool flame rippling on the face of her shield did so with nary a crackle.

Finally, she said, "It's my turn to stand watch while you sleep. You'll need your strength for the last leg of the journey."

He cocked his head. "The which?"

"The last leg. We've come so deep. Eovath can't be too far ahead."

"I wish that were so. But if I'm not mistaken, we're still in the caves that lie just beneath the surface. We haven't even reached the true Darklands yet."

Kagur scowled. "I don't understand. Caves are caves, aren't they?"

"From what I've heard, yes and no. Supposedly, there are three layers to the Darklands: Nar-Voth, Sekamina, and Orv, each in some ways different than the common caverns we've traversed so far, and likewise different from the other two."

She grunted. "Fine. I'll go as far as I have to."

"Good. Because from what Eovath told you, I suspect that's all the way to the bottom."

Chapter Ten
Nar-Voth

Something's following us," Kagur murmured.

It was many days later—how many was already difficult to recall. Kagur didn't bother keeping track.

"Are you sure?" Holg replied. "I didn't hear anything."

"I did. The click of claws on stone, maybe." She pulled the fiery shield off her arm. "Take this and keep walking. Slowly."

It was hard to guess how anyone or anything hunted in these naturally lightless depths. But if the creature behind them was following the fire, maybe Holg would draw it forward until Kagur could both see it and take it by surprise.

She pulled her longbow off her back, strung it, and nocked an arrow. Then she waited while Holg headed on down the passage. With every passing moment, the ambient amber glow seemed to dim, and she scowled away the impulse to scurry after the receding source of the light.

A bone-pale something appeared in the gloom before her. She felt a twinge of surprise even though she was waiting for it. It wasn't creeping on the floor. Rather, it was clinging to the ceiling.

She drew and loosed. The arrow pierced the white creature. In response, still upside down, it charged as fast as a man could sprint right-side up.

The closer it came, the more of it she could make out. It was a ten-legged spidery thing the size of a wolf, with jagged pincers extended to seize her and the double set of vertically aligned mouth parts behind them already gnashing with greed for her flesh.

She drove another shaft into it and still didn't kill or even balk it. She laid a third on her bow, drew it, started to release it, and then the pale creature dropped from the ceiling, twisted in midair, landed on its feet, and continued its charge.

Somehow, she held onto the arrow and adjusted her aim. The spider-thing leaped at her. She shot the shaft into the wet maw behind the scissoring mandibles, then leaped aside, dropping the bow and drawing her father's longsword.

But she didn't need it. The pale creature lay thrashing for a moment, and then the convulsions subsided with a final shudder. It didn't move again even when she gave it a cautious jab.

Holg came back up the tunnel and squinted down at the carcass. "I was hoping for something we could eat, but I wouldn't care to try my luck with that thing's flesh."

As he'd demonstrated when the jerky ran out, his prayers could create food and water, too. But every such exercise of his gifts was an expenditure of power he could otherwise have used for something else, like keeping them on Eovath's trail when nothing else would serve.

Kagur switched her sword for Eovath's dagger, knelt, and dug her arrows out of the pallid thing's body. Two were all right, but one had bent and blunted its steel point stabbing through the creature's shell. She cursed. This was the fifth one ruined, and she had no way of obtaining more.

"It's unfortunate," Holg said, somehow recognizing what had provoked the oath, "but when something tries to kill us, we have to fight back as best we can."

"It's the shield," she said, rising and wiping gore off her knife. "Our torch. The light draws the cave beasts to us, and then . . ." Something occurred to her, and she swore again, this time disgusted not with her bad luck but her lack of wit.

But maybe the underground was actually to blame.

At times, the way became difficult. Chasms split tunnels and chambers, and she and Holg had to clamber down one side and up the other. They'd needed to ford a frigid, roaring stream, too, and it had nearly swept the old man off his feet and into the hole through which it vanished. On another occasion, a shuddering in the stone itself shook rock from the ceiling and nearly bashed her brains out.

But a part of her actually welcomed the obstacles and hazards. They gave her something to focus on. When the going was easy, the smothering darkness weighed on her.

Then, a thought she didn't want to think nagged at her: that Holg had no idea what he was doing. Though he claimed they'd reached Nar-Voth, his so-called Darklands didn't look any different from the caverns above them. He'd gotten them lost, lost and buried forever, and her fists clenched with the urge to beat him until he admitted it.

At other moments, the dark spaces numbed her, and she had difficulty holding any thoughts at all. Bereft of the sky and open vistas, of day and night and any clear sense of the passage of time, she caught herself drifting through the perilous depths in a daze.

Then she bent her thoughts on Eovath and what he'd done, and the resulting surge of rage and grief steadied her. Still, her head wasn't as clear as it ought to be. The fact that she'd only just now thought of her new idea proved it.

"What?" Holg asked.

"Do you remember the glowing red mold?" she asked.

"Yes."

"The shine was enough to light up the space around it for a few paces, anyway. But I couldn't see it from far away like any beast with eyes can see this firelight."

Holg nodded. "That's a good thought. Unfortunately, we haven't run across any since before we last slept."

"I know. But maybe we'll find some more."

She kept an eye out as they continued their descent. They camped three more times, and lost what felt like at least half a day when, despite their certainty that they were on the right path, they fetched up against a blank wall of stone.

At one point, black rats with bristling fur and beady red eyes started trailing them, first one, then four, and then, startlingly, at least two dozen. Belatedly realizing the vermin might truly be dangerous, Kagur gave an echoing shout that failed to scare them away.

She was still wondering if killing one with an arrow would do the trick when Holg turned and brandished his staff. Light flowed through the carved, curling lines and blazed forth from the end. The rodents fled.

The burst dazzled Kagur, too, but afterward, she felt her body relax in the light lingering in the air as it might have after a thirst-quenching drink of water. The glow wasn't the blue dome of the heavens, or tundra stretching out for mile after mile before her, but it was something.

"That might have been an overreaction," said Holg. "But now that I've spent the power, shall we rest here for a while?"

She clenched her will to say no. She and Holg had taken a rest not long ago. She had no business indulging in another so soon, not while the heart still beat in Eovath's chest. In fact, she bristled at the implication that the dark had so worn away at her nerves that she *needed* the comfort of the light.

Then she took another look at Holg, at the slumping way he leaned on his staff and the bruised-looking bags under his eyes, and felt a vague sense of shame. His magical sight notwithstanding, maybe he was the one who needed a respite from the perpetual and omnipresent dark.

"All right," she said, "for a little while." She took another look around for potential dangers, then sat down on a place where the floor humped upward.

She and Holg were quiet for a time. Then she asked, "Why would Rovagug—or any god or spirit—speak to Eovath?"

Holg smiled. "Are you finally persuaded that one did?"

"Just answer the question."

"Well, actually, it's a bit of a puzzle. Generally, the Rough Beast's worshipers are out-and-out madmen who want to slaughter all living creatures indiscriminately.

Eovath just wants to kill humans. Still, Rovagug *does* want our kind to die, and spirits have to treat with people who can help them accomplish their ends in the mortal world. The god likely judged that your foster brother was the right person in the right place to do grievous harm."

She mulled that over. Then: "I wonder . . . did the Rough Beast rot his soul, or was he always full of hate on the inside?"

"Are you searching for a reason not to hate him?"

Kagur glowered. "No!"

"Well, my guess is that the truth lies somewhere in the middle. There was already a seed inside Eovath, but it might not have grown if Rovagug hadn't watered it. But obviously, I can't know that for certain, either."

"For a holy man, you don't know much."

Holg chuckled. "Believe me, I agree." The glow in the air dimmed, and the darkness flowed back like reaching hands, until the flames dancing on the shield were the only light remaining. "Well, that's that." He planted his staff and heaved himself up from his seat. One of his joints popped. "Are you ready to move on?"

Sometime thereafter, they came upon the remains of a colossal snail. Most of the slimy flesh was gone, likely eaten by scavengers, but Kagur could still make out two wounds that looked like they could have been chopped by a giant's axe.

She moved closer for a better look and was only a couple paces away when she noticed that the glistening grease on the putrid carcass was *flowing*. It was alive, albeit a revolting, liquid kind of life such as she'd never imagined.

She backed away and was pleased the slime-thing paid her no attention. It already had its meal.

Later, Holg worked his magic with the fetishes to choose a path when the tunnel split into three. The way he picked brought the travelers to the mouth of a side passage that ran off to the left. The barest hint of red light gleamed from that direction, and water was splashing there as well.

Kagur frowned. The branching tunnel was level and too low for a frost giant to stand up straight inside it. The primary passage sloped downward and had a high ceiling. It seemed reasonably obvious which way Eovath had gone.

But her hesitation only lasted a moment. If she could finally obtain some of the glowing fungus she'd noticed before, and if using that to light her way kept hungry beasts from sighting her from afar, then a brief detour would be worthwhile.

"Come on," she said. She prowled down the side passage, and Holg followed.

The red glow grew stronger, and the splashing louder, until the way opened out into a large cave. Patches of the phosphorescent crimson fungus flourished in profusion, and so did a variety of other molds. Mushrooms grew in the muck on the floor, some normal-sized and others tall as mammoths with caps wide enough to shelter a family like a tent. The water gushed from cracks in the right-hand wall and spilled down to form pools and rivulets twisting through the chamber. The moist air smelled of loam and vegetative growth and decay.

Holg smiled. "You can make your fungus light, and we can refill our waterskins."

Kagur grunted. "We can pick mushrooms, too. I recognize some kinds that are good to eat."

"Excellent. Mind you, I'm grateful for the provender the spirits provide, but it doesn't have a lot of flavor."

"Gather what we can carry, but stay alert."

It would be reckless not to. Nowhere else in the underworld had they come upon such an abundance of plant life. It would be peculiar if no animals dwelled here to eat it, or to prey on the creatures that did.

But the only thing she saw moving in the dim red light were the spores drifting upward as fungus squished and crunched beneath her boots. They tickled her nose and made her want to sneeze.

Relaxing a little but still cautious, she headed for an outcropping furred with shining red. Holg proceeded toward one of the miniature waterfalls.

She studied the phosphorescent fungus and pondered how best to make use of it. If she had a stick, she could jam a piece of it on the end and have a light resembling a conventional torch. But she didn't want to foul her longbow or sword with—

Something whispered, the sound nearly lost amid the constant hiss and gurgle of water. Kagur whipped out her blade, pivoted, and failed to spot anything she hadn't before, except for a plant with pale flowers mostly hidden among mushrooms as tall as she was.

"Did you hear that?" she asked, turning toward Holg. When she got a good look at him, she felt a pang of alarm.

By now, she'd seen the old man strong and eager, and also weary and dogged. She'd seen him resolute in battle, smug as he pontificated and philosophized, and more irritating still when he presumed to offer sympathy or advice. In every humor and situation, his face bespoke intelligence. He even frowned in his sleep, like he was still mulling over the riddles of life.

That wasn't the case anymore. His jaw hung slack, and he didn't respond to her question.

Scanning the dim cavern, she started toward him. Despite her vigilance, she still missed seeing what made the hiss when the faint noise came again.

Suddenly the air around her was thick with spores. They stuck to her face and tingled all the way down into her lungs when she breathed them in.

With that, she realized she didn't need to worry about Holg or herself, either. Everything was fine. Or it would be, once she turned to the right.

So she did, to find her father and Eovath smiling at her.

"What is this?" she asked, stepping toward them.

"It's us," Eovath said. "We came to fetch you back to camp."

"There is no camp anymore," she replied. "You murdered everybody."

"Don't talk crazy," the giant said. "I could never do anything like that."

She wanted it to be true so badly that knowing it wasn't enraged her. Whatever was playing tricks, how dare it use this against her?

"Blacklion!" she bellowed, and her vision cleared. Two figures *were* standing between her and the plant with the pale blossoms, but they weren't Jorn and Eovath. By the putrid look and stench of them, they were dead, but had been freakish and ugly even while alive. One had a pinhead with a single eye, and the other, three arms and a face like a bear. Tendrils like coarse grass grew through their gray, mottled skin.

They shambled toward Kagur with hands outstretched. Taking advantage of her superior reach and quickness, she didn't find it too difficult to stay away from them while she slashed at their flesh. But they were hardy. She had to cut one twice and the other three times before they fell down.

She pivoted to check on Holg. He wasn't where she'd seen him last, but after a moment, she located him. He was supine and bleeding from a gashed forehead, and four more creatures were dragging him toward the back of the cave.

The new creatures looked alive, not dead like the things she'd just dispatched, but in some respects, their appearance was similar. Short and skinny as starving children, they had dangling masses of mold growing out of holes in their skins.

Kagur ran toward them. From the corner of her eye, she saw pale flowers twisting on their stems. Tracking her.

She tried to sprint even faster. Spores or pollen hissed out of the centers of the flowers, and one such spray washed over her.

She stumbled. Her head swam. Her anger and determination faded as a kind of stupefied euphoria welled up to supplant them. Nothing looked threatening anymore.

But everything was. She sank her teeth into her lower lip, and the burst of pain cleared her head.

She whirled and bolted from the cave.

Chapter Eleven
The Face and the Altar

Kagur ran a few strides down the connecting tunnel to make sure no flower could spray her again. Then she poured the remaining lukewarm water in her waterskin onto a fold of her cloak and used it to scrub her face.

It helped. Her thoughts sharpened into focus, and everything looked real. Shapes and shadows no longer appeared on the verge of squirming and flowing into something else. She still had pollen stuck to her clothing, but it wasn't addling her.

And now that it wasn't, she had to reach Holg. Gorum only knew what the small creatures wanted him for, but it couldn't be anything pleasant, not when they'd taken such care to lay a trap for anyone who happened by.

For now that it was too late, she could see that the cave was exactly that. The glow, the splash of flowing water, and the edible mushrooms were all bait, while the profusion of mold hid the pale flowers, the walking corpses that appeared to be their servants, and the stunted fungus men, too.

When the blossoms stunned their prey, the small creatures allowed them to keep some of the victims, but hauled others away. The travelers' dazed condition made them easy to subdue.

Kagur had no way of knowing if she'd already spotted all the flowers or their dead, rotting slaves, but she suspected not. She also had to assume the fungus men realized she'd escaped the cave and were keeping watch lest she return.

In the world where she belonged, she might have tried circling and getting to Holg from another direction, and for all she knew, there might actually be a different way into the cave. But even if so, she'd never find it in time. She was just going to have to enter via the same opening as before.

She tore a strip of cloth from the bottom of her cloak and tied it so as to mask her nose and mouth, then pulled up her hood and tugged it tight around her face in an effort to expose as little bare skin as possible. She took a deep breath, dashed back into the cave, and ran toward the spot where she'd last seen Holg and his captors.

This time, she knew what to look for. Still, a corpse surprised her. Its jaw fallen away, it heaved itself up from inside a boulder-like mound of fungus amid a burst of spores. She bellowed and cut deep into its lopsided skull, and it fell down.

By then, steaming flowers, their color a sickly yellow in the fiery glow of her shield, were twisting in her direction. She lunged, dodging most of the hissing jets of pollen, and what did brush her had no effect.

She slashed the flowering plant as she raced by, and it convulsed. She felt a flash of satisfaction.

Another dead thing stumbled toward her but was too slow to intercept her. Pollen spurted at her but fell short.

An arched opening appeared in the far wall. As she approached, fungus men leveled their spears to defend it.

She was surprised there were only two, but maybe they hadn't believed anyone who escaped the cave would dare to come back. Or that a single foe could make it past the yellow flowers and the shambling dead.

The guards' hides were dark green in the glow of the shield. They thrust at her in unison. Without breaking stride, she blocked one attack with the shield and knocked the other out of line with a downward sweep of her longsword.

Plunging on into striking distance, she cut right, then left, and each stroke bit deep. Both sentries staggered and collapsed.

She ran on down a tunnel that doglegged to the left. Instinct warned her that at least one more guard must be waiting beyond the bend. She positioned her shield to catch a thrust to the midsection and kept running.

As expected, a spearhead rasped off the shield. Clawed hands extended to rip flesh, a second sentry tried to dive under the shield.

She snapped the rim of the shield down on the creature. Something snapped, and the guard sprawled on its belly. She simultaneously stamped on its head and sliced the other fungus man across its snarling face.

Another arch opened on a chamber nearly as spacious as the one she'd just exited, everything once again red, gray, or black where the light of Holg's conjured fire didn't reach. Kagur inferred it was the fungus men's home. She saw no arrangements for cooking, sanitation, or privacy, but many of the sheets of mold on the walls formed recognizable shapes. The inhabitants had sculpted them.

The largest of the fungus carvings had the form of a scowling face. The stuff composing it was a darker red than the growths Kagur had seen hitherto, and seemingly not phosphorescent.

A rocky shelf extended below the face at about the height of Kagur's shoulders. The fungus men had lifted a flat block of stone on top of it, and, still insensible, Holg sprawled on the crude altar. Standing between him and the mold sculpture, alternately turning to each, a creature that was apparently the tribal shaman whirled its hands through complex passes.

Its fellows stood clustered beneath the ledge. Some were still watching the sacrificial ritual. Others had caught the sounds of struggle in the passage and were turning in Kagur's direction.

Hoping to drive through them before they could gather themselves to resist her, she charged. She cut repeatedly with her sword and bashed living obstructions out of her way with her shield. The steel clanked.

Something raked down the lower portion of her back. She knew it must be claws, but her leather armor kept them out her flesh, and now the ledge was right in front of her. She bounded up one of the two natural ramps that led to the altar while the little green shaman scurried down the other.

Unfortunately, the other fungus men were braver. Some rushed for the ramps. Scrabbling with their talons, others swarmed up the nearly vertical surface directly below the altar itself.

Pivoting, lunging, slashing and thrusting, Kagur somehow flung back the first wave. Dead and wounded fungus men toppled back into their comrades, hindering them for an instant.

But only that. Furious and determined though she was, Kagur knew she couldn't hold out for long against them all, especially since, standing at the back of the mob beyond her reach, his clawed hands tearing at the air, their shaman was starting a spell.

Kagur could only think of one ploy that might serve her need. She made a backward hop toward the rust-colored face.

A cloud of spores burst from it. Despite the protection of her makeshift mask and hood, her head throbbed.

But she couldn't let on that the burst had hurt her, not when she was attempting a bluff. She raised her arm and held her shield a finger's length away from the carved face, just as though Holg's cool fire had the power to sear and profane it.

The shaman clapped its hands twice, the first noise Kagur had heard any of the fungus men make. The others hesitated.

But what now? The creatures would resume the attack as soon as Kagur stepped away from their sacred image. They might do it in any case when they simply tired of the standoff.

"Holg!" she said. "Wake up!"

He didn't stir. On the floor of the cavern, a fungus man armed with a javelin sidled to the left. It plainly hoped to throw when she was looking right. Another creature stooped and picked up a stone.

"You said this hunt was the point of your whole life," Kagur continued. "You said your patron spirits tasked you with it. Curse you and them both if you fail me now!"

Holg groaned and raised a shaking hand to the bloody gash in his forehead.

"Do something," Kagur said. "Now. We're out of time!"

Holg turned his head in the direction of the fungus men. Kagur wondered just how much of the scene before him his ruined eyes could actually discern. She hoped that, looking in the opposite direction from the flaming shield, he could make out enough of the details to grasp what was going on.

Holg whispered, then sat up suddenly. At the same instant, his form burned white. The blaze put both the light of the fiery shield and the phosphorescence of the red fungus to shame, like he hadn't merely set himself aglow but turned into a thunderbolt or a star.

The fungus men were as surprised as Kagur felt. Even the shaman backed away from the shelf.

"Thank all those who rose at the beginning," Holg murmured, an edge of strain in his voice. "Let's get out of here. Walk confidently, but don't provoke the creatures."

Kagur found it took an effort of will to move away from the huge russet face and descend from the shelf. But the fungus men didn't rush her and Holg. Instead, they made way and allowed the humans to retreat back down the tunnel.

As soon as Holg stepped back out into the first cave, the light in his flesh went out. He gasped and clutched at the wall.

"Are you all right?" Kagur asked. Turing her head, she tried to assess his condition and watch for pursuing fungus men, yellow flowers, and corpse slaves all at the same time.

The old man wheezed in a couple more breaths, then managed to straighten up and answer.

"Yes. It's just that with age, that trick has grown particularly taxing." He snorted. "I didn't expect I'd ever use it again, certainly not to cow opponents it wouldn't even have hurt. Fortunately, they didn't know that, and I'm told it looks impressive."

"Why not daze them like you did Ganef's men?"

"You can't enthrall a plant. There wasn't anything I could do that would get us out except stack another bluff on the one you were already running."

Kagur shook her head. She and Holg had been lucky, beyond a doubt.

"Thank you for coming after me," the old man continued.

Though she didn't know why, the simple gratitude in his voice—and the assumption of camaraderie that underlay it—rankled.

"I had no choice," she snapped. "I need you."

Holg simply nodded, but as he turned away, she thought she saw his lips twist into a smile.

Chapter Twelve
Sekamina

Illuminated by the glow of a chunk of red mold jammed on the end of a dead man's femur, the stone floor rose and fell like oversized snowdrifts. Kagur and Holg stood at the bottom of one such swell while something padded around on the other side.

Kagur felt a thrill of excitement. Could it possibly be that she and Holg had at last caught up with their quarry?

The sensible part of her said no, not if Holg was correct. He believed Eovath was bound for the very deepest caverns and was still far ahead of them. But the shaman didn't know everything.

She pressed her finger to her lips, and Holg nodded. They crept up the rise. Unfortunately, despite their attempt at stealth, the red glow of the fungus torch was still likely to give them away to whatever was moving on the other side.

But Kagur had to be able to see. The only alternative was to hang back while Holg, with his ability to sense things in the dark, scouted ahead, and she wasn't willing to let the scrawny old man stumble into trouble by himself.

Crouching, they peered over the top of the rise and down into the next depression. An instant later, she reached for her sword. By the Lord in Iron, her intuition had been correct! There was Eovath right in front—

No. Frustration twisted her guts. Vaguely revealed by the red phosphorescence, the creature below her *wasn't* Eovath.

It was taller than any human, yet manlike in the crudest sense. That and desire accounted for her momentary confusion. But the thing was no frost giant, nor anything else she'd ever seen before. Gray fur grew all over its body, and its arms forked at the elbow to allow for four clawed hands. A vertically aligned mouth ran up what passed for a face and over the top of its head.

As it turned and looked up, she spotted two more standing farther away. One held a shepherd's crook, which it presumably used to herd the several goat-sized beetles crouching around it.

Though all but certain she and Holg were going to have to fight—so far, pretty much every creature they'd encountered in the Darklands had wanted to kill them—Kagur nonetheless took her hand away from her sword hilt and raised it in a sign of peace. The old man made the same conciliatory gesture.

The gray things surprised her. They simply stood watching as the two humans withdrew back down the slope.

That by itself wasn't enough to make Kagur feel secure. She and Holg kept retreating until they put three more of the rises between them and the giants.

Then she listened and peered about. Everything was silent, and nothing was moving within the halo of crimson light.

Safety, or at least the appearance of it, evoked another jaw-clenching spasm of frustration. "Curse it!" she snarled. "I was sure those were Eovath's footprints in the mold!" But new growth had blurred the tracks, and she supposed they'd actually belonged to one of the furry creatures.

Holg sighed. "I thought so, too."

"Do you have any idea where we lost the real trail?"

"Honestly, no."

"Then ask your spirits."

"I wish I could. But I've already channeled too much power. I need rest before I perform any more divinations."

She glared at him. "We rested just a little while ago." Or at least she believed they had. It was difficult to be sure in the unchanging darkness, but she still felt relatively fresh.

Holg scowled. "That doesn't change the fact that I've prayed a number of prayers since."

Nor the fact that you're feeble and useless, Kagur thought. But the unspoken retort gave her a twinge of shame. It wasn't fair.

To her eyes, Nar-Voth had looked no different than the caves above it, but she hadn't needed Holg to advise her that they'd passed from the uppermost layer of the Darklands into Sekamina. Here, they discovered chambers far bigger than any they'd encountered previously, spaces where they could hike for miles without ever catching a glimpse of wall or ceiling.

At first, the broad, high spaces eased her. Irrationally so, she supposed, considering that whether a space was large or small, she could see no farther than the reach of her torchlight. Still, the mere knowledge of ample room blunted the nagging feeling that she was in constant danger of being crushed.

Soon, though, she realized Sekamina had presented a new hindrance to the hunt. It had been difficult enough to track Eovath through Nar-Voth, but at least in those confined spaces there had generally only been a few ways the giant could have gone. This hole, or that one? Down the tunnel, or up the cliff?

By contrast, in the huge caves of the middle region, the possibilities were far more numerous, and the floor was often naked stone, with no plants to bend or break and no earth to hold an impression. Thus, the seekers had to resort to Holg's powers of divination more frequently, and it slowed them down.

"You know," Kagur said, keeping watch, "that the longer it takes us to catch up with Eovath, the longer he has to pursue his schemes."

"I do," Holg answered, pulling the stopper from his waterskin. "But if the spirits don't see fit to help me in ways they never have before, I can't force them. Perhaps we should take comfort in the fact that they don't believe they need to."

Maybe, thought Kagur. Or maybe they're just stupid.

Eventually, Holg felt strong enough for the ritual. He whispered the incantation, and a bronze fetish that looked like a wavy flame slithered along the ground.

Following the prompt, they hiked to where the long, regular swells in the ground flattened out. Somewhere out on the plain before them, motes of blue and green glowed in the air like stars. For an instant, the thought of the sky—the real sky—made Kagur's chest ache, and she scowled the feeling away.

"Am I seeing lights?" Holg asked, squinting.

"Yes, and before you ask, I can't tell what's making them. We'll have to get closer."

They prowled onward. Kagur kept her eyes moving, looking for trouble, and listened and sniffed the air as well. The underworld still frequently surprised and confounded her, but she had learned the importance of using her other senses to detect dangers lurking beyond the feeble reach of sight.

Still, despite her caution, she didn't detect the creature until it pounced into the torch's circle of crimson phosphorescence. Pale, stooped, and hairless, with enormous bulging eyes and pointed ears, it gripped a dagger in either hand and gathered itself to spring.

Kagur poised her shield—now wrapped in cloth to mask the cool fire still burning on its surface—to hold the beast-man back, dropped the fungus torch, and reached for her sword. But as the blade hissed from the scabbard, other creatures like her would-be attacker scrambled out of the darkness behind it. They grabbed their fellow, shoved it to the ground, and kicked it until it waved its hands in a gesture of surrender.

As the other creatures allowed it to get back up, some of them glowered in the humans' direction and even bared jagged teeth, but none of the others tried to make an actual attack. Instead, many with net bags of fungus or rock slung over their shoulders, they marched off in the same direction Kagur and Holg were headed.

"First," said Holg, "the giants with too many hands let us go on our way without a fight. Now, these things are doing the same, even though it seems to run contrary to their natural instincts."

"I think we're on some kind of truce land," Kagur said. "Sacred ground."

"Maybe."

As she and Holg stalked on, Kagur glimpsed still other creatures moving in the same direction. More giants with four hands dragged travois laden with glowing green crystal. Dark creatures whose humanoid features ended at the waist, giving way to the bodies and legs of giant spiders, led bear-sized lizards on strands of webbing. Stinking of decay even at a distance, shambling figures pushed carts that were also cages.

In time, when Kagur and the shaman drew close enough, the lights in the air began to illuminate their immediate surroundings. Some shined through doorways and windows. Others spilled their glow on balconies and walkways. In both cases, they revealed patches of a pair of towering cavern walls sculpted into an immense, hive-like habitation.

Kagur shook her head. She'd heard tell of the stone cities beyond the tundra, but had never before seen one. It somehow felt like a strange joke that she was getting her first look at one here in the depths.

"It's not a holy place," she said, "or at least not chiefly. It's a place for trade."

"Interesting," said Holg. "Maybe Eovath stopped here for provisions."

"And maybe he told someone where he was going. Or somebody just happens to know how to find the place where the sun shines in the depths."

Feeling eager, and at least a little more confident that nothing in the immediate vicinity was *too* likely to attack humans on sight, she quickened her stride, and Holg hurried after her. When she noticed that all the other travelers were converging on a cluster of blue lights at ground level, she headed that way, too.

The blue lights turned out to be glowing crystals hanging from tripods made of long, spindly bones. The shining illuminated four hunched, squat figures that walked on two legs but possessed the wedge-shaped heads, tails, and glistening scales of snakes.

Apparently, travelers were required to present themselves to these sentries—if that was the proper term for them—one group at a time. The snake-people looked over the newcomers' possessions, and then the leader made a pronouncement in its sibilant speech.

This often led to one of the wayfarers responding in what even Kagur could recognize as protest. Then they argued back and forth, until the travelers surrendered either a portion of their trade goods or something their spokesman carried on his person.

"Can you see what's happening?" Kagur whispered.

"More or less," Holg answered. "A person has to pay a toll to enter the fair."

"Can we?"

"I hope so. We aren't bringing goods to market. We simply want to buy. For people like us, the fee could be minimal."

Kagur hoped he knew what he was talking about. The whole arrangement seemed like nonsense and thievery to her.

"We need to be able to talk to them," Holg continued. He murmured, and light flowed along the curling lines cut into his staff. He then repeated the prayer and squeezed Kagur's shoulder at the end of it.

Abruptly, despite the inhuman tones and the fact that she was hearing several different languages, she understood all the conversations taking place around her. She even sensed that if she wished, she could join in without difficulty. Though Holg had told her how his magic could open her ears and quicken her tongue, it was still astonishing to experience it firsthand.

The old man grinned at her. "It's reassuring that nobody's saying, 'Those two humans look delicious.'"

As was often the case, his good humor inspired a flash of painful memory, of warmth and laughter shared with her parents, other Blacklions, and even Eovath. She scowled and turned away.

The snake-things—she heard the term "serpentfolk" whispered among the other petitioners—permitted a group of spider-bodied people to pass on through. That brought Kagur and Holg to the front of the line.

The serpentfolk looked them over with their yellow eyes. Forked tongues flickered from their mouths as though to taste the smells in the air. The reptiles had no facial expressions that Kagur could discern, and the way their bodies flexed and twisted at every point made their stances equally hard to read. Still, she sensed they were surprised.

After a few moments, the leader hissed, "Uplanders?" It meant: did they come from the surface world?

"Yes," Holg said. "May we enter?"

"If you pay," the snake-thing replied.

"I'm a healer. If someone is injured or sick, I can tend him."

The guard bared its fangs. "My folk live or die by our own strength." It pivoted toward Kagur. "Your sword."

She shook her head. "No. But this is a good cloak."

It was also a garment she didn't need anymore. Though neither she nor Holg understood the reason, the Darklands had turned out to be warmer than the snowy but sun-warmed tundra high above them.

The sentry gave a short spit of a hiss that, thanks to Holg's magic, she recognized as derision. "A savage's garment. We wear better."

That was debatable. Intricate embroidered patterns adorned what once might have been a vividly purple tunic. But it was threadbare now, and the dye had faded.

Moving in its flowing, unsettling fashion, the serpentfolk turned back to Holg. "Your staff. Or one of the baubles hanging around your neck."

Holg shook his head. "I need them as much as my friend needs her sword."

"You'd better have something." The leader waved a clawed hand at the miscellany of creatures waiting behind the humans. "You're holding up the other travelers. Wasting their time and ours."

Holg's mouth tightened. Then he opened the pouch on his belt and brought out a golden oval with an ivory cameo framed inside it. The carving depicted a smiling woman with a long nose and curly hair. The ornament had a wire loop at the top to string it on a chain or cord, but that part was missing.

"I have this," the shaman said. "A famous artisan made it."

The guard snatched it, then attempted to mask its eagerness after the fact: "It will do. Move along."

As they proceeded, Kagur succumbed to a twinge of curiosity. "Was that a memento of your time in the southlands?"

Holg sighed. "Yes. It bore the likeness of someone dear to me."

They walked on in silence for another moment. Then, feeling like she was lifting something heavy, Kagur said, "Sorry."

The old man squared his bony shoulders. "It's all right. She would have wanted me to part with it if that was what it took to stop your brother. In fact, she would have booted me in the stones if I hadn't."

Carved with rearing and intertwining serpents, the two high, sculpted cavern walls met at a right angle. Now that Kagur was close enough to view them clearly, she was both relieved and obscurely disappointed to realize they didn't constitute quite the teeming habitation of countless reptile-people she'd been anticipating. Many of the windows and doorways were dark, and most of the elevated paths empty, lending the heights, for all their forbidding grandeur, an air of desolation and decay.

The triangle of ground between the walls was livelier, for it was here that diverse creatures were doing their bartering, some from tent-like stalls of hide and bone. The babble of myriad inhuman voices and the grunts, growls, hisses, and screeches of the beasts the speakers had brought to market echoed from the surrounding stone. A tangle of smells, some merely exotic but many foul, thickened the air, with a carrion stink the strongest of all.

The press, the strangeness, and the sheer ugliness all scraped at Kagur's nerves, but it wasn't going to become any more appealing while she stood and contemplated it from the outside. She took a breath and headed into the crowds. His staff tapping, Holg walked along beside her.

Small as a toddler but with a white-bearded face as wrinkled and aged as the shaman's, a little man in a pointed red cap and iron boots called out in a high, quavering voice. "Who will trade, who will trade for my clever helpers?"

The "clever helpers" were an assortment of severed hands, some human-looking and others less so, set out on the ground around him. Many lay motionless, but a couple twitched and flexed, while one was even walking around on its fingertips.

The little man grinned at Kagur and Holg. "I'll bet you can't find these in your Upland markets. You won't believe how useful they are, especially when you have both halves of a set." He clapped his own hands.

All the clever helpers sprang to life. A freakish pair, the left with an extra thumb and the right with seven fingers, reared up on stumps of forearm and threaded a needle. A slender one with gleaming black skin picked up a spoon made of stone and stirred the air. A scaly pair mimed the act of strangulation.

Holg shook his head. "The other folk here at the market don't mind you trading body parts harvested from their own kind?"

The tiny man leered. "We all keep the peace in this cave. Now, if they were to catch me in another . . . but they never will. No ghoul or gug is cunning enough to trap a redcap. So tell me, which pair do you fancy?"

"None of them," Kagur said. "We're looking for a giant twice as tall as I am, with blue skin, yellow hair, yellow eyes, and a battleaxe. Have you seen him?"

The redcap stroked his tangled beard. "I'm trying to remember."

"Do you know where the sun shines in the depths?" Kagur persisted. "That's where he was headed."

"Well, now," said the tiny man, "that almost sounds familiar . . . but no, it's gone again."

"You want a bribe," Kagur realized.

"Indeed he does," Holg said. He pointed his staff at the little trader. "How about this?"

Golden light glowed from the carved swirls on the rod. The redcap hissed, covered his eyes, and recoiled. The clever helpers smoked and flopped about until the radiance faded away.

"You can't do that!" the little man snarled. "Not here!" He looked around. "Guards! Help!"

Kagur put her hand on her sword. "Be quiet."

"Yes," Holg said, "calm down. I didn't hurt you. I was simply making a point."

The redcap glowered. "What point?"

"That I'm a formidable person myself. So is my friend. You should see her wield that sword. As you will if you trade us bad information. We'll come back and find you."

The little man hesitated. "Your blue giant was here. I saw him. But I don't know which way he went when he left, and I never heard of any sun shining in the Darklands. That has to be nonsense, doesn't it?"

"We hope to find out," Holg said. "Thank you for your help."

As he and Kagur walked away, she asked, "How did you know the little man meant to cheat us?"

The shaman grinned. "I actually wasn't sure. But in my experience, the more you look like an outlander, the more likely a merchant is to assume you're gullible and try to take advantage. We're as strange to these folk as they are to us, so I thought I should make the point that we're *not* gormless marks, even if we look the part."

Kagur mulled that over. "We'll have to make the same point to everyone who claims to have knowledge to trade."

"Maybe not everyone. But if somebody stinks of slyness and deceit like that one did, then yes."

"Even if someone can help us, with your ornament gone, we'll need something else to trade."

"My services. The serpentfolk apparently scorn the healing arts, but others may feel differently, especially if they're ailing. Or I can perform divinations." He smiled. "The spirits sent me here, so if need be, they ought to be willing to stoop to a little common fortune-telling."

The potent stench of rot drifted from a spot twenty paces beyond the redcap, where hunched, shriveled vendors dickered with others of their own kind. Despite the fangs in their mouths and the claws on their fingertips, they had a disturbingly human quality to them.

Kagur turned to Holg. "Are these dead *people*?" she asked.

He nodded. "Ghouls. I never knew they burrowed so deep below the graveyards."

One ghoul shambled back to a cage cart, an ungainly conveyance with stone wheels and bones for bars, and dragged out a hairless, bat-eared creature like the one that had attempted to attack Kagur on the plain. This specimen, however, was doughy and obese and had an air of cringing, drooling imbecility. The dead man who was taking possession of it knotted a leash around its neck.

Leading an enormous black scorpion with bound pincers and a capped sting, two more beast-men passed by. One bared its crooked fangs at the transaction, but neither attempted to interfere.

Kagur inferred that no one was allowed to molest people—or things—who entered the market of their own free will. But anyone who came as a captive was livestock, plain and simple.

Down another aisle, one of the gray-furred giants traded dreams. "Dreams of lust!" it rumbled. "Dreams of glory! Dreams of revenge!"

Kagur found it difficult to believe the offer could be anything but a particularly brazen swindle. But the giant had already collected a sizable stack of trade goods and had a dozen disparate folk lined up waiting to consult with it, so maybe it could actually deliver what it promised.

Still, who would want it? How weak and cowardly would a person have to be to settle for a *dream* of revenge?

She and Holg worked their way from one trader to the next, beyond the point where the magic of understanding failed and he had to renew it. Some creatures professed to know nothing of any frost giant or sun shining in the depths. Some, surly, suspicious, or taciturn, proved unwilling to talk about anything but the raw gems, ores, mushrooms, dried bat wings, or slaves they wanted to barter. Others claimed they could help, but generally with a shifty air and always backing off when promised reprisal for a lie.

Finally, frustrated and frazzled by the crowds, the noise, the stenches, and the scenes of cruelty and grotesquerie unfolding on every side, Kagur said, "Let's find a clear patch of ground. Work your magic with the fetishes, and we'll move on."

Holg sighed. "I suppose we might as well. This was a good idea, but it's not working out." He started for the edge of the market, and she followed.

Three serpentfolk warriors stepped out into the street to intercept them. The one in the middle wore a crested helmet with a ratty black plume.

"The Lady Ssa wants you," it said.

Chapter Thirteen
The Lady Ssa

Now that she and Holg were climbing them, Kagur saw that the walkways winding up the cavern wall had no true angles or corners. Neither did the windows and doorways. Every shape was rounded in a way suggestive of the flowing, twisting way a snake would move.

Up close, her surroundings looked even older and more ruined. Invisible from the ground far below, a number of the crystal lamps no longer glowed, while a great many of the chambers beyond the openings were altogether empty. In others, only rats crouched, and lizards skittered.

But the city was plainly inhabited at the very top of the wall, just below the place where it curved out to form the cavern ceiling. Here, sentries flanked the well-lighted entrance to the Lady Ssa's apartments. Piping, rhythmic but shrill and atonal, wailed from inside.

The humans' escorts conducted them on into a big, long room that Kagur supposed corresponded to a Kellid tribe's communal tent. The luminescence of green crystals glinted on pale stone and the assembled snake-people.

The serpentfolk Kagur had seen hitherto were squat and burly despite their inhuman sinuosity. The creatures attending Lady Ssa were, too, but their mistress was willowy enough to make skinny Holg appear fat by comparison. Jewelry glittered on her body, from the spiky tiara on her head to the rings on the lazily shifting end of her tail.

Lounging in a high-backed golden chair, she stared at Kagur and Holg for a few moments. Then, bracelets sliding and clinking on her curling arm, she waved her hand, and the piper stopped the high, discordant droning.

"I've heard tales of your upstart race," said Lady Ssa, "and plainly, the stories didn't lie. You're animals, fit only for slavery, with minds too primitive to endure the touch of an advanced intellect. Be grateful I'm willing to lower myself and converse with you in your own fashion."

Kagur twitched her mantle back, making sure it wouldn't hinder her if she needed to draw her sword. She thought she was being sneaky about it, too, but Lady Ssa threw back her head and made a sibilant, pulsing noise that was just barely recognizable as a laugh.

"I didn't mean that *I* intend to enslave you," the reptile woman said. "Not that I wouldn't enjoy playing with you, infusing you with the rarest curiosities from my collection of venoms one tiny drop at a time . . ." Rattling her countless ornaments, she shuddered as though the mere thought was almost unbearably erotic. "But much as I'd like to, I can't. If the Lady Ssa broke her own hard-won peace, folk would fear to come to market, and that would deprive me of any number of amenities."

"Why did you send for us?" Kagur asked.

Lady Ssa shook her head. "So blunt. So insolent. The stories didn't lie about that, either."

"Do you know any stories about the sun in the depths?"

"Yes," the serpent lady said, "as it happens, I do, and when my guards reported you were inquiring about it, I decided we should talk."

Kagur tried not to show the hope that had just flared inside her. "Others we've met here have claimed the same thing."

"But the others all retracted the claim when you persuaded them it would be dangerous to deceive you."

"Yes."

"Well, you mustn't hope to frighten me. I have warriors and sorcery to protect me. But I wouldn't stoop to lie to creatures so generally inferior. That would be unworthy of my majesty."

"No doubt, my lady," said Holg, "no doubt. Still, it might help to move this parley forward if you gave us a hint of exactly what you know or, at the very least, told us how you know it."

"Couched thusly, your demand is simply a subtler form of insolence." Lady Ssa's forked tongue flickered between the large gleaming fangs at the front of her jaws. "But I'm feeling indulgent. Whether a lady is a ruler or a savant—and I'm both—it's part of her vocation to learn everything she can about the world around her. To that end, I've purchased maps and collected traveler's tales. Thus, though I myself have never descended to the Vaults of Orv, I recognize the one you seek. I believe the surface explorers who made the map called it Deep Tolguth."

"Tolguth!" That was the name of a famed settlement east of her tribe's lands, in a region where eerily warm winds and rivers melted the snow. The Blacklions had never traded there in her lifetime, but all had heard stories of the great lizards that hunted its valleys, larger even than the mammoths. What ties could it have to this lightless realm?

Regardless, it wasn't important. Kagur saw Holg open his mouth to ask just such a question, and cut him off before he could speak.

"And you'll tell us how to get there," she said. "Even though you hate our kind. How convenient for us. What do you want in return?"

The snake woman hesitated as though choosing her words carefully. Then: "The tombs of my ancestors lie far below our feet. Something has . . . infested and profaned them. I want you to clear it out."

"Why haven't you done it yourself," Kagur replied, "you, your warriors, and your sorcery?"

"The crypts are forbidden to serpentfolk except when our faith dictates. Whereas you are beneath the notice of the hallowed dead and the gods."

"How lucky for us," said Holg. "What form does the infestation take?"

"Shining blue mold and a thing like an enormous centipede. My people have only glimpsed it from a distance."

The blind shaman nodded. "I've done my share of poking around in tombs, but in this case, I'm hesitant—"

"We'll do it," Kagur said.

Chapter Fourteen
The Tombs of the Serpentfolk

The door was black except for the scraped edges of the oblong hole on the right side, which gleamed palely. Kagur realized the whole massive panel was actually silver, but tarnish covered the rest.

The snake man with the plumed helmet inserted a wavy bar of similarly blackened silver into the hole toothy end first, gripped the crosspiece on the back end with both clawed hands, and twisted. Something clacked inside the door, and Kagur belatedly understood that the reptile man was unlocking it.

She'd seen locks and keys before, but only in connection to trunks and boxes merchants sometimes carried along when they visited the tundra, not on doors. She supposed that wasn't surprising, considering that to her people, a "door" was a tent flap.

The serpent man took hold of the handle and heaved the portal open. The hinges groaned.

"Go," the reptile said.

Though Kagur had little experience of locks, she understood what it was to be trapped. "We're taking the key with us."

"No," the snake man said. "Knock when you're done. We'll let you out."

Kagur put her hand on her sword. "Give us the key, or we'll take it."

"We'll lock the door behind us," said Holg, "to make sure nothing escapes into the upper reaches of the palace. And if we come to grief in the crypts, surely a sorceress as powerful as the Lady Ssa can devise a spell to open the way."

The guard exchanged glances with its two cohorts. Then they all stepped back from the door, not handing the key over, but offering no further objection when Kagur pulled it from the hole.

As Holg had promised, she relocked the door after they passed through. Then they headed down a ramp, and the gleam of the green crystal lantern they'd borrowed flowed across the floor like water. Though dim to human eyes, it was still brighter than the red phosphorescence of their previous light source. Over time, the torch had faded as the fungus wilted.

At the bottom of the ramp, Holg murmured, "I hope you realize Ssa was lying to us."

"Yes," Kagur asked, looking back and forth at twisting corridors with arches cut in the walls. "She no doubt picked 'Uplanders' to do this because she doesn't want to lose any more of her own warriors, and nobody else who knows what the blue fungus and the centipede-thing are would dare try."

"Yet here we are."

Kagur scowled. "We'll handle this, and then the scaly bitch *will* tell us what we need to know."

"Fair enough." The old man peered about. "I don't see any blue light yet."

"Keep moving, and we'll come to it."

Or so she assumed. But she soon realized the crypts were extensive and confusing. Even the main passages curved and doubled back unpredictably, and secondary ones, easy to miss unless a person checked each tomb carefully, snaked away to chambers that were otherwise inaccessible. Indeed, the layout was so mazelike, it might have been the Darklands in miniature.

Finally, scowling, Kagur said, "Use your magic to find the blue mold. Or the centipede."

Holg nodded. "Let's start with the fungus. We can presumably count on it to stay put once the spirits point to it."

He laid three fetishes on the floor and prayed. As usual, he spoke softly, but by now, Kagur had listened to the incantation so many times that she too knew the words. Thus, she realized when he hesitated and stumbled over a phrase.

At the end of the spell, he squinted down at the talismans on their rawhide thongs. None of them started crawling.

"Ssa lied to us," he said. "There isn't any blue mold."

"No," Kagur said, "you didn't say the words right. Try again."

His voice turned icy: "I know how to talk to the spirits."

"Up until now."

"I'm tired of your disrespect!"

"And I'm tired—" She caught herself. Holg could be odd, garrulous, and patronizing, and all of that irked her on occasion. But was she truly this angry with him, angry enough to drive her fist into his face? If so, why?

She took a deep breath. "Even though the magic didn't point a direction, Ssa must have sent us down here for a reason. If she'd just wanted to kill us, there were simpler ways."

Holg nodded brusquely. "I suppose that makes sense. We should explore the whole place before assuming the worst." He recovered his fetishes, and they prowled onward.

Kagur waited for her anger to fade, and in a sense, it did. But the underlying tension didn't subside. Instead, it changed by degree to a gnawing apprehension of the sort she'd felt when she'd first descended into the earth, a dread of being lost and buried.

She'd thrust the key through her belt, and she found herself touching it repeatedly, making sure she still had it. She assured herself that as long as she did, she couldn't really be trapped.

Like he'd read her mind, Holg said, "I should carry the key."

Her fingers clamped around it. "That's all right."

"You're the warrior. You don't want to be burdened with extra gear when it's time to fight."

"You need your strength for magic." Or at least he had before his skills forsook him. "You shouldn't grind yourself down carrying extra weight."

"I may be old, but I'm not a weakling! I kept up with you just as I promised I would!"

"Then do it now." She stalked onward.

Only to find that it made the skin on her back crawl to have him behind her. From there, he could cast a spell or bash her over the head, and she'd never know until it was too late. Until he struck her down and ran off with the key.

But that was ridiculous. Why would he? He was her comrade.

Yes, and Eovath was her brother. That hadn't stopped the giant from trying to kill her.

She was on the verge of insisting that, even in the narrowest passages, she and Holg must walk abreast. Then she heard a faint clicking coming from somewhere up ahead.

It must be the insect-thing. She dashed forward and burst into a tomb containing half a dozen stone sarcophagi. Carved in bas-relief on the walls and coffins, serpents seemed to slither in the emerald gleam of her lantern.

Something else was crawling, too. All but hidden behind one of the sarcophagi, a long, low, many-legged shape scuttled through a different doorway.

Kagur raced after it. Bounding stride by stride, she narrowed its lead and had all but caught up when she rounded a bend and tripped over something on the floor. As she flailed to recover her balance, she realized it was a dead serpent man—proof Lady Ssa had dispatched some of her own people to deal with the "infestation" before recruiting other agents deemed more expendable.

The stumble cost Kagur a moment. By the time she rounded the next turn and entered another tomb, one containing a single large and ornately carved sarcophagus, her quarry was disappearing through one of the other exits.

Unwilling to waste an instant circling around it, Kagur vaulted over the stone sarcophagus. Dizziness assailed her, and she landed off balance. Her foot rolled under, and pain stabbed through her ankle.

But she didn't let it balk her. She charged onward . . . into a small tomb that had no other doors, and that contained no sign of her quarry, just another dead reptilian warrior. Stinking, the corpse sprawled atop the lone sarcophagus. By the look of it, someone or something had cut the unfortunate creature down from behind.

Her ankle throbbing, Kagur hobbled around and looked behind the stone box for a hole that wasn't visible from the entrance. There wasn't any. She'd just finished her inspection when Holg appeared in the doorway.

"You left me!" he said.

She sneered. So much for a sightless dodderer's boast that he could keep up. "I was chasing the insect."

"So where is it?"

She hesitated. "It got away."

"Or else you never saw it in the first place. Do you *want* to abandon me to die? You *need* me."

Maybe I did at the start, Kagur thought, before senility got its teeth in you, and before I found out Lady Ssa can guide me on my way. But now—

She blinked. Whether she still needed him or not, of course she'd never just leave Holg behind. How had her thoughts drifted in that direction, even for a moment?

And how dare he insult her by suggesting that she was capable of such treachery, especially after she'd risked her life to rescue him from the fungus people? His suspiciousness brought the urge to strike him surging back.

She didn't, though. Instead, she sat down on the sarcophagus and extended her foot. "I turned my ankle. Fix it."

He glanced down. "It looks all right to me. I should conserve my power for when we need it."

"We need it now if we're going to finish our task." Or if *she* was going to finish it, while the charlatan stood helplessly by as usual.

"All right," Holg growled, "if it will stop you whining." He lowered himself stiffly to one knee so he could cradle her ankle between his hands as he prayed.

Something about his touch was noisome, and Kagur had the urge to yank her leg up and out of his grasp, or to snap a kick into his teeth. What if he bungled the magic or perverted it on purpose? What if, instead of taking away her pain, the spell well and truly crippled her?

Warmth tingled into the ankle, and the aching stopped. As he heaved himself back to his feet, Holg scowled at her like he suspected what she'd just been thinking.

She stood up. "Let's move."

As they prowled onward, he muttered under his breath. The sound rasped on her until it was all she could think about.

Stop it, she thought. Stop it. Stop it. Stop it. Stop it. Stop it or I'll stop you. Stop it or I'll stop you. Stop it or—

They rounded a bend, and soft blue light gleamed on the stone ahead.

The sight of it startled and dismayed her. She realized that until that instant, she'd forgotten all about it and the centipede creature—forgotten everything but Holg's incessant drone. Lord in Iron, something was *wrong* with her!

Still feeling dazed and muddled, she nonetheless decided she needed to get out of the crypts, and quickly. But the blue mold, or at least some of it, was right in front of her. After working so hard to find it, maybe she should destroy it before she withdrew to recover her wits. Supposedly, all she need do was sprinkle it with the herbicidal mixture Ssa had supplied.

She advanced into the next Vault. Holg's muttering and the tapping of his staff followed after her.

The shining blue fungus grew in patches on the wall, but primarily encrusted the four sarcophagi. There, it flourished in such profusion that Kagur needed a moment to discern how these boxes differed from the ones she'd seen hitherto.

They had lids made of clear crystal, not stone. The serpentfolk bodies inside appeared perfectly preserved, adorned with gold and gems from their heads to their feet and the tips of their tails just like Lady Ssa. Each box occupied the center of a complex circular design graven on the floor.

Something about the motionless but entirely uncorrupted reptilian forms was horrible. Feeling mired, stupid, *paralyzed* as she sometimes had in nightmares, Kagur couldn't stop staring at them.

Or maybe it was Holg's voice that was draining her of resolve and understanding. At some point, the muttering had gone from irritating to numbing.

"Sullen," the old man said. "Reckless. Heedless. *Ungrateful.* You don't deserve the spirits' help, and I can't fulfill their wishes if you get me killed along the way."

Why, she wondered, struggling to focus, were his spiteful complaints half putting her to sleep instead of angering her? He must be bewitching her the same way he'd befuddled Ganef's men!

And the blow from behind would come next!

Chapter Fifteen
The Centipede

Kagur bellowed, and it broke her free of Holg's spell. She flung herself forward and felt the breeze as the old man's staff whizzed through the air at her back.

She whirled, dropped the green crystal lantern to clash against the floor, and snatched for her longsword. She'd cut the treacherous—

No! She wouldn't! Something was driving both of them mad, but she had to resist it. She left her blade in its scabbard.

Perhaps too addled for any more magic, Holg rushed her. Snarling, he feinted low, then whirled the staff at her head.

She knocked the weapon aside with her shield and shifted in close. She drove her fist into his jaw.

Hitting him was as satisfying as she'd imagined it would be, and more satisfying still when he fell down. Now she'd kick him until—

No! "I'm not your puppet!" she screamed.

That defiant outburst felt right, but just whom was she defying? The blue mold? How could that be? She'd been confused almost since the moment she entered the tombs, before she'd come anywhere near the stuff.

"You're shrieking at me," said Eovath, laughter in his rumble of a voice.

Kagur whirled. His axe dripping blood, more gore spattering his body, her brother leered at her from the far corner of the Vault.

"It's a good trick, isn't it," he continued, "driving people crazy? Rovagug taught it to me."

Trembling, she reached for her sword. Her groping hand couldn't find the hilt.

"But apparently the magic didn't quite take with you," Eovath said. "That's all right. I'd rather kill you with my hands." He started forward.

She dodged left, and he compensated instantly. He was still coming right at her, and the way he was shifting his axe from side to side, she couldn't tell where to position her shield.

But it made no sense that he was lurking here, or that she'd missed spotting someone so enormous the moment she peered into the crypt. It was as crazy as any of the fancies that had been festering inside her head.

And so, as he swung the axe, she croaked out, "You're not real!"

Eovath vanished.

But what had made her imagine he was here in the first place?

The centipede! Gorum, she'd even glimpsed and chased the filthy thing, but then, with her thoughts warping and blurring as soon as she tried to think them, forgotten all about it.

She had to locate and attack it before it could try any more of its tricks. She cast about but couldn't see it.

Where could it possibly be hiding? She strained to think, but nothing came to her.

Not until she realized that Eovath—or the illusion of him—had stood straight and walked without difficulty. The tomb had a high ceiling, and in her empty-headed state, she'd neglected to look up.

The creature was floating above her.

It did somewhat resemble a centipede longer than a man was tall. Dozens of legs dangled down the length of its body. But it had a pair of writhing tentacles, too, each wrapped around a scimitar with a blade of smoky crystal. Set in a triangle, one above the other two, its three jagged mandibles gnashed and dripped a viscous liquid. The glows of the blue fungus and Kagur's lantern glinted on its shell and in its cluster of round little eyes.

The creature was hideous almost beyond bearing, but Kagur sneered at its manifest cowardice. It had fled before her already, and now it imagined it was hovering above her reach.

Resolved to teach it differently, she drew her sword and ran at one of the crystal sarcophagi. She sprang to the top of it, leaped again, and cut.

Her blade lopped off the tip of a segmented leg and swept on to shear into the insect-thing's belly. Then she dropped back onto the coffin. She floundered on the slick crystal lid and moist fungus but managed to keep her footing. She bent her legs for another jump.

The centipede plummeted straight at her.

She dived out from under it and slammed down hard. Her foe crashed down on top of the sarcophagus. As she rolled to her feet, it hopped to the floor.

The creature scuttled toward her and cut with both scimitars simultaneously. She blocked one with her shield and parried the other with her father's sword. The steel rang, and before the centipede-thing could pull its tentacles back, she slashed the one on the left. Dark ichor splashed from the wound. The crystal blade slipped from the thing's grip, and it had to make a fumbling snatch to retrieve it.

Kagur grinned, advanced, and cut again.

As the fight continued, the wormlike insect's mouthparts periodically dripped a thick, viscous drool. Kagur assumed it was poison, and made a mental note to stay well away from those bony mandibles.

But it was still trying to poison her mind, too. A force she now recognized as intrusive tore at her thoughts, repeatedly reducing them to disorientation and bewilderment. She kept forgetting where she was and how the fight had started.

It didn't matter, though. Now that she finally had the centipede-thing in front of her, she didn't need to think to kill it. Fury, loathing, and her training would carry her through.

She pivoted to cut at the centipede's right tentacle, gashed it, and instantly swung back to meet an attack from the left. The crystal scimitar whirled in low and then whipped high, shedding droplets of venom as it traveled.

Crouching, Kagur dropped below the arc of the attack and cut at the same spot she'd ripped already. Her sword sheared all the way through the tentacle. The severed end and the weapon it was coiled around tumbled to the floor. The centipede gave a rasping cry and faltered.

Trusting to speed to carry her safely past the remaining scimitar, Kagur charged with her point extended. The longsword punched into the cluster of eyes.

Before she could pull it back out, the centipede-thing surged forward. Evidently it was willing to drive the blade even deeper into its own flesh if that was what it took to score on Kagur in return. The three mandibles spread wide.

Then the creature's legs gave way beneath it, crumpling from front to back so that the thing fell quickly, but still, discernibly, a segment at a time. The other scimitar made a cracking noise as it too dropped to the floor.

Kagur dragged her sword out of the centipede's head, stepped back, and scrutinized the carcass. It showed no signs of jumping up again, but it was her thoughts coming back into focus as much as the creature's lack of motion that convinced her it was finished.

Toward the end, she'd realized her mind was failing, but it took the recovery of her faculties to make clear to her just how crippled she'd truly been, how close to falling into utter lunacy or imbecility. The threat was now past, but even so, she shuddered.

She moved back to Holg, poured water on his face, and patted his cheeks. "Wake up, old man."

Milky eyes fluttered open, and he groaned. "I'm tired of getting hit in the head."

"Be glad I didn't cut it off." She offered the waterskin. "Drink."

When Holg was ready to stand, he had to go squint at the centipede-thing. Kagur, meanwhile, dribbled herbicide onto the blue mold and watched it wither, the luminescence in certain patches flaring for an instant before flickering out altogether.

The tombs proved to be considerably less extensive and mazelike going out than they'd seemed coming in. Kagur realized it was her burgeoning insanity that had made them so bewildering and wondered with a twinge of disgust just how many times she and Holg had wandered in a circle without realizing it.

She was glad to leave the crypts, but her reaction was premature. She and Holg had to return immediately with Lady Ssa and several guards. The reptile woman wanted to see for herself that her agents truly had accomplished their task.

Kagur considered reminding Ssa of her assertion that the presence of living serpentfolk would offend "the gods and the hallowed dead." But she was tired, and in the wake of the centipede's psychic assault had developed a pounding headache. The gibe seemed like more trouble than it was worth.

She suspected Holg felt no better than she did, but as she might have expected, that wasn't enough to stifle his loquacity. As Ssa surveyed the chamber where the insect-thing had met its end, he asked, "So, what was it really all about?" He pointed with his staff to indicate the centipede's carcass. "What was that thing?"

"Such knowledge wasn't part of the bargain," Ssa replied.

"But will it do any harm to share it?" the shaman said. "I love my tribe in the Uplands, but sometimes, dwelling among them, I missed the conversation of other scholars." He nodded toward her squat, hunched warriors—creatures unmistakably her kin, yet just as unmistakably formed differently than her or the bodies in the sarcophagi with the crystal lids. "Perhaps, on occasion, you feel similarly."

Ssa stared at him for several moments. Then: "The thing you killed is a seugathi. Such creatures serve even fouler and more powerful beings that dwell in the Vaults of Orv."

"How did a seugathi get into the tombs of your ancestors?" Holg asked.

The serpent woman gave a short hiss. "I wish I knew."

"Well, then, *why* did it come in? What did it want here?"

"As best I can judge, it wanted to sow the cytillesh—the blue fungus—on the coffins of the sleepers. I assume that if we checked, we'd discover it shifted the lids slightly as well, so the spores could get inside. Then it remained to defend its handiwork."

Holg frowned. "And why would it want the spores to reach the sleepers?"

"Cytillesh is often called brain mold. Over time, it alters the minds of those who breathe it in."

Intrigued despite herself, Kagur said, "Then the bodies in the boxes really are 'sleepers,' not corpses. They're hibernating like bears."

"Yes," said Ssa, "they're wizards who suspended themselves to await the moment when we serpentfolk are ready to wrest back all that is rightfully ours from your wretched kind."

Holg scratched his chin. "And what do the masters of the seugathi have to gain by driving the sleepers mad or afflicting them with whatever it is that brain mold does?"

"I don't know," the serpent woman said. "I've never met anyone who even had a plausible guess why such creatures pursue the bizarre ends they do. Perhaps they're all mad themselves."

Holg mulled that over for a moment or two. Then he said, "I appreciate you indulging my curiosity. Now, if you'll show us the maps you mentioned, we'll be even more grateful."

"As soon as I complete the cleansing you began," Ssa replied. She faced the sarcophagi and raised her clawed, scaly hands above her head. Emeralds and topazes set in her various ornaments flickered with their own inner radiance. The air grew cold, and her bodyguards scurried to clear the space between her and the coffins.

Averse though she was to any display of sorcery, Kagur recognized that Ssa's present intentions were no concern of hers. Still, driven by an obscure impulse, she said, "Wait—what are you doing?"

"Destroying them," the sorceress replied. "They are *not* going to wake up demented in *my* time to claim or ruin everything I've built."

"You said that brain mold alters the mind *over time*. Maybe the sleepers haven't yet breathed in enough of it."

"Or perhaps they have."

"So you'll just butcher them when they're lying helpless? Your own kin? The only creatures in this whole great cavern that are truly like you?"

Ssa's gaze dripped scorn. "No one is like me."

Then she hissed an incantation, and with a shattering of crystal lids, the bodies in the sarcophagi burst into flame.

Chapter Sixteen
The Orc Child

The green glow of the crystal lantern washed over the rocky floor ahead. None of the serpentfolk had objected when Kagur held onto it. She doubted that was out of gratitude. More likely, for all their claim to be the superior race, they were reluctant to start an unnecessary quarrel with someone who could slay a seugathi.

She peered at whatever the light could show her, listened, and sniffed the air as well. She and Holg agreed that while Ssa's cavern itself might be truce ground, the paths leading in and out were likely prime spots for marauders to wait in ambush.

Thanks to their caution, they'd caught the sound of something padding after them a while back. Then, moments ago, it had made a noise like a cough. Kagur suspected the sound was actually a signal to alert its comrades that victims were drawing nigh.

But if so, she hadn't detected those accomplices yet. With a twinge of reluctance, she hooded the lantern so Holg could peer with his peculiar senses. Blackness engulfed them.

"Well?" she whispered.

"Nothing yet," the shaman replied.

"Look up," she said. One foe floating above her head had nearly made an end of her, but she was in her right mind now.

After a moment, Holg said, "Ah, yes."

"What?"

"It's more brutes like the one that wanted to attack you on the way into Ssa's city. They're crawling on the ceiling, and they've got nets."

"How many are there?"

"Seven I can see."

Kagur opened the lantern. "Walk on like we don't know. When we're close, warn me, then make a bright light."

As they stalked toward the danger, Kagur's nerves were taut, and she had to fight the impulse to look up. Finally, Holg said, "Now."

She closed her eyes. The shaman rattled off a spell, and the resulting blaze turned the inside of her eyelids red. The marauders gave rasping cries.

Kagur opened her eyes. The light in the air dazzled her, but she blinked several times, and then she could see.

The pallid, hairless things on the ceiling, however, still had their bestial faces screwed up like they were at least half blind. She nocked an arrow, drew, loosed, and one fell from its perch to *thud* on the tunnel floor twenty feet below.

She shot another, and it plummeted, too. Then, with roars and grunts, the rest dropped lengths of rope or vine and clambered down as fast a man could sprint.

As the beast-men reached the ground, she dropped her bow, whipped out her longsword, and readied her shield. Holg gripped his staff with both hands. Then, fangs bared, knives and cudgels poised, the creatures surged at them like a pack of starving wolves.

Recalling how the brutes liked to pounce, Kagur watched for the two racing in the lead to gather themselves for a final overwhelming spring. At that instant, she hurled herself at them.

Her slash caught one at the start of its leap, opened its neck, and splashed gore through the air. She rammed her shield into the face of the other. Bone crunched, it staggered, and she sliced it across the back of the knee and hamstrung it.

She took another stride into the midst of the remaining beast-men. She cut one across the belly, and, knees buckling, it dropped its stone club—a broken-off stalactite or stalagmite by the look of it—to yowl and clutch at the wound.

At once, she pivoted, just in time to catch the swing of another stone club on her shield. She riposted with a head cut that sliced away a pointed ear.

The beast-man bared its crooked fangs and struck back. She wrenched herself out of the way and thrust her point into the creature's torso.

Good, but she had one foe remaining, and she'd lost track of it! She whirled to locate it before its bludgeon, blade, or filthy jagged teeth found her.

Something *cracked*, and she turned far enough to reorient on the beast-man just as it pitched forward onto its face. Making sure he disposed of it, Holg hit it a second time.

"I would have caught up with you a little sooner," he panted, "except that the creature that was shadowing us ran up to help its brothers." Flexing the fingers of his right hand, he nodded toward an eighth beast-man sprawled several paces away.

"I managed." Kagur stepped to the brute with the split belly. It snarled and tried to flounder away from her as she thrust her sword into its heart. "You're all right?"

Holg switched his staff to his right hand so he could work the fingers of the left. "Fine."

She grunted. "Then I'll finish off the rest of the beast-men. You see about recovering my arrows."

When they were ready, they trekked onward through the dark and echoing spaces. At a place where a downward-sloping passage split into three, Holg consulted the spirits.

By rights, the maps he and Kagur had seen and the counsel they'd received should prove a tremendous help in finding their way. But they couldn't be sure a creature who made no secret of despising humans hadn't decided to lead them astray, and even if she hadn't, the Darklands were still a maze. Thus, Holg intended to keep performing the ritual from time to time. He'd simply do so less frequently.

The wolverine fang and its leather thong slithered toward the mouth of the tunnel on the left, and the old man smiled. "The directions are good so far."

"So far." Kagur stooped and retrieved the talismans that hadn't moved while he fetched the one that had. Then, as they prowled on, she said, "No thanks to me."

"What do you mean?" Holg swept the tip of his staff back and forth just above the floor.

Kagur scowled. "I shouldn't have antagonized Ssa by asking her to spare the sleepers. Her kind and ours are obvious enemies. What do I care if they slaughter one another?"

"Do you remember what I told you about patterns?"

She tried to recall. Holg said lots of things, and many of them seemed pointless. But this time, she recognized what he was getting at.

"Eovath murdered his own helpless kin. Ssa meant to do the same, and it . . . bothered me."

"Enough to make you protest."

Kagur had never really considered that people could do things without understanding their own motives. She found she didn't much care for the idea.

"The way turns steep up ahead," she said. "We should save our breath for the climb."

Two marches later—at some point, she'd lost the habit of trying to divide time into "days"—she sighted a red worm the size of a man surrounded by a sort of rippling haze. She and Holg waited for it burrow into the passage floor and disappear, and when they advanced and felt the residual heat at the site, she realized it had *melted* its way into the stone.

During the third march after that, they had to traverse the narrow strip of mucky ground between a black lake and the cavern wall. As they reached the far end, several fish-men with crests of fin atop their heads swam to the surface of the water and stared after them with goggle eyes. Fortunately, that was all they did. Maybe they weren't hungry. Or perhaps they preferred to swarm out and catch prey in the middle of the path that twisted around the pool, and they'd already missed their chance.

On the next leg of the journey, the travelers came upon the image of a leering devil or demon with curly horns and cloven hooves carved in bas-relief on a tunnel wall. As far as Kagur could tell, the site was nowhere near the habitation of any intelligent creature, and she had no idea why the sculptor had chosen to place the work here. But someone else had come along after him and taken a chisel to the image's eyes.

Every creature or phenomenon that was new to Holg made him want to pause to learn what he could about it and inspired him to garrulous speculation. Meanwhile, Kagur gritted her teeth against the impulse to grab him and manhandle him on down the trail, or at least growl at him to hold his peace. To her, the unfamiliar things weren't marvels, just delays.

Maybe her feelings were unreasonable, for it appeared Ssa *had* provided good information, and as a result, she and Holg were making faster progress than before. But somehow, that very realization made her even more impatient to find her quarry, and she dreamed of Eovath every time she slept.

Sometimes she relived the butchery in the communal tent. Sometimes a pleasant recollection twisted into bloody nightmare. But the worst dreams were happy memories that simply played out as they had in the waking world.

Ignoring his protests that he was too ungainly to learn, she taught the giant to dance.

Taking advantage of her stubborn refusal to give up, he kept her guessing for weeks at a "riddle" without an answer. When he finally admitted the trick, she launched herself at him and they fell down wrestling in the snow, struggling till her anger turned to laughter.

On a trading visit to Icestair, they climbed the stone steps to the top of the glacier. As she gazed across the expanse of gleaming ice to the north, and back down at the green and brown tundra stretching away to the south, she felt a weight lift from her heart for the first time since her mother's death.

Such dreams were the hardest to bear. She woke from them loving him anew and believing she was still with him, her father, and the rest of the tribe. Then she opened her eyes to stone and darkness, rediscovered the truth, and tightened her jaw lest she make an anguished sound that Holg, standing watch, might hear.

Nine marches out from Ssa's market, the way brought them to a pit as broad and round as the top of the Earthnavel. Red light shined out of it like a fire was burning at the bottom, but when Kagur looked over the rim, she saw patches of the same luminous fungus from which she'd fashioned a torch.

Unlike the Earthnavel, the pit didn't narrow as it went deeper, or at least the part she could make out didn't. A trail, so steep or narrow in places that it barely deserved the name, spiraled down into the crimson haze.

Kagur took a long breath. "The way into Orv."

Holg nodded. "According to Lady Ssa."

As there was red light to see by, Kagur decided it would be foolish for her and Holg to make themselves conspicuous by showing a green one. She hooded the crystal lantern and strode toward the top of the trail.

Then, with grinding reluctance, she made herself turn back around. "We've been traveling for a while," she said, "and even with the path, the climb down doesn't look all that easy. We can rest first if you need it."

Holg grinned. "Even though the wait would drive you mad? Thank you for your consideration, but no. Now that we've made it this far, I want to find out what's at the bottom as urgently as you do."

They started downward, edging along or clutching at the rocky wall when necessary, trying to avoid both falling to their deaths and making noise. But despite their best efforts, they occasionally dislodged pebbles that clattered down into the darkness, and Kagur gritted her teeth whenever they did.

She'd long since decided that *every* part of the Darklands was dangerous, but that wasn't the only reason for her caution. Unless Ssa's information was out of date, dangerous beasts laired and hunted in the lower reaches of the pit. Luckily, there was also supposed to be a way around them.

Eventually, the trail both widened and leveled out into a ledge that curved halfway around the pit before sloping downward once again. Soft clicking and rustling sounds rose from below.

An arrow resting on her longbow, Kagur peered over the edge. Squinting, Holg looked as well.

The eight-legged creatures beneath them resembled spiders or fleas the size of men, with enormous claws and long feelers curling back from their heads. Mostly quiescent at the moment, they crouched on shelves or had squeezed into cracks and depressions in the rock.

"Are they giant insects?" Holg whispered. "I can't tell."

"Yes," Kagur replied. "I'll watch them. You find the fissure."

According to Ssa's information, a natural opening on the ledge provided access to hollow spaces that in turn descended into Orv. Kagur assumed the creatures below her could also find their way into the honeycomb, but hoped that at worst, she and Holg would only run into them one at a time. Which would be better than trying to make their way past several at once.

Although they could in theory exit the pit if they simply kept on the way they were going. Kagur could just make out tunnel openings at floor level. As she was trying to spot them all, a figure, tiny with distance and vague in the red-lit gloom, came through one on her right. The shadow looked around but seemingly failed to spot the insect-things. They must be less visible from below than from above.

The newcomer headed for a pale spot on the floor. Watching, likely preparing to attack, some of the insects shifted position.

When the figure moved into the middle of the space, Kagur could see him better and realized it wasn't just distance that made him look small. He was skinny and only half grown, with elongated canine teeth jutting from his lower jaw, pointed ears, shaggy black hair, and skin that would no doubt be dirty green if viewed in sunlight. He was naked except for the ragged hide kilt wrapped around his waist.

"I found the opening," Holg whispered. Then, evidently perceiving the tension that had come over her, he added, "What?"

"There's an orc down there," she replied.

Which was no concern of hers. The orcs of the Hold of Belkzen were her people's enemies, vicious brutes whose nature it was to murder, rape, torture, and pillage. She had no doubt that the boy below shared the same proclivities, and if the insects were busy devouring him, that would make it easier to slip past them.

Holg squinted down at the floor of the shaft. "Watch out!" he shouted.

Startled, the orc boy looked up. Then he whirled toward the nearest opening at the wall.

"Why did you do that?" Kagur demanded.

"The orc may have useful information," Holg replied. "He can't share it if he's dead."

Meanwhile, on the floor of the pit, something flickered though the air. The orc flopped suddenly backward and then slid flailing over the ground toward a different wall.

In the uncertain light, Kagur couldn't make out what was really happening until the child jerked up into the air. Then she understood that one of the insect-things had thrown a sticky line like a strand of spider web to catch him, yank him off his feet, and drag him bumping and scraping up to its perch. The boy tried clutching the wall to arrest his involuntary ascent, but he wasn't strong enough.

Kagur would still have been happy to watch the wretched orc die. But if Holg had decided there was a reason to help him, she supposed she ought to follow the old man's lead.

She drew and loosed. Her arrow pierced the insect that had snared the orc where its bump of a head fused with its body. The creature jerked but kept hauling in its prey.

Kagur shot another shaft into the insect. It shuddered and collapsed on its shelf.

But the creature's sticky line was still attached to both its body and that of its prey, and its death left the orc boy dangling above the ground. He produced some sort of knife and sawed at the strand but couldn't part it. Meanwhile, clinging to the curving walls, more insects crawled in his direction.

Holg said, "I'm going to make light," and then started quickly reciting a prayer. Judging that she had time for one more shot before he finished, Kagur took it and squeezed her eyes shut.

As before, the magical light shined through her eyelids, and she blinked to help her vision adjust. When it did, she saw that unfortunately, the brighter illumination now flooding the pit didn't appear to have blinded or frightened the insects. They were still heading for the boy.

"Try something else!" she snapped. Laying another arrow on her bow, she stepped to the very edge of the path for a better sightline to the insect closest to the child.

A filament whipped up from somewhere beneath her.

She tried to dodge, but the strand snapped across her shoulder anyway. The creature that had sneaked into position to snare her wrenched her into space.

Chapter Seventeen
Orv

As Kagur plummeted, she banged repeatedly against the wall, dropping her bow to grab at outcroppings. She missed one, then caught another and arrested her fall with a jolt she felt from her hands to her shoulders.

Her elbow and knee hurt, too, where she'd slammed them into the stone, but she barely had time to notice before the creature's strand tugged her upward.

Her impulse was to resist. But she would have no hope of saving the orc boy unless she dealt quickly with the creature that had snared her, and to do that, she needed it within reach of her sword.

So she let it drag her up and concentrated on avoiding any more battering against the wall. Maybe the insect-things depended on such impacts to soften up their prey—but if so, this one was going to be disappointed.

It hitched her closer and closer to its enormous pincers, and she made herself wait to draw her longsword. She didn't want the motion to alarm it prematurely.

She *did* want it to deposit her on its ledge before it actually tried to seize her, but it didn't oblige. She was still hanging when, holding onto the line with one set of claws, it reached for her with the other.

She didn't have her shield. She'd set it aside to use her bow. Instead, she twisted away from the pincers, drew her blade, and cut at them. The weapon crunched through shell and hacked the uppermost claw partway loose from the joint, so it flopped uselessly.

The insect-thing recoiled. Aided by the resulting pull on the line, Kagur scrambled up onto the shelf, where there was barely space for her between the creature in front of her and the drop behind.

The insect lunged at her, the other pair of pincers and its mandibles spreading wide. She hacked at the claws, doing little damage but at least knocking them aside. Then she sprang over her adversary's head and scrambled across its body to a patch of ledge with a little more room for her to stand.

She started to spin back around to face the creature, but the insect was quicker. It gave the strand another jerk, wrenched her off balance, and reached for her sword arm.

Somehow she snatched the limb back, and the pincers clashed shut on empty air. Bellowing, she cut at the insect's head and split its black-eyed countenance in two.

The creature shuddered in a spasm. Then it floundered backward, pulling free of her sword in the process, and backed right off the edge of the shelf. Coils of filament straightened as the insect's fall pulled the line whistling after it.

In one more instant, it was going to drag Kagur over the edge, too. She slashed at the strand, and it parted just as the falling creature's weight drew it taut, enchanted steel prevailing where the orc's blade had failed.

Sucking in a breath, she pivoted to find out what had become of the orc boy. Somewhat to her surprise, he was still alive.

Holg had evidently run on down the spiral trail until he reached the section above the insects that had been heading for the boy. Scurrying back and forth, he had made such a pest of himself that the creatures were now endeavoring to climb the wall to kill him first. As Kagur watched, he hurled a stone down with such force that it nearly knocked a scrabbling insect from its perch. A line whirled up at him, and he recoiled, the cast falling short by a finger length.

The old man was fighting well but plainly couldn't hold out much longer by himself. Two of the insect-things had nearly clambered all the way up to the trail.

Kagur needed to get herself back on the path. She thrust her sword back in its scabbard and climbed.

She was in too much of a hurry to test her hand- and toeholds. She gripped and stepped anywhere she could. Loose stone clattered away beneath her feet. A chunk of rock broke free from the wall just as she was about to trust it with her full weight.

Despite her recklessness, she somehow managed to reach the path. Maybe Gorum thought it would be a waste for one of his worshipers to die in a fall at the very moment she was struggling to rush into battle.

She picked up her shield, drew her sword, and pounded down the trail. As she neared Holg, another strand looped upward, and this one snared the old man and jerked him off his feet.

Holg let go of his staff, grabbed hold of a bulge in the stone surface beneath him, and, his wrinkled face contorted, kept himself from sliding over the edge.

But he could do nothing else as the two insect-things in the lead scrambled up onto the trail.

Kagur sprinted even faster, closed the remaining distance, and cut at the nearer of the creatures from behind. Though her blade cracked the shell on its back, it didn't bite deep, and she doubted she'd hurt the creature badly. She just had to hope shock would balk it for a crucial moment. She lunged on past it and hurled herself at the other insect just as it was about to snip its pincers shut around Holg's head.

Kagur smashed into the creature shield-first to shove it away from its prey, then whirled her blade high and stabbed the point straight down into the insect's head. That killed it, but the blade stuck in the wound. Shouting, she had to pull hard to draw it forth.

She spun back around to confront the first insect. Backing away, it was drawing filament from its underside. She rushed it before it was quite ready to throw and dropped it with a second cut to the body.

Then she slashed the line that had Holg stretched out taut and immobilized. He gasped when the pulling stopped.

"Get up!" Kagur rasped. "The rest are coming!"

Holg fumbled for his staff, used it to heave himself upright, then pointed it over the edge of the trail and spoke to the spirits. Dazzling light lanced from the end of the rod and burned into the body of the insect that had crawled the highest, knocking it loose from the wall to thud on the floor below.

Kagur confronted the next two creatures as they clambered onto the shelf. Shifting back and forth, maneuvering so the beasts kept getting in each other's way, she cut down one and then the other. Killing them was a little easier now that she had a sense of how they moved.

She and Holg assailed the next one together, she slashing and he hammering with his staff until it collapsed. Then she looked over the edge and saw the fight was over. The few remaining insects were scuttling into fissures in the rock.

Holg stumbled backward to lean against the wall.

"Are you all right?" Kagur asked.

He took several wheezing breaths, then managed to straighten up and answer. "Yes. As I keep telling you. Is the orc still with us?"

Kagur took another look down. The green-skinned boy was still hanging and doggedly sawing away. She suspected the glueyness of the strand impeded the cutting action of the blade.

"For better or worse," she said.

"Then we should talk to him." The carved patterns on his staff gleaming yellow, Holg murmured the prayer that enabled him to converse with any creature capable of speech. Then he invested Kagur with the same ability.

She stepped to the edge of the trail to find the boy peering up at her. "Orc!" she called. "Stop trying to cut yourself free, or the shaman and I will kill you."

Holg turned to her. "He knows we just saved his life. Why threaten him?"

"He's an orc," Kagur replied, "and we don't want him running off before we question him. I'm going back up the trail to fetch my gear. Then I'll climb to where I can cut the line. You get to the floor of the pit to keep him there after he drops."

As far as Kagur could tell looking down from above, the threat of Holg's magic was enough to persuade their captive to behave himself. Though plainly wary, poised to defend himself if need be, the orc didn't try to attack or bolt past the old man as she finished her own descent, her knee and elbow aching now that the excitement of combat no longer masked the pain.

Up close, she could see that the boy's features were less coarse and swinish than those of the average orc that came raiding north out of Belkzen. Evidently, he had some human blood in him. Given the circumstances under which such interbreeding invariably took place, that didn't dispose her to regard him any more kindly.

Holg said, "This is Nesteruk. I've given him our names, too."

Kagur felt a pang of irritation. Of course Holg would chatter endlessly with anyone he could draw into conversation, even orcs.

The green-skinned boy eyed Kagur with a tense fascination that even Holg with his weird milky eyes and mystical abilities hadn't quite elicited. After a moment, she sensed it was the sword in her hand that dismayed and intrigued him in equal measure.

"Are you afraid of this?" she asked. "You should be. But if you do as you're told, I won't hurt you." She wiped the insect gore off it and slid it back into its sheath.

Nesteruk hesitated and then slipped his knife back into his kilt. The weapon was a length of whetted flint with rawhide wrapped around the dull end to provide a grip.

"What do you want from me?" he asked in a voice that broke from low to high partway through.

"Lead us to the sun that shines in the depths."

Nesteruk shook his head. "I don't know what that means."

"These aren't 'the depths' to him," said Holg. "They're simply his home." He turned to the orc. "Do you know of any 'sun'? Does the word mean anything to you?"

The boy snorted. "Of course. The sun is what lights the world. But not the edges of the world."

"Is that where we are now?" Kagur asked. "The edges of the world?"

"Yes," Nesteruk replied, in a tone that said, *don't you people know anything?*

"And what were you doing at the edge of the world all alone?" asked Holg.

Nesteruk hesitated, his brief display of adolescent condescension wilting. Kagur suspected that, like her own younger self and probably every other youth since time began, he'd ignored his elders' prohibitions and ventured where he wasn't supposed to go.

"Exploring," the orc said at length. "You can find things sometimes." He glanced at the white spot he'd been approaching when the insect snared him. It was a litter of gnawed and broken bones.

"Keep watching him," said Kagur to Holg. She turned to recover her shield and find her bow.

To her relief, the longbow appeared to have survived its fall undamaged. As she picked it up and examined it, she noticed Nesteruk eyeing it with something of the same fascination her sword had elicited.

Then something clicked overhead. Reminded of the danger, she, the boy, and Holg made a hasty exit from the pit before the surviving insects could rally for a second attack.

Once the orc had led them some distance down a snaking passage, she said, "A giant twice as tall as I am,

with blue skin and yellow hair and eyes, came to Orv—
your 'world'—before us. Have you seen him?"

Nesteruk exploded into a run.

Startled, both Kagur and Holg faltered. Then she
sprinted after the boy. Behind her, the shaman started
a prayer but stopped reciting when Nesteruk vanished
around a bend. Holg presumably couldn't hurl the
magic at a target he could no longer see.

Kagur realized she too might well fail to stop the boy.
Unless she caught up quickly, he could easily give her
the slip.

The lantern swinging, her knee twinging, she made
herself dash even faster. When she rounded the turn,
the green light washed over Nesteruk squirming into a
crack in the wall. In another moment, she likely would
have run right past without ever noticing the opening,
and could never have wriggled through even if she had.

She grabbed the boy by the forearm, heaved him back
out into the larger tunnel, and slammed him face-first
into the wall. He gasped. She pressed her shield against
his back to pin him in place, yanked the flint knife from
his waist, and tossed it clattering to the other side of
the passage.

"What was the idea?" she asked. "To run and fetch
other orcs to kill us?"

"No!" he gasped. "I just wanted to get away."

"Why? I told you Holg and I wouldn't hurt you if you
obeyed."

"I know, and I wanted to believe, even though your
long knife is made of the same stuff as the giant's axe.
But then you *asked* about him!"

Kagur grunted. "He's done some harm to your tribe?"

"He killed three of our warriors on the trail. The axe chopped all the way through their bodies!"

"Then be glad I came here to kill him."

Holg rounded the bend in the passage. Squinting, he asked, "What was *that* all about?"

"A misunderstanding," Kagur said. "Nesteruk is going to lead us properly from now on. Aren't you, orc?"

"Yes," the boy replied.

She backed away from him. "Then get on with it."

As they stalked onward, Kagur practically itched with the urge to ask more questions. But Nesteruk still looked skittish and mistrustful. She didn't want to spook him and set him running all over again, nor was she certain she could trust any answer she wormed out of him.

First, she told herself, get to the last cave. *Then* you can wring more answers out of him.

Eventually, they made another turn and found a slope in front of them. A shaft of light fell through the opening at the top.

The radiance dazzled Kagur. But it was clear and clean in a way that even Holg's most potent magic couldn't quite reproduce, and even as she threw up her arm to protect her eyes, she felt some fundamental part of her opening to it like a flower.

Using his grubby, broken-nailed hands to aid him, Nesteruk scrambled up the rise, and the humans followed. They all stepped through the opening and out onto a rocky hillside.

Though she knew it wasn't so, Kagur felt like she was dreaming yet again. For it appeared there truly *was* a sun hanging in a blue sky above her and blazing too brightly for anyone to look at it straight on.

The sunshine gleamed on the lake at the center of the country below. If Kagur could trust her sense of distance and scale, that deep blue expanse was by far the largest body of water she'd ever seen, just as the lands around it were by far the greenest.

"We *can't* be back on the surface," she said. Everything, from the wisps of cloud to the scent of vegetation on the balmy breeze—*real* plants, not nasty mold and such—insisted it was so.

"We're not," said Holg. "If you recall, Lady Ssa said the Vaults of Orv were bigger than even the largest caves of Sekamina. I thought I understood what she meant, but apparently, I still underestimated. At any rate, turn around and look behind us."

Frowning, Kagur did, at steep brown rocky hillsides and crags that climbed up and up, gradually turning into something she'd grown wearily familiar with: a cavern wall. The wall just started to curve outward into a ceiling at the place where she lost it in the haze that was also the sky.

"I see," Kagur said, and turning once more, she noticed other things that had escaped her first astonished gawking. Shapes—birds, she assumed—soared and circled lazily high above. Most of the greenness had a bumpy texture that indicated dense forests. Hidden inside one of them, something that was surely a sizable animal gave a mournful croaking call.

"I got you here," Nesteruk said. "Now, you go right." He sprang forward. Kagur reached out for him, but her clutching fingers fell short.

Nesteruk threw himself headlong down an especially steep section of the hillside, raising a cloud of dust as he tumbled. Kagur had no chance of keeping up with him unless she was willing to do the same thing and risk more bumps, bruises, and maybe even broken bones in the process, and she realized she wasn't.

For after all, it was by no means certain that Nesteruk even knew Eovath's current location. Whereas she was sure Holg's fetishes could point the way.

The orc sprang up, seemingly unharmed from his rolling descent, and darted left into a stand of pine trees. Kagur lost sight of him a moment later.

"Well," said Holg, "that was unfortunate."

"You could have stopped him with magic," Kagur answered.

"And you could have put an arrow in him. But I guess neither of us actually felt inclined to strike him down." Holg glanced to the right. "He told us to go this way."

To Kagur's eye, the slopes on the right and left looked pretty much the same, a transitional zone between the crags looming behind her and the forests in the bowl-shaped land below. Frowning, she replied, "But we don't know why. I'd rather have your magic guide us."

To Eovath. She imagined how it would feel to finally drive her father's sword into his vitals and shivered with anticipation.

Chapter Eighteen
Eovath

As Kagur and Holg headed down into the lowlands, the air grew steadily warmer, until it was hotter than the tundra even at the height of summer, and they pulled off their mantles and stuffed them in their backpacks. Still, sweat trickled down from her hairline and soaked her armpits, and she wished she could dispense with her coat of leather as well. But she hoped she was going to need the armor soon.

That was by no means certain, though. Holg's magic could only point them in the right direction. It couldn't tell them how far ahead Eovath was. If their luck was running bad, the frost giant had trekked all the way to the other side of the central lake. In that case, they had days or weeks of hiking still ahead of them.

Such a possibility seemed almost intolerable. Against all likelihood, all sane expectation, there *was* a "sun in the darkness," and Kagur had found it. Now that she had, the need for vengeance burned in her like a fever. She could almost hear her father, Dolok, and all the other Blacklions urging her on.

That eagerness made her impatient with the countless trees towering on every side. In the open country she was used to, a hunter might have spotted Eovath, or the pyramid he'd said he meant to seek beneath the second sun, from miles away. In this place, she could sometimes see no farther than she could throw a stone.

Holg, however, predictably found everything about the country fascinating. She didn't blame him for kneeling to consider mounds of droppings or big, clawed tracks in the sod. Despite the nervous energy goading her ever onward, she too recognized the importance of gleaning what they could about the larger beasts in the area. Such knowledge could save their lives. But it set her teeth on edge when he paused to squint at dragonflies the length of her forearm whirring past on glimmering wings. Or at anything else that was strange but harmless, like the star-shaped yellow blossoms growing from a tree with a diamond pattern to its bark and long, dark green leaves flopping like petals from the very top.

"Have you noticed?" he asked. "It was mostly trees around us when we started down—"

"It still is," she said. "That's a tree you're wasting time on right now."

"Is it?" he replied. "Or is it a bigger version of all these ferns on the ground?"

Now that he'd pointed it out, she saw the resemblance. But still: "What difference does it make?"

"I don't know yet. Probably none. But have you noticed there's no birdsong?"

"There are birds. I saw them in the sky when we stepped out of the caves." And sometimes glimpsed them still, when she peered up through a gap in the foliage overhead.

"But no bird*song*. I always hoped to, but I never made it far enough south to see jungle. For a little while, I imagined I was finally getting my chance. But now I suspect this place is even stranger than the Mwangi Expanse."

Kagur had never even heard of "the Mwangi Expanse," but she knew better than to say so and invite a discourse on the subject. "As I said: What difference does it make? Keep moving."

With a snort and a shake of his white-fringed head, he obliged her, and they hiked onward a while longer. Until, despite her avowed disinterest in anything and everything that didn't bring them nearer to Eovath, she faltered in astonishment.

The shadows of the trees—and towering tree-like ferns—had pointed up the slope when she and Holg started down. And even though they'd been traveling for a while, the shadows pointed in exactly the same direction still.

Squinting and shielding her eyes, she peered upward through the mesh of branches and drooping fronds as best she could. Then she was certain.

"What have you noticed?" asked Holg.

"This sun doesn't move."

The old man pondered that for a moment. Then he said, "I don't suppose it *could* rise and set, could it? It would bump into the cavern walls."

His seeming lack of amazement at *her* discovery irked her. Stifling the feeling as best she could, she said, "So it's always light here."

"Apparently so, which makes it seem a strange place for a god of chaos and destruction like Rovagug to work some monstrous evil. But there must be a reason."

Kagur grunted. "Let's catch up to Eovath before he has a chance to show us what it is."

Gradually, as she and Holg marched onward, she realized the seemingly perpetual noon was putting one part of her at odds with another. She'd been exerting herself for a long while, first in the tunnels and pit, and now here in the "Vault." Her body felt sore and awkward, and her belly felt hollow.

And yet, to a Kellid born to the rhythms of day and night and of roaming across the plains, it would also feel strange to make camp while the sun was at its zenith. Despite her weariness, she suspected she wouldn't be able to relax if she did.

Just a little farther, she told herself. A little closer to killing Eovath. Then maybe I'll be able to rest.

A pace or two ahead of Holg, she pushed through a tangle of shoulder-high ferns that grew thickly enough to make walking difficult. A cloud of gnats rose from the fronds. She was still swiping them away from her face when she stepped into the clearing beyond. Maybe that was why, just for a moment, she mistook the creature on her right for a boulder or rock formation covered in dull green moss. Then it lumbered around to face her.

The reptile was as big as a mammoth, if not bigger. It was unquestionably longer, thanks to a snakelike tail with spikes on the end. A double row of triangular plates ran all the way up that tail, over its high, rounded back, and down to its comparatively small head. Its deep-set eyes glared at the intruders.

"So *this* is what Tolguth and the Vault have in common," Holg breathed. "No wonder the mapmakers named it that. And perhaps I understand what the god of fearsome beasts finds interesting in this place."

As he finished speaking, Kagur spotted something that made her feel *slightly* less imperiled. "This 'fearsome beast' eats grass. It has some hanging out of its mouth."

"Then let's stop disturbing it and let it get back to its meal."

"Right." But Kagur didn't want to retrace her steps. If the reptile decided to charge while she and Holg were tangled up in the undergrowth, it would be difficult to run or fight. "Let's *slowly* work our way around the left edge of the clearing."

They made it halfway, with the huge reptile turning ponderously to keep them in front of it. Then the sunlight dimmed.

Startled, Kagur glanced up despite the menace hulking just a few paces away. The sun hadn't shot across the sky in an instant and found itself a horizon to sink behind. Instead, it was simply fading like a fire burning down to embers, only far more quickly.

The reptile must surely be accustomed to the sudden advent of twilight here in its cavern home. Still, as if the change had inflamed its suspicion that the humans meant to harass it into outright certainty, it started forward. The tail with its bony spikes hitched higher into the air.

Kagur and Holg whirled and ran. By the time she took four strides, dusk gave way to night, with only stars—or something like them—shining between the leafy branches and fronds overhead to provide a trace of light.

The ground trembled. She glanced back. Despite its bulk, the reptile was coming on fast. *Maybe* she could outrun it. She doubted Holg could.

"Go right!" she gasped. Possibly expecting her to do the same, Holg obeyed. She veered left, let out a shout, and the creature pounded after her.

As she dashed on, she looked for trees or tree-ferns growing close enough together that her huge pursuer wouldn't be able to squeeze between them. She couldn't spot any amid the gloom.

But animals were afraid of fire! She tore at the wrappings covering her shield. They fell away, and Holg's cool flames leaped forth. She pivoted, bellowed a war cry, and shoved the burning shield at the onrushing reptile's face.

Then, as it kept pounding closer, she realized that, like a charging mammoth, such a huge animal might have difficulty stopping suddenly even if it wanted to. She threw herself to one side barely in time to avoid being trampled.

The gigantic reptile thundered past and wheeled, orienting on her once again. Now! Now was the time for it to notice and back away from the fire.

Perhaps considering such a course, it hesitated. Then the spiked tail whirled through the air. Kagur dodged. The tail thudded into the ground, then, flinging clumps of sod and dirt, immediately heaved back up for another strike.

As she scrambled backward, she tried to think of what to do. The fire hadn't scared the reptile. She doubted she could either outfight or outrun it—not in the dark on unfamiliar ground, not when she was tired and hungry and still ached from the bruising she'd taken in the pit. What did that leave?

She could only think of one thing. The creature might be able to run as fast as she could, but it wasn't as nimble and couldn't change direction as rapidly.

She sprinted *toward* it.

The spiked tail whirled in a horizontal arc. She dived underneath the stroke, scrambled up, and dashed onward along the creature's flank. Now that she was in close, she felt an impulse to draw her sword and cut, but she resisted. Stick to the plan!

The reptile shuffled around in a circle to find her again. She allowed it a glimpse, then charged up the other side of its scaly form, though she had to stop short to avoid another hammering tail strike arcing out of the gloom. The dirt it threw up spattered her face.

At the start of her next dash, she faked left and then ran right. At the beginning of the fourth, she used a double fake.

She wondered if she'd yet succeeded in confusing the beast or tiring it out. But truly, it scarcely mattered. *She* couldn't keep this up much longer. She was panting, and her pulse pounded in her throat. Her knee throbbed, threatening to turn her desperate sprints into hobbling.

"Blacklion!" she snarled, then raced down the length of the reptile's body and dodged the sweeping tail one more time. As her pursuer began another turn, she yanked her arm free of the straps on the inside of the shield, hurled the fiery shield spinning away in one direction, and scurried in the opposite one. Wincing at the rustling of the fronds but unable to prevent it, she dived into a patch of ferns.

The gigantic reptile finished turning, and then, as she'd hoped, lumbered after the firelight. Once it reached it, it looked down at the shield in perplexity or disappointment, then wheeled back around.

Kagur held her breath when the creature peered in her direction. But it evidently couldn't see her, for after some more unsuccessful searching, it made a grumbling sort of noise and prowled off into the dark.

She gave it time to wander farther away before breaking cover to retrieve the shield. Now, she supposed, she needed to find Holg, but the skinny old man came out of the gloom and found her first.

"I didn't realize you meant to take all the danger on yourself," Holg said, his tone vaguely accusatory.

"Do you have any magic left?" she replied.

"Well . . . very little."

"Then I made the right move. And now, since there *is* night here after all, we need to figure out how to pass it safely."

"True enough. I suggest climbing a tree."

They did, and the ascent proved easy enough. The difficult part, Kagur soon discovered, was finding an even slightly comfortable and secure-feeling place to rest while rope bindings protected her from a fall and beasts roared and hissed in the dark.

At one point, a huge, shadowy form stalked underneath the humans, halted, and stared upward. It occurred to her that the creature might be strong enough to shove the whole tree over if it thought the prey hanging in the upper branches was worth the effort. But maybe it didn't, for eventually it moved on.

At first, she thought she wouldn't be able to sleep. But in time, she drifted off to dream of Eovath humming softly, as was his habit when attending to a chore. In real life, the sound had always given her a warm, fond feeling. In the dream, it did the same until she noticed the giant was humming while whetting his axe. Then she looked on tongue-tied and frozen in dread without remembering why.

The abrupt return of daylight woke her, the sun in the center of the sky brightening as quickly as it had faded. Blinking and yawning, she tried to roll over. Her bindings halted her and reminded her where she was.

The climb to the ground showed her the night had left her stiff. But an application of Holg's healing magic fixed that as well as the lingering aches in her knee and elbow.

"Good," she said, experimentally flexing her arm. "Now pray us up something to eat. Then ask your spirits to point to Eovath."

Holg hesitated. "My friend . . . has it occurred to you you're in a little too much of a hurry?"

Kagur scowled. "Why aren't you in more of one? You're the one who stops to study everything even though you claim we're racing to stop a calamity."

"I admit, you may have a point. I've always been curious, and occasionally, it's gotten me into trouble. But other times, it's gotten me out."

"What are you trying to say?"

"That this 'Vault' is both huge and stranger than any place I've ever been, including all the strange places we traveled through on our way down from the Earthnavel. Perhaps, instead of rushing headlong wherever the fetishes point, we should try to learn more about it. In the long run, it might improve our chances of stopping Eovath."

"How would we do that?"

"For one thing, we could take another look at the country from higher ground and really study it this time."

"You mean backtrack?"

"Well, yes."

"That's stupid!"

"Nesteruk and his people are there. Don't you think there's more they can tell us?"

"You think *orcs* will help us?"

"All right, perhaps not. But consider this: Nesteruk seemed surprised by things about us, like my eyes and your weapons, but not *everything* about us. He'd plainly seen human beings before, and likely even has some human blood. And back in the highlands, he tried to send us the opposite direction from the one he was taking."

Kagur scratched a bumped-up insect bite on her cheek. "You think he wanted to send us to our own kind."

"Yes. He wanted to thank us for saving his life."

"An orc wouldn't feel gratitude. And even if there are humans living hereabouts, they might not want to help us, either. Or might not be able to."

"That's true. We don't know anything for certain."

"Yes! We do! We know Eovath's in front of us. We know your fetishes can guide us to him. So let's finish this!"

Holg sighed. "Very well. We'll do it your way. For all I know, you could be right." He hefted his staff. "I'm glad you're at least willing to make time for breakfast."

The new day warmed swiftly as the motionless sun beat down. Insects droned and flitted among the ferns. The way forward led past enormous glimmering spider webs strung between tree trunks, as well as another sort of oversized reptile with a shell like a turtle's and a knob of bone at the end of its tail. Fortunately, this one simply looked at them briefly and then returned to munching fern fronds.

Oblong, red-speckled yellow fruit grew on a low-hanging bough. Holg murmured a prayer over a piece of it, declared it safe to eat, and took a bite that dribbled juice down his chin. The stuff turned out to be pleasantly tart, and he and Kagur carried some with them when they moved on.

Just when Kagur was beginning to think the caverns deserted except for giant reptiles, Nesteruk's people appeared. Armed with spears, javelins, and knives, half a dozen full-grown orcs appeared on a stretch of high ground while Kagur and Holg were traversing the declivity below. She drew her longsword and slashed at the air to make the steel flash in the sunlight.

The orcs retreated to the other side of the rise. She watched for them thereafter, but saw no indication that they were trailing her and Holg.

Which didn't necessarily mean they weren't. She was an expert hunter and tracker in her own sort of country, but not here in "jungle," as the old man called it. It almost made her wonder if he hadn't had a point when he'd advised against pushing onward as fast as they could.

But only almost. Her father, Dolok, Roga, and all the other Blacklions were dead, and every additional breath their murderer drew was an affront to their spirits and a shame to their only surviving kinswoman.

Eventually, she and Holg came to a place where the trees and tree-ferns thinned out. At the end of the clear space, the ground dropped away, plunging to interrupt what was, overall, a long, gentle descent from the crags at the edges of the cavern to the central lake.

From her elevated vantage point, Kagur could once again see that blue expanse of water shining on the other side of still more green jungle. And now that she was closer, she could also discern a cluster of black and purple-red stone towers on the shore, and a triangular shape rising from the center of the lake itself.

She squinted. The object was a pyramid, the sides stair-stepping up to the flat space at the top. As best she could judge, it was directly under the stationary sun where Eovath had expected to find it.

Eager for an even better look, she strode out into the open and toward the edge of the cliff. Likely sensing her excitement even if he couldn't see the reason for it, Holg hurried after her. Birds floated high overhead in the azure sky.

She reached the edge and looked down. Then she caught her breath, and the pyramid didn't matter anymore.

There was a strip of open ground at the base of the cliff, too. Eovath was down there, his yellow hair and steel axe blade gleaming in the sun.

For several moments, the frost giant was the only thing that registered, the only thing that existed in all the world. Then Kagur reflexively took a breath, and the view below widened to encompass other elements, including Eovath's companions.

Those companions were twenty or so stooped, gray-scaled reptile-men somewhat resembling Lady Ssa and her people but not exactly like them. They had ragged finlike crests running from the tops of their heads down their spines, and they didn't move with the seemingly boneless sinuosity of serpents.

The creatures were looking on as Eovath faced the jungle and flourished his axe in a way that reminded Kagur of the way Holg sometimes brandished and spun his staff when working magic. After a moment, an enormous reptile with a horn on its snout, two longer ones jutting from above its beady eyes, and a sort of protruding bony collar sweeping back from its head lumbered forth from the tree-ferns. It was like

Eovath had summoned it—and maybe he really had, for despite the beast's size and natural weapons, no one within reach of the spear-like horns appeared alarmed by its arrival.

Was Rovagug teaching Eovath sorcery? Were the reptile-men? Maybe it was a combination of the two.

"Your brother's companions," said Holg, squinting.

"What about them?" Kagur replied.

"I heard tell of such creatures during my time in the southlands, but the ones my friends spoke of were the crudest of savages. The specimens below appear more advanced."

She grunted. She didn't care about the reptile-people and their accomplishments. She cared that they and the three-horned beast were obstacles on the path to her retribution.

Ever since waking in Holg's tent, she'd yearned to face Eovath again, this time with her father's blade in her hand. It would be the most satisfying and fitting way to kill him.

But it couldn't happen, not while he stood in the midst of his new allies. Yet if she passed up the present opportunity, she might never find her way to another.

To hell with it, then. She'd put an end to him here and now, and when he died miserably, without any warning or chance to defend himself, that too would be fitting in its way.

She readied her longbow and drew an arrow from her quiver. Despite her parsimony on the journey, she only had a few left. But even shooting over such a distance, a few would be enough.

To her dismay, as she pulled the shaft back to her ear, something shifted inside her. The hate in no way diminished. It remained implacable. But love and sorrow welled up in her, too, and though her hands did not tremble, tears blurred her sight.

How had it ever come to this? If only she'd realized how Eovath felt—

No. To hell with useless thoughts like that, too. Kill him and rejoice.

She blinked away the tears, saw Eovath had almost imperceptibly changed position, and adjusted her aim accordingly.

Then a gray-green shape hurtled down at the edge of her vision, and Holg cried out.

Chapter Nineteen
Hunted

Kagur whirled. His flowing blood vivid in the grass and the dirt, Holg sprawled on his back, beating with his staff at the creature that had plunged down on top of him.

At first glance, his attacker looked gigantic. It took Kagur an instant to see it was mostly huge, flapping leathery wings—the reptilian body at their juncture was no bigger than a child's.

Yet the creature was still plainly capable of inflicting ghastly wounds. The backswept vane on its head swinging back and forth, it jabbed and bit at Holg with a straight beak as long and pointed as a sword while its talons dug into his flesh.

No birdsong, Kagur remembered. Why would there be, when the beasts that ruled the sky of the Vault weren't truly birds after all?

Even as she was thinking that thought, she loosed her arrow. It flew straight, and should have taken the flying reptile in the body. But at that same instant, Holg tried to drag himself out from under his attacker, and the creature twisted to hang on to him. As a result, the shaft simply stabbed into its wing and dangled from the membrane. The reptile turned its head to screech at Kagur but didn't let go of its prey.

She dropped her bow beside her shield, drew out her sword, and rushed the creature. Then she heard a snapping sound at her back.

She wrenched herself around and cut at the beast that was swooping down at her. Her blade hit it somewhere, and then it slammed into her, its momentum nearly knocking her over. Talons gouged and clung.

With the reptile's body pressed against her face, it was impossible to see and almost as difficult to breathe. Its wing beats sent her stumbling off balance, its claws gripped painfully, and its beak gouged at the reinforced leather armoring her back.

She stabbed at the reptile again and again. Finally, it screeched and fell away from her, and then she saw that while blind, she'd blundered to the very crumbling edge of the cliff. With a snarl, she lunged back to safer ground, cut at her bleeding assailant as it turned to face her anew, and sheared halfway through its neck. The beast collapsed with a final spastic flailing of its wings.

As soon as its death throes subsided, she sprang over the carcass. It was the quickest way to reach Holg and the reptile tearing at him.

Yet it wasn't quick enough. The creature had time to let go of the old man and wrench itself around to face the danger. Huge wings spread and flapping as though to confuse and contain its foe, long beak alternately stabbing and snapping, it hopped forward.

Kagur met the attack with a cut that sliced the leathery hide on the creature's beak but glanced off the bone beneath. She shifted in and to the side when the next attack stabbed at her, and the beak clashed shut over her shoulder. Bellowing, she cut into the reptile's body, and like its fellow it collapsed with a frenzied lashing and rattling of wings.

Kagur rushed to Holg and threw herself down beside him. "How bad is it?" she panted.

He didn't answer. He was unconscious, and his wounds were plainly quite bad indeed. His attacker had gouged furrows in his mostly hairless head and shredded parts of his torso. His skinny body was bloody from crown to belly.

Kagur held her hand before his nose and mouth. He was still breathing. She told herself that was something.

Rasping cries sounded from the bottom of the cliff. She looked over the edge.

For the first time, she noticed that some distance off to her left, a trail of sorts ran up the cliff face. It was too narrow for the enormous three-horned creature, but Eovath and the reptile-men were running toward it.

Plainly, they'd noticed the commotion on the high ground, as they naturally would if their own winged sentry beasts had caused it. If their arts could tame a four-footed reptile, why not flying ones as well?

It occurred to Kagur that she still might be able to shoot Eovath, but she realized even as the thought enticed her that it was stupid. Hitting him at long range when he was standing still and unaware would have been one thing. Killing him now would be far more difficult.

Besides, though she would gladly have traded her own life to avenge her tribe, it would be despicable to simply let Holg die of the wounds he'd already taken or beneath the spears and claws of the reptile-people. She had to save him if she could, and every moment counted.

So did every bit of weight and bulk. She retrieved her bow but left her shield where it lay, discarded her backpack with the green crystal lantern inside it, yanked Holg's bundles off his back, and thrust his staff through his belt. Then she heaved him off the ground, draped him around her shoulders, and scurried back into the jungle.

She judged she could manage his weight for a while. At the moment, she was more concerned about the blood still dripping from his wounds. It was spoor for their enemies to follow.

"Wake up, old man," she said. "Wake and pray to your spirits to heal you."

He didn't.

So she sought to carry him as far and fast as she could without leaving an obvious trail of footprints, trampled ferns, and broken low-hanging branches. She only made it a short distance before the jungle grew quiet, the faint background noise of small, unseen animals abating. The change surely meant Eovath and his allies had made it up the cliff and entered the trees.

Sweat stinging her eyes, Kagur desperately scanned for somewhere to hide in the profusion of plant life. Lord in Iron, she even knew how to hide on the tundra, where everything was open. Yet she didn't see any blind likely to conceal her for long against a score of determined searchers, and if Eovath had observed just who was fighting the winged reptiles on top of the cliff, he was unquestionably determined.

A rasping cry sounded behind her. She looked back. A reptile man had spotted her and was alerting its companions.

In too much of a hurry to be gentle, she dumped Holg on the ground and readied her bow. The reptile man simply kept crying out, without scrambling for cover, and she realized that, like Nesteruk, it had never seen archery. It assumed that if it was out of javelin range, she couldn't possibly hurt it.

The reptile somehow sensed it was mistaken about that when she pulled the fletchings back to her ear. It lunged for the cover of the nearest tree-fern, but it was too slow. The arrow plunged between its ribs, and it collapsed.

Kagur grinned, but the satisfaction was only momentary. She hadn't dropped the reptile man in time to keep it from calling to its fellows, and now she only had four arrows left, not nearly enough to kill them all.

She wrapped Holg around her shoulders and strode onward. He felt heavier than he had before.

"Sister!" Eovath's bellow came from somewhere behind Kagur and off to the left. She looked but couldn't see him.

"Sister!" the giant repeated. "Give yourself up, and I promise my new allies and I won't hurt you! You know I never wanted to in the first place!"

She sneered and tried to quicken her stride. Eovath knew her too well to believe she'd ever surrender. He just wanted to provoke her into answering back and giving away her position.

"All right!" Eovath called after a time. "We'll do it your way! I understand, you have to walk your path to the end! How could I not, when we two are the same?"

The hell we are! she thought, and then, ahead and to the right, she spied a tangle of red flowers on tall stalks.

Or maybe not precisely flowers, for, ranging from hand-sized growths to those larger than her head, each consisted of just two lobe-like petals with yellow, hair-like tendrils protruding from the edges. But whatever they were, the thicket was one more patch of cover to put between her pursuers and herself. She considered swinging around it, but it looked like she should be able to push and squirm her way straight through.

Taking advantage of a narrow gap in the foliage, she started to do so. She caught a whiff of the flowers' peculiar scent, sickly sweet with a hint of rot, and then a tug brought her up short. She, or more likely Holg, had snagged on something. Scowling, she yanked and twisted to pull loose.

But afterward, she was still caught. She looked back over her shoulder, and her eyes widened. A two-lobed crimson growth had closed around Holg's dangling arm like a pair of jaws and clung with sufficient strength to keep her from yanking him free.

She reached to snap the vine-like stem to which the flower was attached away from the primary stalk. But as she gripped it, a second scarlet growth looped over and down to close around her hand.

The fleshy insides of the lobes were moist. For a moment, the dampness stung, and then her hand went numb.

With a snarl, she jerked it free. But then, as if the more she thrashed about, the more she excited them, additional scarlet flowers twisted in her direction. One closed on her shoulder, and a second strained at the very limits of its reach in an attempt to wrap around her head. Behind her, others were no doubt taking hold of Holg.

Fast, vigorous motion might have roused them initially, but it was the only recourse now. Kagur fumbled for her sword with numb fingers, yanked Eovath's dagger from its sheath with her off hand, and slashed and hacked as best she could with Holg's dead weight riding on her back.

Somehow, it was enough. After a moment, it became clear that once their jaws closed, the plants never willingly let go, but she managed to cut apart enough of them to pull free of the rest. She staggered back out of the thicket.

Voices rasped among the trees and tree-ferns, calling to one another. "Kagur!" Eovath rumbled.

Curse it, the hunters were catching up! And the thicket was no help, just one more obstacle stretched across her path!

Or was it?

The reptiles surely realized the crimson flowers were dangerous, and for that reason, they might assume no one would or could take refuge among them. Yet, maybe because they mainly ate the Vault's oversized flying insects, most of the double-lobed traps grew high on the stalk. So it *was* possible someone could hide in the thicket safely if he or she kept low.

Hating the deadness in her fingers that made every frantic action clumsy, Kagur laid Holg on the ground, pulled the amber bead fetish from around his neck, and swiped wet blood from his body. Then she scurried down the front of the thicket, flicked drops of blood on the ground, pressed a clear footprint in soft earth, and dropped the fetish at the end of the false trail.

Then, with the voices of her hunters growing still louder, still closer, she rushed back to Holg. She dropped to the ground, and, crawling, dragged the unconscious old man into the shadows at the bases of the stalks.

Not all the sweet-smelling crimson jaws grew too high to threaten her. Some coiled down to bite. She shifted away when possible, ripped them from the stem when necessary, and kept moving.

She hadn't penetrated nearly as far as she'd hoped to when something, pure instinct perhaps, told her to freeze. She did, and a moment later, Eovath and three of the reptile-men came into view and peered into the gap.

Despite the cover the plants afforded, Kagur found it all but impossible to believe her foster brother's yellow eyes didn't see her when only a few paces separated them and she could see him clearly. Still, lying absolutely still, she told herself he wouldn't. She and Holg were *not* going to die like this, with the giant unpunished and the Blacklions unavenged.

Maybe Gorum heard and approved of that silent vow, for Kagur turned out to be correct. From the left, where she'd left the false trail, a sibilant voice jabbered. Eovath and his companions turned and headed in that direction. Other reptile-men followed.

Kagur lay still for a while afterward, to make sure her foes were truly gone and simply to catch her breath. Finally, when the numbness in her hand was giving way to a painful jabbing, she hauled Holg back out into the open. The old man was still breathing, and as best she could judge, the bleeding had finally stopped. But he showed no signs of coming around.

Scowling, she hoisted him back onto her shoulders and marched in the opposite direction from Eovath and the reptile-men. When she thought she might have traveled far enough to avoid them henceforth, she turned her steps toward the section of the crags where Nesteruk had tried to steer her.

Arriving with the same startling swiftness as before, night interrupted her trek, and she realized she had no way of carrying Holg up a tree. She simply had to lay him on the ground and keep watch with her bow and sword ready, while great beasts snarled and roared in the dark. Fortunately, none of them happened her way, or if they did, she never spotted them, and they passed her by in favor of other prey.

In time, Holg started to whimper. She touched his brow and felt the fever burning in his skin. Without truly waking, he fumbled for her hand, called her Ulionestria, and insisted the solution to the riddle was in the items on the tabletop in the portrait.

Kagur resumed her march as soon as day returned. Though mottled pink and itchy, her sword hand was essentially well again, but her back ached from carrying her burden.

She happened on more of the tart yellow fruit and gobbled it as she trudged. Eating made her more alert despite her sleepless night.

Gradually—far too gradually to suit her—the ground rose, the vegetation grew sparser, and glimpses of giant reptiles became less frequent. Crags loomed before and then around her. If she peered, she thought she could even make out the spot where they became the cavern wall.

But she didn't sight any human beings, or even orcs. Maybe Holg had been wrong. Maybe no one lived up here.

Maybe. But she stumbled onward even after the way became steep and difficult, and pebbles pattered away beneath her feet. It was too late to try anywhere else. For good or ill, the highlands were the old man's only chance.

And finally, after both the yellow fruit and her water were long gone, when her throat felt full of dust and the ache in her back had spread to torture her hips and knees as well, two figures rose up from behind the rock formation above her. Unfortunately, they were hefting javelins.

Chapter Twenty
The Dragonfly Tribe

Kagur had struggled so long and hard to reach this place that the threat of the javelins enraged her. And the warriors who held them were just a few strides away. She could drop Holg, rush them, subdue them, and *force* them to help.

Then she scowled as she realized exhaustion, desperation, and perhaps her own warrior instincts had her thinking like a fool. Even if she did win the skirmish she'd just envisioned and took the sentries captive, it would still be unlikely she could coerce help from their entire tribe. She had to put aside the lessons of a journey where she'd met nothing but enemies, man-eating beasts, and outright horrors, and comport herself with the courtesy she would have shown to other Kellids at an assembly of the following.

She raised her hands in what she hoped anyone would recognize as a sign of peace. No javelins flew down at her in response. So far, so good.

Next, she laid Holg down and set her longbow beside him. Even if the sentries didn't understand what it was, they might take it for a fighting staff like the shaman's. She took off her baldric and quiver and set down the rest of her weapons as well, even Eovath's dagger.

She waved at the unconscious man and her bow and blades, then held out both hands palms up in a gesture of beseeching. Since she was sure the sentries wouldn't understand the language of her people, it was all she could do.

The sentries spoke back and forth. Then they came down the trail. They still held their javelins in such a way that they could throw or jab in an instant if need be, but if Kagur was reading their expressions and body language correctly, they didn't truly expect or want a fight.

Their hide garments were as crude and scanty as Nesteruk's kilt, and like his knife, the tips of their weapons were made of flint. Still, now that Kagur was seeing them up close, she was surprised at the degree to which they resembled her own people. They were broad-shouldered and muscular, and like most any Kellid warrior worthy of the name, bore their share of scars, which their near nakedness displayed to good advantage. That skin was deeply tanned, and their hair, worn long and loose, was black and straight.

The two men took a closer look at Kagur, Holg, and the weapons on the ground. Then the older one spoke to her.

She shook her head and answered, "I don't understand. But you see the old man's hurt. He needs your healer."

The sentries conferred briefly. Then the older man gave his javelin to the younger and hoisted Holg in his arms. He started back up the trail, and his fellow tribesman motioned for Kagur to follow.

Since the sentries hadn't confiscated her weapons, Kagur inferred that they'd decided she could be allowed to keep them. Moving slowly in case she was mistaken, she picked up her gear and tramped upward. It was a relief not to have Holg's weight draped across her shoulders anymore, but not enough of one to put an end to all her aches and pains.

At the top of the trail, where crags rose in a semicircle around a broad, flat space and the mouths of caves opened in the rock, was the habitation she'd been seeking. A squatting craftsman chipped away at a piece of flint, a half-grown girl cranked the spit roasting a lizard the size of a boar, and two other youngsters wrestled while their friends looked on. But everyone stopped what they were doing to gape at Kagur, Holg, and their escorts.

The older sentry shouted something that was presumably an explanation, reassurance, or both. Then he headed for a cave mouth on the left.

Enough sunlight spilled through the opening to reveal the abundance of drawings rendered in reddish brown, ochre, and white pigment on the walls inside. Kagur noticed hunting scenes and the image of a dragonfly repeated over and over again. Maybe it was the emblem of the tribe.

The older sentry called out, and a stooped, gray-haired woman emerged from the darkness farther back in the cave. Like Holg, she wore fetishes dangling from her neck. She also had dragonflies painted above each eye and on the backs of her hands.

She and the warriors conferred, and the man carrying Holg set him on a pallet made of dry grass with hide spread on top. Then the Dragonfly shaman set to work.

Kneeling beside Holg, her upper body rocking back and forth, she chanted with her painted hands upraised. At the end of every prayer, she pressed them against the old man's body. Although it wasn't always easy to tell beneath the crusts of dried blood, the old man's wounds shrank and puckered, some healing entirely and leaving only scars behind.

Finally, the gray-haired woman stopped rocking and chanting and took a deep breath. Kagur stooped and touched Holg's forehead. He didn't feel hot anymore.

But he wasn't waking up, either.

Kagur looked at the gray-haired woman. "Will he live?" she asked, only remembering as the last word left her lips that she and the healer didn't speak the same language.

But the wise woman seemed to guess what Kagur was saying. She pinched a wisp of Holg's white hair between her thumb and forefinger to call attention to it.

Kagur could interpret that easily enough: Holg was an old man. He'd pushed himself hard ever since leaving the camp of the Fivespears, and now he'd taken grievous wounds. The Dragonfly shaman had done everything she could to help him, but only time would tell if it had been enough.

Kagur nodded, and the wise woman spoke to the sentries, who waved for their guest to accompany them back out of the cave. Kagur was reluctant to leave Holg, but neither did she wish to refuse her hosts, and there was nothing more she could do for the old man anyway.

The sentries conducted her to a place where water hissed down the face of a cliff to form a pool, the runoff from which then spilled away to fill a second one lower down. The warriors cupped their hands in the liquid and drank as a way of inviting her to do the same.

She did. The water was cold, tasted of iron, and so eased her parched body that she shivered.

When she'd drunk her fill, the men took her to the lower pool. There, they washed their hands, then mimed the act of scrubbing all over their bodies.

Kagur hesitated to lay her weapons and even her armor and clothing aside. But the cave dwellers had induced her to divest herself of her bow and sword once already and hadn't taken advantage of the opportunity to harm her.

So once again, she did as they'd suggested, and found it refreshing to scrub away gore, sweat, and the grime of her long, hard trek. Although it was somewhat disconcerting when people gathered to gawk at her.

At first, she had no idea why she was even more of a curiosity naked than when wearing what must to them be exotic clothing. Then she realized the sun of the Vault had bronzed the spectators all over their bodies, whereas she was pale where the sun of the tundra had seldom touched. She must seem a strange piebald creature in their eyes.

But at least they weren't laughing or jeering, and she tolerated their scrutiny as best she could. She did her best to rinse the filth from her clothing, too, and then, seeing little alternative, wrung it out and put it back on damp.

Afterward, some of the cave dwellers brought her lizard meat, mushrooms, and slices of orange melon. She made herself nod in acknowledgment before wolfing down each successive portion of her meal.

When she finished eating, the sentries led her back to the Dragonfly shaman's cave. She gathered they were indicating she was welcome to stay in the same place as Holg if she wished.

She settled herself near the old man's pallet. Farther back in the gloom, the Dragonfly healer muttered to herself and burned something that produced drifting coils of acrid smoke.

Eventually, night seized the Vault in its grip, turning the whole cave black as ink. Sometime after that, Kagur slept and dreamed of Eovath. The giant laughed and laughed at her failure to destroy him.

Chapter Twenty-One
Flint and Feathers

When Kagur woke, the sun was shining in the mouth of the cave, and the Dragonfly healer was washing the blood and dirt off Holg's face with a hunk of gray fungus that held water like cloth. She dunked it in a big gourd whenever it dried out.

"How is he?" Kagur asked.

As before, the wise woman seemed to understand the question. But her only answer was a shrug.

Kagur sighed, reached for her coat of reinforced leather, and then realized that, after all the weeks—or had it even been months?—of marching, she'd finally come to a place where she didn't need it. She still hung her baldric over her shoulder, but left the armor, longbow, and quiver where they sat.

When she exited the cave, people hurried to bring her breakfast. Before, she'd discerned a resemblance between these folk and her own people. Plainly, both groups deemed hospitality sacred.

In fact, as she looked around at men chaffing each other as they set forth to hunt, a mother holding and crooning to a crying baby, and a gangly youth scurrying toward a pretty girl with a snub-nosed impish face just emerging from a cave, nearly everything seemed familiar in its essence. For a moment, she felt bitter grief and longing.

Then those feelings warped into an anger partly directed at herself. She didn't understand why, but neither did she question it. Anger was easier to bear.

She didn't belong here. She should be out hunting Eovath. It was maddening to know she'd been one instant away from shooting him when the winged reptiles hurtled down.

Yet she couldn't just wander off and abandon Holg. She was stuck here, no matter how it galled her.

So, frustrated, full of restless energy, she prowled aimlessly about until she spied the worker in flint she'd noticed the previous day.

He was a man of about her father's age, with pale blue eyes, a humorous cast to his expression, and a twisted leg with old scars creasing it from thigh to ankle. Today, he sat chipping away at a spearhead while a boy who resembled him carved the length of wood likely intended for the shaft.

Kagur decided that perhaps she didn't have to stand idle with worry and impatience gnawing at her. Maybe she could occupy herself with a task that would ultimately help her kill Eovath.

She hurried back to the healer's tent and grabbed her bow and quiver. Then she approached the craftsman and his son. The worker looked up and smiled. Intrigued, other villagers paused to watch and find out what Kagur intended.

She pointed to herself and said her name.

The lame man pointed to himself and said, "Denda." He indicated his son. "Bok."

Kagur drew one of the remaining arrows from her quiver and proffered it for his inspection. The steel head gleamed in the sunlight.

A couple people cried out. Others stepped back or reached for the knives in their kilts.

Apparently, the Dragonfly tribe knew of Eovath and his metal axe. And they didn't like the giant any better than did Nesteruk and his tribe or orcs.

Kagur dropped the arrow, put her hand on top of her scalp, raised it to the sky to suggest someone inhumanly tall, and then violently shook her head. She mimed the act of chopping with an axe and shook it again.

It seemed a wretchedly crude and inadequate way of conveying that even though she too wielded steel weapons, she was no ally of Eovath's. But apparently the cave dwellers took her meaning, for they relaxed.

She cautiously picked up the arrow, indicated the tip, and then pointed to the spearhead. She curled her fingers in a beckoning gesture that she hoped communicated, *give me*, or, *I need*.

Denda snorted, gestured to the arrow, and then to the long, sturdy, finished spear leaning behind him. He was inviting her to compare what he considered the puny, useless article in her hand to a real weapon.

Kagur hated to lose one of her last steel-tipped arrows, but she needed to enlist Denda's cooperation. So she strung her bow, and, followed by the onlookers, walked the few paces to where level ground plunged away to become steep mountainside. She drew, sent the shaft arcing over the rocky slopes, and felt a pang of satisfaction when her audience exclaimed at how far it flew.

She walked back to Denda. He smiled thoughtfully, nodded, and picked through the pile of flints beside him until he found one small enough to make an arrowhead.

Kagur pulled another shaft from her quiver, showed it to Bok, and pointed to indicate the wood. She was trying to ask if he had anything suitable for carving into an arrow. But in so doing, she drew her own attention to what was on the end opposite the head, and then she felt like an idiot.

No bird sang or twittered in the Vault, nor were the creatures soaring high above the crags and tree-ferns actually avian. And if she couldn't procure feathers to fletch an arrow, she'd just wasted one for nothing.

But though Bok was looking at the arrow with interest, it wasn't the astonishment of someone who'd never seen feathers before, and that gave her hope. She touched her fingertip to a fletching and raised her eyebrows.

He nodded and pointed toward the lowlands. He seemed to be indicating that he and his father didn't have any feathers on hand, but that he knew where to get them.

Reassured, she nodded. Bok went into one of the caves and returned with smaller lengths of wood. She sat down and drew Eovath's dagger to help the boy carve. The whisper of their blades made a counterpoint to Denda scraping and tapping stone against stone.

They worked for a while, until a burly man with a shaggy, grizzled beard and a necklace of big, curved claws tramped to the top of the trail. Bok spoke eagerly to his father, and Denda smiled wryly and answered back. The boy jumped up, ran to the big warrior, and then they conferred.

At the end of the conversation, Bok ran back to Kagur, pointed in the same direction he'd pointed before, and motioned for her to stand up. Apparently, he'd persuaded the big man to take them to the place where feathers could be had.

She scrambled up, thanked Denda for his help, and bowed in the hope that even if her tone hadn't conveyed her meaning, the body language would. Then she trotted back to the healer's cave.

Holg was still unconscious. "I promise, I'll be back," she said, then pulled on her armor.

By the time she hurried back out into the sunlight, two more hunters had joined the expedition, the comely lass Kagur had noticed earlier and the lanky lad eager for her company. Bok performed the introductions. The big man was Vom, the girl was Tlee, and the other boy was Rho.

Frowning, Vom addressed his companions. Naturally, Kagur couldn't understand a word of it, but she recognized the stern tone and demeanor from the days when she'd been an eager adolescent and one of her elders was taking her and some of her peers out to hunt. Vom was stressing that *he* was in charge, and by the gods, everyone else had better do whatever he commanded.

When he finished with that, Vom led them all out of the village, past the sentry post, and then down a narrower trail that branched off the primary one. Ahead lay trees that, in the aggregate, were a darker green than the jungle Kagur had traversed before. Gleaming like silver in the sunlight, a river writhed through the forest on its way to the great central lake,

Once the hunters descended to abundant vegetation and softer earth of the lowlands, sign became more abundant. Eventually, they paused to consider big, three-toed marks in the sod.

It irked Kagur that she, a skilled tracker in her own country, was the only one who didn't know the source of the prints. She pointed to them and then spread her hands in a way that she hoped conveyed inquiry.

Vom hesitated as though trying to figure out how to answer without words. Then he spread his fingers wide, stuck his arm back between his legs, and waggled it back and forth in a way that reminded Kagur of the spike-tailed reptile that had pursued her and Holg.

Vom's undignified posture made Bok, Tlee, and Rho giggle, too, until the big man snapped at them. Then, as they all set forth again, he surprised Kagur by tipping her a wink.

As the march continued, all the cave dwellers, now realizing how little she knew about their country, and perhaps discerning a way to amuse themselves on the trek, started instructing her as opportunities presented themselves. This pink fruit was good to eat, but those little dark blue berries were poisonous. Travelers needed to keep their distance from the mounds resembling oversized pinecones, lest black ants as long as her finger come swarming out to sting.

The teaching, incomplete and piecemeal though it was, made her feel more confident, more herself, and she fixed every bit of it in her memory. She likewise strove to retain each name for something her companions gave in the course of their pointing and miming.

The earth grew muddier as they approached the river. Channels of water showed through the trunks of the trees and tree-ferns, and clumps of something that looked like tangled gray-green beards hung from their branches and fronds. Brightly colored flowers grew there too, somehow flourishing high above the ground, while insects hovered, flitted, and droned in even greater numbers than in the jungle Kagur had hiked through before.

She realized this was swamp, a sort of terrain with which she'd had little experience. The landscape's own unique plants, animals, and sign elicited a new wave of instruction from her young teachers. But now they provided it in whispers and kept an eye on their surroundings as they discoursed. Evidently, they believed the game they sought was somewhere close at hand.

Vom spotted it first. He raised a hand, and everyone froze.

Up ahead and to the right, its feathers a mottled brown and green, a bird the size of a raven stood ripping at the carcass of a lizard. It was close enough to shoot, but before Kagur could indicate as much, Vom waved everyone forward, and she decided that was actually better. Why risk losing yet another steel-tipped arrow if one of her companions could kill their quarry with a javelin?

Keeping low and availing themselves of cover, they crept forward. Rho stole a glance at Tlee, then tapped himself on the chest, signaling that he wanted to be the one to make the kill. He straightened up, cocked his javelin back, and cast.

Unfortunately, though he'd moved with commendable quickness, his aim was off. The javelin plunged into the soil beside the bird, and the creature gave a harsh cry, lashed its wings, and took flight.

Bok leaped up, pivoted, tracking the bird's motion, and threw. His weapon stabbed into the creature's body, and it fell like a stone.

The hunters trotted up to it, and Kagur saw it differed from the birds she knew. Little pointed teeth lined its beak, while its tail was as long as its body. But it had plumage, and that was all that mattered.

Vom picked it up and proffered it for her inspection. The quizzical expression on his square, shaggy-browed face asked, *Are you sure this is what you want?* She gathered the bird's meat wasn't good to eat, and the warrior had missed her demonstration of the power of her longbow.

She nodded vigorously. In response, Vom shrugged his massive shoulders, stuffed the bird in a hide bag, and waved everyone onward as if to say, *In that case, we'll go catch some more of them.*

They did, while also killing reptiles the size of hares, digging tubers that grew just under the surface of the damp black earth, and even plucking cocoons from branches for some purpose Kagur couldn't guess, and which her companions' miming attempts at explanation failed to clarify. In any case, she realized she was glad the expedition wasn't purely an act of charity undertaken on her behalf.

But if the day's events were somewhat improving her spirits, they were having the opposite effect on Rho. He was nearly always the first hunter to hurl his javelin and nearly always missed. Maybe he simply wasn't particularly skillful, or perhaps his eagerness to shine in Tlee's eyes was making him jumpy. Whatever the problem, either Bok or the girl herself killed every green-brown bird and most of the other game as well.

Nobody smirked or teased Rho when he missed, and Tlee showed no sign of liking one boy better than the other. Still, as the day wore on, he frowned more and more often.

Kagur felt an impulse to pat him on the back but refrained. When she was his age, she wouldn't have welcomed such an expression of sympathy. Come to think of it, she might not even now.

Eventually, Vom led them all back toward the crags. Kagur wondered how he'd decided the moment had come. Maybe, living his whole life beneath the unmoving sun, he'd developed an innate sense of the passing of time that had yet to awaken in her.

Everyone remained alert. In a place so full of dangerous beasts and insects, only a fool would have done otherwise. But still, their demeanor was more relaxed, and Kagur understood why. Hunters seeking their quarry carried themselves differently than those who'd already found it and were simply making sure trouble didn't catch them unawares.

Rho, however, plainly didn't share his companions' self-satisfaction. Sulking, he said almost nothing until the moment when he suddenly pivoted to the right.

Kagur looked to see what had caught his eye. Well back among the trees and tree-ferns rising from a particularly low and mucky patch of ground, one of the long-tailed birds perched on the stem of a sturdy frond. A few steps beyond it, a channel flowed sluggishly.

Kagur had previously communicated to her companions that they'd already taken enough birds to provide what she needed. Still, Rho shifted his grip on his javelin and stalked toward the new one.

Vom raised his hand for everyone else to hang back, probably to ensure they wouldn't make any noise. The bearded Dragonfly wanted Rho to have the best possible chance to finally kill a bird.

Meanwhile, the boy changed tactics. Seemingly recognizing that throwing at long range hadn't served him well, he circled toward the channel, a course that enabled him to creep up close to the bird from behind.

Rho slowly and silently straightened up, took a moment to aim, and then cast his weapon. It pierced the bird between the wings, and it toppled from the frond.

Pleased to see Rho succeed, Kagur nodded. The youth hurried toward his kill—then plunged into a sandy patch of channel-bank as if the earth beneath him had suddenly changed to powdery snow. Submerged to the sternum, he gave a startled yell.

Vom spat what could only be a curse, shouted instructions to Rho, and then led the other hunters forward. Kagur was relieved to see the boy wasn't sinking any deeper, and that the other Dragonflies were concerned but by no means panicked. Evidently they knew how to extricate Rho from the mire.

Rho lay on his back with his arms spread wide. Possibly, Vom had instructed him to assume that position. Bok started across the sand with his javelin extended butt-first for the other boy to grab.

Vom barked a one-syllable command. Presumably, it was "No" or "Stop." Bok did the latter and then backed up.

The burly tribesman probed the sand with the point of his own javelin. The flint came out wet with bits of grit clinging to it.

Apparently, no part of the sandy patch was safe, which meant Rho's companions needed something longer than a javelin to pull him out. Kagur wished she hadn't abandoned her rope along with her backpack, but maybe they wouldn't really need it. Vom looked around, found a low-hanging branch, and chopped at its base with his hatchet.

Rho screamed.

Kagur spun back around. Gray-black worms the size of men were crawling out of the channel straight toward Rho, and the muck didn't even slow them down. They flowed over the top of it with a motion that was half slithering, half swimming. The fanged circular maws at the front ends of their bodies dilated and puckered, dilated and puckered, the biting, sucking action constant as a heartbeat.

Kagur drove one of her two remaining arrows into the worm in the lead. It kept coming. She loosed her final shaft. That stopped it but did nothing to deter the creatures behind it. They simply nudged the carcass aside.

Meanwhile, Vom, Bok, and Tlee scrambled closer to the morass and raised their javelins. Just before the adolescents could throw, the big man shouted. He'd spotted two more worms crawling up out of the channel, and these were headed in the trio's direction. If the young people had made their casts, it would have left them with only their knives to meet the threat.

As matters stood, Kagur judged that she was the only would-be rescuer still free to come to Rho's aid. Unfortunately, with all her arrows gone, such an effort would require dashing onto ground that might well dissolve into slop beneath her feet. But she was just going to have to chance it. She dropped her bow, whipped out her sword, and sprinted.

She circled around to the far side of the sandy patch. That way, she avoided the worms humping toward Bok, Tlee, and Vom, and besides, no one had probed over there. For all she knew, the ground might be more solid.

Or not. The sand felt soft and yielding as she raced out onto it. Refusing to think about that, she slashed at a worm that was only an arm's length away from Rho.

The longsword sliced open the creature's hide and exposed pale, moist flesh beneath. Thin, dark fluid and a thick, dungy smell spilled out of the wound.

Fanged maw clenching and opening, clenching and opening, the creature twisted and surged at Kagur. She took a retreat that kept it from seizing her foot in its teeth and cut at it once more.

The stroke split the worm's head—if a mouth alone sufficed to qualify a body part as a head. The thing flopped and coiled in what she hoped were its death throes.

That was one foe accounted for. But as she stepped to meet the next, the sand melted beneath her as it must have melted under Rho. Crying out, she slid down into it like it too was a ravenous horror bent on seizing and destroying her.

But she stopped sinking, or at least doing so rapidly, when the muck was up to her hips. She supposed some variation in the consistency kept her from instantly plunging in all the way up to the breastbone like Rho had.

Whatever the reason, though footwork had just become impossible, she could still wield her blade. And she was going to have to, to save the boy and herself.

The next worms heaved and slithered at her. She cut furiously, to hurt them and to balk them with shock, pain, and sheer opposing force when they sought to bite. Some surged close enough to bite anyway, and, fixed in place, she jerked her upper body from side to side in frantic attempts to dodge.

As she would have expected, her efforts at evasion weren't always good enough. Twice, worms clamped onto her. The pressure of the contracting rings of fangs was excruciating, and only the reinforced leather of her armor prevented them from instantly shearing into her flesh. Bellowing, she stabbed and hacked until her attackers released their holds.

Meanwhile, she sank deeper. The sand rose over her navel and then her floating ribs.

A worm tried to hump on past her on its way to Rho. She shifted her grip on her sword hilt so she was only holding it by the pommel, and that afforded her just enough extra reach to jab her point into the creature's flank. Distracted from its intended prey, it writhed around to retaliate.

The worms crawled at Kagur from all sides, and she had to twist at the waist to manage any sort of attacks at the one behind her. The motion seemed to sink her even faster, like she was *screwing* herself into the muck, and she discerned that in another few moments, she'd be in too deep to defend herself at all.

Make the last few moments count, then. She struck as fast and hard as she could while roaring "Blacklion!" with every stroke.

Until the muck engulfed her to the shoulders, and it became impossible to swing a sword. Then, panting, she contemplated the lengths of torn, segmented flesh on every side and discerned that none of them was moving anymore.

Not long after that, Vom, Bok, and Tlee hauled Rho and her out of the mire. When they did, she saw that the Dragonflies had needed to kill four worms before they were finished. In the same time, while floundering in the ooze, she'd accounted for half a dozen.

Her companions offered what she took to be expressions of admiration. Rho, however, spoke with a hangdog air. She suspected he blamed himself for drawing everyone else into danger, and that he might even be offering apologies along with his compliments.

Kagur squeezed his shoulder and gestured to the bird he'd killed. She hoped those crude signals would somehow convey that they'd all survived unharmed and he'd killed the game he'd been after, so as far as she was concerned, all was well.

And maybe they did, or at least some approximation thereof. Brushing wet sand off himself, the boy gave her a smile.

Chapter Twenty-Two
Council of War

Kagur didn't think Vom had originally intended that he and his companions should spend the night away from the mountain village. But everyone needed a rest after the fight with the worms, and afterward, when they'd all marched from the swamp back into jungle, he called for a halt under the spreading branches of a towering, creeper-laden tree.

Night fell with its usual suddenness shortly thereafter, as everyone but Kagur had likely sensed it would. When they all climbed the tree, she remembered she no longer had any rope to tie herself in place. Fortunately, though, she found a fork in the trunk where she could jam herself in half lying down and half sitting up. With wood pressing in on more sides than not, she managed to sleep without rolling over and plummeting to her death.

The rest of the Dragonflies shouted greetings when the hunters reached the village the following day. People waved Kagur toward the healer's cave, and she realized Holg must be awake.

Eager as she was to see him, she hesitated before stepping into the shadowy chamber with its painted walls. She didn't want to find him maimed or dying.

"I know you're out there," the old man called. "I keep telling you, my senses are different than yours."

At least he sounded the same as always. Kagur snorted and strode on in.

In fact, Holg wasn't the same. The beak and claws of the flying reptile had left livid scars. But he didn't appear to be in pain or moving any more stiffly than usual as he sat with his back against a wall sipping water from a gourd.

"My amber fetish is missing," the blind man said. "Do you know what's become of it?"

"Yes." Kagur started telling him about the false trail she'd laid to mislead Eovath and the reptiles.

"Xulgaths," Holg interrupted.

"What?"

"According to our hosts, the reptile-men are called xulgaths." Evidently, the old man had felt strong enough to make use of his translation spell.

"If you say so." She finished her explanation of the fate of the fetish, which led in turn into an account of all that had happened since the fight atop the cliff.

When she finished, Holg sighed and said, "Well, I'm sorry to lose that bead. I had it for a long time. But I'm grateful to you for carrying me all the way up into these mountains."

Kagur scowled. "Don't be."

"All right. I was forgetting, you help me simply because you need me."

"No! That's not what I mean! It's . . ." She groped for words. She wasn't good at apologizing. In the times before Eovath had gone mad and dragged her whole life into madness along with him, she hadn't needed to be.

"I don't deserve your thanks," she said at last, "I've been an ungrateful, surly companion."

He smiled wryly. "I'd rather have a comrade who snaps at me but comes to my aid when I need it than one who speaks cordially but is of no use when some unpleasant creature is ripping out my liver. And I understand how grief and rage still weigh on you."

She shook her head. "It doesn't matter. There's a way to behave, no matter how life is treating you. My father would be ashamed of me."

"I doubt that very much."

She felt something loosening inside her, knotted emotions too complicated to sort out all at once. But she sensed that the feeling, part pain and part relief, might bring tears to her eyes if she let it, and she clenched herself to keep that from happening.

"Anyway," she said, her voice a little thick, "I don't promise to be 'cordial.' But I will do better. Are you able to take up our task again?"

Holg fingered the talismans dangling from his wrinkled neck. "With a little more rest, I will be. Ghethi—the healer here—helped me considerably, and once I was awake, I was able to petition the spirits for myself."

"If you *need* more time—"

"No. We may not have it. Eovath allying with the xulgaths, summoning and commanding that three-horned reptile . . . I don't know where it's all headed, but it's worrisome. We need to stop it—and him—before it goes any further. The question is, how? Now that he knows you're here, we've lost a considerable advantage."

She frowned. "The best plan might still be to shoot him from ambush."

"You may be right, but it's possible that if we knew more, we'd could conceive a better strategy. Let's go talk to our new friends."

Holg gripped his staff and used it to clamber to his feet. Kagur resisted the impulse to help him. He wouldn't want her to, and this was an opportunity to judge how much of his strength he'd truly recovered. It turned out to be at least enough to make it up on the first try and keep his balance without swaying or staggering once he did.

He murmured a prayer, and golden light flowed like water through the incised grooves on his staff. Then he recited the incantation a second time, squeezed Kagur's forearm at the end of it, and, as she had in Lady Ssa's marketplace, she suddenly understood the bits of conversation drifting in from outside the cave.

Thus prepared, they went out into the sunlight. Holg's staff swept back and forth across the ground, and all the folk who hadn't yet seen him up and about clustered around for a look at him.

"Kagur and I are grateful for your hospitality," the shaman told them, "and when we have time, it will be our pleasure to answer all the questions you must have about peculiar strangers like ourselves. But for the moment, we have urgent matters to attend to." He turned his head. "Vom? Ghethi? Are you here?"

Actually, they were close at hand. The shaman's milky eyes had simply failed to pick them out of the crowd. At Vom's suggestion, they all settled themselves at a spot at the edge of the flat space, with a magnificent view of mountainside, jungle, and the central lake spread out below them. Nearby, Denda chipped arrowheads, Bok carved the shafts, and Rho and Tlee plucked the brown and green birds.

"Your people were alarmed when they saw my weapons," Kagur said. "Because you know of a giant with blue skin and yellow hair, and you don't like him."

"Yes," said Vom.

"Please," Holg said, "tell us about that."

The burly warrior frowned. "We don't know where he came from. The same place as you?"

"Beyond 'the edges of the world,'" the old man said. "For now, please, just believe there is such a place and go on with your story."

"We heard tales of the giant before any of us saw him. A lone man wandering, only twice as tall as any man should be, with blue skin and an axe that shined like water in the sun. He slaughtered everyone he met, and not even the strongest warrior could stand against him."

Kagur scowled. "I'll 'stand against him.'"

"Please," said Holg. "Let Vom continue."

"By the time one of our own folk spotted the giant from a distance," the big man said, "something had changed. He was marching with a band of xulgaths."

"Your enemies," Kagur guessed.

Ghethi's mouth twisted. "We have many enemies. Other tribes of men often and the orcs always. But the xulgaths are the worst."

"They live on the pyramid in the middle of the lake and in the cities along the shore," said Vom. "Humans and orcs live in the highlands. And we all fight in the forests in between."

Kagur nodded. "Where the food is."

"And *we* are food to the xulgaths," Vom replied, "and slaves, too. They capture us to row the boats that carry them around the lake."

Holg absently rubbed the purple ridge of a new scar on his temple. "I wonder why creatures who would naturally take Eovath—the giant—for a human being, albeit a freakishly big and strangely pigmented one, would welcome him as a friend."

"Because they worship Rovagug, too," Kagur suggested.

"Perhaps, although the similar creatures I heard about in my youth worshiped the demon lord Zevgavizeb. I suppose the two entities could have forged an alliance. Each is a spirit of bloodlust in his way."

"Or maybe Eovath's craziness prompted him to try to make friends with the xulgaths, they responded by attempting to kill him, and after he butchered enough of them, they decided a partnership would have its uses after all."

Vom grunted. "I don't understand everything you strangers say. But it makes sense if the xulgaths saw the giant as a sign or a blessing from the demon they worship, or if they just decided to use him as a weapon."

"Why is that?" asked Holg.

"They've taken him to live on the pyramid. That's their holy place. And they've been raiding human villages more often, like they believe the time has come to wipe us out."

"Are they succeeding?" the blind man asked.

Vom shrugged. "It's hard to know. But there are stories that the giant and xulgaths together have destroyed some tribes."

"Partly because the giant commands the great reptiles of the jungle," Ghethi said. "The xulgaths have always known arts to call and control them. Perhaps they taught the magic to him, and he learned to cast it even better than they do. For he always leads several of the beasts into battle."

Holg nodded. "That's the sort of gift the Rough Beast would bestow."

Kagur glanced back at the peaceful scene behind her, at Denda and the young people working to craft her arrows, children playing catch and scampering about, and a women scraping a sheet of hide with a stone. "What will you do if the xulgaths come here?"

"Fight," said Vom. "if we think we can win. Otherwise, flee upward into the highest crags."

"Where the xulgaths will likely still hunt us down," Ghethi said.

Vom gave her a sour look. "Then pray to the spirits that something happens to the giant before the xulgaths look our way."

"Me," Kagur said. "*I'm* going to happen to him."

"I trust so," said Holg, "but we still need a strategy."

"My thinking hasn't changed," Kagur replied. "We've just heard that Eovath comes into the jungle often. I'll shoot him the next time he does."

"Eovath comes into the jungle at the head of patrols and war parties," Holg replied, "with flying reptiles and probably other beasts playing outrider. In addition to which, he now knows you're here. I don't say your scheme is impossible. You have a knack for accomplishing difficult feats. But it's unlikely."

Kagur scowled. "Then what's your idea?"

"For starters, reinforcements."

It took Kagur a moment to interpret that. Then she turned back to Vom and Ghethi and said, "Excuse us. Holg and I need to talk alone."

Both the bearded man and the wise woman frowned. They didn't like being abruptly excluded from the discussion any more than Kagur would have appreciated it in their place. But neither made any objection. Rather, Vom nodded brusquely.

Kagur and Holg repaired to a patch of shade where ten paces separated them from the nearest potential eavesdropper. Keeping her voice low, she said, "No."

"Eovath found himself an army," Holg replied. "We could use one, too."

"These folk are brave. But they're no match for these xulgaths *and* Eovath *and* packs of huge reptiles."

"Neither are we, by ourselves. But if we all join forces—"

"I said *no*."

Holg frowned. "I understand that you don't want to place them in danger. But they already are, and they can either work with us to eliminate the threat or sit and wait for the xulgaths to come for them. Which option gives them the better chance?"

"I *don't* care about placing the Dragonflies in danger. They aren't my tribe." Her tribe was dead. "But killing Eovath is *my* task. It's bad enough that I had to involve you."

Holg smiled a crooked smile. "It's just as well you didn't promise cordiality."

She grimaced. "I shouldn't have said it that way. But you're a tribesman of the tundra. You understand what I mean."

"I do, and I sympathize. But as I keep telling you, you have to accept that our mission is about something greater than revenge."

"Why? I kill Eovath either way."

"As I've also told you, we have patterns running through our lives."

"And?"

"And a person needs to know when to follow a pattern and when to break it."

Kagur sighed. Holg's mind worked in a twistier fashion than hers, and as was so often the case, she hadn't understood him. Yet she couldn't help feeling he'd somehow won the argument, perhaps simply by heaping on the glib and cryptic utterances until, befuddled, she could no longer see how to continue.

"All right," she growled, "we'll ask them." And for some reason, during the few steps back to Vom and Ghethi, she came around to thinking it the right choice and resolved to ask persuasively.

"I told you," she said, "that Holg and I came here to kill the giant. Will you help us?"

Vom frowned and fingered a tuft of his beard. "We've never been afraid to fight the xulgaths. But now . . ." His eyes widened abruptly. "You have Denda making the little spears that fly from your . . . spear thrower. Can we make spear throwers, too? Enough for every warrior in the tribe?"

"No," Kagur said. "I mean, if I found the right kind of wood, then yes. But it would take too long for your folk to learn to shoot."

"That's not a judgment on you," Holg added. "It takes a long while for anyone to master the bow."

Vom grunted. "Then we'll have to fight the xulgaths as we always have." He forced a smile. "Why not? We've beaten them before."

"Wait," Kagur said as a notion struck her. "Maybe there's a better way."

Holg cocked his head. "Tell us."

"Eovath lives on the pyramid. Why not attack him there where he doesn't expect it?"

"That would require penetrating a whole city of xulgaths," the old man replied. But his tone wasn't dismissive.

"Xulgaths who keep human slaves," she said. "At night, sneaking, we can avoid notice."

Vom shook his head, and Kagur recognized the regret in his frown. He was about to reveal the flaw in her scheme as she'd pointed out the defect in his.

"We live in the highlands and hunt in the forest," the big man said. "We don't have boats."

"Who does?" Kagur asked.

She didn't like Vom's answer.

Chapter Twenty-Three
The Skulltakers

The four shriveled heads sat in a row on poles driven into the earth. The fresher ones stank and sweated slime, and insects crawled in and out of the openings in their flesh.

Vom glowered at the boundary markers. He surely recognized at least one or two of the twisted, rotting faces.

Kagur sympathized with the anger no doubt burning inside him. But it wouldn't do anyone any good to let him stand here and feed the fire. She tapped him on the shoulder and, when he turned his scowl on her, waved to the trail that ran on past the rotting heads.

Vom nodded curtly, and the four of them stalked on. He led, carrying a spray of sweet-smelling flowers with long white petals tinged pink at the base. Supposedly, they constituted a request for a peaceful parley. Kagur and Holg followed, and Dalk, a Dragonfly with a broken nose and a missing upper incisor, brought up the rear.

The trail wound downward through the transitional zone between highland and lowland. Though tree-ferns were scarce, true trees were reasonably common, as was brush. In time, Kagur spied a green face with two fangs jutting up from an underbite glowering at her from the other side of a thicket.

She stifled her initial reflex, which was to nock one of her new arrows and let it fly. Meanwhile, the watcher ducked out of sight.

"They've found us," she murmured.

"Then it's time for this," Holg replied. He signed to Vom and Dalk that he wanted a halt, then murmured the prayers that would enable him and Kagur to converse with the orcs and the Dragonflies, too.

When he finished, he grinned at the cave dwellers. "Now, if the orcs hack off *our* heads, Kagur and I will be able to understand when you say, 'I told you so.'"

Vom's lips twitched upward into a grudging smile. "Everything's good, then."

As they marched on, Kagur spotted more orcs along the trail, each glowering from what was nominally a hiding place, although they became less and less concerned about genuine concealment as the humans penetrated deeper into their territory. Vom brandished the white flowers at them in a way less suggestive of peaceful intent than contempt. Like he meant to convey that if they ignored the sign and attacked, they were even more despicable than he'd imagined.

It wasn't how Kagur would have conducted herself in his place, but maybe it was proper etiquette among the peoples of the highlands, for the orcs didn't throw any javelins or stones.

They did start to call out, though: the word "humans" over and over again. Kagur decided that, infused as it was with scorn and ill will, it was all they needed to say.

As the path began to climb again, the taunt came more and more frequently, until it was like a drumbeat, and it was plain dozens of orcs were snarling it. Then a final scramble up a steep bit of trail brought Kagur and her companions into the orc village.

The habitation was on lower ground than that of the Dragonflies, low enough to support a fair amount of grass and even a couple fruit trees. A single mossy cave entrance, maybe leading to one communal living space, opened in the ground that sloped on upward on the way to ultimately merging with the wall of the Vault itself.

Dozens of orcs *had* turned out to glower at the humans who'd arrived under sign of truce. Kagur assumed one of the watchers on the trail had run ahead to alert them. A fair number of the creatures showed signs of human blood, which, in her eyes, only made them that much more repulsive.

As she and her companions strode to the center of the open space, the green-skinned creatures encircled them. "Humans!" they chanted, emphasizing each syllable. "Hu-mans! Hu-mans! Hu-mans!"

Vom ran cold eyes over the ranks of green faces. Then he spat in the dirt.

The chanting stopped, but apparently only so the orcs could move on to a different sort of harassment. Several particularly big creatures, one wearing a necklace of dried human ears and another with his hair plastered and reeking with old, clotted blood, prowled forth from the ring of onlookers to inspect the visitors at close quarters. Vom and Dalk matched them sneer for sneer, and Kagur followed her companions' lead.

It was easy enough. Her expression simply mirrored the loathing she felt on the inside.

She attracted the attention of the orc with the dried gore stiffening his twisting, tangled spikes of hair. Up close, it was apparent the reeking mane harbored a thriving community of bugs.

For a moment, a flicker of genuine curiosity supplanted the ritual hostility in the orc's expression as he registered her exotic appearance. Then he jabbed his finger at her longbow and thrust out a filthy hand.

Kagur pretended to hesitate. Then she swallowed and held out the weapon.

When the orc reached for it, she simultaneously snatched it back and punched him in his snout of a nose. He reeled backward and groped for the flint knife thrust in his loincloth. His fellows roared.

Shouting at the top of her lungs, Kagur called them all the filthiest and most imaginative obscenities she knew, and from the looks of it, Holg's magic did a fair job of translating. Surprised and maybe even intrigued or amused by insults different than any they'd ever heard before, the orcs fell silent.

When she ran out of epithets, Kagur sucked in a breath. "We came to talk. Listen or try to kill us, but don't waste my time striking poses!"

Clad in only a ragged kilt, a female orc stepped forth from the crowd. She was at least as big and brawny as any of the males, and deeply scarred where some animal had clawed her left breast away. She carried two flint knives tucked in her garment, and a club with stone chips jutting from the head dangled from her grimy hand.

She fixed her bloodshot eyes on Vom. "Who's the screecher?" she asked.

"Kagur of the Blacklions," Vom replied, "and the other stranger is Holg of the Fivespears." He turned to them. "This is Ikolch."

As far as Kagur had been able to determine, the tribes of the Vault didn't formally acknowledge a single chieftain the way the folk of the tundra did. But she inferred that Ikolch was a leader among her people the way Vom was influential among his.

Ikolch spat. "I never heard of those tribes."

"Knowing how stupid orcs are," Kagur said, "I didn't think you would have."

Ikolch snorted. "I like the way you throw insults around, screecher. I wonder, if I eat your tongue, will the knack pass to me?" She shifted her glare back to Vom. "What do you want?"

"With the blue giant to help them," said Vom, "the xulgaths are killing whole tribes. The Dragonflies mean to stop it. But we need the Skulltakers' help."

The orcs stood silent for a moment, as if Vom's words were so strange it took time to decipher them, and then burst into laughter.

Kagur waited for their mirth to run its course. Then she sneered and said, "Cowards. Like all orcs."

"No!" Ikolch snapped, seemingly genuinely affronted for the first time. "But the xulgaths are mostly raiding humans. Why should we care?"

"Have you considered," Holg asked, his tone mild and his stance relaxed amid all the truculence, "what would happen if the xulgaths did succeed in slaughtering all the humans?"

Ikolch leered. "Orcs would have more room and more food."

"For a while," the shaman said. "But as I understand it, the xulgaths are the enemies of *everyone* without scales, and it's always been orcs *and* humans pushing back that kept them from overrunning your world. If the tribes of men fall, the balance shifts."

"But if we kill the giant," Kagur said, "the xulgaths lose heart, and life goes back to the way it was."

Ikolch frowned like she was actually mulling that over. But her hesitation gave another orc the chance to push to the front of the circle of spectators and join the deliberations. He was losing his coarse black hair in the front, which had the effect of making him look like he had a higher forehead than his brutish fellows, and he bore a regular pattern of zigzag scars on his chest that someone must have cut there on purpose.

"That's Yunal," Dalk murmured, "the orcs' shaman."

"This is stupid," Yunal said. "*I* haven't seen the future the strangers foretell."

"Maybe because we're going to prevent it," Kagur said.

The orc seer ignored her. "*Humans* are the cowards, and they want to trick us into fighting the giant and the xulgaths *for* them!"

"Wrong," said Holg. "What we actually need from you is your boats."

Yunal blinked. "Why?"

Holg explained.

Afterward, Ikolch frowned. "We use the canoes to fish the river. We don't take them out on the lake."

Kagur shrugged. "Water is water."

Yunal sneered. "Says the fool! The reptiles in the lake are more dangerous than the ones in the river."

"We'll kill what we need to kill," Kagur replied.

Ikolch chuckled. "I do like the way you talk."

Yunal shot her a sour look. "Talk is all it is. It would be stupid to help *humans*!"

"It will only be one time," said Holg, "and we promise not to tell."

"Maybe their words are only talk," said Ikolch to Yunal. "But with the ghost-giant to help them, the xulgaths *are* stronger than before."

"The humans will lure Skulltakers to their deaths!"

"The plan is reckless," said Vom. "But that's good. That's why the xulgaths won't be expecting it."

Ikolch scratched at a stain on one of her tusks. "They'd never expect orcs and men to ally against them, I'll give you that. And folk would remember our names forever."

"Not if we fail," Yunal snarled, "and we would, following humans."

"No one's asking you to follow," Vom replied. "Our people may not like each other, but we'll do this as comrades, fighting together."

"No," Yunal said. "We orcs would be carrying out *your* plan."

"*My* plan," Kagur said. "And if someone needs to lead, it *should* be me. I've known Eovath—the giant—my whole life. I know how he thinks, and that's why I can kill him."

"And," Vom added, "she fights better than any warrior I've ever seen."

Yunal snorted. "The strongest human is puny compared to the weakest orc." Some of his tribe laughed or clamored in agreement.

But then a youthful voice said, "Kagur fights better than anyone *I've* ever seen, too."

Kagur turned to discover it was Nesteruk who'd spoken and wondered fleetingly how she'd missed spotting him hitherto. Maybe he'd been standing behind someone taller.

But though she was surprised at him speaking up, Ikolch looked even more so. "What do you know about it?" the orc leader demanded.

Nesteruk hesitated, and Kagur abruptly sensed he was the hulking female's son, and that she was the one who'd forbidden him to explore the tunnels running out of the Vault. In his place, Kagur wouldn't have cared to confess disobedience, either.

He did, though. He told about the fight in the red-lit pit in a way that made Kagur sound like a true daughter of Gorum, although Holg and his magic came in for a share of the praise as well.

When Nesteruk finished, Ikolch's fist clenched the shaft of her war club so tightly that the wood creaked. "You and I will talk later," she promised.

"Yes," Kagur said, stepping forth from her companions, "let's finish *our* parley first. You just heard one of your own vouch for my prowess. And much of that is skill. But I also have weapons better than yours. Weapons that make me a match for any foe, even a giant and the beasts he commands." She slapped herself on the chest. "Hit me with your club."

Ikolch eyed her. "It will kill you."

"What do you care?"

"You saved my whelp. But have it your way." Ikolch lifted the club, and the orcs howled encouragement.

The coat of leather was protection. But no armor afforded *complete* protection, particularly if a carnivorous plant had previously gnawed patches of it thin. So, though the point of the demonstration was to show the efficacy of the reinforced leather, Kagur had no intention of letting the club bash her squarely or strike her breasts or vitals. She twisted and caught the blow on her forearm at an angle that made it glance down and off. She hoped the resulting noise, a sort of smacking thump, was still loud enough to impress.

Habit, frustration at her failure to pulp human flesh and smash human bone, or a combination of the two made Ikolch swing the club back up for a second blow. Kagur sprang backward, whipped her father's longsword from the scabbard, and, extending her arm, put her point in line.

Orcs exclaimed to see a blade so long, or maybe at the flash of steel. Poised to rush into striking distance, Ikolch stopped short just in time to avoid spitting herself.

"Touch it," Kagur invited. "Feel how sharp it is."

Ikolch did. A bead of blood welled from the resulting cut on her fingertip.

"I also have this," Kagur said. Pivoting, she thrust the sword back in its sheath, nocked an arrow, drew, and loosed at the trunk of a tree on the other side of the open space.

Flint, sadly, wasn't steel. But the longbow was as powerful as ever, and the points Denda had shaped were razor sharp. The arrow punched through bark and into the wood beneath.

Many of the orcs goggled, and why not? They recognized that none of them could throw a javelin as fast and hard.

But if Yunal was impressed, Kagur couldn't tell it from his sneer. "Is that all?" he asked. "Are these the tricks that will help Skulltaker warriors defeat giants and beasts as tall as trees?"

"Eovath's not as tall as a tree," Kagur replied, "but yes."

"Then prove it!" Yunal snapped. "Kill Old Scar. By yourself. *Then* the Skulltakers will help the Dragonflies."

"Agreed," Kagur said.

"No!" cried Vom. "That's mad! *No one* can kill a longstrider by himself! Especially not Old Scar!"

"I will," Kagur said. "What is a longstrider, anyway?"

Chapter Twenty-Four
The Black Jungle

Holg shook his head. "I don't like this. Even if you succeed, I'm not certain the orcs will keep their promise."

"I am," Kagur said. "The filthy things have no honor, but they do have pride. If I pass the test they set me themselves, it would shame them to go back on their word."

The old man frowned. "Hm. Maybe."

"Besides, they *are* worried about Eovath and the xulgaths, and they crave the glory they'll win by hurting the reptiles in a way no one has before. They just need convincing that the scheme can work."

"Well, then, if you're sure you have to try, I should be coming with you."

"You can't. I said I'd hunt alone. Spend the time talking to the Dragonflies. The Skulltakers too, if they'll let you. Find out everything they know about the xulgaths."

"All right." Holg raised his staff to the sky, chanted a prayer, and laid his hand on her shoulder. Warmth tingled through her, clearing her mind and infusing her with a feeling of vitality. The shaman had given her his blessing.

And with that, she supposed, she might as well set forth. She gave a nod to Vom, Dalk, Nesteruk, Ikolch, and Yunal—she assumed the adult orcs were there to make sure she didn't take a whole hunting party of Dragonflies along with her—turned, and headed down the trail.

Below her lay what the cave dwellers called "the Black Jungle." The thick canopy of branches and tree-fern fronds looked green enough to her, but Vom had explained that from time to time, dark flowers bloomed among them in such profusion that the foliage appeared murky from a distance.

Which was the way the folk of the highlands generally saw this particular forest, even though it teemed with game and edible plants. Few hunters were reckless enough to trespass on Old Scar's territory.

Longstriders were apparently huge carnivorous reptiles that walked on their hind legs, so dangerous they put even spiketails and threehorns to shame. But even compared to others of his kind, Old Scar was a terror. For some reason, he hated both humans and orcs, and would even stop gorging on a fresh kill to pursue either through mile after mile of forest.

Living on the tundra, Kagur had heard stories of dragon-like creatures called linnorms, and a land to the west where lords proved their fitness to rule by killing them single-handed. She told herself that if those hunters could do that, she could bring down Old Scar. She'd make a start by scouting his territory and hope she didn't run into the longstrider himself before she was ready.

As she stalked along, she drew on everything Vom, Bok, Rho, and Tlee had taught her to stay clear of other dangers. Their haphazard instruction was by no means enough to enable her to make her way with the same casual certainty she would have felt on the tundra. But it kept her downwind and at a safe distance from an oblivious threehorn and forestalled any urge she might otherwise have felt to sample a glossy red fruit that would have given her belly cramps and the runs.

It didn't, however, prevent something from spotting her, hearing her, or catching her scent. In time, she caught a glimpse of the creature pacing her while slipping from the cover of one tree-fern to the next.

At first, even though by now she was well inside the jungle they allegedly avoided, she thought her stalker was a man or an orc. It was the right size and walked on two legs. But as, trying not to let on that she'd noticed it, she continued to watch from the corner of her eye, she eventually made out that it was a reptile with a stripe of ragged-looking crimson hide running from its snout all the way to the tip of its tail.

To a degree, it resembled Vom's description of a longstrider, and for a moment, she wondered if she'd attracted the attention of a young one. But the Dragonfly leader hadn't mentioned a streak of red, and the forelegs looked too long, so she decided this was more likely something else.

Whatever it was, it was plainly interested in her, and she wondered if she should shoot it before it made up its mind to attack. But she was reluctant to risk losing any of the arrows on which she, Denda, and the three youths had labored. She intended them for larger game.

She set her longbow and quiver against a tree so they wouldn't hinder her and to make sure they wouldn't be damaged. Then she drew her father's sword and, slashing it back and forth to make the steel flash in the sunlight, strode straight toward the reptile.

At first, it simply stared back at her, and she thought her aggressive display might convince it to go look for easier prey. Then it exploded into a charge, and a second such creature, one she *hadn't* spotted, burst from the ferns behind it.

They were quick, coming on faster than a man could sprint. Their speed inspired a witless urge to get out of the way *now,* but Kagur resisted it. If she dodged too soon, the reptiles would only compensate.

So she waited until the creature in the lead sprang, the claws on its forefeet and the larger spurs on the back ones poised to rip simultaneously. Then she spun herself out of the way and cut open its flank as it hurtled by.

The longsword sliced deep, and the reptile screeched and landed badly. But then, staggering, it caught its balance and whirled back in Kagur's direction.

She lunged and slashed at its neck before it could quite finish turning. Her blade spattered blood through the air as she yanked it back out of the wound, and the reptile went down thrashing.

The second creature leaped at her right over the spasmodic body of its dying packmate. Grunting, she wrenched herself out of the way and somehow sensed at the same instant that by avoiding one attack, she was making herself vulnerable to another. She *kept* spinning and discovered a third reptile pouncing to tear her head off.

She dropped to one knee, and as the beast leaped over her, she slashed open its belly. When the beast landed and pivoted, its intestines started sliding out of the gash. Seemingly addled by the sudden shock of the wound, it scrabbled at the glistening lengths of gut, which had the effect of yanking them out faster.

The creature *might* still pose a threat, but Kagur had no choice but to turn her back on it anyway, to face the reptile she had yet to strike. She jumped up and pivoted just in time to meet the swipe of a forefoot with a cut that severed a clawed toe.

The reptile lifted a hind leg and swung its dagger-like spur in a horizontal arc. Kagur simultaneously retreated a step and slashed. Her sword cut deep, and when the creature set its foot back down, the limb gave way beneath it. As the beast toppled, she lunged and drove her point up under its ribs, surely piercing a vital organ of some sort.

Instantly, she turned, surveying the battleground. No fourth reptile was rushing in to threaten her, and the one she'd sliced from ribs to crotch lay in a pile of its own guts, croaking and shaking. Panting, heart thumping, she finished killing it, wiped her sword on a fern, retrieved her bow and quiver, and then continued on her way.

She spent the night in another tree and realized she'd started to feel comfortable doing so. Maybe that was why she slept soundly enough to dream.

She stood on a hillside looking down at a settlement walled with a log palisade, and though she'd never seen the place in waking life, she somehow knew this was Tolguth. The cluster of wooden buildings stood at the foot of the Tusks and in the strangely lush northeastern corner of the country her people claimed for their own.

Generally speaking, her nomadic folk had no use for such fixed abodes. But Tolguth wasn't just a town. It was a fortress, a defense against the great creatures of these unnaturally warm valleys and abominations spawned by the Worldwound farther east.

Intermittently aware that she was dreaming, she contemplated the settlement for a time, and though no sound, smell, or shadow alerted her, she gradually came to feel the weight of a presence behind her. It was disturbing from the start and grew steadily more so, as though enemies were massing in greater and greater numbers.

She needed to turn and face the danger like a proper Blacklion. But that realization was only a thought and nothing more, as if she'd forgotten how to translate ideas into action.

Then Eovath's voice rumbled at her back: "You really should see them as they are in this final moment before the killing begins."

The words freed her, or perhaps compelled her. She turned and caught her breath.

His golden hair and steel axe shining in the sunlight, Eovath grinned at her like he wanted her to share in his exhilaration. All around him, the gigantic reptiles of Orv, threehorns, spiketails, redstripes like the ones she'd recently fought, and others she had yet to encounter in waking life, awaited his command, while overhead, spearbeaks soared on leathery wings.

"This is wrong," Kagur said. "The guards on the walls see you. They must."

Eovath shrugged. "They mainly watch the east, where the demons are. But if you think they'd spot us, then they can. It won't make any difference."

Suddenly, down in the village, horns blared and blatted. Men ran to arm themselves and report to their battle stations like ants scurrying around a damaged nest.

Eovath raised his eyebrows. "Is that better?"

"You don't have to do this," Kagur said. "You avenged your blood kin when you killed the Blacklions. The folk down there have never wronged you."

"That's one way of looking at it, I suppose. But the pack has made a long, hard trek on short rations. They're hungry." The giant swung his axe over his head to point at Tolguth. Roaring and snarling, the reptiles surged into motion like an avalanche of huge, scaly bodies, gnashing fangs, and claws. Their strides shook the ground under Kagur's feet.

As they charged, arrows flew at them, and despite the protection leathery hide afforded, some faltered or even fell down thrashing. But then spearbeaks swooped at the archers on the wall-walks, knocking them from their perches, and the defensive volleys abated.

Somewhat resembling the redstripes but standing so tall that even Eovath looked small in comparison, the longstriders bounded across the ground and could have been the first of all the truly enormous beasts to reach the wall. They stopped short, though, deferring to even huger four-footed reptiles with little heads on the ends of long, flexible necks.

The long-necked reptiles simply crashed into the palisade. Some suffered as a result, pierced by the points carved at the tops of the logs composing the barrier or by the jagged shards of wood resulting from its demolition. Lowing like oxen, blood pouring out around their stamping feet and lashing tails, several creatures hung impaled on the wreckage.

"That's too bad," Eovath said. "But snakenecks aren't really all that good at killing, and I won't need to knock down any more walls after this."

The redstripes rushed through the breach, if that was the right term when in fact scarcely any of the north wall was still standing. Hunting in groups of two, three, or four, they assailed any humans within reach.

Though quite possibly shocked by the destruction of the wall, the people of Tolguth were seasoned warriors, and they met the redstripes' onslaught with equal ferocity. For a moment, had Kagur been cognizant only of that aspect of the battle, she might have believed the defenders had a reasonable chance of prevailing.

Then the longstriders followed their smaller cousins through the breach. Their forelegs were stunted, seemingly useless things, but they didn't need them to wreak havoc. Their jaws and fangs were huge enough to scoop up a man, chew him to shreds, and swallow him down in an instant. Stooping and straightening, they did so repeatedly. Meanwhile, they crushed other folk beneath their three-toed feet or pulped them with sweeps of their tails, maybe without even realizing they were doing it.

Suddenly, trumpeting of a different sort shrilled through the air. Mammoths and their riders ran to engage the attackers, and for the first time since the battle started, Kagur felt a thrill of hope. Huge as the reptiles were, the woolly beasts with their deeply curved tusks were big and strong enough to contend with them. They had to be!

But hope gave way to a pang of concern when she discerned that Grumbler was the mammoth in the lead. After she'd turned him loose in the foothills of the Tusks, he must have found his way here.

A longstrider wheeled to meet him, and the two animals lunged at one another. The reptile struck like a snake, but Grumbler twisted his head to the side, and the great jaws snapped shut not on flesh but on the point of a tusk.

Grumbler yanked the tusk free amid a shower of blood and broken fangs. Meanwhile, the warrior on his back thrust repeatedly with a long spear. Most of the jabs either fell short or glanced off the longstrider's scales, but a couple pierced the flesh around its nostrils.

Undeterred by any of the wounds, the reptile roared, spraying a mist of blood in the process, and gathered itself to lunge. But Grumbler acted first. He rushed forward, bulled into the longstrider, and knocked it reeling.

Don't let up! Kagur thought. Keep attacking!

Grumbler started forward to do precisely that. But then a threehorn rushed at the mammoth's flank. It was, Kagur now saw, one of two such beasts that had entered the town after the redstripes and longstriders.

Grumbler turned and narrowly avoided the attack. He raised his trunk, perhaps to bash at the threehorn as it lumbered by, and the rider hefted his long spear to stab.

But now the mammoth had presented his flank to his first opponent. Recovering its balance, the longstrider lunged, snapped its jaws shut on Grumbler's neck, and, with a wrenching motion, flipped him off his feet.

The spearman flew from the mammoth's back. The fall likely killed or crippled him, but it didn't matter even if it hadn't. Two redstripes pounced on him the instant he hit the ground.

Grumbler struggled to break free of the longstrider's grip, but without his legs under him, even his strength wasn't equal to the task. The reptile kept holding him down while gnawing its fangs deeper and deeper into his neck. Blood poured out until the mammoth shook in one last spasm and lay still. The longstrider straightened up and roared.

Kagur's fists clenched.

"It's sad," Eovath said, "but Grumbler chose his fate. You freed him, and he was stupid enough to return to slavery."

Down in the streets of Tolguth, the other mammoths were dropping one by one, bitten apart by longstriders, pierced by threehorns, or battered by spiketails. As the enormous beasts assailed one another, they smashed into or fell atop houses that sometimes then collapsed, likely trapping folk inside in the rubble.

That might have been how the fires started, too, although it was also possible some desperate soul set them on purpose in a final effort to drive away the reptiles. If that was anyone's notion, it worked after a fashion. The attacking beasts did withdraw.

They didn't go far, though. They surrounded Tolguth and killed anyone who fled the conflagration, attending to the task until nothing remained of the fortress town but charred sticks, ash, and the column of gray smoke fouling the azure sky.

"Well," Eovath said, "I call that a good start."

"The start of your death," Kagur replied. "Your beasts are strong, but some fell today. More will drop in every battle you fight, until none are left."

"You have a point. To be honest, I'm not even sure how well the reptiles will fare out of the jungle, even though I led them up here in high summer. But I brought plenty. If need be, I'm willing to gamble the tundra will run out of humans before I run out of beasts. But I doubt it will come to that. When other frost giants hear of my victories, they'll come running to help me wipe the humans out."

For a moment, the prospect of such a thing made Kagur feel numb with dread. Then her head cleared, and she sneered.

"No," she said, "this is just another nightmare. Another piece of nonsense. I traveled the caves that connect Orv and the Earthnavel, and you could never get the biggest beasts through the narrower tunnels or find enough food to feed them along the way."

"It certainly wasn't easy, but I managed. Remember, Rovagug guides my steps, and besides, years have passed since you and I last saw one another. I had plenty of time to plan the trek to the surface after I helped the xulgaths wipe out the humans of the Vault." He smiled. "Those were good times, although there was never a moment when I wasn't impatient to return here and get on with my true work."

"None of that will ever happen, either. I'll stop you."

"You tried, but you failed. Again. I want you to know I wept when I found your severed hand still clutching your father's sword. I suppose it fell from Old Scar's jaws when he was chewing you up."

"Brother, if you cried, that proves you don't belong on your devil's path. What do you think awaits you at the end of it?"

"Maybe peace. Maybe nothing. Either way, it doesn't matter. If you fight for something hard enough, you *become* the fight. You know that better than anyone."

"Then let's fight." She reached for her sword but couldn't find the hilt.

Jorn Blacklion's blade was hanging from Eovath's belt, even though she hadn't noticed it until this moment. The giant sighed and shook his head.

She snarled and grabbed for Eovath's own black-handled knife, the dagger that had nearly slain her, but for some reason, she couldn't grip that, either. She looked down and saw that her arm ended in a stump.

"Poor little ghost," her brother said. "It hurts my heart to see you like this." He walked on down the slope.

Stubbornly, frantically, she tried over and over to pull an arrow from her quiver to drive into his back. But an arm without a hand couldn't do that either.

She was still trying when, her arm flailing, she jolted awake in her tree.

Chapter Twenty-Five
Old Scar

The three-clawed track was over half as long as a man was tall. The reeking mound of droppings behind it was fresh.

Kagur double-checked that the warm breeze was still blowing in her face. It was. It wouldn't carry her scent to any beast lurking up ahead.

That was good as far as it went, but it didn't mean a longstrider might not detect her presence anyway. According to Vom, they had sharper eyes than most of the other giant reptiles of the Vault, and keen ears as well.

Keeping low, taking care not to rustle ferns or step on twigs, she crept forward. She peered, listened, and sniffed the air for a first indication that her quarry was close by.

Intent though she was on the task at hand, last night's nightmare nagged at her like a stone in her boot. Had it foretold the future?

Surely not. Even befuddled by the vagaries of dream, she'd managed to list reasons why Eovath's scheme would never work, and besides, asleep or otherwise, she was no seer. That was Holg's province.

Yet both her brother and the old man had warned her something extraordinary was happening, something gods and spirits had a hand in. If such madness was truly what her life had become, then maybe even a simple warrior *could* catch a glimpse of one of Holg's hidden patterns.

She scowled and told herself it didn't matter if the nightmare had had any truth in it. At worst, it was a conditional kind of truth. Tomorrow had no final form as yet. She would shape it by what she did today, and when Eovath lay dead at her feet, she could rest easy knowing the Blacklions were avenged, the Dragonflies would thrive, and the beasts of Orv would never menace the tundra.

Up ahead, something swished through grass. The breeze brought her a musky smell.

Moving even more cautiously than before, she crept onward. She pulled down a frond just far enough so she could peek between it and the one hanging above it. Then she caught her breath.

Old Scar, the first longstrider she'd seen in reality, was shaped very much like the ones in the nightmare— an indication, perhaps, that the dream had been more than just the churning of a restless mind. But standing in a clearing and looking sunward, maybe in the hope of detecting prey, he was even huger than the beasts that had descended on Tolguth. The scar that gave him his name was a white groove in his dark green hide running from just under his left eye down his short, S-shaped neck to his shoulder.

Kagur suspected he'd taken the wound when he was still growing. It was hard to imagine anything hurting him now.

Except me, she thought, shaking off the awe the gigantic reptile inspired. *I'm* going to hurt him.

The question was, how?

She certainly hadn't scouted all the overgrown and beast-infested reaches of the Black Jungle. But she'd already found a couple patches of ground that might serve her need. Unfortunately, at the moment, she and Old Scar weren't especially near them.

But longstriders had sharp ears, and a creature that delighted in killing men could presumably recognize the human voice. She'd retreat back the way she'd come and, when she had a sufficient lead, give a shout to draw her quarry after her.

Her pulse ticking in her neck, she turned and skulked away. Common sense insisted a beast so huge couldn't possibly come stalking after her without making the slightest sound, yet from time to time, she succumbed to the urge to glance over her shoulder even so.

She crept into a kind of arch made of creepers, with meshed vines linking the tree trunks on either side and winding through the branches over her head. The tangles provided cover of a sort, and she felt marginally safer until she glimpsed stealthy, sliding motion above her head.

She looked up. Colored the same brown as the creepers in which it evidently liked to lie in wait for prey, a snake longer than she was tall dropped right on top of her.

Few snakes lived on the tundra, so Kagur knew little enough about them. But every serpent in any traveler's tale she'd ever heard had been dangerous by virtue of a venomous bite. So she dropped her longbow, grabbed hold of the reptile's body just below the wedge-shaped head, and, for an instant, imagined she was safe.

But only until the snake's heavy coils writhed and slid around her body, pulled tight, and squeezed with appalling strength.

The constriction around Kagur's legs made her stumble into a mass of creeper and then fall to the ground. If she gave the snake a chance, it would bind her completely, then crush the breath and life out of her.

She still had the reptile gripped with her right hand. Snarling, she strained until her left arm flailed free of the coil wrapped around it. Then she snatched out Eovath's dagger. It wasn't enchanted, but when she and a foe were wrestling on the ground, it was still a more manageable choice than a longsword.

She stabbed out one of the snake's eyes and then the other, each time hoping the knife would pierce the brain. And perhaps it did, but the reptile's coils kept tightening anyway.

The snake made another try at entangling her knife arm. She heaved the limb free, set the blade under the base of the snake's skull, and sawed. Blood flowed, the dagger scraped on a vertebra, and the reptile convulsed.

For the person caught in the snake's coils, those spasms were bruising punishment in their own right. But they were better than constant, relentless pressure. They allowed Kagur to wriggle and flounder free.

When she did, she spotted Old Scar, who'd apparently heard the rustling, rattling disturbance of the vines, coming through the trees and tree-ferns. He broke into a bounding run at the same instant.

She thrust Eovath's dagger back into its sheath, leaped up, recovered her bow, and sent an arrow flying. The shaft plunged into Old Scar's chest just under one of the stunted forelimbs, but he didn't even seem to notice.

Kagur shot again, scored another hit, and the beast still didn't falter. She didn't have a time for a third effort before he rushed in close.

Lord in Iron, he was *big*, and it seemed to her that his deep-set eyes, yellow as Eovath's, did indeed glare down with a hatred of humankind as implacable as the giant's. The massive head plunged down at her, the great jaws spreading wide.

She dodged to the right. The longstrider's fangs clashed shut in the space she'd just vacated.

She scrambled, circling, trying to confuse her foe while dodging his sweeping tail and stamping feet. After a moment, she got him pivoting away from the area she needed to reach while she was in position to bolt toward it.

The trick won her an instant's head start. Then the earth shook like a titanic heart beating as Old Scar pounded after her.

Vom had told her longstriders ran fast and tirelessly, but, no doubt due to their weight, had trouble turning abruptly. So when Old Scar's shadow fell over her, or she simply felt him looming at her back, she veered right or left, running a zigzag course that lengthened the distance to her goal but kept the reptile from quite overtaking her.

And it would continue to do so. Right up until the moment when she mistimed a dodge or fatigue slowed her down.

A pinecone-shaped anthill appeared amid the greenery before her. Hoping that even an angry longstrider would be leery of the nest, she dashed right past it. For several steps, big black insects popped and crunched beneath her soles while their fellows scurried around her feet.

When she glanced back, she saw her ploy had failed. Old Scar *didn't* swing wide to avoid the anthill. Rather, one striding foot caught it and smashed it to flying grit and dust.

Curse it!

Suddenly, Kagur felt a fiery jabbing in her right thigh. She looked down and discovered two of the finger-length ants clinging to her leg. They must have scuttled onto her foot when she was racing through their territory and crawled upward, maybe after their mandibles failed to penetrate her boot. Unfortunately, they were proving quite capable of biting through her breeches.

Though it was awkward to swipe at the ants and run at the same time, she managed it. But even after she knocked the insects off, the bites continued to burn and itch.

Breath rasping in her throat, she told herself she wouldn't let *that* slow her down, either.

The riotous masses of vegetation, her zigzag path, and the sweat stinging in her eyes all made it difficult to be sure she was even still running in the right direction. But finally she spotted what she was heading for: a patch of ground where the tree-ferns grew more thickly than on the stretch she'd just traversed.

Sensing something changing, she glanced back just in time to see Old Scar break stride. He was no fool. He realized a creature his size would find it difficult to maneuver amid such dense and sturdy growth. But after an instant, he resumed the chase anyway, his malice overcoming his good sense.

Kagur ran several paces into the thick stand of tree-ferns, turned, nocked an arrow, drew, and released.

The shaft pierced Old Scar's torso just as he started to follow her in. Like the previous wounds, the new one didn't appear to trouble him.

Lodging an arrow in the longstrider's scales wasn't too difficult. But driving it deep enough to penetrate the leathery hide and the muscle beneath and reach a vital spot was plainly a different matter.

All right, Kagur thought, panting, I'll do better.

Laying another arrow on her bow, she backed away from Old Scar's earth-shaking advance and waited until the moment when his body stuck between two tree-ferns. Plainly, they would only hinder him a moment before he bulled his way through. But in that moment, he roared in vexation, and she loosed her missile into his open jaws.

She could just make out that the arrow stabbed into the tissue at the back of his mouth. Surely the flesh was soft and vulnerable there. Surely Denda's sharp flint would cut an artery or something else important.

But apparently it didn't. Old Scar lashed his head back and forth, spat the arrow out, and heaved himself free of the tree-ferns.

Kagur dodged left, then right, then left again, winding her way through the thickest growth, keeping just ahead of the longstrider and shooting at those moments when an especially tight squeeze hindered him. She hoped short range and the beast's relative immobility would enhance her aim.

But those advantages didn't seem to matter either. Likely because of the arrow that had flown into his mouth, Old Scar now appeared to understand which shots had the best chance of hurting him, and even wedged between tree-ferns, he could snap his jaws shut and jerk his head when she aimed at it. The defense kept her from driving a second arrow into his mouth or putting out a mad yellow eye.

Retreating, she circled left. The reptile followed and caught in yet another narrow space. She darted forward. Maybe if she got right under Old Scar and loosed a shaft up into the spot where his neck met his lower jaw, that would be the killing shot.

But before she could get that close, Old Scar strained and thrashed, and suddenly, one of the tree-ferns that was holding him in place pulled out of the ground. Cracking and rattling, it toppled at her.

She threw herself to the side. A stiff, dark green frond the size of a blanket swatted her anyway and knocked her reeling. Her foot caught on something, and she fell on her back.

Gaping jaws plunged down at her. She started to shoot up at them, then realized the arrow was gone from her bow.

She rolled. Old Scar's fangs snapped shut beside her, close enough to spatter her with spittle.

At once, the longstrider twisted his head and took a pivoting sidestep for a second try. She rolled to her feet and sprinted away from him.

Pure luck, or maybe Gorum's favor, carried her into another thick knot of tree-ferns just as Old Scar caught up with her. The tall plants snapped and groaned as he jammed in among them.

Gasping, Kagur reached for another arrow. Her groping hand discovered she only had three left.

She supposed that shouldn't surprise her. She could, after all, see arrows sticking in Old Scar's body pretty much everyplace except where his relentless struggles to reach her had snapped them short. Still, it seemed impossible that she'd loosed so many to so little effect.

She remembered Eovath telling her in the nightmare that Old Scar was the beast fated to kill her. Then she spat the thought away.

Old Scar was an animal, she was a hunter, and *she* was going to kill *him*. If arrows wouldn't do the job, she had another weapon in reserve. It was just going to take another little trot through another stretch of jungle to reach it.

Now keeping a safe distance from old Scar, she headed in the appropriate direction. Rubbing her smarting ant bites, she halted to catch her breath twenty paces beyond the clump of tree-ferns.

Unfortunately, seemingly as strong and indefatigable as ever, it only took the longstrider a few moments to shove his way nearly to the edge of the denser growth. She drove another arrow into his scaly breast—why not?—and then dashed onward.

As before, she ran as fast as she could and zigzagged periodically. Old Scar pounded after her.

A shimmering sheet of spider web stretched between two tree trunks. Sure Old Scar would catch her if she swung around it, she simply plunged on through. Swiping sticky strands off her face, she hoped that neither of the fist-sized spiders she'd seen lurking in the web was now crawling on her the way the ants had.

She rounded a tree-fern and found herself running straight at several bear-sized, four-footed reptiles with fin-like crests rising from their backs. Fortunately, they scuttled out of the way, no doubt leery not of her but of the huge beast bounding along at her back.

She veered left and then sensed something was wrong. Instantly, she flung herself back to the right, and Old Scar's fangs clashed shut in yet another near miss.

The longstrider had anticipated when and which way she was going to veer and adjusted his own course accordingly. He kept on learning her moves and tricks.

That was bad, but at least she didn't have much farther to go. Realizing she must have unwittingly fallen into a pattern of evasions, she tried to deviate from it for the final leg of her race and make herself unpredictable once more.

Apparently, that worked, for at last she drew near a stand of slender young tree-ferns—saplings, give or take—crowned with a few dark buds of the plant that gave the Black Jungle its name. The flowers must be coming into bloom. She told herself she was going to live to see it, and Old Scar wasn't.

Not slowing down, she plunged on through the wall of saplings and out the other side. Abruptly, there was empty space before and below her, a place where the ground fell sharply away. Twisting, she grabbed hold of one of the young tree-ferns. The sudden stop jolted her arm, and she hung with her right foot barely planted on the edge of the drop-off, the left one dangling.

Before she could haul herself to a safer position, Old Scar crashed through what was, to him, no obstruction at all. It likely wouldn't have hampered his vision, either, if he'd bothered to look over it, but he'd been too intent on his quarry.

He roared, and as he toppled, the tip of his tail whipped at Kagur's head with enough force to smash her skull or snap her neck. She wrenched her upper body out of the way, and the extremity missed her, although it arced by close enough to fan her face.

Old Scar slammed down on the bottom of the depression in the earth with a thud that shook dirt pattering down from the rim.

Got you! thought Kagur, grinning. Got you!

Vom had told her that if a longstrider fell while running, it often suffered a grievous injury. And she'd done better than that. She made Old Scar run and plummet down a hole as deep as he was tall.

She heaved herself back onto solid ground. Then she peered down into the depression.

For a moment, Old Scar lay as still as she'd expected. Then one of his hind legs jerked.

She insisted to herself that meant nothing. She'd seen how the great reptiles of the Vault sometimes shivered and twitched for a while after they expired.

But Old Scar's flanks pumped in and out, demonstrating that he *hadn't* expired. He was still breathing. But surely he was on the brink of death.

The longstrider lifted his head, then tried to struggle to his feet. Kagur took hold of her next-to-last arrow, let it fly, and drove it into his back. He floundered up anyway.

Old Scar stood favoring one leg and roared up at her, a deafening thunder that seemed to shake the entire jungle. Then he peered about, oriented on a side of the depression that was just a slope, not vertical like the one she'd tricked him into tumbling over, and hobbled in that direction.

Kagur pulled the last arrow from her quiver. The point was gone. Maybe the snake had broken the shaft when it was squeezing her, or maybe she'd snapped it short herself when rolling on the ground.

In any case, it was useless, and maybe that meant the only sane thing to do was flee. At least Old Scar was limping. Maybe, weary as she was, she could still keep ahead of him.

But even if so, what would be the point? She needed the orcs' canoes, and there was only one way to get them.

She set down her bow, drew her father's sword, and walked to meet the longstrider.

As she did, she swung wide, out of the saplings and toward a tree with branches that started growing fairly low on the trunk, spread wide, and had more black buds sprinkled along their lengths. She hadn't quite reached her goal when Old Scar finished clambering out of the hole. He looked about, spotted her, and hesitated like he was surprised to find her standing her ground at last.

"Come on," she rasped. "I hurt my leg, too. It'll be a fair fight."

The longstrider charged.

Even limping, he was fast. Kagur scurried under the spreading branches. Old Scar caught in them. She rushed him and slashed at the injured leg.

But she only had time for one cut. The mesh of branches was even less able to withstand Old Scar's strength than the dense stand of tree-ferns had been. As soon as he thrashed, broken pieces of limb came showering down, and his jaws hurtled down along with them.

Kagur leaped back, and the bite missed. She struck and scored, gashing her foe above the nostrils. He was clumsier than before.

But not all that much. He lunged again, and though she dodged, his fangs snapped shut on her sword midway down the blade. Fortunately, she was able to yank it free—the weapon sliced the longstrider's gum as it slid out—and found it unbroken and unbent.

Maybe Old Scar hadn't caught it squarely between the hammer of one tooth and the anvil of another, or perhaps its enchantments had protected it.

The longstrider pivoted to strike at her yet again. She ducked behind the tree. Circling after her, he tangled for an instant in more low-hanging boughs. It gave her another opportunity to dart in and cut at his foot.

The trick worked for a little while longer. But Old Scar's hops and lunges soon ripped all the lower branches down, and after that, they hampered Kagur, not the longstrider. The litter of sticks and scraps kept threatening to trip her while her huge foe simply crushed it underfoot.

Under *bloody* foot. By any sensible estimation, she'd cut up Old Scar's extremities pretty badly. But he was still upright, and so long as that remained so, she wouldn't be able to even reach his vitals.

She ducked behind the tree trunk for what felt like the hundredth time. She faked left, scurried right, and gaping jaws shot down at her. Old Scar had guessed which way she actually intended to go.

She sprang, and the longstrider's teeth clashed shut behind her. She scrambled on forward, longsword poised to cut, and then, even though it meant putting all of his weight on his bad foot, her adversary lifted the good one to stamp on her.

Instead of rushing on, out from underneath the threat, she halted. As the foot plunged down, she thrust upward.

It was a risky move. Her point might fail to pierce the target. Or, even if it did penetrate, the impaled extremity, impelled by Old Scar's determination or sheer momentum, might finish its attack and squash her anyway.

But in fact, Jorn Blacklion's sword stabbed deep into the sole of Old Scar's three-toed foot. The longstrider jerked it back up and away from the source of the sudden, unexpected pain.

The reflexive action cost him his balance and toppled him. His fall jolted the ground as he slammed down on his side.

Kagur bellowed, "Blacklion!" and sprinted at his chest. When she got within range, she thrust repeatedly. Thrusts were more likely than cuts to slip between ribs and damage something vital.

Old Scar writhed, and the hitching motion knocked her staggering. It also brought her closer to her foe's forelimbs.

When she'd been looking up at the longstrider's immensity from the ground, those two-clawed limbs had looked puny and useless, but not anymore. They were as long as her legs and corded with muscle, and, scrabbling, the left one grabbed hold of her sword arm.

The pressure *hurt*, and the talons cut into her leather armor. Old Scar bowed his neck and lifted her toward his jaws. His breath smelled of his own blood, but she would have sworn by the Lord in Iron and Holg's nameless spirits that she saw triumph and gloating cruelty in the blazing yellow eyes.

She shifted her sword into her left hand. Then, swinging her dangling body, twisting her immobilized arm and making it throb, she drove the blade into Old Scar's throat.

The longstrider faltered for an instant, and then his huge body started bucking in spasms. It was almost like he was vomiting, and the gore that gushed from his jaws reinforced the impression. In reality, though, it was likely coming from a torn blood vessel in his neck, not his stomach.

The longstrider tried again to bring her within reach of his gnashing, red-stained fangs, but apparently the action was now beyond him. When he failed to complete it, he raked at her with the right forelimb.

His talons snagged in the reinforced leather of her armor and tore a sheet of it away. A repetition of the action would surely shred much of her torso. But Old Scar gave a shudder that rattled her bones, and the forelimb and all the rest of him stopped moving.

At first, dazed, Kagur found it difficult even to comprehend the longstrider's death. Then, feeling more numb than anything else, she wondered what had actually contributed to his destruction. Had all the arrows accomplished anything? Had he injured not just his leg but his insides plummeting down the hole? Had she nicked the heart or pierced a lung stabbing into his chest? Or had it really all been that final desperate sword stroke?

She had no way of knowing and decided it wasn't important. What mattered was that now the orcs would give her boats and warriors to paddle them, and that in turn would put Eovath in reach of her sword.

Chapter Twenty-Six
On the Water

Old Scar's carcass stank and had attracted a cloud of buzzing flies and other vermin. Despite that, and the fact that a number of Dragonflies and Skulltakers had already visited the site to verify the creature's death, Kagur had assembled the two tribes here. Warriors might feel more inclined to follow her when the proof of her prowess—or at least her luck—was in plain view. And besides, the Black Jungle was neutral ground, avoided by every tribe for as long as the longstrider held sway.

Surveying the assembly, sun-bronzed humans to her left and green-skinned orcs on the right, she could mostly already tell who meant to accompany her, though it wasn't that those warriors bore more weapons. No warrior of the crags descended into any forest or swamp for any reason without arming herself to the best of her ability. It was the resolve, and in some cases, the eagerness on their faces.

Even knowing it shouldn't take long, the prospect of addressing the assembled warriors made her feel an unaccustomed twinge of awkwardness. She'd inherited her father's talent for fighting and hunting, but little of his knack for facile speech. And it didn't help that she felt strange in her new garment, a crudely stitched sleeveless tunic of reptile hide.

She took a breath. "Well, then. You wanted Old Scar dead, and there he lies. Now, who's going to help me kill the blue giant?"

"I am," said Holg, "but you knew that already."

"I'll go," said Vom.

"So will I," said Ikolch. She gave Kagur and Holg a leer. "I've always wondered what the xulgaths get up to in their sacred place."

"They kill and eat orcs," Yunal said with a scowl.

Fortunately, as far as Kagur could tell, the Skulltaker shaman's words didn't discourage anyone who wasn't dubious already. More orcs and humans volunteered, until she had over a dozen. Based on the meager information she and Holg had gleaned about the island pyramid, that might be about the right number. Many more would increase the risk of detection.

She was just about to declare she had all she needed when Rho and Nesteruk stepped forward together. From expressions on the faces of the adult Dragonflies and Skulltakers, Kagur gathered they were as surprised as she was.

Even though Kagur had persuaded the two tribes to unite against a common threat, they made it clear through scowls, muttered insults, and spitting on the ground that their longstanding blood feud was merely in abeyance. Still, at some point over the course of the last few days, the two youths must have struck up, if not a friendship, at least an acquaintance.

"We'll go, too," said Nesteruk, his voice breaking.

Ikolch scowled. "No, you won't."

"Kagur and Holg saved my life," the orc boy said.

Kagur felt a pang of surprise, and maybe even a tiny hint of guilt. Perhaps she'd done Nesteruk an injustice. Perhaps some orcs *were* capable of gratitude.

If anything, his words made his mother glare even more venomously, but to Kagur's surprise, she seemed at a loss for a verbal retort. Maybe, according to Skulltaker tradition, Nesteruk now owed a debt that rendered all other considerations unimportant.

"Kagur saved my life, too," said Rho.

"I didn't do it alone," Kagur said, "or to get you killed a few days later."

"We heard you talk about the plan," said Rho. "It's all about looking like slaves. You'll look less like a war party if you have a couple boys mixed in with the grownups."

"He has a point," Holg murmured. "The xulgaths certainly wouldn't expect us to bring anyone that young to the ziggurat. To a degree, it would disguise us."

"I thought that was why we were bringing a blind old man."

Holg smiled. "I suspect I actually hinder us in that regard. Any xulgath that gets a good look at me is apt to wonder why a thrall so seemingly useless wasn't eaten before he got old and stringy. We'll hope it doesn't come to that."

Frowning, Kagur pondered. Then, addressing the entire gathering, she said, "The boys' futures are at stake, too. It's a reason to bring them if they want to go. But only if their elders agree."

Dalk with his broken nose and missing tooth was one of the Dragonflies who'd volunteered to go on the raid, and now he raised his javelin to draw attention to himself. Kagur, who was still learning all the ties of kinship within the tribe, realized he must be Rho's father or a guardian of some sort.

"Rho's been initiated," he said. "He's a man in the eyes of those who came before. I won't shame him by forbidding him to go . . . unless Vom, who's been teaching him, tells me I should."

The big man's mouth tightened inside its shaggy border of mustache and beard. Plainly, he felt as reluctant to risk being responsible for Rho's death as Kagur did. But after a moment, he said, "We'll need to sneak. Rho did that well when we hunted for feathers."

"Fine!" Ikolch snapped. "If even a useless human child is coming, Nesteruk is, too. No one will say only a Skulltaker was deemed unfit. Now, let's move out. I want to make it partway down the river before dark."

The members of the war party shouldered the bundles necessary for the expedition, and humans bade one another farewell while orcs sneered at what they seemingly considered contemptible displays of softness. Then Kagur and her companions set forth.

Hiking through jungle was more comfortable without the weight of her armor, but when she spotted a spearbeak soaring overhead or the spoor of some dangerous beast on the ground, she missed the protection anyway. Unfortunately, she was far from adept at leatherworking, and even a crude repair was beyond her. She was lucky Denda and his young helpers had managed to make her some more arrows.

Maybe she would have enjoyed the cool comfort of her unencumbered condition more if the stain on her bare arms and legs hadn't to some degree counterbalanced it. A diluted version of the same pigment the Dragonflies used to daub pictures on cave walls, the stuff felt itchy and unpleasant on her skin. But she was willing to put up with the coloring in the hope that it, an additional layer of rubbed-on dirt, and darkness would hide the pallor of her limbs.

It wasn't long before Nesteruk and Rho advanced up the column to walk along with her and Holg. She discouraged them with a glower, and they fell back again.

"Are you sorry we let them come?" Holg asked.

She shrugged.

"I don't know if it was the right decision, either," the old man said. "But I believe we all felt something moving in the moment. A pattern either advancing itself or breaking apart to form a new one."

She sighed, irritated, yet, she realized, resigned to his cryptic utterances as well. Perhaps weeks or months of them had finally worn her down.

In time, the raiding party reached the river. Reflecting the blue sky and the trees and tree-ferns that made green walls along its banks, the watercourse was considerably wider and clearer than the brown channels Kagur had seen in the swamp. She suspected it flowed faster, too, although nowhere near as fast the frigid streams that hissed down from the Tusks and the Crown of the World. An insect as long as her forearm swooped, skimmed across the surface, and climbed back skyward clutching a little squirming fish.

The Skulltakers kept three canoes hidden under a pile of fallen branches and fronds. Hollowed and carved from sections of log, the boats were long and narrow and had paddles, spears with barbed points of wood and bone, and old fish scales and stains in the bottoms.

As Kagur and her fellow humans soon discovered, one first pushed a canoe into the shallows and then hopped inside while trying not to tip it over. The orcs laughed and jeered at their companions' lack of facility.

Kagur had still only learned a few words of the speech of the highlands, and Holg's most recent spell of translation had run its course. So she failed to grasp the substance of most of the taunts. But the orcs' tone didn't seem quite as nasty as she might have expected, while the humans tolerated the chaffing reasonably well. No one was raising a hatchet or clenching a fist.

Maybe the simple act of traveling together while contemplating the perilous exploit to come was at least *slightly* blunting the warriors' traditional hostility. Kagur hoped so. Before the raid was over, they might need any hint of camaraderie and mutual trust they could muster.

And with that thought came the sudden, surprising realization that perhaps *she* was growing at least a little accustomed to the Skulltakers as well. The sight of them no longer elicited the same reflexive surge of disgust.

She wondered if she should cling to her animosity. It was, after all, simply what every Kellid felt, and for excellent reason. But if she and the Skulltakers were working to bring down a common foe, what would be the point? Especially when said foe was the creature she *truly* hated.

She decided that if her old antipathy was drowsing, she might as well let it. She could resume detesting lesser enemies when Eovath lay dead at her feet.

Shortly after she came to that conclusion, it occurred to her that if she actually wanted orcs and humans to regard one another as comrades, such feelings were more likely to flourish if the two groups shared all labors equally, paddling included. So, kneeling toward the front of the lead canoe, she studied how Ikolch dipped her paddle and stroked when she deemed it appropriate.

The Skulltaker didn't do it constantly, and it was plain that, heading downstream, the orcs weren't much concerned about pure motive power. The current bore them along at a fair pace. But they needed to steer.

When Ikolch had labored and Kagur had watched for what seemed a reasonable time, she tapped the orc on her grimy, brawny shoulder. Her expression as vicious as usual, Ikolch looked around. Kagur pointed to the paddle and then held her hand palm up to signal, "Give me."

Ikolch hesitated and then handed the implement over.

Kagur shaded her eyes with her hand and turned her head to mime the act of keeping watch on what lay ahead. Then she pointed to the orc. She hoped that conveyed, "I'll paddle, but you need to tell me which direction to steer and when."

Ikolch grunted and gave a nod.

In fact, Kagur didn't always need the orc to warn her. Some hazards were unmistakable, like floating logs, snakenecks—more beasts that looked much like they had in her nightmare—standing submerged to their bellies, or carnivorous plants dangling spiny two-lobed appendages over the water.

Yet at first, other perils were far from obvious. But gradually, studying the parts of the river Ikolch indicated even as she paddled to avoid them, Kagur came to recognize shallow places where a canoe could grind against hidden rocks or tangles of sunken deadwood.

Her improved understanding pleased her. Although maybe that was stupid since she doubted she'd ever do this again.

She was going to kill Eovath. Any other outcome was inconceivable. She was less certain she'd survive him by more than a moment, and as long as she avenged the Blacklions, that was all right. But if she did survive, she and Holg would presumably attempt the long climb back to the tundra, where canoeing would be about as worthless a skill as she could imagine.

Still, doing her fair share and knowing herself competent were preferable to being useless and ignorant, and maybe the Dragonflies felt the same way. For in time, they too started offering to spell Skulltaker paddlers.

Eventually, presumably knowing night was nigh thanks to the inner reckoning that still eluded Kagur, Ikolch turned the lead canoe toward a little treeless island in the middle of the river, and the other boats followed. After dragging the vessels onto the muddy shore, the travelers walked from one end of the place to the other swishing spears and javelins through the ferns, reeds, and brush, checking for any dangerous beast that might have swum or flown here since Skulltaker fishermen had last visited the place. They found none and made camp.

Kagur gathered it was rare but not unknown for the xulgaths to venture this far upriver, and so it was a camp without a fire. Still, her companions sat in the usual circle to gobble their rations, and in time, Vom started a joke. Kagur only caught a word or two, but she recognized it for what it was. Just visible in the dark, the burly Dragonfly's impish smile reminded her of Roga's.

But Vom's sense of humor was apparently superior. Other men actually laughed, and after a moment, even some of the orcs gave a grudging chuckle. Then a Skulltaker began a joke of his own.

The moment made Kagur feel strange, like something was hurting and easing her at the same time. Then her insides clenched in a spasm of anger that impelled her to get up and walk to the edge of the black water. She stared out across it at the equally dark forest on the other side.

After a while, not bothering to feel his way with his staff in the murk that was clarity to him, Holg came to join her. "I can cast another charm of speaking," he murmured. "You don't have to be left out."

She scowled. "Somebody needs to stand watch."

"Somebody else already is. The boys volunteered, remember? You know, I'm fairly certain that allowing yourself to enjoy something won't weaken your determination to kill Eovath."

She spat. "Of course it wouldn't."

"What's wrong, then? Do you believe it would be disloyal to your father and the other Blacklions to form new attachments?"

"I don't *want*—" Realizing she didn't truly want to say what she was about to blurt out, she stopped short. "Old man, you and I both come from the same land. And you're a staunch companion."

"Thank you."

She waved the interruption away. It was annoying enough to say such mawkish things without him stretching out the moment. "The point is, you and I are friends. But these others . . . they're our comrades for the time being. But they're *not* my kin or my friends. They're a weapon in my hands."

"If you say so," Holg replied, and then something made a little splash a stone's throw away from the shore. "Did I ever tell you that when I was in the southlands, I learned to catch a fish with just my hands?"

"Despite your eyes?"

"Having to rely on one's sight may actually be a handicap. Things can look like they're in the wrong place under the surface of the water. Iacobus, a sage from Absalom, hypothesized that . . ."

Grateful for the change of subject even though the shaman's rambling discourse became incomprehensible almost immediately, Kagur watched the night and let him drone.

Even after the sun flared back to life, the travelers lazed on the island. It would be useless if not dangerous to depart prematurely. The xulgath city that stood where the river met the lake was less than a day's travel away, and they needed to slip past it in the dark.

Though Kagur understood the reason, the delay rekindled the seething impatience that had possessed her at intervals ever since waking in the camp of the Fivespears. She prowled around and around the island until Ikolch finally declared it time to depart.

At one point, the current carried them in front of five canoes heading out of an inlet. Kagur's companions set down their paddles and took up their javelins. But the strangers, perhaps astonished to see men and orcs journeying together, simply goggled and let them pass by unchallenged.

Eventually, darkness again engulfed the Vault, and, not trusting humans with their inferior night vision to steer clear of hazards, the Skulltakers took possession of all the paddles. Not long after that, clustered towers appeared amid the gloom.

Since she and her comrades were trying to keep well clear of the city, Kagur couldn't make out much of it except for the vague shapes of the nearer spires, a step pyramid, and a tame spiketail grazing on the shore. But numerous points of firelight shined through windows and atop battlements, and a shrill atonal whining—was it truly supposed to be music?—set her teeth on edge.

Suddenly, Ikolch stopped paddling, and the other orcs in the lead canoe did the same. For a moment, Kagur couldn't see what had made them cease, but she could hear it. Up ahead, something else was swishing through the water in the same rhythmic fashion.

Its high prow carved with some sort of image, a larger boat emerged from the blackness. Much longer paddles—she thought they must be what Holg, in one of his many reminiscences, had called "oars" or "sweeps"—stuck out of the sides to push it along.

Ikolch made a fierce slapping motion at the bottom of the canoe. Kagur crouched low, and her companions did the same. She assumed the men and orcs in the other dugouts were taking the same precaution.

But even if so, someone aboard the patrol boat still noticed something amiss. Inhuman voices hissed back and forth, and then one rasped a command. The oars on one side of the craft stroked while those on the other lifted out of the water, turning it in the raiders' direction.

Kagur scowled. She had no idea if she and her comrades could contend with the bigger boat while fighting from canoes. Even if it was possible, could they manage it quickly and quietly enough to keep anyone on the shore from noticing the skirmish?

Hoping for a magical solution, she glanced back at Holg. Unfortunately, the old man was simply bending low like everybody else. He evidently didn't have a prayer for the occasion.

But then, from somewhere behind the lead canoe, something made a sound midway between a growl and a cough. After a pause, the noise repeated.

The xulgaths on the patrol boat did more hissing back and forth, and then the leader snarled another command. The rowers maneuvered again and headed straight upriver, between the drifting canoes and the towers on the shore.

Ikolch waited until Kagur couldn't hear the splash of the oars anymore. Then the orc straightened up, and everyone else in the lead canoe did the same.

Ikolch pointed at the next canoe in line. "Nesteruk," she whispered.

Kagur guessed the boy, perhaps merely for his own amusement, had taught himself to imitate the call of some river beast with a long, low shape, and he'd just done so. Duped into believing they were peering at such creatures, the xulgaths had decided they didn't need a closer look.

Kagur nodded to show she understood. "Good trick."

The acknowledgment seemed to remind Ikolch that even a hint of maternal pride was at odds with her customary surliness. She scowled, spat in the river, and took up her paddle once again.

Once they reached the lake, the orcs paddled hard. They needed to reach the xulgaths' holy site with most of the night still before them.

Motionless as its sun, the Vault's stars silvered the water falling from upraised paddles, while enormous beasts periodically rose to the surface of the lake. The breaching only made a little noise, but for the most part, Kagur could still hear the creatures better than she could make out their shadowy forms.

Once, just a stone's throw to the right, a relatively small head reared high above her, and she wondered if a snakeneck had waded or swum this far offshore. Maybe not, for after the head plunged back under the surface, it stayed there as the canoes sped onward.

Gradually, at first visible only because of the fire that burned atop it, the dark pyramid came into view, and then took longer to reach than Kagur expected. It was bigger than she would ever have imagined, and, like a mountain, kept looming larger and larger.

A lengthy approach gave sentries plenty of time to spot the raiders drawing near, but as far as she could tell, nobody did. Maybe she had the darkness to thank, or maybe she'd guessed right that the xulgaths had grown complacent in the assumption that their foes could *never* assault them here.

The canoes glided parallel to one face of the ziggurat as their occupants looked for a likely place to put in. Holg spotted it first, a row of small boats perched on the edge of the bottom tier. With luck, their canoes would sit unnoticed beside the others.

The ledge was about waist high above the water, and though it was impossible to be certain in the dark, Kagur had the impression the pyramid simply continued stair-stepping into the depths. She wondered if it did so all the way to the bottom of the lake, and just how far down that was.

The raiders tried to lift the canoes out of the water quietly, but the bottom of one still scraped on the wet, dark stone. Kagur gritted her teeth, and Rho's wince confessed that he was to blame.

Fortunately, no one came rushing to investigate the noise. Kagur took another glance around, and then she and Holg pulled off their boots and stashed them in their canoe. The humans and orcs of the Vault didn't wear anything on their feet, so their new allies couldn't, either.

Nor could folk who were supposedly slaves openly carry weapons. The raiders stowed theirs in the bundles that, they hoped, looked like innocuous burdens for thralls to haul around. Holg stowed his staff as well. But he needed to keep his fetishes ready to hand for magic.

First, whispering, he restored the gift of universal speech to Kagur and himself. Then, murmuring another incantation she'd come to recognize, he set three talismans on the stone.

The one pointing straight ahead at the core of the ziggurat was the one that crawled.

Chapter Twenty-Seven
The Ziggurat

The raiders shouldered their bundles and trudged along the tier. Kagur resisted the urge to touch the hilt of her longsword inside the roll of hide to make sure the blade was still where she could find and draw it quickly.

In time, boats like the one that had nearly caught them on the river emerged from the gloom ahead. Unlike canoes, these were too big to haul in and out of the water on a daily basis, and the xulgaths had built railings along the water to tie them to. Some sort of paste glued the wood in place. Perhaps that was easier than drilling holes in the stone. Pads of woven reed kept the vessels from bumping and scraping their hulls to pieces.

Holg pointed and murmured, "There."

Squinting, Kagur just made out what he was indicating. A rectangular opening led into the pyramid. A xulgath sentry stood there, its spear leaning ready to hand against the wall.

"Here we go," Kagur whispered. "Hang your heads and act scared."

As she and her companions shuffled forward, she realized she *was* scared, or at least uneasy. She didn't fear the reptile itself, but she feared all the holes in her plan. What if slaves were expected to greet or salute their masters in a particular way? Or what if the xulgaths never assigned men and orcs to the same work crew? Or—

She wrenched her mind away from such thoughts. It was too late for them. She, Holg, and the cave dwellers were here now, and if things went wrong, they'd simply have to cope.

This was the first time she'd seen a xulgath up close. Had the scaly gray reptile straightened up, it would have stood as tall as a man. But it hunched forward like it was on the verge of dropping to all fours, and its arms were long enough that maybe that was how it sometimes shambled around. It didn't pick up its spear as the raiders drew near, but it did finger the coiled whip hanging on its knotted belt.

Seeking to pass through the doorway, Kagur kept as far from the xulgath as possible. The expression on its face—if the reptilian eyes and jaws were even capable of expression—was impossible for a human to decipher, but it stepped back as though giving her and her companions room to pass. When it reached for its hip, she realized it was actually giving itself room to use the lash.

Her sword hand twitched with the impulse to draw her own weapon. She made herself cower instead.

The xulgath flicked the whip. The lash snapped across her bare calves. The sting made her go rigid.

She pointed to her bundle. "Please! A master ordered us to take these things up!"

The xulgath brandished the whip to wave her onward, and she realized it hadn't struck her to punish her for some proscribed behavior. It had simply felt the urge to hurt her.

If fate was exceptionally kind, maybe she could do likewise on the way out.

On the other side of the doorway, lamps of luminous green crystal in wicker cages glowed at intervals along the walls. She and her companions wouldn't have to grope their way through total darkness. That was reassuring, but even so, after several paces, something started nagging at her.

She knew nothing about xulgaths or immense stone structures, either. But she realized she'd expected the interior of the ziggurat to reflect the same simple symmetry, straight lines, and right angles as the outside.

Had she simply turned out to be mistaken, she would have discerned as much and forgotten about it. What was bothering her was an irrational feeling that she was right and wrong at the same time.

The shadowy green-lit passage before her was level and ran at a right angle to the tier outside. Yet she *felt* that it diverged infinitesimally from true. No matter how she peered and squinted, though, she couldn't spot the discrepancy, and the effort threatened to put an ache in her head to go with the smarting in her legs.

"Does everyone feel that?" she whispered.

"Yes," Holg answered. "It may be the aftereffect of some evil working. Or countless demonic rituals performed over generations. Ignore it as best you can, and keep moving."

That sounded like good advice, and they heeded it. Their progress took them toward another sentry stationed at a doorway.

The new xulgath was guarding orc and human slaves huddled in the chamber beyond the opening. The space stank of filth and sickness, and the captives were packed in tight, even though other rooms nearby were empty.

Like Kagur, her companions trudged past the opening trying not to display any obvious interest in the prisoners. Still, she suspected they were peeking from the corners of their eyes and deciding that if the things went awry, death in battle was preferable to the wretchedness they saw before them.

Not far beyond the slave cell, they came to a point where the strings of crystal lamps ended. Fortunately, at the same spot, a doorway in the left wall granted access to a flight of stairs leading upward.

Holg fished out the fetishes he'd hidden under his tunic, laid a couple on the floor, and whispered his prayer of finding. The wolverine fang on its knotted thong slithered toward the steps.

"How often can you do that?" Ikolch asked.

"Not as often as we'd like," the old man answered, picking up the talismans. "But the magic should at least guide us to Eovath's general vicinity."

Ikolch sneered. "I can do that much just by beating some answers out of a sentry."

"But then," Kagur said, "you'd leave a corpse behind for other xulgaths to find. Stick to the plan."

The stairs led them onto the second tier, out under the stars once more. Drawing a breath of fresh, moist air, Kagur felt a trace of queasiness depart. She'd escaped the indefinable and possibly hallucinatory skew inside the ziggurat. She and her comrades crept onward, looking for another way into the pyramid, or, better still, an external staircase, ladders, creepers, or even weathered, broken spots running up the tiers. While trying not to be obvious about it, they stuck close to the wall to make it more difficult for creatures on the ledges above to see them.

From time to time, bits of sibilant conversation drifted down from overhead. Then something snapped, drums pattered, and a line of xulgaths came whirling down the shelf in a frenzied, capering dance. Each reptile repeatedly cracked a whip consisting of a peculiar-looking length of leather—the preserved tentacle of some creature like a seugathi?—with a long, curved talon at the end, and periodically, it lashed a fellow dancer or one of the several tom-tom players who marched behind them. The claws snagged and tore flesh, but no one cried out or faltered for more than an instant.

Kagur assumed the xulgaths were shamans of Zevgavizeb conducting a rite. She likewise assumed that if they were willing to flog one another, slaves were fair game, too. Though the xulgaths were out toward the center of the ledge some distance from the next stair-step up, she and her comrades pressed themselves against the wall to make themselves as inconspicuous as possible.

Unfortunately, the procession veered toward them anyway. Kagur wondered if her companions, particularly the Skulltakers, had the forbearance to endure the stroke of a whip without retaliating. She also wondered how many of them would still be fit to fight after the dancers finished with them.

Maybe she and her companions *needed* to fight. Just hope it went fast and quietly and they could hide the bodies afterward. She slipped her hand into her bundle, and then Holg stepped toward the xulgaths.

"Noble masters," he said, his words timed to the drumbeats, "all praise to the mighty lord of caverns . . ."

For a moment, Kagur's eyelids drooped. When they snapped up again, she realized Holg was trying to beguile the xulgaths as he had the Fivespears warriors.

Seized by the magic, the reptiles apparently didn't see anything strange about an old human slave with cloudy eyes offering praise to their demon god. Nor did they balk when Holg managed a clumsy imitation of their capering and led them safely past the rest of the raiders.

But he couldn't dance their dance without suffering the consequences. One whip ripped open his tunic and scored the skin above his ribs, and another snagged and gashed his thigh.

Still, he maintained the lulling rhythm of his prattle while he gradually allowed the other dancers and the drummers to pass him by. Then he cavorted and spun in place until they disappeared into the dark.

Kagur ran to him. "Are you all right?" she asked.

"I didn't know if that would work," he wheezed. "If their ritual hadn't already been stup . . . stupefying them in its own way, I don't think it . . ." His knees buckled.

Kagur caught him and sat him down. "I said, are you all right?"

"I will be. I just need . . ." He clutched his fetishes through his tunic and gritted out a prayer. The bleeding stopped as the gashes closed.

Still, he lost his balance when he stood up, and she had to catch him again. "Sit back down," he said. "Catch your breath."

He shook his head. "We can't afford to linger in one place. It's too risky. I just need a little more magic." He recited the same restorative prayer as before. "There. That's got it."

She let go of him but stood ready to grab hold once more if necessary. "Are you sure?"

"Yes." He frowned. "I just hate to spend so much power when we're likely to need it for other things. There was a time . . . never mind. Onward!"

Not long after, they found a way back into the pyramid. Presumably, if they entered, they'd eventually come upon a set of stairs that ran up to the next tier.

Kagur wondered why they couldn't just find one long staircase that went all the way from the bottom to the top. Maybe there was a defensive or religious reason. Or maybe such an ascent did exist, but it was hidden in the lightless core of the structure.

As before, the green-lit corridors and the chambers to either side gave her the nagging sense that the right angles and basic symmetry masked some festering peculiarity. She tried to concentrate on other things.

Though she didn't see any signs they cooked it, this appeared to be the area where the xulgaths prepared their food. Fruit and tubers sat in baskets of woven reed, and lizards and beetles the size of badgers crouched, hissed, and clicked their mandibles in wooden cages.

There were no caged men or orcs, but she did spot two corpses with much of the flesh flensed away, the ribs cracked to permit removal of the heart, liver, and other organs, and the eyes scooped from their sockets. Presumably, when the xulgaths hungered for such meat, they simply brought slaves up from below.

No one was preparing any meals now, though, and as the raiders trudged past a series of doorways opening into one large chamber, they were afforded a look at how the xulgaths that presumably worked in the area spent their leisure time. Seated in a circle, several were passing a flat, sharp-edged piece of flint around. Each swallowed the stone and regurgitated it before handing it to the next.

As Kagur passed the last opening, one xulgath failed to bring the flint up. Retching, it clutched at its throat, and a mix of blood and spit spilled through its fangs.

None of the other xulgaths tried to help it. They didn't even laugh. They just stared, drinking in their fellow's distress.

As before, the raiders eventually came to a place where blackness lay before them, but stairs ascended on the left. When they reached the next tier, Kagur once again savored the fresh air and the relief from the oppressive atmosphere inside.

She assumed these wouldn't last, and she was right. She and her companions still couldn't find a way up the outside of the ziggurat, and when they came to another opening, they exchanged resigned glances and crept back inside.

Into an area where xulgath warriors lived. In one room, the reptiles sparred with staves, two against two. In another, half a dozen administered a beating to another that had its hands bound behind its back and its fanged jaws tied shut. In an armory stocked with spears, javelins, and hatchets, a craftsman swung a club to test the weight and balance, then went back to whittling it.

Wide-eyed, Rho slipped up beside Kagur. "The blue giant's a warrior," he whispered.

"But not an ordinary one," Kagur replied. "A sacred one, in the xulgaths' estimation. He'll be at the top of the pyramid."

She had no way of knowing that for certain. But with slaves at the bottom, xulgath laborers above them, and warriors next, it seemed a likely progression, and when she happened to glance at Holg, he gave a slight nod of agreement that pleased her and made her feel patronized in equal measure.

Above the habitations of the common warriors was a tier where, by the looks of it, their chieftains lived with more privacy and amenities. On the level above that, the shrines began.

Many contained a vertical spike of bloodstained stone jutting from the center of the floor. The demon god to whom the sacrificial implements belonged was a blend of longstrider, worm, and bat, with tentacles thrown in for good measure.

The xulgaths had carved and painted Zevgavizeb's image on freestanding wooden screens, but not the walls. Maybe even they recognized the wrongness lurking in the stonework and feared to agitate it.

In time, Kagur spied what she assumed to be the doorway to another staircase at the point where the green light failed. But like the entry on the bottom tier, this one was protected.

In fact, it was better protected. A guard with a spear stood to either side of it, while a shaman armed with a claw-whip perched on a stool, studying the writing on a sheet of hide. But the truly impressive guardian was a giant reptile of the breed the cave dwellers called clubtails. Somewhat resembling a turtle, only with rows of pointed extrusions lining its shell, it swept its long tail back and forth on the floor, scraping the ridged knob at the end against the stone.

Obedient though the clubtail evidently was, Kagur wondered fleetingly how the xulgaths had conveyed such a huge beast to its present location. Probably when it was a baby or even an egg. And here it would stay in the gloom for the rest of its life, too huge ever to pass through the opening onto the exterior walkway and see the sun.

Together with its keepers, it seemed a formidable obstacle. Still, the raiders' imposture had fooled every xulgath so far, and so Kagur opted to press on.

The reptilian warriors noticed the newcomers first. The one of the right said, "Look," and they leveled their spears in a casual way. The clubtail grunted and lumbered around to face the intruders, too.

The shaman hopped off the stool. "What are you doing?" it snarled.

Kagur tried to cringe convincingly and speak humbly. "Bringing things for the masters up above."

The xulgath blinked. "What are you talking about? Slaves aren't allowed that high. You shouldn't even be here without an acolyte overseeing you."

She bobbed her head. "Sorry. We're lost, then. We'll go back down." She turned, and her companions followed her lead.

"Stop!" snapped the shaman. "I want a better look at you."

If the creature scrutinized the intruders closely, that would be the end of the deception. Even if it didn't examine the bundles, none of the raiders were gaunt enough to pass for slaves, and though most bore scars, the scars weren't whip marks.

Kagur glanced at Holg to ask without words if he had any magic likely to fool the reptile and keep it fooled. The old man gave a tiny shake of his head.

They had to fight, then. And even though it would have been far better to avoid any fight short of the one with Eovath, a part of her was glad to stop groveling before xulgaths and start killing the filthy things.

She took hold of the hilt of Jorn Blacklion's longsword. When the reptilian shaman padded up behind her, she drew, turned, and cut in one smooth motion. The blade sheared through the xulgath's throat, and it fell down thrashing with blood spurting from the wound.

At her back, Holg chanted to the spirits. Behind the fallen shaman, the two warriors faltered, then came on guard and retreated back down the passage. Their jaws opened, presumably to cry for help.

But though their mouths worked, nothing came out. In fact, Kagur could no longer hear sound from anywhere. Evidently, Holg's magic had enveloped the corridor in supernatural quiet to keep other xulgaths from hearing the fight.

Kagur dodged around the still-convulsing shaman to silence the warriors permanently. Now gripping their own weapons, her comrades charged with her.

But the xulgaths kept scrambling backward while the clubtail ran forward until its bulk and lashing tail virtually blocked the passage. Suddenly, *it* was the foe the intruders were closing with, and with their enormous ally now covering their retreat, the sentries bolted for the staircase.

With only her sword in her hand and the clubtail barring the way, Kagur had no chance of stopping them. She hoped Holg could do it with a prayer, then realized the silence likely precluded further magic.

Rho had a javelin, though. He scurried close to the oncoming clubtail, and then, despite the looming peril and the fact that the guards had nearly reached the doorway, took a moment to aim as he had when he'd finally killed his bird. Then he threw, and the javelin arced over the giant reptile and pierced a sentry between two of the ragged frills on its spine. The xulgath collapsed.

Just as dangerously close to the clubtail, Ikolch sidled to find a spot from which she could make a throw. By the time she did, the remaining xulgath was scrambling through the doorway. Still, her javelin caught it in the ribs. It stumbled a final step and collapsed, most of it hidden inside the opening but its twitching feet and tail protruding back into the passage. The orc leader leered.

Then the clubtail smashed her head and flung her to the floor.

Kagur cut at the giant reptile, and her blade slashed it between the beak and eyes. Vom and a Skulltaker wounded it, too. Still, it kept coming.

The confines of the corridor sometimes fouled the huge reptile's tail when it tried to strike and hindered it when it tried to turn. Unfortunately, they hemmed in the creature's foes as well.

Perhaps looking for a vulnerable spot to chop with his hatchet, a Dragonfly darted along the clubtail's flank. Reacting to a different threat entirely, the reptile lurched sideways and shoved the warrior into the wall. The claw-like growths jutting from its shell punched through his torso.

His mouth working, bellowing even though neither he, the clubtail, nor anyone else could hear it, Dalk jabbed at the reptile's beak. The tail whirled through the air to bludgeon him.

Dalk jumped back and dropped his spear. When the appendage hammered down in front of him, he pounced, wrapped his arms around it, and held on as the creature heaved it back up into the air.

Seemingly startled, the clubtail balked. In another moment, it would no doubt pound its tail down again, or else lash it into a wall, pulverizing Dalk. Except that Kagur didn't intend to give it the chance. She charged and drove her sword point into the base of its neck, just shy of the place where the plated shell began.

The clubtail shuddered. Dalk dropped from its tail and reeled backward just before the appendage started whipping back and forth, but no longer at anything in particular. The battering only chipped and cracked the surrounding stonework and knocked a green lamp down. When the flailing subsided, the reptile collapsed.

Now gripping his staff, Holg hurried to the warrior who lay against the wall with his shredded viscera bulging from the tear in his chest. The shaman surveyed the body, then shook his head.

Kagur felt obliged to make a similar inspection even though Ikolch's head was nothing but blood and mush. But Nesteruk beat her to the corpse. As he peered down at it, she couldn't help remembering how it had felt to peer down at her own butchered kin. She hesitantly put her hand on his shoulder.

He pivoted toward her with no sign of tears welling in his bloodshot eyes, nor any hint of weakness in his face. Just rage. Just hate. For some reason, that ferocity made her feel approval and regret at the same time.

Nesteruk tried to speak and then remembered the silence. He jabbed his fingers at the stairs.

She nodded. It was time to finish their climb and claim their revenge.

Chapter Twenty-Eight
The Chamber of Spikes

Bundles abandoned, every weapon now ready to hand, Kagur and her surviving companions climbed the steps. Sound returned. Though he appeared to be trying to control it, Holg's breath wheezed in and out of his skinny chest.

As before, the raiders skulked along a shelf seeking a doorway. When they found it, Kagur peeked in and gasped.

When she'd first glimpsed the Vault in all its verdant, sunlit vastness, she'd had the disorienting feeling that some agency had whisked her back to the surface world. Now she could almost imagine she'd magically stumbled back into one of the caves of Nar-Voth, with countless stalactites hanging and stalagmites stabbing upward.

But when she looked more carefully, the flatness of the ceiling and floor marred the illusion. The xulgaths had either harvested genuine stalactites and stalagmites from real caves elsewhere or sculpted imitations, then glued them here to create a fitting holy of holies for their demon master.

Once Kagur figured out that much, it likewise occurred to her that the internal layout of the ziggurat, which had varied little through the tiers below, had finally changed significantly. She wasn't peering down a corridor, but rather into a chamber so big it might well take up the entire level, although the countless spiky obstructions and the green-tinged darkness made it impossible to be sure.

Sibilant chanting and a padding sound echoed from somewhere inside.

Eovath was among the xulgaths performing the ritual, whatever it was, and Kagur didn't need to see one of Holg's fetishes crawl to confirm it. She could feel it. She took a breath, laid an arrow on her longbow, and led her comrades through the opening.

They fanned out as they advanced, the better to watch for trouble and find the quickest path to their quarry. Still, they sometimes had to squirm their way through narrow gaps between one stalagmite and the next or stoop under clumps of exceptionally long stalactites. Occasionally, a cluster of stony spikes was simply impassable, and then they had to backtrack.

In fact, the chamber was enough of a maze that Kagur was glad they had the chanting to lead them onward. Otherwise, they might have gotten turned around.

At the periphery of her vision, a shadow shifted. She pivoted. Its crimson markings gray in the emerald glow, a redstripe had oriented on her and was opening its jaws to screech.

She drove her arrow into the back of its mouth, fortunately to more effect than when she'd hit Old Scar in the same spot. The redstripe fell.

Rolling and thrashing against stalagmites, the reptile still threatened to make enough noise to warn Eovath and the xulgaths. But Vom rushed up and thrust his spear into it until its convulsions subsided.

Kagur listened. She couldn't hear any change in the noise up ahead.

She looked at Vom. He gave her a nod to indicate that he, too, believed their foes were still unaware of their approach.

As she and her comrades skulked onward, she watched for the zone where green phosphorescence and shadow would give way to utter darkness. Beyond that point, Holg would have to ask the spirits for light, making further stealth impossible.

But they never came to such a threshold. As Kagur had suspected, the top of the pyramid was all one room, and unlike the levels below, crystal lamps glued to the wall, stalactites, and ceiling glowed all the way across.

She realized as much when she finally caught sight of the open space at the center.

The xulgaths had apparently left it uncluttered so they could perform ceremonies like the one in progress. In the heart of the space rose a longer version of the bloodstained stone spikes Kagur had seen in the lesser shrines. The naked body of an orc—she couldn't tell if he was still alive—hung impaled on it.

Clad in voluminous but ragged layers of scaly hide—intended, she suspected, to suggest the wings, tentacles, and tail of Zevgavizeb—a dozen xulgaths were simultaneously chanting and capering around the sacrifice. Eovath wore the same tattered vestments but stood apart in front of several carved and painted screens. Maybe his devotion to Rovagug precluded him taking an active part in observances to another power.

Kagur felt the same fierce urge she had atop the cliff, to forgo archery and fight him face to face and blade to blade. And it might be feasible. She and he had about the same number of allies. It would be a fair fight.

Fair, but stupid and selfish. She couldn't ask Holg, the Dragonflies, and the Skulltakers to run even greater risks just so she could drink as deeply as possible from the cup of revenge. Even the orcs deserved better.

She looked back and forth at her comrades, each crouched behind cover of one sort or another, each ready to hurl a javelin or, in Holg's case, to flick and spin his staff through mystic passes. Then she stepped into the open, drew, and loosed.

The arrow hit Eovath in the center of the chest. A volley of javelins followed, and some of those struck Eovath, too. The cave dwellers were happy to slaughter xulgaths whenever possible, but they understood their mission was to kill the blue giant.

As surely the barrage had done. Even a frost giant couldn't survive an arrow in the heart and half a dozen javelins stabbing into his body. Kagur was so sure of it that it took her an instant to realize her eyes were telling her something different.

The impacts staggered Eovath. But her arrow snapped, and the javelins glanced off. He was evidently wearing some sort of armor under the ragged vestments, and flint arrow- and spearheads couldn't pierce it.

Kagur wondered where he'd obtained the protection. Lady Ssa's marketplace, maybe. She wondered, too, why he hadn't been wearing it when she'd found him summoning the threehorn at the bottom of the cliff. But at that point, he hadn't known she'd tracked him to

Orv, and, like her coat of leather, his armor was likely uncomfortable in the jungle heat.

Such thoughts, though, didn't slow her hand as she reached for a second arrow. This time, she'd shoot him in the face.

Eovath, however, denied her the opportunity. As she drew the fletchings back to her ear, he dived behind one of the screens carved and painted with Zevgavizeb's likeness. Meanwhile, the xulgaths that had come through the initial attack unscathed—about half of them—also scrambled for cover.

Kagur drew her sword and bellowed, "Get them!" She and her comrades plunged out into the open.

Now hidden, a xulgath snarled an incantation. Eovath shouted, "Come! Kill!" and his words too bore a hammering weight of power that made a listener want to twitch.

Utter darkness smothered the dim green phosphorescence. A Dragonfly cried out. In surprise, Kagur hoped, not distress.

She herself shouted, "Holg!" Needlessly, for at the same instant, the old man started praying.

He did so rapidly enough that it only took him a moment to restore the emerald glow. Still, by that time, three more redstripes were racing into the open space.

One of the reptiles sprang at Kagur. She sidestepped and slashed open its flank. It whirled to come at her again, and a Skulltaker swung his stone hatchet into its spine. The redstripe fell.

Kagur looked around. Her comrades were holding their own against the remaining redstripes. She ran toward the screen where Eovath had taken cover.

He wasn't right behind it anymore. But despite the stalagmites in the way, she spotted him making a hobbling retreat with blood running down his thigh. One of the javelins had found him where his new armor didn't cover.

The brother she'd loved would have stood and fought regardless. But Rovagug's corrupted minion had more pragmatic inclinations.

She plunged after him. Spotting her, he halted and came on guard. As she closed the distance, she caught a first glimpse of the architectural feature toward which he'd drawn her.

It was the staircase she'd conjectured might exist in the core of the ziggurat. But was the patch of floor surrounding the stairwell slanted or level? Was the opening itself square or trapezoidal, and did the flights of steps descending into blackness lie straight or dogleg? Everything shifted from one instant to the next, or maybe everything was every way simultaneously, in a manner that hurt and dazzled the eye.

The sight stunned her. At that moment, his wounded leg plainly less of an impediment than he'd made it appear, Eovath rushed her, whirling his axe at her head.

She leaped away, a frantic effort that carried her too far to permit an immediate riposte. But with the spectacle of the stairwell muddling her, she was lucky she'd managed any defense at all.

The axe whizzed by short of its target. Eovath grinned the way he had when they'd merely been practicing in the Blacklion camp and she'd impressed him with deft blade- or footwork.

"Amazing, isn't it?" He shifted his axe to indicate the stairwell, probably in the hope that she'd glance back at it. "Fascinating and repulsive at the same time. Think of all the miraculous things you would never have seen if you hadn't followed me into the Darklands. And yet you still can't forgive me the circumstances."

She sidestepped in an attempt to put the staircase behind her, so she wouldn't have to worry about seeing it and Eovath wouldn't be able to avoid it unless he turned his back on her as well. But he shifted right along with her, which left the vile seething at the edge of her vision.

"What's wrong with this place?" she asked. She didn't care, but she could use one more moment to shake off the lingering disorientation.

"The xulgaths don't know," Eovath answered. "They didn't build the pyramid. They just discovered it and claimed it for their own. Why not? It's directly under the sun, and they know power when they feel it. But even they won't go all the way to the cen—"

He lunged, feinted to the head, and struck at her waist. She slipped the blow, sliced his forearm, and cut at his chest.

Her sword rang and glanced off some dull black substance under the tattered clothing. Whatever the cuirass was made of, it could withstand even enchanted steel.

"Do you like my breastplate?" Eovath asked. "The xulgaths found it when they first came here. A seer prophesied that one day the champion who could wear it would lead them to greatness."

He feinted low and cut high. Kagur pivoted out of the way.

As she did, the stairwell swung into her field of vision. For an instant, she suffered the dizzying sensation that it was actually the world that was spinning while she was standing still. Snarling, she refused to let the rippling distortion into her head. She kept pivoting until Eovath was in front of her again.

When the giant too finished turning, he rushed at her, and she put her point in line. He lurched to a halt to avoid spitting himself. The green glow of the crystals gleamed on their weapons.

"You're slower than I remember," she said. "No wonder, with all the blood pouring down your leg."

Eovath leered. "I don't remember you ever using taunts to rattle an opponent. I thought you believed such ploys were beneath you."

"Anything," Kagur said, "to finish this quickly. I want to kill you all by myself. And my companions are almost done with the xulgaths."

She *was* saying it to unsettle him, but it was also true. She'd caught glimpses of the rest of the battle as the two of them advanced, retreated, and shifted to one side or the other.

All the redstripes were down, which obliged the surviving xulgaths to defend themselves with knives, claws, fangs, and magic. The latter was potent. Spell-induced terror had sent Dalk recoiling from one of the reptilian shamans, and though it barely grazed its target, the swipe of a different xulgath's hand ripped an orc's arm from biceps to wrist. Yet the raiders had their own magic in the person of Holg, and so their superior numbers still gave them an edge. One by one, their foes were dropping.

But now hissing voices sounded from the direction of the doorway. A fresh redstripe raced out of the stalagmites, and Vom spun around to meet it.

Despite the evidence to the contrary, a part of Kagur had still doubted Eovath—her companion since childhood, a constant in what had once been a simple, normal life—could truly become the anointed champion of some mighty supernatural entity. But she believed it at this moment, for surely the giant possessed luck that only an evil god could give.

If the spearbeaks had attacked just a moment later, Eovath would have died beneath the cliff. If she'd only glimpsed the armor under his scaly vestments and shifted her aim accordingly, he would have perished when she loosed at him tonight. And now this!

One of the reptilian shamans had slipped past the intruders and gone for help. Or maybe someone had found the dead bodies on the tier below. However it had happened, xulgath reinforcements were arriving.

But by Gorum, except for the one redstripe, they hadn't worked their way through the thickets of stalagmites yet! Kagur had a little more time to kill Eovath, and nothing else would matter after that.

She hurled herself at the giant. His blue skin itself tinged green by the crystals, he gave ground before her. He heard fresh xulgaths coming, too, and so was fighting defensively and playing for time. It made it even more difficult to penetrate his guard.

"Coward!" she panted.

"Surrender," he answered, likewise sounding winded. "I swear by the Rough Beast, I'll spare your life."

It occurred to her then that, just as she'd never truly known him, he'd apparently never understood her, either.

She drove in hard, striking relentlessly, dodging his infrequent but vicious ripostes and counterattacks by the narrowest of margins. If she kept it up, some attack would score in the time she had left. It had to!

As they maneuvered, she caught more glimpses of the rest of the battle. Some of her allies had turned to confront the reptiles advancing through the stalagmites. Holg jabbed with his staff, and white light lanced from the end to burn a redstripe's jaws and eyes. His spear point shifting back and forth, Vom battled two xulgaths at once. Screaming, Nesteruk hurled himself at one foe after another while Rho struggled to keep anyone from taking advantage of the other boy's recklessness and flanking him.

By now, the warriors of the highlands must realize they were about to die. But no one faltered. They meant to go down fighting.

Good. That was what they needed to do to buy Kagur time to finish Eovath.

Yet as she made one attack after another, her brother parried, and steel clanged on steel, she realized it was just possible her allies *didn't* have to die. Even with the oncoming xulgaths between them and the door, there was still a way out of here. The cave dwellers just couldn't see if it from where they were standing.

Maybe that was just as well. But curse it, Rho and Nesteruk were still boys, even if they were fighting like full-grown men. Their young lives shouldn't end like this, especially the orc's.

She stepped back from Eovath. "This way!" she shouted. "Down the stairs!"

Eovath snorted. "You're not doing your friends a kindness. In times past, xulgaths tried to explore the inner chambers. None ever came out."

"We will," Kagur said.

And maybe the giant believed they actually had a chance. Shifting his axe from side to side, he came back on the attack. She advanced to meet him.

As they struck, parried, and evaded, her allies made a fighting retreat toward the stairs. Some of them cried out when they saw their goal. Some even balked. His voice harsh and breathless, Holg urged them on.

Meanwhile, Kagur still couldn't slip another cut past Eovath's guard. Willing to take a stroke from the axe if she could kill him in the same moment, she forsook defense for pure aggression.

Yet even that wasn't sufficient. She pushed the giant back, but that was all.

From the corner of her eye, she spotted a pair of xulgaths advancing on her with spears leveled. She realized all her comrades had retreated past her, and thus were no longer in position to hold the reptiles back.

Her every instinct told her to keep assailing Eovath anyway. One more moment, one more slash, might be all it took to drop him.

Still, she whirled and bolted for the stairwell, dodging and twisting through stalagmites as she fled. Her sudden dash caught Eovath by surprise, but after a moment, he pounded after her. So did the xulgaths. A thrown flint knife spun past her head.

A redstripe lunged from behind a cluster of stony spikes. She dodged, twisted at the waist, and snatching foreclaws clicked shut just short of her cheek.

She slashed at a leg as she plunged past and thought she heard the beast fall, although she wasn't sure. The thump, if indeed there was one, was hard to distinguish from the overall noise of the pursuit.

She rounded more stalagmites and the stairwell appeared before her. Maybe all her comrades had already descended. As far as she could tell, no one else was near the edge anymore.

It was difficult to tell anything for certain, though, with her sight addled. Alternately pentagonal and so acutely trapezoidal as to be nearly triangular, the opening revolved like a wheel.

Where did the actual steps begin? Like everything else, their position wavered from one instant to the next.

Reptiles hissed and screeched at her back. Eovath bellowed the name of his god.

Kagur leaped down at the spot where she *thought* there was a stair, and one foot landed at the very edge of it, half on and half off. Her balance shifted, and she toppled toward the empty space at the center of the shaft.

Chapter Twenty-Nine
The Heart of the Pyramid

Wood clattered, and hands gripped Kagur's sword arm. Though she hadn't seen him when she jumped, Holg had caught hold of her. He strained to heave her to safety, but instead, her weight dragged him toward the drop, too.

He'd delayed her fall for a moment, though, and that was time enough for Vom to scramble up a couple steps, grab each of them with one hand or the other, and yank them toward him. They all fell on the hard stone steps in a tangle, but that was better than plummeting over the side.

"Get up!" Kagur gasped. "Keep going!"

Holg fumbled up the staff he'd dropped so he could grab her, and they staggered on down the writhing stairs. Kagur sheathed her sword and ran her fingers along the cold stone wall. She was afraid that if she didn't, she still might blunder off the opposite side of the steps.

A moment later, the xulgaths demonstrated that though they feared to pursue their foes into the core of the ziggurat, they were willing to fling missiles after them. Flying in impossible snaking trajectories, javelins and hatchets cracked and rattled on the steps. Fortunately, none found its mark.

The rest of the surviving raiders were waiting in a space adjacent to the foot of the flight of stairs. At first glance, Kagur wasn't sure how wide the room was or if the ceiling was high or low. But she was reasonably certain no one at the top of the steps could throw a javelin into it. That made it a reasonable haven in which to regroup, especially since only the slightest hint of green phosphorescence reached down this far. The gloom mercifully masked some of the flickering inconstancy.

Unfortunately, Nesteruk was apparently unwilling to allow her a moment simply to catch her breath. Tusked mouth snarling and eyes glaring, bloody hatchet clenched in one fist and gory knife in the other, he stalked toward her while Rho scurried after as though he still needed to protect him.

"You stopped us!" Nesteruk snarled. "The blue giant is still alive, and you made us run!"

"Shut up," Kagur said, the smells of blood and sweat in the air churning her stomach. They wouldn't have bothered her normally, but despite the partial protection the dimness afforded, they were nauseating in combination with the warping of her sight. For a moment, Nesteruk's neck extended from his torso at an unnatural angle, like someone had broken it.

"You said killing the giant was more important than anything!" the boy ranted. "But—"

Kagur punched him in the nose. He floundered back into Rho, who lifted his hands to restrain him if he started forward to strike back. But the punch appeared to have startled the orc out of his fury, not heightened it, and he simply gaped at her.

"I made a decision, and I gave an order," she said. "Soon, I'll give more, and you'll obey. Understand?"

Blood sliding from his left nostril, Nesteruk mumbled.

"I asked if you understand."

"Yes!"

She looked around. Dalk was watching up the stairs. Good. Someone should, even though she was fairly certain the xulgaths wouldn't summon up the nerve to follow them down.

The next step was to take stock of her allies. In addition to the boys, Dalk, Vom, and Holg, she had three Dragonflies and five Skulltakers left, which was better than she'd expected. But one of the humans, a warrior named Bolta, was turning his club over and over in his hands like he'd never seen such a strange object before, while two of the orcs were bleeding.

She was about to ask Holg to help them when Eovath gave an echoing call down the stairwell: "Sister!"

Her whole body clenched. "What?"

"Good! You're still alive. From the tales the xulgaths tell, I was afraid you might be dead already."

"What do you want?"

"To challenge you to finish what we started. Come back up. We'll fight in single combat for your life and the lives of your friends. I promise, the reptiles won't interfere."

"You must not be sure we're going to die down here. Otherwise, you wouldn't offer."

"You're wrong. I'm offering you a choice between a quick, honorable death and a horrible, uncanny one. This is my one last attempt to show you kindness."

She sneered. "Or maybe you're afraid I *will* escape and come at you again."

"Or," said Holg, loudly enough for Eovath to hear, "he knows he botched his first great sacrifice to Rovagug by letting you survive, and he's worried he won't come into the full measure of his powers unless he makes it right."

Eovath didn't answer right away. Holg smiled as he often did when he believed he'd said something clever. Then the shifting rotated the expression into a nearly vertical grimace.

"The reinforcements told me about the bodies on the level below," Eovath called. "They recognized the she-orc with the missing breast. They're looking forward to amusing themselves with the carcass."

Nesteruk looked like he was gathering himself to run back up the stairs. Rho gripped his shoulder.

"What's your point?" Kagur called.

"The point, sister, is that the xulgaths know it's Skulltaker warriors you brought here to profane their sacred place. Them and Dragonflies, the Skulltakers' neighbors. So they know where to retaliate."

Some of Kagur's companions winced. Others traded somber glances.

"They'll focus all their strength on exterminating those two particular tribes," Eovath continued, "unless I talk them out of it."

"Which you will," Kagur said, "if I accept your challenge."

"Yes."

"Then I accept on one condition. You come fight me down here. I never betrayed my own kin. You can trust my promise that *my* companions won't attack *you*."

"And in addition," Holg called, "you'll find out what it's like in the center of the pyramid. Aren't you curious?"

Once again, Eovath didn't answer right away.

After a moment, the warriors of the crags filled the silence. "Coward!" shouted Vom. "The giant's pissing down his leg!" Others laughed, or spat so noisily their foes might hear the wet hawking sound even at a distance.

"Think what you like," Eovath answered, "but I can't break the xulgaths' laws and keep their friendship. Goodbye, Kagur. I love you, and I hope you find your way to Gorum's hall."

Kagur looked to Holg, then indicated Bolta, who was still fascinated by his own weapon. "What's wrong with him?" she asked.

"One of the xulgath shamans cursed him and stole his wits."

"Can you mend him?"

"Probably, but not right away. I barely have any power left."

She gestured toward the wounded Skulltakers. "Can you at least help them?"

"I'll try."

While the old man inspected their injuries and prayed over them, everyone else rested. Or at least Kagur tried. But she felt like something was twisting tighter and tighter inside her.

When Holg returned to her side, he squinted at her face and then whispered, "Other than the obvious, what's wrong? Surely you don't believe you should have gone back up the stairs, or that anyone blames you for staying put. We all know the xulgaths would have swarmed on you in an instant."

She scowled. "It's not that. It's what I did before. Nesteruk was right. We *did* still have a chance to kill Eovath, and I threw it away."

"A very slim chance, I think."

"Still . . . for an instant, I felt it would be wrong for Nesteruk in particular to die as he was about to. And that makes no sense. He was fighting to avenge his mother. Of all of our warriors, he had the *best* reason to stand and slaughter xulgaths until he dropped. So what was I thinking? Is the madness in this place addling me?"

"I don't believe so." The old man paused in the manner of someone framing his next words carefully.

"Do *not* start prattling about 'patterns.'"

Holg's lips twitched into the fleeting hint of a smile. "I can't answer a question if you deny me the use—"

"Then don't answer. It was a stupid question anyway. It doesn't matter why I did what I did. It's done. Tell me why we can't see clearly. Is there magic here that interferes with our sight?"

"Not exactly, or at least I don't believe the answer is that simple. Otherwise, I could close my eyes, rely on my other senses, and the distortion wouldn't bother me. I think space itself is kinked or broken here."

"What does that mean?"

He frowned, thinking, and then asked, "Where is Gorum?"

"Elysium."

"And where is Elysium?"

She had no idea what he was getting at. "I don't know. Up in the sky? The real sky?"

"Have you ever seen it there?"

"You know I haven't."

"So it can't be up there in the same simple way as a cloud or a star. Still, we know Gorum and his realm have to be somewhere. The homes of all the gods and devils must be somewhere, yet you could walk the world for a thousand ages and never catch a glimpse of any of them."

"Are you sure you're answering my question?"

"I'm trying. According to certain philosophers, the answer to the puzzle is that space itself is more complicated than we imagine. It has extra directions to it we don't ordinarily experience, and our inability to look in the right direction is what keeps us from beholding the Lord in Iron's fortress."

"But we're experiencing the 'extra directions' now."

"Some of those same sages believed that under certain conditions, one level of being could overlap another, or that a patch of space could simply contort in the throes of its own special kind of sickness. Then folk in the area might perceive the effects in a muddled sort of way."

Most of Holg's words sounded like nonsense, holy-man speak, but she thought she grasped the essence. "All right. What makes it so dangerous no xulgath ever survived it?"

Holg scratched his chin. "It's possible our outsides don't entirely enclose our insides in such a place. Perhaps, if we step wrong, the blood will simply spill out of our veins or the hearts will fall out of our chests through one of the extra directions."

"If that's the problem, can we do anything about it?"

"I don't know."

"Then assume it's not. What else could it be?"

"If space twists back on itself and perception is undependable, it might be the reptiles simply wandered around lost until they died of thirst."

"Maybe. But if paths lead in, the same paths lead out. Bright steel, we're sitting at the bottom of one right now! It's just not one we can use. Do you have enough magic left to guide us to another?"

"No. Sorry."

"Can you make cold fire like you put on my shield?"

"No. But I can make something comparable. A light we can shine or cover as needed."

"Do that, then."

She rose from the place where she'd been squatting. The warriors of the highlands looked at her, and she struggled to think of what her father might have said to them in her place.

"We did what no men or orcs have done before us," she began. "We came to the xulgaths' stronghold and butchered them by the dozen. That's why they're frantic for revenge. Why they plan to march on your tribes and slaughter every last one of your kin.

"But we," she continued, "are going to prevent that. We're going to find a way out of this pile and warn everyone the xulgaths are coming. So on your feet! We need to move!"

The warriors clambered up and hefted their weapons. Their faces looked grim, but not panicky. Under the circumstances, it was as much as she had any right to expect.

She pressed her fingers to her lips and then led everyone back to the staircase. Dalk shook his head to signal that he hadn't seen or heard any signs that a foray from above was in the works. Then he served as rear guard when she led her companions down the next flight of steps.

By the time they groped their way to the bottom, the darkness was all but absolute. By rights, Kagur thought, that should have made it easy to spot green phosphorescence marking a way out. But, turning, she couldn't see any such glow.

She glanced back at Holg. "Pray your prayer," she said.

"Brace yourselves," the old man said. He murmured, and a pale shining flowered on the head of his staff to reveal more of the distortion's writhing, flowing indeterminacy.

An orc grunted, a human hissed as if at a sudden pain, and Kagur wouldn't have been surprised to learn that his head had actually started throbbing. Hers hadn't, quite, but it felt like it could at any moment. Despite the need to survey her surroundings, she was glad the light was relatively dim.

Beyond tall doorways lay interconnecting chambers with murals on the walls. Most of the faded paintings depicted things with barrel-shaped central masses, an abundance of snaking limbs, and several fan-shaped projections—wings?—sticking out of them, shapes so bizarre Kagur's mind balked at even recognizing them as representations of living creatures. In some pictures, they were on the ground, in some, swimming beneath green waters, and in still others, flying against starry skies.

Some of the rooms contained objects positioned toward the center. Although the shifting and flickering made their precise forms uncertain, the articles appeared at least vaguely drum-shaped more often than not, while many were simply metal frames with empty space at the centers. They were apparently furniture of some sort, but Kagur couldn't guess the function of any particular item.

"What can you tell me?" she asked.

Holg shook his head. "I picked up a fair amount of lore in my travels, but nothing that even hints at the creatures in the paintings."

"Well, they must be long gone, or the xulgaths couldn't have taken over this place. So we'll hope we don't *need* to know about them. My guess is, these stairs run all the way down to the bottom level."

The shaman frowned. "Shouldn't we try to escape the distortion by the shortest path possible? To avoid the hazards, whatever they are?"

"The reptiles expect that. They know how unpleasant it is in here. So when they station warriors to catch us just in case we do make it out, they'll put their best on the upper tiers. And when we break out on the bottom one, we'll already be at water level."

"All right. That makes a certain amount of sense."

"To me, too," said Vom.

Kagur jumped. The burly, bearded Dragonfly had apparently moved closer to hear what she and Holg were saying. That was fine, but it unsettled her that she hadn't registered his change of position until he spoke. What else might sneak up on her while her eyes were undependable?

Hoping Vom hadn't noticed her display of nerves, she crept down the next flight of stairs with her companions trailing along behind her. As she made her way along, it seemed to her that the inconstancy, while no less pervasive, was becoming somewhat less disturbing on a visceral level. Her queasiness had abated, and her head no longer felt like it might start pounding at any moment.

She suspected her mind was learning to shield itself from strangeness and impossibility by not looking at anything too long or too carefully. A doorway was a doorway, and that was enough. She didn't need to determine whether it was rectangular or skewed to the side.

When she reached the next level, she peered about and found more chambers, more murals depicting the barrel-things, and another assortment of their inexplicable furnishings. She asked Holg to quell his light, just in case that would enable her to spot green phosphorescence; if so, she'd at least reevaluate her plan. He wrapped his fingers around the head of his staff, and blackness swallowed everything.

There was still no green light. She told the old man he could let the white one shine.

When it did, she gasped, and others did as well. Rho yelped.

Before Holg had plunged them all into darkness, it had been obvious despite the distortion that one flight of stairs, the one they'd just negotiated, ran upward, and the next one descended. That was no longer the case. Though still extending in opposite directions, they lay at right angles to their former attitudes, except Kagur sensed that wasn't really true. They weren't horizontal. They stretched off in some extra direction people were never supposed to see. Horizontal was merely the way her eyes were struggling to make sense of what was before them.

"Something did this!" snarled an orc named Passamax, whose tusks jutted almost up to his eyes and who wore fangs, talons, and finger bones in the long greasy ponytail dangling down his back. "To trap us!"

"No," Kagur said. "We've seen how everything changes. This was just an especially big change."

"Kagur's right," Nesteruk said. Either he'd gotten past being angry with her or his own judgment impelled him to agree with her anyway. "We aren't trapped. Both ways are still there, the same as before."

"That's true," said Vom, scratching in his beard, his tone thoughtful rather than contentious, "but which one do we take?"

Kagur realized with a jolt of dismay that she didn't know. Even with the staircases rotated to lie on their sides, their positions relative to one another should provide a solution, but with impermanence and paradox baffling her, she couldn't work out what it was.

She looked to Holg. Even he appeared flummoxed.

But Dalk was rear guard. That meant that even though everyone had already stepped off the last flight of stairs, he was likely still closer to it than to the next one. Kagur looked around and located him, though it took a moment. Distortion had gnarled his face and upper body, making them lopsided and nearly unrecognizable.

Wondering if she looked equally hideous, Kagur pointed to the flight of stairs that, judging by Dalk's position, was the correct one. "This way."

Setting her feet on steps that appeared to stand on end instead of lying flat was a bewildering, awkward business. She worried that if she made the wrong move, she could pitch herself down the empty center of the stairwell, but she couldn't even tell what such a misstep would entail.

She finally sat on the floor, closed her eyes, and scooted her way along. After a moment, she felt an indescribable twisting that reminded her of Holg's notion that in this place, a person's insides might fall out even if his skin was intact. Fortunately, though, that didn't happen. Her rump simply slipped off one surface and bumped down on another.

The flight of stairs felt and looked more normal once she and her companions managed to shift themselves onto it. They descended successfully and then peered around. The pale glow of Holg's staff revealed more chambers, murals, and skeletal metal frameworks, and that was all. Nothing was moving or manifestly posed a threat.

Holg briefly covered the end of his staff. Kagur still couldn't see any green glow.

"All right," she said as the old man restored the light, "on to the next tier." She turned toward the stairs and then spun back around.

"What's wrong?" asked Holg.

She took another look at her companions. Unfortunately, she really had belatedly noticed what she'd thought she had. "Bolta's missing. Who was watching over him?"

The Dragonflies looked back at her in dismay, and though she felt anger flare inside her, she also realized she deserved to feel its sting every bit as much as they did. Yes, one of them should have tended to his demented kinsman, but as leader, she should have made certain somebody did so. Disordered space was gnawing at everyone's mind.

"Don't answer," she continued. "What matters is finding him. Dalk, you've been walking behind everybody else. When was the last time you saw him?"

"Well . . . not on this last descent. On the one before it."

"That means he wandered away one tier up, when we were all trying to figure out which stairs were which. We'll go back up and get him."

Passamax glowered. "The rest of us need to get out of here, not waste time searching for a simpleton."

"The Dragonflies would search," said Vom, "if a Skulltaker had gotten lost. Are our warriors are braver than yours?"

A muscle in Passamax's arm jumped with the urge to answer the suggestion with the hatchet in his fist, but he controlled himself. "If we're going to do it," he growled, "let's go."

By the time they climbed back up, the stairs had reverted to approximately the proper attitude relative to their terminus. Unfortunately, Bolta was nowhere in sight. Kagur and her companions called his name, and the shouts echoed away in a halting, unnatural fashion that gave her a chill.

Bolta didn't answer.

Kagur picked a doorway at random. "Keep together." She slipped Eovath's knife from its sheath. "I'll mark the walls to make sure we can find our way back."

Holg stepped up to her side and murmured, "Bolta could have wandered up the next set of stairs, too. He could have gone all the way back up to Zevgavizeb's holy of holies. He could even have stumbled through a hole in the weave of things and fallen out of the world entirely."

Kagur scowled. "We're still going to look."

"I know. I'd decide the same if I were leader. I just wanted you to be aware."

Venturing away from the stairs reminded Kagur of searching the tombs of the serpentfolk. She had the same feeling of confusion and frustration, but this time, it wasn't *only* because an inimical force was scraping at her mind. The arrangement of the painted rooms with their occasional peculiar accoutrements was simply beyond human comprehension, as she realized anew when she entered a chamber and spotted one of the marks she'd been scratching along the way.

She was sure that mere moments before, she'd moved away from this room in a straight line. Thus, it was impossible for her to have returned, and yet she had. Maybe a person *could* get so lost in this place she never found a way out.

She reassured herself that even if the trail she was blazing doubled back on itself, it must ultimately lead to the stairway. Still, even assuming she was right, how long should she continue searching?

Her every instinct told her not to abandon a comrade. But if the raiders were still inside the ziggurat when morning came, escape would likely be impossible.

Five more rooms, she decided. After that, if they still hadn't found any trace of Bolta, they'd turn back.

Counting them off by making a fist and then uncurling the fingers one at a time, she'd just prowled into the fourth one when a soft cry like a whimper sounded from somewhere up ahead.

Chapter Thirty
The Ancient Armory

Straining, Kagur listened. She didn't hear anything more.

"Bolta!" she shouted. Her companions did the same.

After the strange, staggered echoes died away, the afflicted tribesman's cry—if that was what it was—came again. It still didn't have any words to it.

Vom shook his head. Due to the distortion, his shaggy mane flopped around him in a way that was somehow disturbing, although Kagur couldn't define why. "Why isn't he *talking*?"

"He wasn't talking before," Passamax replied. "We found him, let's go get him."

"We are," Kagur said.

As they stalked onward, she kept marking the walls despite the urge to hurry now prodding her on. The cry came at intervals, and sounded closer each time.

Until finally, Holg's light washed into a large chamber with two drum-shaped constructions of silvery slats and wire in the center. Bolta sat in the corner rocking back and forth, his eyes squeezed shut and his hands covering his ears.

"Bolta," Kagur said.

He didn't answer. Maybe he couldn't hear her. Although that would be strange, considering that he'd heard and answered in his wordless fashion when she and the others had called from a distance.

She strode across the room, and Holg and the warriors hurried after her. She took hold of Bolta's wrists to pull his hands away from his head.

He thrashed, and other cave dwellers restrained him. "Easy!" said Vom. "It's us!"

Bolta's struggles subsided into shuddering. He gaped at Vom, and his mouth worked, but nothing came out.

Kagur was suddenly certain Bolt *hadn't* made the whimpering cries they'd heard. Something else had. Something that wanted to draw the rest of them to the same spot as their addled, helpless comrade, maybe so it could creep up behind them while they were all paying attention to him.

She turned, and at that instant, at least a dozen voices started howling and babbling all at once.

The hideous raving battered at a mind already beleaguered by the effects of twisted space. And the sight of the creature responsible was nearly as hard to bear.

A shapeless, limbless mass of flesh, it heaved and oozed through a second doorway, simultaneously stretching sideways so as to block the opening through which the raiders had entered. Its dozens of eyes glared, while the deafening yammer issued from countless slavering, jagged-toothed mouths. The floor softened, and Kagur's feet sank into it like the mere presence of the creature was corrupting its surroundings.

Something—the shrieking and braying, Kagur judged—was unquestionably corroding the ability of her companions to defend against the threat. The others were reeling. Some covered their ears like Bolta. Some wept. Some screamed, adding to the din.

Kagur might be in the same helpless state if she hadn't earlier weathered a comparable psychic assault when she faced the seugathi. But she had, and since she was still capable of battle, it fell to her to kill this horror as well. She reached for the hilt of her sword.

Some of the creature's bulging eyes shifted, tracking the motion. One of the larger mouths stopped raving long enough to spit.

Kagur leaped aside. The gob of spittle splashed against the wall, then sizzled and smoked as it trickled downward.

The vigorous evasive action thrust Kagur's lead foot halfway into the softening floor. She heaved it out before it could stick fast, finished drawing her blade, and rushed the creature.

She had to dodge another wad of acidic spew before she closed the distance. Then she landed a first cut on writhing flesh.

The resulting gash was deep, but she wished she knew where to aim. Unfortunately, though, she had no way of telling where within the formless body the vital organs lay—or if the creature even had any.

A portion of the beast simultaneously reared higher and curled outward to encircle her. Mouths opened wide to bite.

She tried to step back from the threat, and the sticky floor held her in place. She strained and broke free, but the sudden release made her stagger off balance.

The creature made a flowing lunge to seize her before she recovered.

But Holg scrambled between the two of them. He drove the butt of his staff into one of the creature's eyes.

Kagur recovered her footing, and then she and the old man attacked the beast together. She slashed it repeatedly, and he either put out more of its eyes or thrust his staff in one or another of the howling, gnashing mouths as opportunity allowed.

Over time, the latter attacks, and the fact that the shapeless thing needed some of its mouths to spit and bite, somewhat diminished the volume of its wailing. Maybe that helped the warriors of the crags recover from their incapacity, for one by one, they too joined the fight. Vom jabbed with his spear. Nesteruk and Passamax chopped with hatchets.

Flailing with a deceptive lack of grace, the creature flipped two extrusions of its substance around Passamax and gathered him in like a drunkard forcing an embrace on someone reluctant to receive it. Crooked teeth sank into the orc's green skin, and he gave a cry midway between a roar and a scream.

Sure that in another moment Passamax would be maimed if not dead, Kagur sprang on top of the shapeless creature, where its rippling, humping flesh made her stagger and nearly drop one of her feet into a gnashing mouth. Recovering her balance, if only for an instant, she raised her sword high and thrust it down into the shapeless thing's mass all the way to the cross guard.

The creature convulsed and tossed her tumbling down its heaving flank. It didn't take advantage of her momentary helplessness to bite her, though, and when she rolled to her feet, she saw it had stopped moving.

She scrambled up to see how Passamax was. "Get me loose," he gritted, still wrapped in the creature's flesh.

She and a couple of the others extracted him. His bites were ragged and bloody, but when Holg tried to examine one, he yanked his arm free with a snarl.

"You're all right?" the old man asked.

"Of course! I'm a Skulltaker!" Passamax paused. "But it was close. The thing was sucking my blood."

Vom looked down at the creature's carcass. "It wasn't just getting lost that kept the old xulgaths from making it out alive. But now the real threat is dead."

Passamax sneered. "Unless there are twenty more of them crawling around."

If we meet more, Kagur thought, we'll kill them, too. But she hoped it wouldn't come to that.

"Get Bolta up," she said. "We're leaving."

"Wait," said Holg.

She turned. The old man was looking in the opening through which the shapeless thing had come. He held his staff out to the side so the wall blocked its glow from illuminating what lay beyond. That way, his clouded eyes could see more clearly.

Kagur sighed. "We don't have time to poke around."

"Do we have a moment to rearm ourselves?" Holg replied. "We've long since thrown all our javelins, and dropped or broken other weapons along the way."

"What?" She strode past him into the next room, and he brought the light in after her. Cave dwellers followed him.

Three tall, barrel-shaped latticeworks stood in the center of the floor, and for the first time, Kagur discerned a purpose for the frames. These had prongs hooking up from the bars to hang things on.

Some of the hanging objects combined curves and angles into shapes so strange she had no idea of a particular item's function or which part of it, if any, a user was supposed to grip. But others were recognizably javelins cast all in one piece from point to butt from a metal that gleamed like either brass or bronze depending on how the light caught it. A few of the weapons hung by themselves, but dozens more reposed in quivers made of the same yellowish substance.

The cave dwellers came forward to inspect them more closely but hesitated to touch them. Kagur remembered that *any* metal weapon was a wonder to them, and these partook of the ziggurat's eeriness and unimaginable age.

Passamax broke the general feeling of awe by snorting, picking one up, and holding it out for everyone to see. "It's got an angle in the shaft," he sneered, and Kagur realized he was right. All the javelins did. "It won't fly true."

"In here," said Vom, "nothing does."

"You know what I mean." The orc turned, cocked the weapon back, and chucked it at the wall.

As the javelin left his hand, it became a length of glare. The lightning bolt blasted the wall with a dazzling flash and a boom that made the raiders recoil and peppered them with bits of flying stone.

For a moment, in the aftermath, no one moved. Then an orc led a general scramble for the doorway.

"Stop!" Kagur bellowed. Somewhat to her surprise, everyone heeded her. "We're taking the javelins. We can use them."

Vom peered at her uncertainly. "Are you sure we can carry them?"

"I am," said Holg. He lifted one of the javelins from the two prongs that supported it, then twirled it in his fingers and tossed it from hand to hand. Even Skulltakers tensed, but the yellow metal stayed metal.

"See?" the shaman asked. "You have to throw them properly to trigger the transformation."

After a moment, Passamax's mouth stretched into a grin. He grabbed a quiver from its prong, and others followed his lead.

As she and Holg looked on, Kagur whispered, "Were you sure it was safe to play with the javelin like that?"

"Fairly sure, and our friends needed more convincing. I take it you're over your wariness of enchanted weapons."

Apparently she had, for it had never even occurred to her that it might be prudent to leave the javelins behind. Maybe the Darklands, where sorcery was no stranger than most everything else she encountered, made her former mistrust of it pointless.

On the way back, she and her companions followed the blazes scrupulously, even at the points where common sense indicated a shortcut was available. And in due course, their caution brought them to the stairs.

They descended the next flight without incident. Halfway down the one after that, the section of steps below them suddenly elongated and twisted into a spiral that made it look like no one could traverse it without walking upside down like an insect.

"It's all right," Kagur said, proceeding onward without hesitation. "The stairs will be normal once we're on them." She was glad when it turned out to be so.

Finally, the raiders reached the tier on which they'd begun. The stairs continued, but into water. Holg's light reflected on its black surface just a few steps farther down.

Kagur had kept count of the levels. But with the distortion scratching at her thoughts, she was glad to have her reckoning confirmed.

Holg invited the darkness, and as usual, no one could see any trace of a green glow. So they all had to search for it as they'd looked for Bolta, prowling through a honeycomb of painted chambers and marking the walls along the way, meanwhile listening for howling, raving voices.

To Kagur's relief, she couldn't hear any more of the formless creatures. Maybe, in the times before the xulgaths had given up trying to explore the core of the ziggurat, the place had been full of the things, but most had died in the long years since.

Suddenly, blackness shrouded everything. As Kagur jumped, she realized Holg had covered the head of his staff. "We're close," the old man whispered.

Even now, she couldn't see any green phosphorescence. "How can you tell?"

"I feel space straightening out. We're nearing the edge of the damage."

"Then we sneak and feel our way from here."

She skulked forward and caught the tiny padding sounds of the others following. Sliding her fingertips along the wall, she found a doorway and peeked through.

Off to the left, points of green light, dim but steady, with no shifting or paradoxical aspect to them, strung away into the gloom. As Kagur looked at them, she felt what Holg had: an easing of the malaise that bent space engendered.

But she also saw figures waiting at the edge of the phosphorescence. She was pondering how to deal with them when a groping hand fumbled at her waist.

"Sorry!" breathed Rho.

"We're stopped," whispered Vom from somewhere close at hand. "Why?"

"We found the way out," Kagur said, "and the xulgaths blocking it. I want one lightning bolt—*only* one—and then we charge. Passamax, you do the throwing."

"Out of my way," said the orc. Kagur felt people shifting in the dark to clear a path for him.

With farther to travel, the streak of lightning writhed like a snake and crackled in the instant before it struck. The blast tossed bodies into the air.

"Now!" Kagur said. She lunged through the doorway, and her comrades pounded after her.

The lightning had killed some xulgaths and thrown the rest into confusion. Still, the survivors glimpsed their foes rushing out of the darkness and scrambled to defend themselves. A javelin flew at Kagur, and she dodged. That saved her, but someone behind her gave a strangled grunt as the weapon struck him.

She avoided a second such missile, then sprang in among the creatures hurling them, where the reek of lightning-burned flesh hung in the air. A xulgath screeched and rushed her with gaping jaws and outstretched talons. She sidestepped and cut its head as it plunged by. It staggered, and Nesteruk, screaming, finished it with a knife thrust to the chest.

That left the orc boy's flank exposed to another xulgath, but Kagur and Rho lunged at the same time and cut the reptile down together. She sensed danger at her own back and spun, her blade slashing a xulgath across the snout. She cut again and tore its midsection open.

She looked around. As far as she could tell, only two xulgaths were left, both running away. She started to drop her sword and ready her bow, but before she could, Passamax and another Skulltaker hurled ordinary flint-tipped javelins the reptilian guards hadn't had a chance to use.

The weapons caught the fleeing xulgaths in the backs. One fell instantly. The other managed two more stumbling steps, and then it too collapsed.

Kagur looked around at her companions. A couple had fresh wounds, but they were all still on their feet. "Onward!" she said.

As they raced down the passage, more xulgaths lunged from a doorway to attack them, but to no avail. Escape was at hand, and despite all the raiders had endured, the knowledge energized them. They stabbed and hacked through their foes in a matter of moments.

A murky rectangle appeared in the gloom ahead. It was the way out into the open air, and Kagur felt fierce satisfaction at the sight of it. Then the doorway blazed white as the Vault's sudden morning flooded it with sunlight.

Chapter Thirty-One
The Slaves

Someone snarled. Kagur's comrades understood as well as she how daylight diminished their chances. But they'd come too far to do anything but press on.

They burst out onto the shelf above the water. Hissing voices clamored overhead as xulgaths on the upper tiers caught sight of them. Pivoting, squinting and blinking, Kagur looked for their canoes.

They were nowhere in sight, nor were any xulgath boats of comparable size. Evidently, more than one opening led into the ziggurat at lake level, and the raiders had emerged on a different side from the one on which they'd landed.

But one of the larger xulgath boats sat some distance down the shelf with several of the reptiles moving around on deck. Either the craft was just about to depart or it was just putting in.

Kagur had no idea how to manage such a vessel, and was sure her companions didn't, either. But she sprinted toward it anyway, and the other raiders pounded after her.

For a few blessed moments, the xulgaths aboard the boat seemed oblivious to the fugitives' approach. Then something—most likely the cries from the upper tiers—roused them to action. One cast a javelin, but the hasty throw fell short. Two more pushed the boat away from the pyramid with poles.

Like most natives of the tundra, Kagur had never learned to swim, but she didn't let that balk her. She ran even faster, leaped off the tier and over the water, and thumped down in the prow of the boat.

At once, a xulgath spearman lunged at her. But she'd landed well, with her balance intact, and she parried the thrust and slashed the reptile's neck. It fell with blood pumping from the wound.

She pivoted and looked down the length of the vessel, at more xulgaths preparing to hurl javelins—and at the human and orc rowers bound to their oars with coarse lengths of rope or vine.

She shouted to the latter: "You can be free! Just get the boat closer to the ledge!"

The captives gawked at her. Then a grizzled orc covered in lash marks both old and new roared, "Do it!" Other slaves dipped their oars into the water.

Hissing and screeching, xulgaths swung cracking whips. A couple even jabbed with spears or chopped with hatchets. Still, the rebellious thralls swung the vessel back toward the ziggurat, near enough for Kagur's companions to jump aboard.

The xulgaths were dead a few breaths later.

"Now go!" shouted Kagur, still to the slaves. "Get us to shore!"

"Which shore?" asked one of the human slaves.

"The closest one without a xulgath city sitting on it," panted Vom.

Kagur looked back at the ziggurat and all around the lake and decided they actually had a good chance of reaching safety. No xulgath boats were giving chase. Only one was even in view, and it was just a speck on the shining blue water, too distant to intercept her vessel even if the reptiles onboard somehow realized it had fallen into the hands of their enemies.

That meant she had no one left to fight, no more decisions to make, and no more mysteries to try to comprehend. In fact, since she wasn't rowing, she had nothing to do, and with that realization, she suddenly felt how sore and weary she was.

She flopped down in the bow of the boat with her back against the gunwale. There, spent though she was, she set about wiping the blood from her father's sword.

Grubby green feet planted themselves in front of her, and she looked up. Swaying slightly with the motion of the boat, a quiver of javelins swinging on his back, Nesteruk stood before her.

"You're the leader," he said in a tone of sullen contrition. "It was for you to say whether we fought or run."

Kagur sighed. "Sit."

He did.

"Your mother was a brave warrior," she said. "So was my father. We *will* avenge them, and it will be a better vengeance than what we could have had in the pyramid. The blue giant and a pile of xulgaths will be lying dead while we're still alive to eat, drink, laugh, and hunt. Do you see?"

Before Nesteruk could answer, Dalk came thumping down the walkway that ran the length of the boat between the rowers' benches. "Look!" he said, pointing back at the ziggurat.

Kagur scrambled to her feet. A point of brightness danced atop the pyramid in the way that only metal could catch the sun.

Eovath was up there brandishing his greataxe. Using it to work magic like Holg employed his staff.

Kagur turned to the rowers. "Faster!" And although they'd already been pulling the heavy oars vigorously, they picked up the pace a little more. But it still wasn't fast enough.

Something jolted the boat from behind. Kagur staggered. Men cried out, and then another impact jarred the vessel.

Kagur exchanged her sword for her bow and peered down into the water. Nesteruk reached for his quiver.

"No!" she said, then raised her voice to carry down the length of the boat. "No lightning! Not unless it looks like the beast is truly going to sink us!"

She didn't check to see if her comrades were obeying. She kept her gaze on the water. Come on, she thought, show yourself.

When the creature obliged, it was swimming away, and for an instant, she wondered if Eovath's magic had lost its grip on it and it had decided to break off the attack. Then it wheeled, and she realized it had swum under the boat, then risen to the surface to ram the bow as it had previously slammed into the stern.

It was every bit as long as the boat, with the fins of a fish but long reptilian jaws somewhat like those of a spearbeak. If it failed to knock a hole in the vessel by banging into it, it might well be capable of chewing one, or just seizing hold of the boat and flipping it over.

Kagur shot an arrow into the scaly hide above one eye and reached for another shaft. That one pierced the flesh a little farther back on the head. Vom and Dalk threw javelins.

The creature dived deep enough that missiles were unlikely to hurt it and glided under the bow. "It's coming back at you!" Kagur shouted to the warriors at the stern, and they hefted their weapons.

But the creature didn't simply swim all the way down the length of the vessel as it had before. When the boat jolted upward, Kagur realized their foe had given them a bump from underneath.

Fortunately, that attack didn't crack the hull or capsize the boat, either. But it boded ill that the beast was already trying new tactics.

She tried to think of a new tactic of her own. Then something else burst out of the water.

Bounced around to the extent their bound hands would allow, their oars tangled and their rhythm disrupted, the slaves had stopped rowing, allowing a serpent-like head atop a long, twisting neck to rear up between two of the sweeps. It plunged down and snapped a man's head off, splashing his bench mate with his blood.

Kagur loosed at the new threat. One arrow stabbed into the reptile's neck just beneath the jaws. It screeched, and chunks of the head it had just bitten away spilled between its fangs.

Her next shaft drove deep into one of its nostrils. It roared louder, twisted away from the boat, and plunged back under the surface of the lake.

Had she killed it? What had become of the other beast? She looked around, and then Vom shouted, "Behind you!"

She whirled to find the long-necked creature's head plunging at her with bloody jaws agape. It had swum under the boat to reach for her from the other side. She dodged toward the stern, and at the same instant, the vessel lurched as the fishlike reptile rammed it. She reeled backward, and the gunwale caught the middle of her calves. She realized she was going over.

She threw her longbow into the middle of the bow. Then she plummeted and splashed down in the water. Dislodged from her quiver, an arrow floated in front of her face.

Hoping that what she was doing was swimming, or at least an approximation thereof, she flailed. Her head broke the surface, and she coughed out water. But before she could suck in a fresh breath, she slipped back under the surface.

Fighting not to panic, to see and to think, she suddenly registered the row of oars sticking out of the side of the boat. She'd splashed down just a short distance from the vessel, and the nearest sweep was only a couple steps away, if stepping were only a possibility.

Her chest aching with the urge to breathe, she kicked and pulled at the water and dragged herself forward. Her fingertips touched the rounded oar shaft, and then it jerked away from her as the fishlike reptile rammed the boat. The next oar in line clipped her shoulder.

She tumbled, and the dregs of air left in her lungs erupted from her mouth in a burst of bubbles. Half stunned, she just barely glimpsed yet another oar coming at her as momentum carried the boat along.

She clutched hold of that sweep and dragged herself up its smooth length until her head broke water. Then she clung and gasped until the fire in her chest cooled.

Meanwhile, its four flippers stroking and tail rippling, the long-necked reptile swam under the boat. Then it turned in her direction.

Javelins flew over Kagur's head and pierced the creature's back, but they neither killed nor distracted it. It surged forward, this time without lifting its head. It didn't need to when most of her body was under the water, too.

She drew up her legs and heaved with her arms. Together, the two actions sufficed to keep her whole for another moment. The bite that would have clipped her feet off gnashed shut just under them instead.

Now that Kagur was mostly above the surface, the reptile's head came curling up between her perch and the oar in front of it. The beast snorted, and red mist sprayed from the arrow wound in its snout.

"Row!" Kagur bellowed.

She didn't expect everyone to hear or heed her amid the general chaos, and in fact, some oars didn't move, while others, caught on one another, cracked or snapped outright when the slaves pulled them. But the sweep behind her gigantic assailant curled through its normal action and clouted the reptile in the back.

The beast jerked its head away from Kagur to see what had struck it. She pulled her longsword from its scabbard, leaned out as far as she could, and cut with all that remained of her strength.

The blade shed sparkling droplets of water as it whirled through the air. The reptile started to look back around, and then the edge sheared into its neck.

The reptile convulsed and slipped lower in the water. The next sweep of the oar cracked bone when it slammed into its head. The beast stopped floundering and sank.

"Kagur!" called Vom. She looked around to see his shaggy head and broad shoulders sticking up over the side of the boat. "Climb!"

She slid her sword back in the scabbard and shinnied up the oar. When she was close enough, Vom reached over the size of the boat and hauled her into the space between one rower's bench and the next. She was clumsy with exhaustion, and her feet bumped one of the slaves.

Then she heard three crackling sounds in quick succession, and a frenzied splashing in the water. When the noise subsided, Passamax, who was now standing in the bow, shook his fist in the air and bellowed.

Kagur started to clamber up onto the elevated walkway that ran between the benches. Vom moved to help her, and she waved him away.

She hurried up the deck and beheld the cause of Passamax's jubilation. Floating, or maybe just sinking more slowly than its long-necked ally, the fishlike reptile now looked equally inert.

Kagur sighed. "You had to do it. But—"

The orc raised a scarred hand still bloody from all the killing he'd done since arriving on the ziggurat. "I leaned over the side and tossed the javelins low so the boat blocked the view from the pyramid. And the flashes don't stand out in the sunlight as much as they did in the dark."

She blinked. "You understood what I was thinking."

"Why wouldn't I? Orcs aren't just tougher than humans. They're smarter." He bared his teeth, and she realized he was joking.

She turned and looked down the length of the boat. Someone had cut the bindings of the gray-haired orc. Standing on his bench for a better view, he was directing his fellows in their efforts to untangle fouled oars and jettison broken ones. Under his supervision, it only took a little while to get the boat moving again.

Kagur looked across the water for new threats. She didn't see any.

But she did spot Holg, sitting with his back against a gunwale, eyes closed, looking gaunt and wrinkled as she'd ever seen him. Afraid some harm had befallen him, she caught her breath—and then he mocked her anxiety with a soft, rattling snore.

Tired as she was herself, she couldn't imagine how anyone could fall asleep so soon after they'd all been fighting for their lives. But maybe it had something do with the fact that she was young and he was old.

She sat down beside him, and dried her father's sword and her brother's knife as best she could without a scrap of dry cloth anywhere about her. Over time, the rhythmic rocking of the boat loosened her tight muscles almost like a massage, and the warm sunlight eased her, too.

Maybe she *could* sleep if she permitted it. Some of her comrades had settled down to doze. But she preferred to keep watch until they all were safer.

Watching was all she did, though. She was happy to leave it to Rho and Nesteruk to work their way down the length of the boat and cut the captives free.

The oarsmen brought the craft to shore by the swift expedient of running it aground on a white sand beach. The resulting bump jarred Vom, Dalk, and other warriors awake and made them rear up blinking in confusion.

The former slaves spoke to their bench mates, gripped their hands, or even embraced them, but all of it quickly. Then they started jumping off the boat and scurrying toward the green jungle beyond, scattering as they went.

Despite the need for everyone to vanish, Kagur hadn't expected people to depart quite this hastily. Fortunately, they weren't gone yet. "Stop!" she shouted.

Some of the rowers looked back to smile, wave, or nod. Then they kept going.

She looked to Vom and said, "They can't leave yet!"

The Dragonfly warrior shook his bearded head and replied with words she couldn't understand.

The charm that allowed her to communicate with the cave dwellers had worn off. She pivoted back toward Holg. Now more lying that sitting, he was still snoring, sleeping so soundly even the jar of running aground hadn't woken him.

She squatted and shook him by his bony shoulders. "Wake up!" she shouted.

He opened his milky eyes partway. "What?" he mumbled.

"I need you to cast speaking magic!"

Alert now, he frowned and sat up straight. "I slept some, but I haven't meditated. That's generally—"

She hauled him to his feet and waved her hand to indicate the departing rowers, some of whom had nearly reached the tree line. "I need to talk to them! Otherwise, we lose, and Eovath wins!"

Holg grunted. "Well, we can't have that. Stand clear." She did, and he chanted, shifted his staff back and forth, and clutched her shoulder at the end of the prayer. Abruptly, she understood the conversation of the warriors who were looking on wondering what she was so agitated about.

"Stop!" she bellowed. "Please!"

The rowers turned.

"I need to talk to you," she continued. "For all our sakes."

They exchanged glances and then tramped back down toward the water, and while they did, she decided the bow of the boat was as good a place from which to speak as any. When they were clustered beneath her, she began.

"Holg—the old man with the white eyes—and I come from the same faraway place as the blue giant. We attacked the pyramid to kill him."

Standing at the forefront of his comrades, the gray-headed orc said, "I figured you and your band were a raiding party. Did the xulgaths cut you off from the canoes you came in?"

"Something like that," Kagur said.

The orc grinned. "Well, I'm not sorry about how that worked out."

"I'm not sorry about that part of it, either," she replied. "But I'm *very* sorry we didn't kill Eovath—the giant.

"While we were inside the ziggurat," she continued, "the xulgaths figured out that most of us are Skulltakers and Dragonflies, and they mean to strike back at us. They'll bring all their strength to bear to wipe out both tribes."

The scarred orc grunted. "Tell the folk to scatter. With luck, the xulgaths won't catch all of them, and some might find other tribes willing to adopt them. I'm Unlak of the Thirsty Knives. If Skulltakers come to our hillsides, I'll speak for them."

"That's kind," Kagur said. "But my companions are no more willing to dissolve their tribes and run from

337

their enemies than the Thirsty Knives would be in their place."

"What else can you do?" a woman asked. Her whip scars crisscrossed the black tattooed designs on her shoulders and forearms.

"Fight," Kagur said. "Lure our enemies into a trap and kill them."

"How?" called a man who held his hands before him with fingers half curled, like he was still gripping an oar. "If the reptiles attack with all their might, that means warriors from the stone cities, the blue giant and his shining axe, threehorns, longstriders—"

Kagur drew her longsword and raised it to catch the sunlight. "My blade shines, too. And as for the longstriders and other beasts, we killed the pair that just attacked us." She turned. "Show them how, Rho."

The boy took a javelin from his quiver and flung it a tree-fern some distance away. The weapon became a crackling twist of glare that blasted the plant in two. The top fell to the ground with a thump and a rattling of fronds.

Some of the rowers recoiled. They all gaped at the destruction and the little dancing flames it left in its wake. Rho grinned at their astonishment.

"The best part," said Kagur, "is that the xulgaths don't know we have this power. The ones who saw us use it in the pyramid are dead, and Passamax hid what he was doing when he killed the water beast."

Unlak shook his head. "What *are* those things?"

"Weapons from long ago," she answered. "That's all we know, but all we need to know."

"Until touching them brings a curse down," the tattooed woman said.

Kagur indicated Holg, who was paying heed to the conversation even though, since he hadn't prayed a second prayer on his own behalf, he couldn't really understand it. "My friend is a shaman," she said, "and he says the javelins aren't evil or forbidden. Just strange."

"And useful!" Passamax said.

Unlak leered. "I believe it. So why waste one on a tree-fern?"

"To show we have a surprise in store for the xulgaths," Kagur said, "To prove we have a chance of crushing them if other tribes stand with us."

The rowers looked back up at her. Then the tattooed woman said, "I'm grateful to be free, and my kin will be glad to have me back. But we live on the opposite side of the lake from the Dragonflies and Skulltakers. We barely even know the names."

"And my folk," called an orc, "have fought Skulltakers when we met them along the river. They'd laugh if I asked them to go to war to help an enemy."

"Then don't," Kagur said. "Ask them to fight for themselves."

Vom stepped up beside her. "The coming of the giant," he said, "has inspired the xulgaths to try to kill or enslave every last human. They're attacking the highlands like never before. The Dragonflies and Skulltakers have angered them, so we're the next targets. But in time, they'll pick off every tribe of humans and then move on to the orcs."

"Unless we stop them," Kagur said. "If we defeat them and kill the living symbol of their hopes, they'll lose heart and give up their ambitions."

"The xulgaths have always fought the peoples of the highlands," said the man who held his hands like they still gripped an oar. "But they don't try to take *everything*. That would be . . . new."

"Sometimes new things come into the world," Kagur replied. "The giant and his axe are new. So are my sword and the lightning spears. And when you go home, your kin will tell you life has changed for the worse. It's up to us to change it back."

Unlak picked a little crawling insect out of his gray and tangled mane. "By uniting the warriors of many tribes into one big war party."

"Yes."

"It will never happen. I wish it could. I'd take any chance to hurt the xulgaths, and I trust you, odd as you are. But folk who aren't standing here with us today won't feel the same. They'll say, 'We don't *know* that the xulgaths will ever come for us.' Or, 'How can we trust strangers?' Or, 'How do we know any other tribe will even show up?' Or—"

Kagur raised her hand. "But will you be my messenger?" She looked around at the other rowers. "Will all of you tell your tribes what I ask?"

They hesitated. Then the man with the curled fingers said, "Yes. But it won't do any good."

Kagur turned to Passamax. "Give me your quiver," she said.

The orc glared. "They already said their tribes won't come. That makes the lightning our only chance!"

"It's not a chance. Not by itself. Even the mightiest weapons can't win a battle if your side doesn't have enough warriors."

Passamax's scowl deepened. "If this doesn't work, the giant won't have to kill you. I'll do it myself." He jerked the yellow metal cylinder off his shoulder.

Meanwhile, Holg gave Kagur a little nod.

She sheathed her sword, took the quiver, and jumped from the bow down into the sand. The shifting white grains were hot beneath her feet. She pulled out a javelin and offered it to Unlak butt first.

The orc's bloodshot eyes widened. After a pause, he started to reach, then hesitated.

"It's all right," Kagur said. "A person can handle them without harm." She waved to the other galley slaves. "Everybody, come take one."

"Why would you give such things away?" Unlak asked.

"When you return to your tribes, you'll find they're worried about the xulgaths and want to strike back. They only need proof that it's possible."

Unlak frowned. "And the javelin will convince them?"

"Yes. Together with the tale you have to tell. If need be, throw the javelin and show what they can do. But if you can, save it for the battle to come."

Unlak took hold of the weapon. "My folk will hear your request. That's all I can promise."

"Fair enough."

Two of the rowers simply couldn't bring themselves to touch a javelin. But the rest took one, some with bravado and some gingerly, then trotted for the trees and tree-ferns as they had before.

Kagur looked back at Passamax and hefted the quiver. "You still have a couple left," she said.

The orc spat, and she wondered if his disgust was justified.

Chapter Thirty-Two
The Last Dream

Drums pounded out a frantic rhythm while skirling flutes supplied the melody. Angry at missing the festivities, Kagur sat apart from the musicians and dancers and rubbed the aching soles of her feet.

His blue skin nearly black by night despite the full moon shining overhead, Eovath tramped up and extended his hand.

She shook her head. "I can't. I left my boots on the ziggurat, and I'm not used to hiking without them."

"That didn't happen yet," her brother said, "unless you insist that it did. This can be last year. In fact, it is." He waved his hand at the revelers, the tents, the mammoths, and the vague, flat grayness of the tundra extending for mile after mile beyond. "Because you want it to be."

She realized he was right. This was exactly what she wanted, and her feet didn't hurt a bit. She took his hand, he helped her up, and they walked toward the music.

The dancers capered in a circle, which reversed direction whenever one of the drummers decided to call out the command. Folk who didn't react fast enough ended up jostled or even knocked to the ground. Blacklions particularly inspired by the music sprang from the ring to the space inside it, where they turned cartwheels, flipped, and threw one another into the air.

Knowing Eovath needed a fair-sized patch of ground to execute the steps, other dancers opened a gap in the ring for him and Kagur. Jorn and Taresk smiled at them.

Kagur and Eovath spun and kicked to the beat. "This is better, isn't it?" he said.

"Yes," she answered. "It's everything a sane person could want. That's how I know you're mad. Only a madman would poison it and chop it to pieces."

He sighed. "I thought that by now, you might understand. It's *all* a dance, everything that's happening. Maybe it started when your father killed mine, or when the Rough Beast first whispered to me. Anyway, the music carries us along."

The drumming and piping were still whirling all the Blacklion dancers along, but though the tempo was becoming ragged, and the flutes were starting to screech and squeal.

"Would you have stopped dancing if you could?" Kagur asked.

"Would you forgive me if you could?"

"No."

"There's your answer."

She frowned. "It's not an answer I understand."

The night darkened. No matter which way she and Eovath turned, the moon no longer shined over the giant's shoulder.

"When you give yourself over to a purpose," he said, "and decide nothing else matters, it sets you free by making everything simple. In its way, it makes you drunk as Tian brandy. I know you've felt the exhilaration, too."

"All I feel is hate."

"That's what I mean." Somehow gleaming even with the moon extinguished, his golden eyes peered down at her. "But I see it was only true for a while. Now you're reverting. It's sad that I wasn't able to give you the gift of purity, either."

The music had slowed to a dragging atonal whining with seemingly random drumbeats underneath. It was only Kagur's memory of how the tune was supposed to sound that kept her kicking and pivoting in time.

"The only thing I want from you," she said, "is your life."

"Then why haven't you taken it? No, never mind, that isn't really fair. Neither of us could kill the other. We haven't reached that part of the dance. We're coming to it, though. This is the last time you'll dream about me. Your last chance to understand."

Mere shadows in the gloom, dancers shuffled, stumbled, and lurched. The smell of rot tinged the air.

"Understand what?" she asked.

"Anything you want. If you like, I'll even tell you how to kill me."

"Why?"

He grinned. "Maybe I'm choking on guilt and regret. Or maybe I decided I hate you after all, and I want you to die knowing you had the answer but not the strength to use it."

"Tell me, then."

On the other side of the circle, dancers toppled to the ground.

"Fight the coming battle to kill me and for no other purpose," Eovath said. "Hammer me with every warrior and weapon you have."

"You do have to die," Kagur said, "but we need to throw back the xulgaths and their beasts as well."

"If you try to win everything, you'll lose everything. Fight the battle close to the red pit. Kill me and then abandon the cave dwellers to die. Go home to the tundra where you belong."

"If I did that," she said, "it would truly be the end of the Blacklions. I'd stop being one if I threw away everything our father taught us."

"The Blacklions are already ended, sister. Look around."

All the dancers were collapsing, sometimes falling to pieces in the process. Despite the darkness, Kagur spotted her father just in time to see the head tumble from his shoulders.

For a moment, she felt dismay and a numbing bewilderment. Then a surge of rage snapped her thoughts into focus.

She snatched for her knife, but Eovath grabbed her arm and squeezed with a frost giant's strength. The bones in her wrist ground together, and she gasped.

"I told you," he said, "we have to finish the dance. It ends like this." He threw her to the ground amid the fragments of reeking carrion that were all that remained of her kin.

Something squeezed her shoulder, and she cried out knowing it could only be a dead man's hand. But then her eyes popped open, and the starlight filtering through the canopy revealed Nesteruk crouching over her.

He whispered to her. At the moment, she didn't have Holg's magic to enhance her understanding, so she only caught a few words. But she assumed the orc boy was telling her he'd heard her muttering or shifting restlessly, realized she was having a nightmare, and climbed down from his branch to hers to wake her.

Fortunately, she'd learned enough of his people's language to thank him. He nodded, reached up for a bough, and climbed back to the fork where he was spending the night.

Since Kagur couldn't fall back asleep, she was glad when the sun flared back to life not long thereafter. But she would have been gladder if she weren't expecting a sorrowful day.

When she and her companions had fled the pyramid, they'd simply tried to get off the lake as quickly as possible. They might not have survived if they'd worried about anything else. Fortunately, the effort still landed them on the same side of the lake as the Dragonfly and Skulltaker villages, and after several days of pushing hard, she and the other raiders were nearly home.

She, Holg, and their fellow humans returned to their territory while the orcs went home to theirs. Upon her arrival at the painted caves, she set about the task of confirming to the kin of those who hadn't returned that yes, just as they feared, their loved ones were dead.

Vom and Dalk made the rounds with her to embrace those who wept and praise the valor of the fallen, and she sensed they would have performed the whole task had she asked it of them. But she'd led the war party, and it was her responsibility.

Insofar as it was possible, though, she put off explaining everything that had happened and all that was about to. She deemed it better to wait until she could talk to Dragonflies and Skulltakers together.

The opportunity came the following day, when dozens of folk from each village met by Old Scar's remains as they had before. By now, scavengers had mostly picked the longstrider's bones clean, and they no longer stank. Around their gleaming whiteness, the Black Jungle was truly black, with dusky flowers shrouding the greenery and perfuming the humid air with a pungent sweetness.

Kagur surveyed the crowd. The last time she'd spoken here, she'd only been talking to warriors, but that wasn't the case now. Somehow sensing that the tribes were in imminent peril, old folk, nursing and expectant mothers, and children had descended from the crags to listen, too.

"All right," Kagur said. "You all know some of us journeyed to the pyramid to kill the blue giant. I'll tell you what happened when we got there." Omitting irrelevancies like how it actually felt to experience twisted space and all the tricks it could play, she sketched the events as clearly as she could.

The Dragonflies and Skulltakers were as alarmed as she'd expected by Eovath's threat to annihilate them. But they were less heartened than she'd hoped by her effort to recruit allies for the struggle to come.

Leaning on the spear that also served him as a walking staff, Denda asked, "Will anyone really come?"

Vom answered, "I think some of them may."

"But even if they do," asked an orc, "will they get here in time? You say the xulgaths are already bringing their warriors together."

"From all around the lake," Kagur said. "That will take time, too. It's a race, but our allies may win it."

"You don't lack for gall," Yunal sneered.

"What do you mean?" Kagur replied.

"You lured Skulltakers away on a crazy venture with our sworn enemies. Naturally, it failed, and we lost some of our bravest, Ikolch included."

"My mother wanted to go," Nesteruk said. "And she always told me that anytime a warrior—"

"Be quiet!" Yunal snapped. "A shaman is talking. This stranger, this *human*, got Skulltakers killed, and now the giant and the reptiles are coming to slaughter the rest of us." She glared at Kagur. "Your fault! Yet you *still* want to tell us what to do. *That's* what I mean by gall!"

"The xulgaths," Kagur said, "were coming in time, no matter—"

"You claim that, but how do we know?"

Kagur wanted to punch Yunal. She took a breath instead. "A warrior of the Blacklions is talking. *You* be quiet. Maybe the raid was a bad gamble, but it's too late to rethink it now. We can only decide what to do next. If you don't like my plan, what's yours?"

"I don't care what humans do, but my folk will scatter and stay alive!"

Passamax scowled. "Skulltakers don't run away."

"I know, warrior," Yunal said, "and it angers me to give such counsel. But the stranger there forced this on us, and no one can call us cowards for doing what the spirits say we should."

"How are they saying it?" asked Holg, leaning on his staff with all of his left foot but the ball and toes off the ground. The shoeless trek from the lakeshore had been hard on Kagur's soles but harder still on his, just as the fast pace had taxed his endurance.

Seemingly caught by surprise, Yunal hesitated. "What?"

"I asked how you learned the will of the spirits," the old man said. He shifted his weight to lift the blistered heel of his right foot off the ground. "Kagur just now explained the current crisis and the new plan. You haven't prayed in the moments since. How can you know what you claim to know?"

Yunal waved his hand at the forest around them. "Are you *so* blind you don't see how the darkness of death chokes the green of life? This is our future if we stay and face the doom rushing to claim us."

Orcs muttered to one another, and even Passamax abruptly seemed less full of fighting spirit. But Holg smiled the way Jorn Blacklion had when he was practicing swordplay and an opponent fell into a trap.

"Funny," the old man drawled. "I thought it was just nature being nature." He shifted his clouded gaze to the crowd. "Haven't you watched the black flowers bloom over and over again for as long as anyone can remember? What makes this time special?"

Yunal shivered like a warrior on the brink of going berserk. "A blind, feeble old human is calling me a liar."

"What I'm saying," Holg replied, "is that it's easy for seers to slip into bad habits. We want people to heed our counsel, and they often will if we're relaying messages from the spirits.

"Unfortunately," the old man continued, shifting his weight again, "we can't go around casting divinations *all* the time, the results can be puzzling when we do, and it's rare for the powers to speak of their own accord. But I suspect we all realize early on that if we simply claim to hear their whispers in the wind or read their warnings in the way a spearbeak circles in the sky, people will give excessive weight to what are actually just our own opinions."

"You *are* calling me a liar!" Yunal snarled.

Holg shrugged. "If you insist on putting it that way, maybe. Back in my homeland, the spirits really did speak to me. They told me to help Kagur and stop the blue giant. And if I say they want us to fight and you say they want us to run, well, we can't both be right, can we?"

"We can prove which of us the spirits favor." Yunal looked to the crowd. "Clear a space!"

"It always comes down to this," Holg murmured, "at least when you're arguing with orcs."

"You're limping," Kagur replied, "and you have trouble seeing in sunlight. Are you sure about this? We could take some of the orcs to hear what Ghethi has to say." The Dragonfly healer had stayed behind in her cave to tend two children weak and dizzy with fever.

"They wouldn't go," said Holg. "If I don't fight, they'll take it to mean Yunal is brave and right, I'm cowardly and wrong, and that will be the end of it." He smiled. "Don't worry. After all the foes and beasts we've faced already, surely you trust me to knock some sense into this fellow."

Unless his magic is stronger than yours, Kagur thought. She had no idea of the extent of Yunal's powers, and she didn't see how Holg could know, either.

But she did trust the old man, and he'd also convinced her he was right: this was the only way. She squeezed his bony shoulder, and he closed his eyes and hobbled forward to meet his adversary.

For a few moments, each shaman simply stood and seemingly took the measure of the other. Then they both started reciting incantations at once. Yunal snarled his prayers and swung a large, intricately carved bone like he was smashing heads. Holg spoke softly and shifted his staff through tighter, subtler passes.

The old man finished first, but nothing overt happened as a result. An instant later, Yunal completed his prayer by lashing the bone down to point at his opponent.

A pillar of yellow flame roared up from the grass around Holg's feet to engulf him completely. Kagur caught her breath. Bolta, whose wits the old man had untangled on the trek back from the lakeshore, said, "No!"

Then the fire subsided except for a few small flames crackling in the blackened grass, and Holg stood unscathed in the middle of the scorched spot. He waved his hand at Yunal palm up as if to ask, "Is that the best you can do?"

The orc's jaw muscles bunched, and then he and his adversary launched into new incantations. But this time, Kagur discerned that they weren't quite starting simultaneously. Holg waited to hear the first word and observe the starting gesture of Yunal's prayer before beginning his own. Like a swordsman fighting defensively, he was sacrificing a bit of speed in order to gain knowledge of his opponent's intentions. It wasn't Kagur's preferred method, but she could only hope the strategy would serve him well.

A hornet as long as her arm shimmered into existence between Yunal and Holg, then, wings droning, shot toward the human shaman. Holg spoke the final word of his prayer and flicked his staff at the onrushing creature in a casual-looking way, like he was shooing away an insect of normal size. The hornet vanished.

Yunal roared and lashed the bone in an arc. A second bone, shiny and translucent like it was made of ice, flew out of the first and hurtled at Holg.

Somehow the orc had produced the flying bone considerably faster than he had the burst of flame or the huge hornet, without needing to speak a prayer, and the abrupt acceleration in the tempo of the fight appeared to catch Holg by surprise. He tried to dodge the weapon's strike, but it clipped the top of his bald head anyway, and he stumbled.

Blood streaming from his gashed scalp, he raised his staff and parried the next blow, and the one after, but seemed capable of nothing more. Meanwhile, Yunal advanced, and Kagur assumed that when he closed the distance, Holg would have two hammering cudgels to dodge instead of one.

She wanted to dash forward and intervene. Scowling, she held the urge in check. From the expressions on the faces of Vom, Dalk, and other members of the raiding party, and the white-knuckled way they gripped their spears, javelins, and hatchets, they were having to hold themselves back as well.

Then, however, Kagur noticed something that eased her fears at least a little. She tilted her head sideways to whisper to Rho: "Holg's lips are moving. He's blocking and whispering a prayer at the same time."

The boy grinned. "He's drawing the orc into a trap."

But it was a trap that would only work if Holg articulated the prayer properly, and with blood streaming down from his split scalp and the flying bone clacking relentlessly against his staff, that couldn't be easy. He blocked another strike, and although he thus averted a second blow to the head, the conjured bludgeon smashed down on the knuckles of his left hand. Kagur winced, but the shaman's mouth kept working, *maybe* without a stumble if his nameless patrons were looking out for him.

Yunal stepped closer and nearly into striking distance. Holg retreated a space, and thick gray fog swirled into existence around him, concealing him from view.

Yunal hesitated at the edge of the cloud, peering in. The conjured bone flew back to him and floated above him. Then the butt of Holg's staff leaped out and thumped him in the forehead.

The orc reeled backward. Holg lunged out of the mist and landed a second cracking blow to Yunal's forearm. The other shaman fumbled his grip on his weapon but clutched it before it could flip out of his fingers.

Holg landed, or half-landed, one more attack, a glancing blow to the shoulder. Then Yunal struck back, and for the next few moments, they swung, jabbed, blocked, and evaded like ordinary combatants.

Kagur frowned. It was good that at least Yunal hadn't yet commanded the flying bone to resume attacking, but she suspected the orc didn't really need the help. He was younger and brawnier than his opponent, and in a purely physical confrontation, he had the edge.

Apparently recognizing the same thing, Holg retreated toward the cloud, which still held its shape like a bubble instead of spreading and thinning as it should. Whipping the bone in his hand back and forth, Yunal shouted words of power.

Holg waited until Yunal was several words into the incantation—deep enough, perhaps, that it was difficult to stop short of the ending, deep enough that the music carried him along. Then the old man started another prayer of his own.

The orc swept his weapon over his head and pointed. The cloud shredded into nothingness.

As the last wisps of mist dissolved, Holg finished his prayer and stabbed with his staff. The resulting flash was both difficult to see in sunlight and the first offensive magic the old man had attempted. Maybe it caught Yunal by surprise, and that was why he didn't even try to dodge. The beam of light caught him in the torso, and he doubled over.

His limp erased by the urgency of the moment, Holg rushed forward and repeatedly slammed his staff down on Yunal's head, shoulders, and spine. In another moment, surely, the bashing would drop the orc to his knees.

Except that despite the punishment, Yunal managed to silently command the hovering bone, and it hurtled at Holg. Rho called, "Look out!"

But if the old man even heard, he didn't react in time. The bone bashed him just above the ear, and he reeled. A second blow caught him in the ribs, and Kagur heard one of them snap.

Holg blocked the next strike and the one after, but he had to turn away from Yunal to do it. Bleeding, swaying, the orc straightened up, gripped the carved bone with both hands, and swung it over his head.

At the same moment, the weapon's flying counterpart vanished as the magic that had created it ran out of strength. Eyes still shut, face painted with blood, fetishes swinging on their thongs, Holg lurched back around and, the whole weight of his body behind the blow, smashed his staff into Yunal's face.

The orc fell on his back and stayed there long enough for Holg to stagger to him and press the butt of his staff against his neck. One hard thrust would crush the windpipe.

"I don't want to kill you," Holg said. His voice was thick, and between that and the wheezing, it was difficult to understand him. "But I will."

"What do you want?" Yunal panted.

Holg spat blood. "You know."

The orc took a breath and then called, "I surrender and admit I was wrong. On this day, the human heard the words of the spirits plainer than I did."

"Thank you," said Holg. He tried to sit down but couldn't manage it gracefully. One foot slipped on the bloody grass, and he landed with a bump that made him gasp.

Kagur hurried to him with Rho, Vom, and others following close behind. When the old man opened his eyes, she saw that the white of the left one had turned red.

"That wasn't quite the elegant triumph of strategy I had pictured in my head." Holg spat more blood.

"Are you bleeding on the inside?" Kagur asked.

The shaman started to shake his head, then winced when that evidently made it hurt worse. "I don't think so. I just bit my tongue one of the times that our friend here clouted me. But that's not to say he didn't beat me half to death, and talking like my mouth is full of mud, I'm not sure I can manage magic." He smiled at Yunal. "Perhaps you could heal both of us."

The orc looked surprised, but did so. Fearing some spiteful trick, Kagur watched and listened carefully, especially when Yunal actually laid his hands on Holg's body. But it was all right. Cuts closed, and scraped places smoothed into healthy skin. The sections of the old man's broken rib clicked back together in a way that made him grit his teeth.

Afterward, as both shamans clambered to their feet, Holg thanked the orc in a voice that was clear once more. "The spirits have graced you with a great deal of power. I hope we can count on it in the battle to come."

Yunal glowered. "I told the Skulltakers to flee. I thought it wise. But I'm *not* afraid to fight."

"Believe me," said Holg, rubbing his battered knuckles, "I know that as well as anyone could."

The orc hesitated like he wasn't sure what to make of his fellow shaman's friendly manner. Finally, gruffly, he said, "Maybe it will come out all right. If the spirits truly did speak to you."

Holg smiled wryly. "Unfortunately, Rovagug, or something akin to him, spoke to Eovath, and for all I know, Zevgavizeb spoke to the xulgaths."

For once, Kagur understood what the old man was getting at. "The gods and demons balance each other out. That leaves it up to us."

Chapter Thirty-Three
The Trap

The area in front of the Skulltakers' cave was noisy with all the warriors packed into it, even though the youngest orcs and a few of their caretakers had relocated to the Dragonfly village to await the outcome of the coming battle.

Kagur and Holg stood at the edge of the flat space and gazed lakeward. She couldn't actually see the shore, but she could imagine what was happening there. Scouts had kept her apprised, and she'd been to see for herself two days ago.

Some xulgaths arrived aboard boats, which the slaves then rowed away to fetch more. Other warriors and shamans came by land, marching along the edge of the lake with longstriders and spiketails in the vanguard and spearbeaks flying overhead. The reptiles all congregated in a sprawling camp clamorous with hisses, roars, and screeches, reeking of reptilian musk and waste.

"We still have time to move," Kagur murmured. "We could fight from the Dragonfly village. We'd be able to see farther, and the creatures would have a steeper climb to get at us."

She was really talking to herself, but if Holg recognized as much, he saw fit to answer anyway. "As I recall, you considered all that when you were making the decision, and you still liked this battleground better."

That doesn't mean I was right, she thought. But maybe she was, and it was unlikely to inspire confidence among her warriors if she started reversing her decisions.

"My father," she said, "good a man as he was, never rose to command a following. So I never had the chance to watch him do it."

Holg smiled. "That's as close as I've heard you come to confessing you're worried you might be out of your depth."

Kagur scowled. "I was just talking."

"My mistake. Still, look at it this way: if you never saw it, then neither did Eovath."

She grunted. "That's a point."

It wasn't the largest point, though. Neither she nor Holg had mentioned that, for after all, no one could do anything about it. As cumbersome a process as it was for the xulgaths to mass their strength at one spot along the lake, they were still assembling more quickly than Kagur's largely hypothetical allies. So far, only two liberated oarsmen had turned up with their kin, and two additional war bands simply weren't enough.

At her back sounded a steady chip-chip-chip; Denda and Bok were laboring from sunrise far into the night to ensure their comrades were well armed. His voice breaking, an adult's one moment and a boy's the next, Nesteruk chattered excitedly.

Curse it, Kagur *had* to win, for the sake of the living who trusted her no less than her own murdered kindred. Even for the sake of the orcs, who somehow had come to seem just as important as the human cave dwellers. Experience had shown her they weren't entirely like the marauders out of the Hold of Belkzen.

But *how* could she win? Her plan had seemed good when she conceived it, but plainly—

"Someone's coming," said Holg. He used his staff to gesture down the trail.

After a moment, she heard the same jumble of voices that he'd evidently caught. Dalk, who'd been out scouting, strode around a bend in the trail with Unlak beside him and dozens of men and orcs hurrying along behind. Spying Kagur and Holg, the former slave saluted them with a wave of the gleaming yellow javelin in his hand.

"I met these folk in the forest," said Dalk as he reached the end of the path.

"We sent our own messengers to other tribes that are friendly to us," Unlak said, "and warriors joined up and traveled together for safety's sake. It slowed us down some, but we made it."

"Not by much," said Dalk. "The xulgaths were getting ready to march. They might even be on the move by now."

Kagur scowled. "Then we may not have much time to get our new warriors ready." She looked at Unlak. "Come with me."

She led everyone to the mouth of the orcs' communal cave, where Rho sat with the gleaming quivers she'd left in his charge. "How many new tribes?" he asked.

"Nine," Unlak said, and the boy started counting out nine piles of lightning javelins.

"The warriors of each tribe will fight as their own war party," Kagur said, "but cooperate with other groups, too. And I'm the leader of everything. Do you see?"

Unlak nodded and watched Rho finish laying out the javelins. "I just won a bet. My brother was sure you wouldn't share any more of those. Certainly not with orcs."

"Orc or human," Kagur said, "we're all the same in this fight. Don't attack until the signal comes. Then throw the javelins at the creatures that are hardest to kill."

"What signal?" he replied

She explained, then handed him and all the other newcomers off to Nesteruk. The orc youth would help the various war bands find the places where she wanted them to wait and make sure they had water and food while they did.

For her part, Kagur strode about making sure people knew the reptiles were on the move and double-checking that they understood the plan. In the process, she verified that caches of javelins and other weapons were where they were supposed to be and brandished her "shining" blade for anyone who cared to see it.

It all seemed to take an inordinate amount of time, and she kept worrying the reptiles would suddenly appear before she even finished. But that was just edginess, not good sense. It was a fair distance from the lakeshore to the Skulltaker village, and Eovath's great following wouldn't cover it as quickly as Dalk, Unlak, and their companions had.

When she completed her tasks, she retrieved her longbow and quiver. Then she told Holg she was heading out.

The old man shook his head. "You could die down there before the real battle even begins. It's not how the commanders of the southlands lead their armies."

Kagur shrugged. "It's how my father led, and I don't think either Kellids or these cave dwellers would follow a leader who did it any other way."

Holg sighed. "Fair enough. Really, I just wish I were going with you. But it's true: I don't run fast enough. So just do me a favor. Don't kill *every* xulgath. Leave me a couple."

As Kagur departed the village, Vom, Passamax, and Yunal came trotting to join her. The three of them descended the winding trail together.

It didn't take long to reach the stretch of wooded hillside she'd selected, and somehow, she knew she still had some daylight left. Apparently, she was finally learning to judge the passage of time without a sun that rose and set.

She prowled along the slope checking on the humans and orcs who'd arrived before her and taken cover behind trees, tree-ferns, and thickets. All the warriors seemed well hidden from anyone peering from farther down the hill. They also understood what she required of them.

After the inspection, she and Passamax crouched behind their own blind, a thick stand of ferns as tall as she was, and kept watch with the others. When night was nigh, they made a cold, chewy supper of smoked jerky and raw tubers, then climbed a tree.

Passamax took the first watch, and she, the second. As she peered into darkness nearly as profound as any she'd encountered in Nar-Voth or Sekamina, with scarcely a trace of starlight filtering through the mesh of leaves and branches overhead, she wished she possessed the night vision of her orc companion. But it was sound that provided a first warning of the enemy's approach.

During the early part of the night, the forest had roared, snarled, and screeched with the cries of nocturnal beasts. Now, though, the creatures were falling quiet, and it could only mean the xulgaths were coming.

Kagur scowled. Since the reptiles saw as well or perhaps even better in the dark than orcs did, she'd anticipated they might make their final approach under cover of night. It was still a complication, though. Her human allies in particular might come to harm or bungle the execution of the plan when they couldn't see.

But it was too late to worry about that, either. Things were what they were.

She clambered along a branch to rouse Passamax, but he reared up by himself before she could. Either he hadn't been asleep, or the quiet had woken him. He started down the tree trunk, and she climbed after him.

When he was low enough to do so without breaking a leg, he dropped to the ground. Keeping low, he darted along the hillside to make sure everyone knew the xulgaths were on their way. Kagur strung her bow and crept back to her chosen patch of cover.

For what seemed a long while after that, nothing happened except that Passamax skulked back and gave her a nod to convey that all their allies were ready. Then, finally, she caught padding and rustling noises farther down the hill. Vague shapes moved, only barely distinguishable from the ambient gloom and one another.

Passamax touched her hand and pointed. Kagur squinted and then turned her head to peer from the corner of her eye in the hope that the night hunter's trick would help her discern what the orc wanted her to see.

It did. She glimpsed a shadow prowling some distance ahead of its fellows. If the xulgath scout spotted the warriors lying in wait, it would hiss a warning, and Passamax looked to Kagur to prevent that. The reptile was out of javelin range, but she should be able to hit it with an arrow.

As she nocked a shaft, she took note of the breeze and fixed her gaze on the slinking, still only barely visible form. She drew the fletchings back to her ear, exhaled, and loosed.

The scout dropped without a sound, to all appearances killed instantly. Seemingly failing to notice anything amiss, the loose ranks of murky figures behind it kept advancing, and Passamax gave Kagur an approving punch on the forearm.

As she pulled a special arrow from her quiver, she wasted a moment trying to spot Eovath. His hulking form should show up even in the blackness, shouldn't it? But she couldn't pick him out and forced herself to focus on other matters.

Like judging when the enemy had come near enough. She needed the vanguard within javelin range, but much closer than that would be too close.

The xulgaths were still a little farther out than seemed ideal when, by bad luck, one creature's course led it straight to the body of the scout. The living reptile didn't appear to understand exactly what had befallen its comrade, but it bent over the corpse for a closer inspection, and Kagur had no doubt it would rasp the alarm in a moment.

She stripped the hide wrapping off the arrow Denda had made and Holg had infused with magic, and it glowed white. She drew, released, and the luminous shaft arced through the air and buried itself in the chest of the inquisitive xulgath. An instant later, four of her orc allies hurled glowing javelins at other targets in the front rank.

The purpose was twofold. Kagur wanted to illuminate the enemy so that even night-blind humans could throw with a fair chance of hitting the target. She also hoped to startle and dazzle the foe for a critical moment.

The tactic appeared to succeed in both respects, but it also clearly revealed portions of a xulgath war band larger than any in cave-dweller memory, with at least four longstriders looming over the warriors and threehorns and spiketails lumbering in their midst. Kagur, Dalk, and other spies who'd viewed the host previously had tried to warn of the force's size and composition, but perhaps their eloquence had been unequal to the task. Somewhere along the hillside, someone let out a cry, and Kagur suspected that particular warrior wasn't alone in his astonished dismay.

"Blacklion!" she bellowed. She nocked, drew, released, and reached for the next shaft, fast as her hands would do the work. Let her allies see xulgaths falling one after another, quickly as the beats of a racing heart, and maybe that would hearten them.

Passamax roared, "Skulltakers!" and Vom, "Dragonflies!" They hurled javelins and felled more xulgaths.

The demonstration of fierce resistance served its purpose. Recovering from their consternation, other warriors started shouting and throwing, too, and javelins rained down on the xulgaths.

Meanwhile, Yunal snarled a prayer and hammered the air with his pale cudgel. On the final word, he thrust the bone at the nearest longstrider.

The gigantic reptile staggered a step, then tilted its head and peered at all the creatures clustered around it. Then, suddenly, it roared and lunged at a spiketail, trampling xulgaths in the process. It bowled over the other huge beast, held it down, and tore at it with its jaws. The spiketail tried to strike back, but maybe it needed its feet under it to aim properly, for its tail merely pulverized more xulgaths two and three at a time.

Reptilian warriors recoiled from the barrage from above and the frenzied struggle of the two enormous animals. Other longstriders roared as though the sight of the fight and the smell of gore were stirring their own aggressive instincts. Threehorns rumbled, balked, and shied.

For a moment, it almost looked like the horde might fall into complete disarray. Then Eovath strode from the darkness behind the first ranks of xulgaths, and even their shamans, with staves in their clawed hands and fetishes dangling from their scaly necks, looked to him in the clear hope that he'd put an end to the chaos.

Kagur loosed an arrow. Passamax and several others threw javelins.

Eovath pivoted and all but vanished behind a wooden tower shield sized for a giant. Kagur had never seen a xulgath use such an implement, but evidently the same craftsmen who built the reptiles' boats could make one if someone gave them direction.

The missiles all either stuck in the shield or bounced off. Eovath shouted, "You had your chances to kill me from afar, sister! Now you'll have to make another try at doing it the hard way!"

His face a mask of fury, Yunal chanted and whipped the carved bone around like he was battering his most hated enemy to death. Then he pointed it at the blue giant.

Yellow and blue fire shot up from the ground at Eovath's feet. But the flames curled and, to all appearances, slid into the giant's black breastplate like snakes disappearing into a hole. In an instant, the conflagration was gone, and Eovath wasn't even singed.

"Told you!" called Eovath with laughter in his voice. Still presenting the shield to his foes, he regarded the rebellious longstrider and, to a lesser extent, all the huge, restive beasts and began an incantation.

Unable to understand what her brother was saying, Kagur realized the power of universal speech had forsaken her again. But she didn't need to decipher the meaning to sense the power of the magic. Delivered in a voice that combined the deep tones of a frost giant with the sibilance of a xulgath, the words of command throbbed in the air and scraped at her nerves. Passamax slapped himself in the face like the spell had put some unpleasant sensation in his head and he needed to smack it out.

Kagur kept shooting. Long and wide as it was, the tower shield didn't quite cover Eovath completely. She should be able to drive an arrow into the top of the head.

Except that every time she would have hit him, he stepped or lifted the shield a little higher, and the shaft streaked harmlessly by or broke against his protection. No one could strike him with a javelin, either. Considering that he must be devoting as much of his attention to magic as to protecting himself, his impenetrable defense had something uncanny about it, like the Rough Beast truly was watching over him.

Kagur scowled that demoralizing notion away. Eovath was lucky, that was all, and nobody's luck lasted forever.

But the giant's good fortune lasted long enough for him to finish the prayer. The disobedient longstrider straightened up from its kill, its gory jaws still chewing a final mouthful of flesh. The other huge beasts quieted.

And their renewed docility steadied the xulgaths. The slackening of the harassment from above likely helped, too. Kagur's companions had assailed the front ranks of their foes to lethal effect, but now they were running out of javelins.

Eovath pivoted and glared back up the hill. He shouted something in the hissing language of the xulgaths, then brandished his axe at the orcs and humans. The reptiles charged.

"Go!" Kagur bellowed, and she and her comrades ran.

The reptiles had a steep slope immediately before them, while the first section of hill the humans and orcs had to traverse was considerably less so. In addition, the xulgaths didn't know the ground the way the folk of the highlands did. Slim advantages, but Kagur hoped that together, they'd be enough to keep her comrades and herself ahead of their pursuers.

She dashed through a stand of ferns, the smallest waist-high, the largest taller than a mammoth. Fronds rustled behind her. Hoping Passamax or one of her other allies was following in her tracks, she glanced back.

It wasn't Passamax. It was a redstripe. The xulgaths had sent the fast, nimble creatures racing ahead of them.

Kagur turned and reached for her longsword but only had it halfway out of the scabbard when the man-sized creature sprang high, the talons on its hind feet poised to catch and rip. She threw herself sideways, avoiding the attack, but ended up with fronds the length of her forearm dangling and flopping all around her, impeding her vision and hampering her movements.

She simultaneously finished drawing her blade and floundered clear of the vegetation. But by then, the redstripe had already spun around and leaped back into the air.

It was too late to dodge or duck. Kagur lunged with the point of her sword extended.

She and the reptile slammed together. The impact broke her grip on the hilt of her weapon and knocked her backward.

But the redstripe's claws didn't tear her flesh. The snatching, rending attacks passed to either side of her, whereas her sword punched into the base of the reptile's throat and out the other side. The creature fell down thrashing.

She hovered just beyond the reach of its flailing, whipping limbs, awaiting the moment when she could retrieve the sword safely. She was still waiting when a second redstripe charged her.

Retreating, she grabbed for Eovath's knife. Then Passamax rushed in on the redstripe's flank and plunged his spear into its body. His momentum bowled the beast off its feet, and he leaned on the weapon, pinning the reptile in place and sinking the point deeper until his foe expired in a final screeching convulsion.

Passamax pointed up the hill and jabbered. Without the benefit of Holg's speaking magic, Kagur only caught one of the words, but she was certain she grasped the gist: "Keep going!" She recovered her sword and ran on.

Someone screamed. Off to the left, just visible in the foliage and the dark, a longstrider held a writhing figure in its gnashing jaws. The shrieking stopped abruptly, and then the gigantic reptile gulped what was left of the warrior down.

Elsewhere, a female voice roared, "Dragonflies! Dragonflies!" as the xulgaths or their war beasts caught up with her. Kagur wanted to rush to her warrior's aid, but couldn't see where the woman was and didn't have time to go searching. Dozens of advancing foes would overtake and overwhelm her if she tried. So, hating the necessity, she kept fleeing toward the Skulltaker village.

The hillside steepened again into the final arduous climb that helped make the orc habitation defensible. She felt winded by the time she scrambled to the top and squirmed through a narrow gap between barricades woven of branches and briar. Flimsy defenses, in her judgment, maybe not worth the labor that had gone into them. But Holg, whose idea they were, claimed they could hold back foes for at least a moment or two.

Somehow, the old man himself was waiting for her at the exact spot where she finished her ascent. "How many others made it back?" she panted.

He shrugged. "Maybe half? My hope is there are others still coming behind you."

"Mine too. But we can't wait for them." She took a deep breath to calm her pounding heart and restore the strength of her voice. Then she shouted. "They're coming! You know what to do! On my order!"

The men and women in charge of handling the cross sections of log rolled them to the point where the hillside dropped sharply away. Another of Holg's ideas, laboriously cut with axes, mallets, and wedges, the barrel-shaped weapons were as tall as Kagur. It remained to be seen whether they'd travel far enough to accomplish their purpose, but Nesteruk had at least identified relatively clear, straight paths through the trees and tree-ferns.

Two more warriors clambered up onto into the flat space in front of the Skulltakers' cave. Kagur was glad to see that one of them was Dalk. Blood flowed from a gash below his knee, and more of it dripped from the hatchet in his right hand and the knife in his left. But he gave her a gap-toothed grin like running and fighting for his life was good sport.

Orcs shouted to one another, and after another moment, Kagur could just make out the stirring and churning in the darkness that was the xulgath horde coming up the slope. The sight reminded her of the numberless, implacable black ants from the pinecone-shaped nests. But that comparison was no more encouraging or otherwise useful than the idea that Rovagug was personally shepherding Eovath through the battle, so she pushed it out of her head as well.

Wanting the foe to climb just a little higher, she silently counted to five. Then she shouted, "Now!"

Along the drop-off, humans and orcs heaved the wooden rounds forward.

Some performed as poorly as Kagur had thought they might, bouncing and tumbling off course, crashing into tree trunks and thickets, and hanging up short of the foe. But others rolled on, faster and faster, until they slammed into one xulgath, and, often, rolled right on to crush other reptiles behind it.

Even the enormous war beasts weren't entirely impervious to the onslaught. One piece of log bounced high and smashed down on a spiketail's tiny-looking head. The beast didn't fall down afterward, but something was plainly wrong with it. It simply stood and shuffled in place no matter how its handler urged it onward.

But, brutally effective as they were turning out to be, the sections of log weren't only weapons. Their banging, thudding, crunching progress, and the xulgaths' rasping cries of alarm, signaled Unlak and the warriors who'd arrived with him to make a different sort of attack.

Javelins flew from the vegetation to either side of the reptile horde. Some of them finished their arcing flights as they began, as shafts of wood terminating in points of flint, and pierced the bodies of xulgaths. But others dissolved into lengths of dazzling, crackling glare, and the latter burned into the forms of the gigantic war beasts. The creatures staggered, convulsed, and bellowed in rage and pain. Blasted by three bolts of lightning simultaneously, a longstrider fell and squashed a dozen xulgaths beneath it.

Lightning blazed down from the Skulltaker village, too, as Vom and Rho threw metal javelins. Other warriors sent more log sections rolling and bouncing down the hillside. Holg and an orc wisewoman chanted prayers, and the latter gashed her forearm with a knife, possibly spilling her blood as an offering to her patron spirits.

Kagur and her companions on the slope had met the xulgath horde with some approximation of the strength two allied tribes might reasonably be expected to field. After a show of resistance, they'd fled from the reptiles' manifestly superior might, and the bloodthirsty creatures had given chase.

As a result, she now had the enemy surrounded on three sides by a war band that, while still smaller than the horde of reptiles, was much larger than they could have expected. The warriors in front of the xulgaths had the advantage of high ground, those on their flanks had cover, and everyone was attacking with potent weapons unlike any the creatures had ever seen. Taken altogether, it was as deadly and daunting a trap as she and her comrades had been able to devise.

Down on the slope, Eovath laughed.

"Well done, sister!" he called. "*Very* well done! You're dying the way a great warrior should!"

He bellowed commands, and some of his allies turned to confront the warriors assailing their flanks. The rest charged uphill.

Chapter Thirty-Four
The Battle

Kagur spotted Eovath on the hillside. She aimed an arrow, and then a spiketail lumbered in front of the giant and blocked her view. Cursing, she shot an oncoming xulgath instead.

She dropped two more after that, then glimpsed or perhaps merely sensed motion overhead. She looked up and saw a gliding shadow, visible chiefly when it occluded one star and then another. It could only be a spearbeak.

"Watch the sky!" she shouted, pointing upward. She then realized that with so many folk yelling, xulgaths hissing, longstriders roaring, lightning bolts crackling, and log sections thumping and banging, it was likely no one had noticed. She loosed two shafts at the spearbeak, and it thudded to earth in front of one of the branch and briar barricades. Presumably, someone noticed that.

Kagur looked back down the hillside just in time to see xulgaths that had charged high enough to hurl javelins. She ducked, and two such missiles arced over her head. Off to her right, someone less fortunate cried out in pain.

The first wave of xulgaths raced onward. Kagur drew her sword.

As Holg had promised, the barrier in front of her hindered the foe. One xulgath tried to scramble over, its feet tangled in the mesh, and she slashed its throat as it floundered. A second darted for the gap between her barricade and the next one, but as it squeezed through, a tribesman smashed its skull with a club. A third had a spear long enough to reach across the top of the obstruction, and it thrust the point at Kagur's torso. She sidestepped, grabbed the weapon, yanked the reptile forward, and hacked into its spine.

Then a redstripe sprang high enough to clear the barricade and rip her head off, too. She sidestepped, cut, and caught the beast in the leg. When it landed, the wounded limb made it stagger, and an orc speared it in the guts before it could catch its balance.

After that, the pressure on Kagur's position let up, although she could see it would resume as soon as more xulgaths completed the scramble up the slope. She used the momentary respite to try to survey the battle as a whole.

But that was difficult. The flares of lightning reduced the lower reaches of the hillside to dazzling confusion. She could tell that a couple of the gigantic war beasts were down, but not what kind or how many were still on their feet. About all she was sure of was that, at the rate her allies were flinging the magic javelins, they were bound to run out soon.

Even closer to hand, it was difficult to decipher what was happening. Humans and orcs battled xulgaths across the barricades with dead and wounded comrades sprawled or crawling at their feet. But who was winning? It was all just howling, screaming chaos, and she wondered fleetingly if her father or even Lord Varnug, with all his experience leading the Blacklions' following, would have understood it any better.

At least she could see that her shamans were still alive. Every tribe had contributed at least one, and they chanted and jabbed with the spears, clutched the carved fangs and claws, or brandished the quartz crystals that lent force to their prayers.

A young girl pointed, and blades of grass shot up tall, thick, and bristling with thorns to catch the xulgaths who were scrambling through them.

Ghethi filled the air with a piercing shriek that, audible even above the general din, knocked half a dozen reptilian warriors reeling backward.

Spiders the size of wolves, no doubt controlled by one of the enemy shamans, swarmed over a barricade, and Holg rattled off an incantation and lashed his staff at them. The scuttling creatures abruptly shrank until Kagur could no longer make them out and they were presumably too small to hurt anyone.

But a couple human shamans had already stopped fighting to drag wounded warriors back from the battle line and tend them. Kagur assumed they'd used up all their battle magic, and it wouldn't be long before their fellow spellcasters did the same.

She hoped the xulgath shamans were running out of power, too. Then more reptilian warriors rushed at her spot on the battle line, and she no longer had thought to spare for anything but killing the next foe, and then the one after that.

Still, she noticed when the blasts of lightning came to an end, and constant dark engulfed the slope once more. Sometime after that, xulgaths stopped rushing up to try to slaughter her.

She looked around. No one else was fighting across the barricades, either, although two Dragonflies were dispatching a spearbeak that was thrashing around on the ground nearer the cave mouth. Mostly, warriors slumped weary and panting amid the mingled stinks of blood, sweat, charred flesh, and the thunderstorm smell of the lightning bolts responsible for the charring. The wounded moaned and whimpered, or, in the case of the maimed xulgaths littering the slope, croaked and hissed.

But what was going on farther away? Kagur didn't *think* there were any longstriders still towering over all the other reptiles, but what about the other war beasts? Were any of them still alive? And were her allies still harassing the xulgaths' flanks? She could hear cries and make out hints of movement that suggested they were, but it was impossible even to guess how they were faring.

She turned to Holg and felt a shock of dismay. As far as she could tell, no enemy had wounded him. But he was wheezing, hanging his head, and leaning on his staff like he'd fall over without it.

But she knew the old man wouldn't want her to remark on his exhaustion or hold back from seeking his help. "What do you see," she asked him, "and what do you think it means?"

"We held them and hurt them," Holg answered, "but they hurt us, too."

"Did we hurt them enough to make them run away?"

The shaman shook his head. "I doubt it. Not while the giant with the shining axe is still alive to lead them."

"Good." Win or lose, live or die, it was time to dance the final measures of the dance.

Down below, the xulgaths in the center of the hillside, the ones not busy fighting on the flanks, raised a hissing, screeching clamor. Then they cleared a path. Tower shield on his left arm and greataxe in his right hand, Eovath rode out of the darkness.

Mounted just behind the bony ruff, which further shielded the lower portion of his body, the frost giant rode the hugest threehorn Kagur had yet seen. As far as she could tell, the steed didn't have any lightning burns or other wounds on its hide. Maybe Eovath had kept it well back, holding it in reserve, or perhaps he'd just now summoned it out of the forest.

For all its bulk and thick legs and the steepness of the slope, the threehorn accelerated until it was lumbering fast as a man could run. Xulgaths screamed and charged alongside it.

Kagur aimed at a beady eye and let an arrow fly. But the beast's head bobbed up and down as it ran, and her first effort struck the bony beak, pricking the creature but nothing more.

At first, no lightning bolts leaped at the threehorn, and she assumed her comrades had expended them all. Then Rho scrambled up to the barricades and cast the one he'd evidently held in reserve.

As the weapon dissolved into a streak of burning light, Eovath shifted the tower shield to the side to uncover the black breastplate beneath. The lightning disappeared into it as the earlier magical fire had, without seeming to do the wearer the slightest harm.

Rho should have thrown at the threehorn, Kagur thought. But she understood how the creature moved now, its rhythm. She could accomplish what the youth hadn't. She nocked one of her last remaining arrows and drew it back to her ear.

The longbow writhed in her grip, twisting and locking into a contorted shape incapable of propelling a shaft. A xulgath shaman had evidently cast a spell on it.

Kagur pivoted back toward Holg. He shook his head to indicate that he couldn't restore the weapon to usefulness. With a curse, she dropped it and her quiver as well.

Meanwhile, Eovath, his mount, and the allies charging with them pounded into javelin range. Men and orcs threw relentlessly, exhausting the last of the missiles. Xulgaths dropped, but the shield protected the giant, and the threehorn only suffered scratches.

Vom bellowed commands, and warriors massed and extended spears over the section of barricade Eovath was charging. The threat didn't deter him or the war beast, either. They kept coming, and when they smashed into the spear points, the weapons gouged the reptile's visage but then snapped or glanced away.

An instant later, the threehorn rammed through the barrier and trampled the center of it flat. Humans and orcs scattered, but some weren't quick enough. Swinging its head back and forth, the beast battered warriors with the sides of its two longer horns, flinging them about. It tossed its head and ripped an orc open from crotch to throat with the curved horn on its beak.

Xulgaths poured through the breach the threehorn had opened. Howling tribesfolk rushed to meet the threat, and where they only fought enemy warriors, they held their own. But when the war beast turned its horns in their direction, they had to scurry out of the way or die.

Kagur circled. The threehorn was all but invulnerable from the front but might prove less so if she attacked its flank.

A xulgath screeched and lunged at her with outstretched claws. She sidestepped, cut at its spine as it blundered past, and it dropped.

Two more reptiles spread out to flank her. She shifted her front foot to make it look like she was retreating, then rushed them. Surprised, they faltered. She slashed left, then right, and they too fell.

She stepped over bodies as she maneuvered, and one of them fumbled at her leg. She sprang beyond its reach without looking to see if it was an injured xulgath trying to hinder her or a wounded ally seeking help. She had no time for either.

Finally, the surging back and forth of frenzied combatants opened a path to the war beast. And Eovath was busy swinging his axe one-handed at targets on the right side of the threehorn while Kagur was approaching on the left. Perfect.

She charged, longsword extended for a thrust that momentum ought to drive deep into the war beast's body. Xulgaths pivoted to chop and stab at her as she passed, but the quickest of them was still a shade too slow.

Eovath, however, was not. Just as the blade was about to reach its target, he somehow sensed the threat. He turned, leaned down, and blocked the attack with his shield. Kagur lurched to a halt just shy of slamming into the barrier herself.

The axe spun at her head, and she stepped back from the blow. Eovath, she thought, was using a weapon intended for two hands with only one. He was also striking across his body, and that was always awkward for a mounted warrior. Maybe she could kill the threehorn even with him fighting to protect it, or better yet, kill him!

She advanced, inviting an axe chop, then swayed back far enough to let it whiz by. She slashed at his hand, just missed, then cut at the threehorn. Jorn Blacklion's sword gashed scaly hide and the flesh beneath. But a rib blocked it from slicing as deep as she'd hoped.

Then the threehorn wheeled toward her, and its bulk was like a shifting mountain, impossible to resist. She scrambled to keep it from knocking her off her feet.

The frantic evasion landed her in the midst of a clash between two orcs and three xulgaths. She parried a spear thrust, cut her assailant's belly open, pivoted, and slashed a second reptile's throat. One orc seized and immobilized the remaining xulgath's knife hand while his comrade bashed its skull in.

All together, it only took a moment. But when Kagur whirled back around, she was right in front of the threehorn's bloody spikes and glaring eyes.

She and the orcs scattered. As she expected, the beast ignored her fellow warriors and stamped after her.

It advanced with a measured tread that allowed it to compensate when she dodged. Under other circumstances, she could still have outmaneuvered it as she had the spiketail her first night in Orv. But the rest of the battle hemmed her in, whereas the giant reptile could simply wade through anyone who failed to get out of the way without even slowing down.

The creature stepped and thrust its horns at her. She lunged between them and slashed it across a nostril. Maybe that part was tender, and the pain would balk it.

No. It flipped its head, and she leaped back to keep the beak horn from goring her. Eovath grinned down like they were playing a game together.

"Coward!" she shouted. "Come down on the ground and fight fair!"

He laughed. The war beast lumbered forward, and she retreated.

But she couldn't just back away forever. Soon she was bound to fetch up against a tree or some other obstacle. Or xulgaths would take her down from behind while she was focused on the threat in front of her.

She charged. A horn shifted to catch her, and she dodged past it.

The giant reptile lowered its head to rip with the curved horn. But before it even finished the preliminary motion, she leaped on top of the beak and scrambled onward toward the bony ruff and the rider behind it. At last, wide-eyed surprise wiped the smirk from Eovath's square blue face.

Kagur raised her sword to cut and reached for the base of one of the long horns to anchor herself. But then, even though she was no longer in front of it, Eovath's mount, completing the action it had begun, tossed its head and flung her into the air.

She slammed down on her back, and her head banged into a stone or something equally hard. Suddenly, everything seemed hazy and far away.

The threehorn lumbered around to face her. A part of her screamed that she had to get away from it, but when she tried to jump up, her limbs were numb and sluggish.

Chanting, eyes closed, Holg stepped between the threehorn and her. The swirling lines on his staff glowed, and as he swung it over his head, the end burst into crimson flame.

Seemingly startled, the threehorn hesitated. Then Eovath snarled a sibilant command and it started onward, evidently to spear Kagur and trample the old man at the same time.

But its foot was just leaving the ground when Holg shouted the final word of his prayer and brought the fiery rod down across its beak. The staff snapped into three pieces. The threehorn froze. Then it shuddered, groaned, and fell over sideways with an earthshaking thud.

Swaying, Holg regarded the huge, now motionless body for an instant. Then he too toppled.

His collapse jolted the fumbling slowness out of Kagur's limbs. She scrambled to the old man and asked, "Are you all right?"

Judging from the way he was shuddering and the blood pouring from his nose, he wasn't. But he gasped, "Fine! Get Eovath! You're the only one who can finish this!"

As she dashed around the threehorn's mound of a carcass, she thought Holg might be mistaken. Even a frost giant could be crushed or pinned if astride such a colossal mount when it fell.

And that would be all right. Ever since the night of his betrayal, she'd craved the most complete and personal vengeance she could take, meeting Eovath blade to blade in the fullness of his might and pride and outfighting him, humbling him, slashing his blue flesh over and over till she ended with his heart's blood staining their father's sword. But now, with her allies' lives in jeopardy, she simply wanted him dead, no matter how.

Unfortunately, when she rounded the threehorn's body, Eovath was on his feet and to all appearances unharmed. He grinned and called, "I'm impressed. Who *was* that old man?"

She advanced. He tossed away the tower shield, gripped his greataxe with both hands, and came to meet her. Perhaps sensing something of destiny or expressive of the will of spirits, gods, and demons in the moment, neither humans, orcs, nor even xulgaths moved to intervene.

Eovath feinted high and swung low, the true attack a stroke meant to reap the legs out from under Kagur. She retreated and slashed his forearm as the greataxe whizzed past, then, before he could ready it for a second blow, lunged to slash at his knee.

But he too defended by retreating. His long legs made it easy, and now the axe came hurtling down at her head. She wrenched herself out of the way and flicked her blade at the giant's wrist. The axe snapped sideways to parry, and steel clanged on steel. The jolt stung her fingers.

Eovath followed up with a chop at her face. She sprang back out of range, and he pursued, whirling the axe at her torso. She dropped under the blow, then exploded forward with her sword extended for another try at slicing his knee.

He pivoted out of the way, and from the corner of her eye, she glimpsed a flicker that told her the greataxe was in motion. She dodged, spun, and cut to the ribs. Her sword rang harmlessly against the black cuirass.

Eovath cut, and she pulled her sword arm back to keep him from lopping it off. They stepped back from one another and started to circle.

She initiated the next three exchanges, and he, the four after that, neither scoring. But by the end of the last one, Kagur was panting. Sweat stung her eyes, her pulse pounded in her neck, and her actions were a hair less precise than before. Meanwhile, except for the superficial cut on his arm, Eovath seemed as fresh as ever.

She supposed it only made sense that he was wearing her down. She was human and had been fighting since the initial skirmish below the village. He had a giant's might and endurance and had saved them for this duel.

But she had to find a way to win! She knew his style and his favorite tricks. That ought to mean she could make him react as she wanted him to.

She shifted in and slashed upward at his fingers. He spun the greataxe in a way that both evaded her attack and caught her blade where the head of his weapon met the shaft. Without pausing, the axe began a second rotation intended to twist the sword hilt out of her grasp.

She cried out, grabbed her weapon with her off hand, and strained against the pressure. Such resistance could only delay the inevitable, and that not for long. Whether she used one arm or two, her strength was no match for his, and, knowing that, he grinned.

The greataxe tore the sword from her fingers. No doubt rejoicing, xulgaths hissed and screeched, while humans and orcs cried out in dismay.

Either way, the responses were premature. After a moment of pushing back, she'd intentionally loosened her grip, and the sudden lack of opposition tipped Eovath off balance. She sprang in close, pulled his knife from her belt, and drove it into his groin, where the black cuirass didn't cover.

Blood spurted, painting her arm to the shoulder. The watchers roared. She stepped out of the way as Eovath tottered forward and fell to his knees.

He turned his head. He was still smiling, but a different smile, with something dazed and incredulous in it. "My own trick," he croaked.

Give or take, she thought. Keeping her eyes on him, she maneuvered to pick up her sword.

"It's still not enough," her brother said. "The xulgaths will heal me. Or Rovagug will."

No, she thought, he won't. And then she charged.

To her surprise, Eovath's shaking hands managed to raise the axe and interpose its curved edge between them. She twisted past it and cut at his neck.

More blood sprayed, and the giant fell forward onto his face. She stood over him and kept hacking.

When the head came off, she lifted it by its yellow hair and pivoted to show it to those nearby. Then she looked for a higher spot from which to display it to everyone.

The body of the threehorn would do. She scrambled up its tail onto its ribs and brandished both the severed head and her father's sword in the air. "Blacklion!" she roared, with all the breath she had left. "Blacklion! Blacklion! Blacklion!"

Xulgaths gaped up at her. Then they fled—first one, two, or three at a time, then the entire horde running back down the hillside.

Chapter Thirty-Five
The Farewell

The Skulltakers' cavern branched into multiple chambers on the inside. Holg had an alcove to himself, with a pallet made of moss, leaves, and hide, plus gourds full of water and red and yellow berries ready to hand.

The healers were doing their best to make him comfortable. But the wavering light of the torch in Kagur's hand revealed a face just as gray and sunken as when she'd looked in on him previously.

"How was the patrol?" he wheezed.

"We didn't find any stray xulgaths," she said, kneeling down beside him. "We did find a couple more of our wounded . . ." She realized she didn't want to finish her thought.

So Holg finished it for her. "But the shamans don't expect them to live, either."

She scowled. "Don't talk like that. No one even hit you."

"No, not last night. But I'm old. I pushed and pushed, and then I drew down more power than I can handle anymore. It's fine, though. I accomplished what the spirits wanted, and you took your revenge. Was it what you expected?"

She thought about it. "I thought I'd burn with the hate I've carried all along, and it would feel good. But everything was too urgent and complicated. I don't know if I felt anything."

"What about now?"

She had to think about that, too. "I just feel tired. Like I'll always love my father and my tribe, but now I can let go of them, too. Even Eovath. I'll never understand how he could do what he did, but I don't need to hate him anymore."

"Believe it or not, that's better . . . than gloating." Holg drew several shallow breaths. "I said before I have no regrets. But maybe I should have one."

"What?"

"You won't have my magic to help you . . . return to the tundra. Still, perhaps you . . . don't need it."

For a moment, she wondered what he meant. Then it came to her. "It would be stupid to go back when everyone I have left is here."

She'd tried not to care about Nesteruk, Rho, Vom, and the others, but somehow she'd come to do so anyway. So why not stay and let her new friends teach her to hunt the jungles? It could be a good life if she let it.

Then something else occurred to her. "You knew I'd decide that if you made me think about it."

He smiled his sly, smug smile. "I want to leave you in as good a shape as I can."

"You're the sick one, fool. I should take care of you. What can I do?"

"There is one thing . . ."

"Tell me."

"In all the time we . . . traveled together, you never smiled."

For some reason, that made tears spill from her eyes. But she managed the smile, too. Then, mindful that the torchlight might be blurring his sight, she took his hand and raised it to trace the bow of her lips.

"You have a good smile," he said.

Outside, drumming clattered.

"The victory celebration," Holg whispered. "Go."

"In a little while."

When the wheezing stopped, she closed his milky eyes. Then, as she'd told him she would, she went to join the living.

About the Author

Richard Lee Byers is the author of more than thirty novels, including the first book in R. A. Salvatore's War of the Spider Queen series and *Blind God's Bluff*, the first installment in his new urban fantasy series. In addition, he is also the co-creator of the critically acclaimed young adult series The Nightmare Club. His short fiction has appeared in numerous magazines and anthologies, including the Pathfinder Tales story "Lord of Penance," available at **paizo.com**.

Acknowledgments

Thanks to James Sutter, Erik Mona, and Andrew Zack for all their help and support. And thanks to Edgar Rice Burroughs. When I was a kid, I thought ERB was the greatest author who ever lived, and I doubt I'd be a writer without his influence. It was great fun to do a story that pays homage to his work.

Glossary

All Pathfinder Tales novels are set in the rich and vibrant world of the Pathfinder campaign setting. Below are explanations of several key terms used in this book. For more information on the world of Golarion and the strange monsters, people, and deities that make it their home, see *The Inner Sea World Guide*, or dive into the game and begin playing your own adventures with the *Pathfinder Roleplaying Game Core Rulebook* or the *Pathfinder Roleplaying Game Beginner Box*, all available at **paizo.com**. Fans of Kagur and Holg's subterranean adventures may particularly want to check out the Pathfinder campaign setting book *Into the Darklands*.

Absalom: Largest city in the Inner Sea region, far to the south of the Realm of the Mammoth Lords.
Blacklions: Small tribe of Kellids on the Ginji Mesa.
Cytillesh: Also called brain mold—a subterranean fungus with strange mind-affecting properties.
Darklands: Extensive series of subterranean caverns crisscrossing much of the Inner Sea region, known to be inhabited by monsters.

Deep Tolguth: One of the Vaults of Orv—a strangely tropical subterranean cavern populated by uncivilized humanoid tribes, demon-worshiping Xulgaths, and prehistoric beasts.

Demons: Evil denizens of the plane of the afterlife called the Abyss, who seek only to maim, ruin, and feed on mortal souls.

Demon Lord: A particularly powerful demon capable of granting magical powers to its followers. One of the rulers of the Abyss.

Desna: Good-natured goddess of dreams, stars, travelers, and luck.

Earthnavel: Legendary tiered pit in the Realm of the Mammoth Lords, leading down into the Darklands.

Following: Term for the collected tribes that follow a specific Mammoth Lord.

Frost Giant: Fifteen-foot-tall humanoids native to cold regions, with white or blue skin and a famous propensity for battle.

Ghouls: Undead creatures that eat corpses and reproduce by infecting living creatures.

Giants: Race of exceptionally tall and brawny humanoids.

Ginji Mesa: Massive expanse of frigid tundra in the Realm of the Mammoth Lords.

Gorum: God of battle, strength, and weapons. Also known as Our Lord in Iron.

Gug: Bizarre, four-armed humanoid monster with a vertical mouth splitting its head.

Hold of Belkzen: A region populated primarily by savage orc tribes.

Inner Sea Region: The heart of the Pathfinder campaign setting, centered around the eponymous inland sea.

Kellid: Traditionally uncivilized and violent human ethnicity from the northern reaches of the Inner Sea region.

Lands of the Linnorm Kings: Northern kingdoms ruled by the Linnorm Kings, warriors who have managed to slay draconic linnorms single-handed. Sometimes called the Linnorm Kingdoms.

Lord in Iron: Gorum.

Mammoth Lord: The ruler of a following of Kellid tribes in the Realm of the Mammoth Lords.

Muster: Ceremonial meeting of the tribes making up a Mammoth Lord's following.

Mwangi Expanse: Massive jungle region at the southern end of the Inner Sea region.

Nar-Voth: Level of the Darklands closest to the surface.

Orcs: A bestial, warlike race of humanoids originally hailing from deep underground, who now roam the surface in barbaric bands. Universally hated by more civilized races.

Orv: Deepest level of the Darklands, characterized by enormous caverns called Vaults.

Realm of the Mammoth Lords: Cold and relatively uncivilized land at the far northern end of the Inner Sea region, inhabited by loosely confederated tribes of Kellids.

Redcap: Fey creatures that look like tiny, angry old men with bloodstained, pointed caps and metal boots.

Rough Beast: Rovagug

Rovagug: The Rough Beast; the evil god of wrath, disaster, and destruction. Imprisoned deep beneath the earth by the other deities.

Sekamina: Middle level of the Darklands, characterized by seemingly unending caverns and tunnels that can span continents.

Serpentfolk: Ancient race of reptilian humanoids with heads and tails like snakes, which once claimed a vast empire but is currently in decline, with most of the individuals left slumbering in underground chambers.

Seugathi: Subterranean race of intelligent, tentacle worms with magical powers.

Song of the Spheres: Desna

Sorcerer: Someone who casts spells through natural ability rather than faith or study.

Tian: Someone or something from the Dragon Empires of the distant east.

Tolguth: Settlement in a region where the cold tundra of the Realm of the Mammoth Lords is warmed by geothermal activity, resulting in strangely lush valleys filled with prehistoric beasts.

Tusk Mountains: Mountain range that acts as the northern border for the Realm of the Mammoth Lords.

Varisia: Frontier region at the northwestern edge of the Inner Sea region.

Vaults of Orv: Enormous and ancient subterranean caverns, often with their own unique ecosystems, found in the deepest reaches of the Darklands.

Witch: Spellcaster who draws magic from a pact made with an otherworldly power, using a familiar as a conduit.

Wizard: Someone who casts magical spells through research of arcane secrets and the constant study of spells, which he or she records in a spellbook.

Worldwound: Constantly expanding region overrun by demons a century ago.

Wraith: Formless undead creature born of evil and darkness, which hates light and living things.

Xulgaths: Intelligent and evil reptilian humanoids that dwell in caves. One of the oldest intelligent races, long since outstripped by other races, and now viewed as feral savages.

Zevgavizeb: Demon lord worshiped by xulgaths. Also the patron of reptiles and caverns in general.

Once a student of alchemy with the dark scholars of the Technic League, Alaeron fled their arcane order when his conscience got the better of him, taking with him a few strange devices of unknown function. Now in hiding in a distant city, he's happy to use his skills creating minor potions and wonders—at least until the back-alley rescue of an adventurer named Jaya lands him in trouble with a powerful crime lord. In order to keep their heads, Alaeron and Jaya must travel across wide seas and steaming jungles in search of a wrecked flying city and the magical artifacts that can buy their freedom. Yet the Technic League hasn't forgotten Alaeron's betrayal, and an assassin armed with alien weaponry is hot on their trail . . .

From Hugo Award-winning author Tim Pratt comes a new adventure of exploration, revenge, strange technology, and ancient magic, set in the fantastical world of the Pathfinder Roleplaying Game.

***City of the Fallen Sky* print edition: $9.99**
ISBN: 978-1-60125-418-4

***City of the Fallen Sky* ebook edition:**
ISBN: 978-1-60125-419-1

CITY OF THE FALLEN SKY

TIM PRATT

In the grim nation of Nidal, carefully chosen children are trained to practice dark magic, summoning forth creatures of horror and shadow for the greater glory of the Midnight Lord. Isiem is one such student, a promising young shadowcaster whose budding powers are the envy of his peers. Upon coming of age, he's dispatched on a diplomatic mission to the mountains of Devil's Perch, where he's meant to assist the armies of devil-worshiping Cheliax in clearing out a tribe of monstrous winged humanoids. Yet as the body count rises and Isiem comes face to face with the people he's exterminating, lines begin to blur, and the shadowcaster must ask himself who the real monsters are . . .

From Liane Merciel, critically acclaimed author of *The River King's Road* and *Heaven's Needle*, comes a tale of darkness and redemption set in the award-winning world of the Pathfinder Roleplaying Game.

Nightglass print edition: $9.99
ISBN: 978-1-60125-440-5

Nightglass ebook edition:
ISBN: 978-1-60125-441-2

Nightglass

Liane Merciel

Luma is a cobblestone druid, a canny fighter and
spellcaster who can read the chaos of Magnimar's
city streets like a scholar reads books. Together, she and
her siblings in the powerful Derexhi family form one of
the most infamous and effective mercenary companies in
the city, solving problems for the city's wealthy elite. Yet
despite being the oldest child, Luma gets little respect—
perhaps due to her half-elven heritage. When a job gone
wrong lands Luma in the fearsome prison called the Hells,
it's only the start of Luma's problems. For a new web of
bloody power politics is growing in Magnimar, and it
may be that those Luma trusts most have become her
deadliest enemies . . .

From visionary game designer and author Robin D. Laws
comes a new urban fantasy adventure of murder, betrayal,
and political intrigue set in the award-winning world of the
Pathfinder Roleplaying Game.

***Blood of the City* print edition: $9.99**
ISBN: 978-1-60125-456-6

***Blood of the City* ebook edition:**
ISBN: 978-1-60125-457-3

Blood of the City

Robin D. Laws

In the deep forests of Kyonin, elves live secretively among their own kind, far from the prying eyes of other races. Few of impure blood are allowed beyond the nation's borders, and thus it's a great honor for the half-elven Count Varian Jeggare and his hellspawn bodyguard Radovan to be allowed inside. Yet all is not well in the elven kingdom: demons stir in its depths, and an intricate web of politics seems destined to catch the two travelers in its snares. In the course of tracking down a missing druid, Varian and a team of eccentric elven adventurers will be forced to delve into dark secrets lost for generations—including the mystery of Varian's own past.

From fan favorite Dave Gross, author of *Prince of Wolves* and *Master of Devils*, comes a fantastical new adventure set in the award-winning world of the Pathfinder Roleplaying Game.

***Queen of Thorns* print edition: $9.99**
ISBN: 978-1-60125-463-4

***Queen of Thorns* ebook edition:**
ISBN: 978-1-60125-464-1

QUEEN OF THORNS

DAVE GROSS

PATHFINDER TALES

With strength, wit, rakish charm, and a talking sword named Hrym, Rodrick has all the makings of a classic hero—except for the conscience. Instead, he and Hrym live a high life as scoundrels, pulling cons and parting the weak from their gold. When a mysterious woman invites them along on a quest into the frozen north in pursuit of a legendary artifact, it seems like a prime opportunity to make some easy coin—especially if there's a chance for a double-cross. Along with a hooded priest and a half-elven tracker, the team sets forth into a land of witches, yetis, and ancient magic. As the miles wear on, however, Rodrick's companions begin acting steadily stranger, leading man and sword to wonder what exactly they've gotten themselves into . . .

From Hugo Award-winner Tim Pratt, author of *City of the Fallen Sky*, comes a bold new tale of ice, magic, and questionable morality set in the award-winning world of the Pathfinder Roleplaying Game.

Liar's Blade print edition: $9.99
ISBN: 978-1-60125-515-0

Liar's Blade ebook edition:
ISBN: 978-1-60125-516-7

Liar's Blade

Tim Pratt

PATHFINDER
TALES

PATHFINDER TALES

PRINCE of WOLVES

DAVE GROSS

PATHFINDER TALES

Winter Witch

Elaine Cunningham

PATHFINDER TALES

Plague of Shadows

Howard Andrew Jones

PATHFINDER TALES

the WORLDWOUND Gambit

ROBIN D. LAWS

PATHFINDER TALES

Master of Devils

DAVE GROSS

PATHFINDER TALES

Death's Heretic

JAMES L. SUTTER

Subscribe to Pathfinder Tales!

Stay on top of all the pulse-pounding, sword-swinging action of the Pathfinder Tales novels by subscribing online at **paizo.com/pathfindertales**! Each new novel will be sent to you as it releases—roughly one every two months—so you'll never have to worry about missing out. Plus, subscribers will also receive free electronic versions of the novels in both ePub and PDF format. So what are you waiting for? Fiery spells, flashing blades, and strange new monsters await you in the rest of the Pathfinder Tales novels, all set in the fantastical world of the Pathfinder campaign setting!

PAIZO.COM/PATHFINDERTALES

Paizo Publishing, LLC, the Paizo golem logo, and Pathfinder are registered trademarks of Paizo Publishing, LLC, and Pathfinder Tales and the Pathfinder Roleplaying Game are trademarks of Paizo Publishing, LLC. © 2012 Paizo Publishing, LLC.

THE INNER SEA WORLD GUIDE

You've delved into the Pathfinder campaign setting with Pathfinder Tales novels—now take your adventures even further! *The Inner Sea World Guide* is a full-color, 320-page hardcover guide featuring everything you need to know about the exciting world of Pathfinder: overviews of every major nation, religion, race, and adventure location around the Inner Sea, plus a giant poster map! Read it as a travelogue, or use it to flesh out your roleplaying game—it's your world now!

EXPLORE YOUR WORLD!

paizo.com

Paizo Publishing, LLC, the Paizo golem logo, and Pathfinder are
registered trademarks of Paizo Publishing, LLC, and the Pathfinder
Roleplaying Game and Pathfinder Campaign Setting are trademarks
of Paizo Publishing, LLC. © 2012 Paizo Publishing, LLC.

PATHFINDER
ROLEPLAYING GAME
BEGINNER BOX

THE ADVENTURE BEGINS!

Designed specifically for beginning players and packed with must-have accessories including dice, monster counters, and a slimmed-down, easy-to-understand rules set, the *Pathfinder RPG Beginner Box* gives you everything you need to set out on countless quests in a fantastic world beset by magic and evil!

AVAILABLE NOW!
$34.99 • PZO1119
ISBN 978-1-60125-372-9

Photo by Carlos Paradinha, Jr

PAIZO.COM/BEGINNERBOX

Paizo Publishing, LLC, the Paizo golem logo, and Pathfinder are registered trademarks of Paizo Publishing, LLC, and the Pathfinder Roleplaying Game is a trademark of Paizo Publishing, LLC. © 2012 Paizo Publishing, LLC